Enthusiastic praise
for *New York Times*
bestselling author

CHRISTINA DODD

"CLASSICS NEVER GO OUT OF STYLE.
A LITTLE BLACK DRESS,
A STRING OF PEARLS,
AND A CHRISTINA DODD ROMANCE."
Lisa Kleypas

"CHRISTINA DODD IS EVERYTHING
I'M LOOKING FOR IN AN AUTHOR—
SEXY AND WITTY,
DARING AND DELIGHTFUL."
Teresa Medeiros

"DODD TRANSPORTS READERS
INTO ANOTHER ENTICING
PLACE AND TIME."
Publishers Weekly

"CHRISTINA DODD
KEEPS GETTING BETTER AND BETTER!"
Deb

"TRE
TO A FA
ANYTHING

By Christina Dodd

CHRISTINA DODD

Candle
in the
Window

AVON BOOKS
An Imprint of HarperCollinsPublishers

AVON BOOKS
An Imprint of HarperCollins*Publishers*
10 East 53rd Street
New York, New York 10022-5299

Copyright © 1991 by Christina Dodd
ISBN: 978-0-06-104026-9
ISBN-10: 0-06-104026-6
www.avonromance.com

First Avon Books paperback printing: February 2007
First HarperTorch paperback printing: July 2000
First HarperCollins special paperback printing: February 1999
First HarperCollins paperback printing: April 1991

Avon Trademark Reg. U.S. Pat. Off. and in Other Countries, Marca Registrada, Hecho en U.S.A.
HarperCollins® is a registered trademark of HarperCollins Publishers.

Printed in the U.S.A.

20 19 18 17 16 15

To Scott
Who supported and encouraged me
through two word processors
and
ten years of writing
I Love You

Medieval England
Springtime, 1153

one

"Do you want her?"

"What?" Lord Peter turned his gray head to his host, surprised by the question, jolted by the interruption.

"I said, do you want her? You keep staring at her." Theobald wiped his nose with the hand that held his knife.

"That girl? The one at the foot of the table?" Lord Peter tread warily, unsure of his host, unsure of the hostility he saw mirrored in the man's eyes. "She's very pretty."

"Pretty?" Theobald snorted, holding his knife clutched tight in one hand and lifting his cup with the other. "Aye, look at her. Her mouth is so wide and red and smooth, and her hair is black, long, clear down her back. It looks magnificent against that skin of hers. Plague take her, Saura's body is the kind poets sing about. She's got legs up to her rump. A very nice rump, it is, too. A tiny waist and these. . . ." Theobald used both hands to gesture, sloshing ale into his lap and cursing.

Repelled by the catalog of her charms and by the thought of the lout laying hands on the girl, Lord Peter apologized stiffly. "I'm sorry, I didn't know she was your concubine."

"Concubine!" Theobald sniggered with contempt, hating the girl with his darting eyes. "I wouldn't have her in my bed, nor give her to you for yours. She's useless, can't you see it? She's blind, blind as a treble-bandaged mole. She's the daughter of my first wife and Elwin of Roget, and I can't even marry her off. A stone hanging around my neck, worthless!"

Worthless? Lord Peter wondered. What had drawn his attention was the way she seemed to manage the production of dinner from her seat. The movement in the great hall swirled around her; the serfs spoke to her respectfully, bowed, and did her bidding. She murmured to her maid and the woman hurried off in the direction of the kitchens. The servant returned and whispered in Saura's ear, and Saura climbed off her bench. Lord Peter watched with close attention to see her stumble, but she moved gracefully, lightly touching the arch that divided the great room and disappearing into a stairwell.

"I'm interested in her woman," Lord Peter told Theobald, never taking his eyes from the spot where Saura had vanished. "What's her name?"

"Saura's woman?" Theobald hooted. "You brave soul. We can do better for you than old Maud."

Lord Peter turned his head to his host once more, smiling thinly. "I prefer my meat well seasoned."

"Aye, it covers the rank smell, doesn't it?" Theobald grinned at his young wife, shrinking beside him, and Lord Peter felt sorry for the girl who would share her lord's bed tonight.

"Maud?" Lord Peter stepped out of the alcove and examined the woman his squire had brought him. Her gray braids hung down her back, her round face was wrinkled with middle age, and she stood tall. Remembering how the retainer had towered over the blind girl, he realized he had found whom he sought. He waved his man away. "You're Maud? You're the woman who serves Saura of Roget?"

Bright blue eyes combed his figure, seeking his credentials in the cut of his clothes and the condition of his body. "I am Maud. Saura's my mistress. I served her mother and I'll serve her until the last breath is left in my body, and if that ass Theobald has offered her to ye—"

"No!" Lord Peter roared, infuriated by her assumption. "No. She's young enough to be my granddaughter."

Maud peered at him quizzically, amazed at his vehemence, and Lord Peter explained with a sheepish shrug, "My lady wife would slice my gizzard on a platter."

"A good woman," Maud said. "Come, walk with me. We're too conspicuous standing in this drafty hall. Why do ye want m'lady?"

Lord Peter fell in step with the woman. "I will speak to her."

"Why?"

"That is between me and the lady." Under Maud's dubious gaze he continued. "Methinks I cannot harm her with you standing guard, or is she so timid she requires a shield?"

"Timid? God, no, not Lady Saura. She has the heart of a lion."

"Good, she'd be of no use to me if she weren't brave. She seems to run the household."

"Oh, aye. She seems to." Maud walked beside him, her face set straight ahead.

No further comment was forthcoming, and Lord Peter insisted, "Well, does she?"

"As ye know, Lord Theobald has married young Lady Blanche and she's the lady of the castle."

Lord Peter examined her, amazed at the cautious answer. "I don't give a damn about Lady Blanche! I'm not a relative of Lady Blanche. I'm only interested in Saura of Roget. Now, does she run this household?"

Maud stopped and searched his honest, exasperated face. Pushing her hand against the door beside her, she suggested, "Why don't ye ask her?"

Lord Peter entered the chamber, gaining at a glance the worth of Saura to her family. The tiny room contained only the space for a straw palliasse and a bahut chest made of iron and wood. Still, a small fire burned on the hearth and no smoke blew in—the sign of a clean flue.

Seated in the only chair, Saura was wrapped clear to her chin in a coarse wool blanket. Her feet were raised off the cold floor with a footstool. Her ears were covered by a fine linen cap, tied beneath the chin. But the headwrap was frayed and no longer white, and almost too small for her tiny head, as if it had been hers since her childhood and never replaced.

Her face! Good God, what had been an admirable portrait of the Madonna seen from a distance was, in fact, the work of some more profane artist. She was beautiful in an earthly way; she was beautiful in the way that made men long to indulge themselves with her. Her white skin shone clear and unmarked by the pox, lifted by exotic cheekbones that bespoke her Norman ancestors. Long and straight, her nose twitched with the scent of him. Her lips were chapped from the cold, as were his, as were everyone's, but hers turned up in a wide, enticing mouth. Black eyelashes which swept her cheeks were a foil for the great violet eyes that turned to him so inquiringly.

No wonder Theobald snarled about her, no wonder he stared at her with hunger and hate. This girl lived beneath his hand, but away from his touch, and it would be beyond the will of any man not to desire her. Until some man branded her as his possession, Saura would be a bone of contention in any household.

If only William—Lord Peter broke off his thoughts with a sharp sigh.

"See enough?" the woman beside him asked with astringent emphasis.

In surprise, Lord Peter realized the two women had been quiet, waiting for his appraisal to end. "Are you always so patient?" he queried, smiling at Maud as he moved to the trunk to sit down.

With a gesture, Saura stopped him. "A moment," she ordered, as she reached into the roomy bag on the floor beside her and pulled out a cushion. Handing Lord Peter the carnation-scented pillow, she said, "The slant of the lid makes the trunk less than comfortable."

"Thank you, my lady." Lord Peter adjusted the cushion on the trunk and sat, amazed that she knew his location with such accuracy.

"I have brought ye Lord Peter of Burke, Sire of Burke, m'lady. He wishes to speak with ye."

"Lord Peter!" Saura rose with a flurry, aware of the man's wealth and prestige. "Why didn't you tell me at once, Maud? He shall have my chair."

Putting his hand on Saura's shoulder, Lord Peter pushed her back. "I am quite comfortable, I assure you, and better able to bear the cold than one so fair."

"He's a big, strong man," Maud added drily. "And has seen worse conditions, I'm sure."

"Maud, you're incorrigible," Saura scolded, but Lord Peter agreed.

"I have seen worse conditions, just today, with the snow-storm that drove me to take advantage of the hospitality of Pertrade Castle. I assure you, Lady Saura, I'm dry and well clad, and as your maid pointed out, I'm a big, strong man." Lord Peter smiled directly at Maud with such charm that the older woman stepped back in surprise.

"Then how can I favor you, my lord?" Saura cuddled back into her blanket.

"I need information. You can help me."

Discomfort and trepidation colored his voice, and when he said no more, she prompted, "I would be glad to give you any information I have, my lord."

"You seem to be. . . ." Lord Peter paused, unsure of how to proceed. Glancing at Maud, he observed the waiting amusement that lit the woman's eyes. "It appeared that you ran the serving of dinner from your place at the foot of the table. Did you?"

A slight frown crossed Saura's face. "As you know, my stepfather has married Lady Blanche and she—"

"No!" Lord Peter stopped her, blunt with impatience. "You don't understand. I don't care if Lady Blanche doesn't lift a finger, it's you I'm concerned with. You! Are you blind?"

Saura lifted a finger and touched one ear, as if she could not believe the question, and Lord Peter raked his fingers through his thinning hair. "I didn't mean it like that. In sooth, I came to the vicinity hoping for an encounter, for Raymond of Avraché remembered hearing tales of you. I know you are blind, but you manage so well, it almost seems a hoax."

"Ye wouldn't say that if ye had seen the times she has fallen over a bench or walked into a door," Maud said without inflection.

"Or the times Maud has beaten some poor idiot for leaving his bench out," Saura added with a clear laugh.

"Have you been blind all your life?" Lord Peter asked, intense with concern.

She blessed him with her slow smile and answered, "Not yet."

Lord Peter whipped his head around. Realizing the irony of it, he sighed. "You handle your lack of sight so well." Almost in despair, he added, "You're so young. You move gracefully, you feed yourself, you dress neatly. You run this household?" Maud nodded to him. "Does your maid do it all for you?"

Maud scowled, but a flattered smile flitted across Saura's face. "No, Lord Peter. Maud is my strong right hand and my eyes, but I'm self-sufficient. My mother taught me to care for myself, for my servants, for my family, and for my home."

"How?"

"My lord?"

"*How* did she teach you these things? Was she blind also? Did she talk to someone, learn from someone? How did she know what to do?" His voice quavered, thick with a private anguish.

Disturbed, Saura heard his trouble but couldn't diagnose the source. "My mother was a canny lady, and if she ever worried about me, I didn't know of it. I did the things she told me because I never knew I couldn't, and if I had ever given in to despair, she would have disciplined me out of it."

"How do you discipline a blind person? Knock them a

blow that they can't see coming and are unable to duck?" Lord Peter asked, his question bitter on his tongue.

"You're not talking about me, sir. Do you have a loved one who has lost his sight?"

"A loved one. Yes. My son, my only child, as strong and robust a man as has ever walked this earth, now cannot walk this earth without stumbling and cursing, falling, walking into something." He buried his head in his fists. "He needs help, my lady, help, and I have no help to give him."

Silence permeated the room, save for the crackle of the fire, while the doughty warrior fought his emotions to a standstill. Saura laid her hand on his elbow and when he raised his head, she held out a filled cup of cider, warm from the fire. Maud stood beside her, smiling encouragement, as Saura invited, "Tell me."

"Since Stephen of Blois claimed the throne from Queen Matilda, there's been nothing but trouble. Nothing but trouble." He rubbed his belly as he remembered. "William and I are balanced on a sword's edge, trying to keep our vows and our properties and our honor. We are forever putting down some bit of rebellion from a tenant or cracking heads with one of the barons who thinks he owns an acre of land he does not."

"Did your son have to go and fight in any of those endless royal battles?"

"No, no. Matilda has retired to Rouen. Why should she fight Stephen, when his barons are doing such a good job of destroying England with these endless, petty wars?" he asked bitterly. "She sits across the Channel and watches and waits. Her revenge is coming. She's raised up her son to fight."

"He tried to take England before," Saura pointed out.

Lord Peter was surprised. "Do you follow the great follies of our sovereigns, then?"

She lowered her head, as befitting a modest maid, yet her voice rang firm. "I own lands that rest beneath the march of armies. With my feeble woman's mind, I seek to understand what I can, but we're at the end of the world here. I hear very little, and that two years late."

Lord Peter suspected her disclaimer hid a keen interest, and so he explained, "Henry was only fourteen last time, but they say he's matured into a powerful leader. He's made plenty of trouble for Stephen from his lands in Normandy, and some say he's already landed in England with an army." Watching her closely, he added, "He was invested with the duchy of Normandy after his knighting by the king of Scotland." He was rewarded by the way her face lit up.

"The king of Scotland is his uncle, is he not?"

Recalling herself, she lowered her head again and folded her hands, but Lord Peter could no longer be deceived. Here was a bright and inquiring mind, languishing in ignorance. He was never a man to let such a mind go to waste in a man, and his wife had taught him the dangers of ignoring that asset in a woman. "Aye, he's Henry's uncle. Henry's related to every great lord and king in Europe, I believe. From his mother, he received the duchy of Normandy. From his father, he received the provinces of Maine and Anjou. 'Fore God, the boy has inherited so many lands, so many responsibilities, and still he seeks the position of king of all England."

"King Stephen won't yield the throne on Henry's behest."

"Nay, but these years of struggle have aged Stephen. The man can't live forever," he said, but he was hopeful, not convinced.

"What's going to happen to our poor England?" she asked.

"I don't know." He sighed. "I don't know. Nineteen years ago, it all seemed so clear. Queen Matilda was good King Henry's only surviving child, and he made the barons swear to uphold her claim on the throne. But she is a woman, and a haughty woman at that."

"That's a bitter dose for haughty men to swallow," Saura answered with humor.

"You show a formidable insight." His humor acknowledged hers. "When Henry died—the present Henry's grandfather—Stephen claimed the throne in London, and England hailed him. He seemed to be the perfect solution. He was the grandchild of William the Conqueror, just as Matilda was. He was charming, generous, and brave. The barons thought Stephen would bring prosperity. We soon found out that charm, generosity, and bravery are poor substitutes for the unscrupulous sternness needed by a monarch."

"I can't even remember a time of prosperity," Saura said. "I was born the year good King Henry died."

"Aye, a whole generation of children have grown up with strife. There's been no law, and the powerful terrorize those they should protect. The memory of these last years chills my blood."

"I understand. My own lands, the lands my father left me, are slowly being eaten away by the 'kind neighbors' seeking to care for them."

"Doesn't Lord Theobald fight?"

Saura's mouth lifted in a sneer, all the more effective for being natural, unseen by her on any other human. "It is too cold for Lord Theobald to go out."

"I see."

"Forgive me for my petty interruption. My hunger for news dissolves my manners and my sincere interest in your son's tale."

"Do not apologize. Your interest in the country's welfare has given me a moment to steady myself. I still can't talk about William, you see, without a pain in my heart. It makes me so angry, for he was injured for nothing. Nothing!" He turned his head back and forth, seeking to dispel the tension that knotted his neck. "We had a battle with a neighbor, a modest skirmish. The most minor of fights."

"Your son was hurt?"

"God, yes. Bashed in the back of the head. His mail hood left bloody imprints on his neck, his basinet helmet crumpled. We had to cut him out. It would have killed a lesser man, but not my Will. He lay like a stone for two days, and we were scared, Kimball and I." Lord Peter shrugged his shoulders, uncomfortable with the unaccustomed sensation of fear, uncomfortable with the volatile emotion of love. "Well, he's my only surviving son, and Kimball's father. And there he sprawled, white and still and barely breathing, like a great oak knocked to the ground. He woke up, though. Just came roaring up, demanding breakfast and demanding that we light the damn torches. With the fire flickering on the hearth and the daylight streaming through the slits in the walls."

Saura bent her head in thought. "How long ago?"

"Two months."

"He has his health, my lord?" she queried, tender with his grief.

"Healthy as a horse. Well, he does have pain in his head. But what good is his health? He's too old to adjust gracefully. He's damn near twenty-seven years old. He earned the colée when he was fifteen, knighted for bravery in the field of battle. He's overseen the management of his mother's lands all these damn dark years since old King Henry's death. He's a big man, by God, he has legs like tree trunks and shoulders that bulge with muscle. He's a fighter and a man of action, but now he won't go outside, he's ashamed to have the folk see him and afraid of making a fool of himself. He won't do anything inside."

"Because he's afraid of making a fool of himself?" Saura understood, her insides clutching as she recalled moments of being a fool, moments filled with the sound of careless laughter at her own pain.

"Exactly. And because he wants to be outside. He won't accept help, he won't help himself; he just sits and broods and drinks."

"He's pitying himself." Maud snorted.

"He's tangled in it." Saura nodded, touched by the real torment in Lord Peter's voice, the gruff call for help. "There's only one thing to cure it, my lord, and that's a swift, brutal kick in the seat."

"I can't! I'm crippled too, crippled by my love for the boy." Responding to the sway of the women's bodies as they bent protectively to him, he stuttered with awkward emotion. "I know you not, barring the little I have seen tonight, but I can see, Lady Saura, that you're a good woman caught in a bad situation. Your stepfather leers at you, and he's a weak man."

"Ye decided that quickly enough," Maud said.

"I'm a warrior. There are times when my life depends on my judgment of character and circumstances." He stared at Maud, and Maud stared back at him and nodded. "I can help you, and what I'm going to suggest will assuage all of our discords. I admire you. I admire the way you handle yourself, your life. I admire your spirit. I would like you to come and live with me."

A growl from Maud interrupted him and he held up his hand. "Peace, old woman. I don't want her for any dastardly reason. Just to live at my castle for a while. She could help me with William, tell me how to help him, perhaps she could help him herself."

"And if this William of yours refused her help, ye old fool, then where would we be?" Maud blazed. "That slimy whoreson downstairs would never let us return."

"Which would be worse?" Saura twisted her mouth with disdain. "Starving to death in the wilderness or living beneath Theobald's roof?"

Lord Peter stroked his chin. They raised a legitimate complaint. If Saura left her home of her own free will and William would have none of her, what would they do with her? A stray bit of humor brightened his face.

"I could take Maud as my mistress and refuse to part with her."

Maud snorted.

"Does she always express herself so disdainfully?" Lord Peter asked Saura, touching her hand with an indulgent finger.

"Always. It's the way she gives her opinion of the world." Saura smiled into his face, an amused and thoughtful smile. "But I expect you would be good for Maud. She's not nearly as old and tough as she would have you believe."

"I thought your lady wife would have your gizzard on a platter," Maud snapped.

"For dealings with a young woman. And Lady Saura is too young. My wife painted quite a vivid picture of an old goat like me with a girl. But were she alive today, rest her soul, she would approve of you, Maud. Believe me, you and she are two of a kind."

Glaring at the man, Maud was jolted into awareness of the warrior before her. His skin was mottled from too much sun and scarred by too many battles, but his fighter's build was attractive. His thinning hair shone with health and his brown eyes twinkled. He had most of his teeth, and he used them all when he smiled knowingly at her.

"I am a widower. So is my son, and his son is not yet married. Kimball is only eight. What we have is a bachelor household, and a dingy mess it is. Perhaps if you're not happy here, you could be prevailed upon to come to Burke Castle as a housekeeper."

"Housekeeper?" Saura exclaimed.

He slapped his knee enthusiastically. "Aye, that's it! Because I fear William will refuse to accept help from you. You're blind, and he doesn't want to be taught by someone sharing his experience, doesn't want to acknowledge his own plight. I've suggested it before. And you're too young, and a woman."

"I can't hide the fact I am a woman," Saura said, "but there's no need to tell him my age."

"Not tell him? I've never deceived him," he answered, troubled.

"But it's necessary?"

"Aye," he agreed slowly. "Aye, it's necessary. We'll not tell him you can teach him, at least not at first. First, we will let you prove what a magnificent housekeeper you are. You could get that damned castle cleaned and the kitchen in better shape. If we didn't tell him you are blind, he would never know, how could he? After you had been there a sufficient time and he was accustomed to you, we could tell him you are a dedicated teacher of the blind, a woman of, perhaps, forty, who has handled many students and taught them everything. He respects age and efficiency. Damn! I believe that is it!"

"What does my mistress get out of this, ye old fool? A passel of hard work, all for a man she has never met," Maud said.

Lord Peter shifted, abruptly uncomfortable with the slope of the trunk. "In my household, women who dwell therein are treated with respect and not beat all out of reason or imprisoned for a peccadillo. Lord Theobald has a new wife, one who will some day be well enough versed to take over the housekeeping, whether any of you wish for it. And Theobald has no fondness for you. It is too easy to die by disease or accident. Have you given any thought to that?"

Giving Lord Peter his first glimpse of the mettle beneath her quiet exterior, Saura impatiently slapped her hands together. "I'm not such an idiot that I never thought how a trip down the stone stairs would affect me. But I do have my own meager salvation. My half brothers were all trained by my mother to protect me, and they have done so vigilantly."

Maud's mouth turned down; she stared at Saura. "Aye, m'lady, but John has been sent for fostering, and Clare is seven and not much help."

"Rollo—" Saura began.

"Rollo is your stepfather's heir, and a good man who cares for ye, but he's just married and in training for his knighthood. He manages your mother's lands. He is so busy that something could happen to ye and it would be a month before he knew. Or longer. He avoids Lord Theobald at all costs. And Dudley studies for the Church. After Clare there is only Blaise, and he's four. He's attached to your new stepmother, and your dear mother's teachings are no good to him."

"Make your point, Maud," Saura murmured drily.

"M'lady, don't ye realize? Your brothers aren't . . . ye're teasing me," Maud accused.

"You do twist the knife a bit, my dear. We've refused to discuss my imminent demise for a reason. There were no choices. Now Lord Peter offers me an alternative to this wretched existence and my unreasoning reaction is to snatch it with both hands. Do you know how long it has been since I was beyond the boundary of this little castle? The seasons pass and I languish here, paying with the money from my lands for the privilege of keeping house for a drunken sot. Still, I wonder if you can convince my stepfather."

"Aye," Maud agreed. "Theobald will not let her go, just for spite."

"Let me talk to your stepfather." Lord Peter grinned in anticipation. "I'm a rich man, a powerful man. He'll pay heed to me one way or another. If he fails to see that having a connection in my household would add to his consequence, perhaps the threat of a summer siege would move him to sense."

Maud laughed out loud. "That'll make the sorry lout see reason."

"I wish I could hear it," Saura said. "Well, if you can convince Theobald, and if sober, conservative Maud thinks I should go, then go I will."

Maud answered with a glimmer of humor. "Ah, m'lady, I never planned to go haring off with this gentle lord without references. I shall check Lord Peter's reputation with his servants."

Saura reached out and caught Maud, sliding her hand down the arm to Maud's hand. Lord Peter watched the grace with which Saura lifted the old maid's gnarled hand and kissed it fondly.

That was what he wanted for his son. That ease of movement, the ability to judge the limitations and adjust. She had to come. She had to. William was desperate and dirty and lost. He needed direction, and this accomplished girl was the one to guide him. Lord Peter decided to rush the defences. "I'll give you my wife's apartment—a private chamber with a huge hearth. We keep fires burning day and night. Burke is close to the coast, and I have many ells of material from France we bought for William's late wife, Anne. You'd be welcome to them."

"Bribery isn't necessary, Lord Peter."

"We'll want to take Alden, too, Lord Peter," Maud interrupted firmly. "He's Lady Saura's man and her mother's before her."

"As you wish." Lord Peter nodded at his ally. "My home is three days' ride from here, and the snow is deep, but I would gladly buy a cart."

Saura winced. "I can ride, sir, on a leading rein, and I assure you I prefer the motion of a horse to the hard bumpings of a cart."

"I go to arrange both at once." Lord Peter rose hastily.

"Wait!" Saura commanded, holding out her hand. "The snow is deep."

"Dress warmly and pack all your clothes, Lady Saura. As soon as the storm weakens I must go. Burke is my primary keep, stronger than the others, but even so I worry about William, alone and in the dark. He's helpless in a way you cannot imagine, still endowed with strength and determination but unable to find a way to proceed."

"Do you want me to pity him, my lord?"

"Yes, pity him. He has always been clear and direct, full of hearty laughter and great rages. Now his rages are unrelenting and self-directed and his laughter has disappeared. Please, Lady Saura," Lord Peter took her hand in his trembling grasp, rubbing his calloused fingers across her chilled skin. "Please come. I know my William is there somewhere, buried beneath the mountain of anger and disgust. My son is still there, but only lost. Please help me find him."

Shaken by his appeal and his unexpected eloquence, Saura

quelled her doubts. Sighing, she rubbed her fingers across her forehead and nodded. "I will think, and I will pack. Your situation cannot be worse than mine is here, and perhaps I can help your son. No doubt I can set your house in order, with the assistance of my good right hand, Maud. See what you can do, my lord. See if you can convince Lord Theobald to wish me Godspeed."

"What is that smell, Maud?"

"I'm not sure, m'lady, but I have my suspicions." Maud marched into the rushes that covered the floor and gingerly lifted them with the toe of her shoe. "Decaying rushes, I suppose, and God knows what underneath."

Pinching her nose, Saura answered, "Well, I know what's underneath, I don't need the Almighty to tell me. Is this the great hall?"

"If ye want to call it that. Hospitality's not the strong suit in Lord Peter's castle."

As if to give the lie to her words, two gigantic dogs bounded toward them, barking an enthusiastic welcome. Maud swatted at them with her open palm. "Back, sirs."

One dog bounded away, the other stood sniffing at Saura's skirt as if it were a meat-laden bone.

"Away, dog!" Maud clapped her hands at the animal, but its growl sounded deep and clear, and she stepped back.

Calmly, Saura reached out her hand and let the dog assess it.

"M'lady, that lolloping beast will bite it off," Maud objected.

"Nonsense," Saura returned. The dog tasted her with a dainty lick of the tongue and then fought to get his head under her hand. When she obliged by scratching around his ears, he quivered with ecstasy.

Maud laughed with unwilling amusement. "If ye could only see him, m'lady. He stands with such a clottish look of heaven on his droopy face."

Snapping her fingers, Saura ordered the dog behind her, and he obeyed with all the eagerness of a devoted servant. Placing her hand on Maud's shoulder, Saura inquired, "Does this place look as bad as it sounds?"

"I'll not close my eyes on this group to find out how it sounds, thank ye. I thought Theobald fed a rough bunch, but it seems no one is in control here. We got here just in time, m'lady. They are taking advantage of Lord Peter."

The heavy clomp of feet behind cut them off. "Find your way, Lady Saura?" Lord Peter asked heartily. "Come in by the fire. You're dripping with snow and shivering with cold. I hope this is the last storm before spring."

"I doubt I would have had the courage to come, my lord, if I had known the condition of the roads," Saura advised him.

"Dreadful, aren't they?" he agreed. "Since the breakdown of the government, nothing's been done for them, and they were none too fine to begin with. Did the cart help?"

Exasperated, Maud voiced her displeasure. "A bumpy, uncomfortable ride most of the way."

"Most of the way?" he asked.

"Aye, except when it stuck in the snow and the mud and we had to climb out to let the horses pull it out. What manner of madman would ignore the signs and go out in such a tempest?"

"You should be grateful I did." That silenced Maud, and he continued, "If it weren't for the storm, we undoubtedly would have been set on by brigands. That's another price we pay for the disorder that rules us."

"Lord Peter," Maud snapped, "you'll frighten m'lady."

"Damn, that's right. I don't want her to run away now that she's had a glimpse—or a whiff—of the mess I've got her into. The place looks even worse than when I left." Lord Peter took Saura's elbow, but she gently disengaged her arm.

"Please, let me hold on to you," she directed, putting her hand into the crook of his arm. "It is more effective."

"Grandfather!" The shout echoed across the smoky room, and a tall boy tripped across the rushes in his excitement. "Grandfather, you're back at last! We were worried."

"Kimball, surely you weren't worried about an old warrior like me?" Lord Peter leaned down to embrace the smiling youth. "I've been absent only three weeks. And you've grown since I left."

"You say that every time you come back. I can't grow all the time. But I did lose another tooth, see?" Kimball contorted his lips to show his grandfather the gap, and then lowered his voice. "I wasn't worried, not really. But when it started to snow, Father began to fret. He said the cold pained your joints and that he should be touring the estates and when you didn't return promptly—" Glancing at the unknown ladies, he finished lamely, "Well, you know."

"I know. Thank you for supervising your father." Lord Peter laid a solemn hand on Kimball's shoulder.

"You are welcome, sir, but who is that?" Kimball pointed a finger at the seven-year-old boy who trudged through the door with a manservant at his heels.

Lord Peter swung around to see the miserable group from Pertrade huddled together, unwilling to approach the fire until properly directed. "Good God, Lady Saura, forgive me. Take my arm." He again offered his elbow. "Let me take you to the hearth. Kimball, this is Lady Saura. She has come to be our housekeeper. She is a distant cousin of your grandmother's. That boy is Clare, Saura's half brother. I've taken him for fostering. Will you make him welcome, Kimball?"

"Of course, sir. It is an honor to meet you, Lady Saura." He bowed from the waist. "I hope you will be happy in our home."

Kimball obediently dropped back with Clare, and Saura heard him tell her brother, "Many thanks for coming. Grandfather's a popular man for fostering, and I've always had boys to fight with. But since my father's trouble all my friends left." The boy grimaced dramatically, and continued, "You've saved me from boredom."

"Your grandson is as courteous as his grandfather," Saura said.

"I hope that's a compliment." Lord Peter laughed, and Saura laughed back.

"I certainly meant it to be."

Maud chimed behind them, "Pleasant! Lord Peter is only pleasant if ye discount the blackmail and the bribery."

Lord Peter stopped and Saura could feel the warmth of fire on her left side.

"A chair, Lady Saura," he offered.

She touched the back and slid into the seat, and before she was settled the dog flopped at her feet.

"Bula! Back!" Lord Peter commanded.

The dog snorted in response, lying against Saura's legs in a wallow of comfort.

"That dog, Lady Saura, is supposed to be a hunting animal," he said in irritation. "God knows, he's never even brought in a rabbit, but that doesn't mean I wish him to become a lapdog. You mustn't encourage him to behave like one."

" 'Tis a way she has with the animals," Maud chided, and

he turned back to the maidservant to pick up their bickering where they'd left off.

"My bribes can be very pleasant."

"So far all I've heard is words," she returned. "Ye promised a private chamber for m'lady, with a fire which we'd better get burning if there is to be any warmth in there tonight."

"Hawisa!" Lord Peter's shout made Saura wince. "Where is that damned Hawisa?"

"Probably down in the straw of the stable making another of her everlasting brats."

The voice from the other side of the fire startled Saura. It resounded deep and as rich as imported cloth, the kind of masculine voice that made her melt with pleasure. Yet it contained elements she detested: sarcasm and pathos and fury.

"No." Lord Peter laughed a little. "It's too cold in the stable. She's probably using my bed, if I know that slut." His tone grew serious. "How are you, William?"

William grunted, and his lack of courtesy stretched into an uncomfortable silence that ended only when Maud intervened. "If ye can command a few of these lazy churls to carry firewood and show the way, I can get those fires built and the chill out of the room. M'lady's feet must be like ice."

"My feet are always like ice," Saura interjected.

Maud ignored her. "And have them bring up m'lady's trunks, she's wet to the skin."

"Wet to the skin! My, my, that could be interesting," the glorious voice drawled again. "If only I could see it."

"The trip went well, William." Lord Peter's voice lowered, deceptively projecting calm. "I wish you had come with me."

"Riding in a cart like an old woman, how the vassals would have laughed at me," the voice said bitterly.

"Merwyn asked after you most tenderly. He invited you to come when next I visit, and Raoul wished he could have your military expertise to guide him when the raiders come in the summer."

The deep voice warmed with eagerness, bitterness vanquished by interest. "Is he sure they will come again?"

"Why would they not? They had rich pickings last winter, cleaning out the harvest barns and raping the peasant women."

"And no one to stop them, with me lying helpless in the keep and you hovering over me like a mother hen. God damn their souls all to hell! The day I lay hands on the man who bashed me on the head is the day he meets his Maker."

Saura liked the voice better now. No longer sarcastic, it echoed with resolve. Seeking to perpetuate his proud defiance, she snapped, "But what will you do afterward? Come back and sit next to the fire and stink?"

It was quiet. God, it was so quiet. She could hear his gasp, and not another sound. Was everyone in the giant room holding his breath?

"Madame, I do not know who you are, nor do I care."

Laden with fury, his voice caused shivers up her spine. It was menacing, but patient, willing to wait for the moment he could tear her heart out.

"No one has told you, apparently, that I'm blind, and unable to do anything but to sit by the fire and stink."

Trusting her instincts about his slovenly appearance, trusting that Lord Peter would protect her, Saura assured William cordially, "I knew you were blind right away. It seems you haven't learned to feed yourself without slopping sauce on your clothes. It seems you can't find your hair with a comb or a bath with your body. It seems all you can do is drink and stink." The servants' shocked murmurs filled the hall.

"Who are you?" The low snarl interrupted her.

"I am Lady Saura, a distant relative of your mother's, and the new chatelaine. Your father thinks his home is in chaos and that my order will prevail." To Saura's satisfaction, the serving folk quieted. Not a sound escaped them. Let the servants as well as the raging beast across from her prepare to deal with her challenge.

"Listen to me, Lady Saura." The golden voice rang clear and low. "I'm not one of your housekeeping chores. Stinking or drinking or an eyesore, nevertheless, don't try to clean me up. I'm happy as I am."

Sticking her little nose in the air and sniffing haughtily, Saura replied, "I believe in turning to good use everything available to me. I'm sure we can think of some use for a blind half-man."

A firm hand beneath her armpit jerked her erect and Lord Peter issued an inarticulate command.

"But we can dust around you for a while," Saura conceded graciously, moving away under Lord Peter's constraint. "Just as if you were part of the furniture."

two

"What in God's name possessed you to say such things to him?"
Lord Peter's question echoed in Saura's mind as she learned
the layout of the castle. It pursued her as she ventured down
the privy stairs to the undercroft below the great hall, and as
she visited the dirty, appalling kitchen hut in the bailey.

True, she could have used William's support. She had Alden, whose stick coerced, and she had Maud, whose salty
tongue converted cowering serfs into soldiers against filth.
She had Bula, whose guard-dog adoration convinced more
than one servant to cooperate with her wishes. Those three
were worth more than a dozen pikemen, but what she
needed was a legion of knights. As Lord Peter had hoped,
spring followed fast upon the heels of the late snowstorm
and the time for a thorough cleaning rushed upon them. He
presented her the keys of the house with great ceremony, but
the serfs were sunk in sloth, without direction since the
death of William's wife. They took a very human advantage.

Led by the slovenly Hawisa, they displayed a sly perversity when given Saura's orders. Sometimes they misunderstood them; sometimes they were terribly slow about completing them; sometimes they remembered the different ways Anne had ordered things done.

Lord Peter endorsed her authority, but the warming of the weather brought a miscellanea of work for him also, and he seldom stayed within the walls of the keep. He did take the time, however, to impress upon the churls the need for silence about Saura's blindness. Content with the alacrity with which they obeyed him, Maud noted which servants helped enforce his command and which ones gave him only bare obedience.

Yet, if Saura had been able to tap William's still-towering authority, it would have expedited her housekeeping chores.

"What in God's name possessed you to say such things to him?"

Everyone treated William as if he were ill. Everyone treated him like fine glass, tiptoeing around him with sympathy and pity, and not one person had any empathy. Their pity blinded them to his robust health and his sharp mind, their pity spoiled William for any useful chore. So what in God's name had possessed her to say such things to him? Merely an unthinking desire to jolt him from his stupor and make him function again.

She listened for a reaction from the lump called William, but heard only grunts and curt commands. Nothing she had said made any difference. Nothing she had said had reached him, she decided.

But the things Saura said had jolted William.

For the first time since his accident, he was angry at someone besides himself. Every warrior knows unavoidable incidents occur in battle, but most warriors are not forced to face such ghastly results of their accidents. Illness and infection he could face, had faced before. But this *blindness!* The poor fool of a priest told him to resign himself to God's will; only his own humility would earn him the kingdom of heaven. In the same breath the priest suggested God was using him for His own good purposes. Good purposes!

William cursed God. What kind of God would humiliate him, handicapping him when he was most needed? The Isle of England writhed in agony, rent by the struggle between Stephen of Blois and Queen Matilda. Guilt haunted him for leaving his father to supervise and defend their far-flung lands and castles. Since his return to Burke Castle in a horse-drawn cart, he had refused to set foot out of doors. And now That Infernal Woman accused him of fear and weakness and uselessness.

That Woman had stolen his guard dog and tamed it to her hand, but she'd never do the same with him.

"God's teeth!" William slammed his hand against the trestle table before him. That Woman was the bane of his life. She brought the winds of change sweeping into the fetid air of the castle and there was nowhere he could go to escape. Unbidden, the thought slipped into his mind.

Hide?

Is that what he was doing? Hiding? Like a cowardly ox, dumb and plodding unrelentingly toward the great nothingness?

"God's teeth!" he swore again. That Woman was making him think: think about his roles here, think about what he could do to help his father, think about the son he had forsaken.

In the far reaches of his consciousness, her voice and the activity it stirred commanded his attention.

"Today we are going to scrub the kitchen," Lady Saura announced. "All the walls, the ceiling, the floors; all the pots, the pans, the spit, the ovens. We'll be done by sundown."

And at sundown:

"We are not finished cleaning the kitchen. I'm sorry, Lord Peter, there is nowhere else to cook for the castle. Until the serfs are done, we must all go hungry."

William grinned at his father's bellow and realized how long it had been since his mouth had stretched back in pure amusement. The sore muscles elongated, and he grinned again for the joy of grinning.

Actually, That Woman didn't say much to him. Actually, she ignored him. There were no more challenges like the one she had flung the first night. As she had promised, he appeared to be no more to her than a piece of furniture, his rehabilitation a poor second to the purging of the keep. Perhaps he had imagined her interest in him. Perhaps she didn't care about a blind beggar like himself.

Still, her voice delighted his ear. A rare feminine voice, soft and strong, it supported a range of emotion that clearly foretold her moods. It was as if she had stopped and listened to herself and modulated her voice to be pleasant.

He liked to hear her exasperation as she scolded the giant dog who adopted her, adored her, tripped her, and protected her with an amiable fierceness. He especially liked to hear the iron in her as she dealt with the churls' deliberate incompetence.

"The trestle tables need to be placed against the walls after breakfast," Lady Saura announced. "Good people, today we remove the rushes from the floor. They abound with fleas. I'm tired of hearing the dogs scratch and I'm tired of hearing you scratch."

In the muttering and shuffling one woman's complaint echoed up to the arches. "That's foolish. New rushes won't grow tall till late summer, an' th' floor'll be bare. Lady Anne never made us change th' rushes in th' spring."

"When did she make you change them, Hawisa?" Lady Saura asked courteously.

"Why, in th' fall, of course." Hawisa snorted with derision, leading the chorus of laughter that jeered at the lady's ignorance.

"*Last* fall?" Saura's voice dripped sarcasm, and when the laughter died, her voice cracked the whip. "The floor will be bare until new rushes are grown, and you'll clean the floor daily as atonement for your sloth. Today, we will remove the rushes and brush the floor."

The work proceeded at a crawl, and once when Alden shouted at the slow servants, Lady Saura hushed him. Pricking his ears, William listened for That Woman's retribution, and as bedtime approached she did not disappoint him.

"Where're our blankets?"

"Blankets?" Lady Saura asked blankly.

"Th' blankets we wrap ourselves in t' sleep."

"The blankets have been taken for washing. The servants will be finished with them." William could almost see the pucker on her face. "About the time these rushes are burned and the floors purged."

"We can't sleep on those benches without blankets. 'Tis still too cold."

"I suppose you'll have to lie in the rushes you have piled up," Lady Saura answered without interest.

"But they're rotten."

"Aye."

Listening to her, day after day, he became quite fond of the clever way she dealt with the childish evasions of the serfs, hearing their grumbles as they began to do as she ordered without question. Only a few held out, still sidestepping her authority, and William began to feel impatience boil within him. These flunkies were questioning the authority of a woman of his class, a woman who spoke Norman French and understood whole phrases of the barbaric English tongue. This woman demanded nothing more of them than that they earn their supper.

"Today is the day we have longed for," Lady Saura announced at breakfast. "As soon as the trestle tables are removed, we will shovel out the garderobes."

A universal groan rose from the assemblage.

"Aye, I knew you would be pleased." William could hear the grim determination in her voice. "They're full, and this practice of shovelling out the top layer of dung is over as of today."

"I'll do it not." Hawisa made her last stand. "I'm a sewin' maid; me job's not carting shit, an' ye can't make me."

William heard the defiance in her tone, heard Alden step forward and the rustle among the serfs as they waited to see her fate for open defiance. He didn't know what compelled him, but with grinding patience he called, "Hawisa, come here."

Instantaneous silence fell, caused by the unprecedented intervention of their blind lord. William listened to the shuffle of her feet as Hawisa approached him. It was a tribute to his acute, new hearing that he knew where she came from and how close she was, but he did not realize that the days of brooding had gained him some ability.

"Kneel down where I can touch you," he instructed, and she pressed her body against his leg as she sank to her knees before his chair. Carefully, he lifted his hand to her face, locating her features with a light touch. When he had run his thumb across her broad cheek he pulled his hand back and slapped her flat-handed. The sharp sound echoed up the stone arches and the girl whimpered and ducked. Quickly, he caught her shoulders, raised her to face level and shook her until her neck snapped. "If you are too good to clean my house," he said clearly, "you can step out into the bailey and see if mucking out the stables would suit you better."

Hawisa's round face bobbed with earnest terror and the craftiness of a vixen run to ground. "I'll clean! 'Tis loyalty t' your dear wife that makes Lady Saura stick in me craw. 'Tis the airs she feigns t' convince us that she's th' new mistress of Burke. Aye, and she nothin' but a blind case of charity Lord Peter has taken on."

The scullions gasped, and Maud muttered, "Here's trouble," but William heard only Hawisa's jibe about the blind and took it as a slur to himself. His next slap knocked her away from his knee and made her head ring. "Out!" he roared, raising himself to his feet in one vital motion. "Out, you poison-fanged viper, and don't let me hear your voice again."

The scurrying of feet rewarded him as Hawisa fled the great hall, and he turned to face Lady Saura and her assembly of rebels. For the first time in months he stood erect, his broad shoulders back and his head up. His blond beard bristled with indignation and the dimples in his cheeks creased with the grimace of command.

"I have listened," he began ominously, "to the insolence and the complaining and the disobedience of the serfs of this castle. I know those of you who are clever enough to obey Lady Saura. I know those of you who are not. And to those who have been sluggard and rude, I tell you now, the time of retribution is at hand. Lady Saura is your better. Lady Saura has taken my wife's place in the management of the house. You will obey Lady Saura as you obeyed Lady Anne. I don't give a damn how old and ugly Lady Saura is. I don't give a

damn whether her blood is vinegar and she sweats butter-
milk. This woman is the chatelaine, chosen by my father and
endorsed by me, and the next insolent serf will answer to me.
I have the leisure to monitor your behavior, and by our Lady
of the Fountain, my blindness has not destroyed my good
right arm."

He finished with a shout that jarred the wall hangings and
blasted the guilty back against the wall. "Well?" he roared.

The hustle of many feet answered him. Maud ordered the
men outside to clean the cesspit from beneath. She divided
the women into scrubbers and shovelers and set them to
work above. One boy went scurrying to prepare the garden-
ers for a sudden influx of dung and another ran for the
garbage carts. William sank back into his chair, seeking with
his ears the Lady Saura, wanting her praise for his media-
tion. In the hubbub he did not hear her approach, but her
light touch on his shoulder alerted him to her presence.

"Perhaps more than a blind half-man, my lord," her gracious voice said directly above his head. "Perhaps more than
a piece of furniture after all."

"Lady Saura?"

She turned her head away from her consultation with
Maud, toward the respectful voice of Bartley. "Aye?"

"M'lord's askin' for ye."

"Is Lord Peter home already?" She rose with a frown.
"Dinner is not ready."

"Nay, Lady Saura. 'Tis Lord William. He's wishin' t' speak
with ye."

She puckered her lips in dismay. Had he thought of his
response to her taunt of the morning? She hadn't forgotten

the sound of his hand on Hawisa's flesh, nor the bellow of his rage. Still, this day had been profitable. Hawisa had been given the very chore she detested. She'd leaned deep into the holes and shoveled, moaning all the while. Then she'd been ordered to clean herself before reporting to the kitchens to turn the spit and scrub the pots. She was no longer required in the keep.

The garderobes smelled cleaner, the floor seemed to have scrubbed itself, the servants moved smartly to the new drill of discipline.

And William; William had responded at last to the bustle around him, to the real world outside his own head.

She had no feel for him yet, for the man who endured inside. She could not observe anyone, their mannerisms and habits, she could only listen to them and draw her conclusions from their voices and intonations. In her own home, the family and retainers she dealt with acknowledged her intelligence and perception, but William seldom spoke and so she groped when she dealt with him. To touch another being was her best insight, but because of the role laid on her, that of a middle-aged woman, she could never benefit by the perceptions open to her with grasp of hand or kiss on cheek.

"Lady Saura?"

Bartley spoke, reminding her of her duty, and she rose with a hidden tremble of her knees. "Aye, of course. Is he still hunkered by the fire?"

Bartley nodded. Maud glared at him and he realized anew that the noble Saura couldn't see him. "Aye, m'lady. He never leaves there."

Saura moved toward the servant, catching his shoulder and then his arm, showing him how to guide her. "Please take me to him," she asked courteously. "And as we go tell me about yourself."

The man started with doubtful steps across the room. "I'm just one of th' churls here," he volunteered, and then fell silent, unused to conversing with women, especially young, beautiful women who stood head and shoulders above him.

"Are you married?" she prodded, matching his hobbling gait with her own.

"Oh, nay, never had time for that, what wi' chasin' around m'lord's estates after thieves an' poachers an' such."

"You were a soldier?"

"Aye, an' I had me own horse th' lord let me ride—that was Lord Peter's father, an' then Lord Peter—till I got too crippled t' ride in winter." His voice sank. "Then I got too crippled t' ride in summer, an' I got banished."

"Banished?" Saura encouraged him with the gaze of her violet eyes, and the elderly man forgot she was blind.

"Stuck in th' keep like some old horse they're too kind t' kill." His bitterness bled into his voice, into the agitation of his limbs. "I'm grateful. Not many lords keep their old men-at-arms in where 'tis warm when they aren't of any use. But 'tis hell t' be old. Don't ever get old, 'tis just one long day after another, an' not enough work t' fill th' time."

"But, Bartley! What would I have done without you these last weeks?" Saura clasped his arm close to her side and shook it. "You've been such a support, helping me with the balky servants and caring for Lord William so I was free to order the cleaning."

"And where would I be without you sitting with me in my corner and telling me stories about the battles of your youth?" The warm, golden tones of William's voice were rich with sincerity and gratitude.

The old warrior trembled a little more, struck with the

palsy of age and embarrassment. "Good master, I didn't know ye listened."

"It's been the only thing that's kept me sane."

Bartley blushed, his papery skin darkening. "Here, m'lady. That damned dog's on your heels again, m'lady, don't trip on him." He assisted Saura to a chair and stood back as the mastiff lowered itself to the floor at her feet. Stepping in front of William, Bartley said, "Been a long time since I taught ye t' ride a horse without fallin' off. We shared some things, m'lord, an' since ye can't fight anymore, an' I can't fight anymore. . . ."

"Come to the fire tomorrow," William invited, "and we'll reminisce."

Pleased beyond all recognizing, Bartley wandered off to boast that Lord William had spoken to him, just like the old days, and cordial as ever.

The silence between lord and lady hummed eloquent with accord.

"Very gracious," Saura approved. "Did he really teach you to ride?"

"Everyone had a finger in that pie," William answered, stretching out his legs to the fire. "If he wants to remember his tutelage, I'll deny him not."

Saura grinned, and rubbed a finger across her lips to erase it. To her mind, a grin didn't go with the image of somber housekeeper. "You asked for me, my lord?"

"Are you laughing?"

She scrubbed a little harder at her lips. "Not laughing at you. But you made that old man so happy!"

William's voice turned frigid. "I can make anyone happy these days, just by speaking civilly."

The grin snapped off her face. "Then spread a little cheer, my lord."

"Now, why is it," he mused, "that when the servants displease you, you are distressingly polite and soft-spoken? When I displease you, you fly into a rage."

"Because I expect better from you!"

"Why?"

"My lord," Saura said with thin forbearance, "you are a warrior. What do you do with a soldier who loses a leg?"

"Teach him another trade."

"And if he will not learn?"

"Let him turn to begging."

" 'Tis a hard world. What do you think of a man who has all the privileges of a loving family, a home and enough food, but must be forced to care for himself? What do you think of a man who refuses to take the burden of work from his father's shoulders, a man who abandons his son?"

"Enough!" William's voice started at her level and rose above her head as he stood in ready ire. "My God, who are you? Saint Genevieve who through the grace of God restored sight to her own mother? Perhaps blindness is a puny thing to you, you haven't experienced it."

" 'Tis as big as you make it."

"But everything I am is bound up with my sight. You said it, I was a warrior. A knight! I had to fight to protect my home, my family, my people. They've no use for me now!"

"Oh, don't they?" Saura relaxed, on steady ground. "Did you arbitrate their quarrels, hand down judgment for their crimes?" William didn't answer, and her grin blossomed again. "You have a reputation for fairness in arbitration. Did you leave the education of your son to others? He pines for you, for your support, as he grows into maturity. Your father needs a man to talk to, to ask advice of, to be with. Your tenants need guidance. They are a bunch of lost and bleating sheep without your firm hand. You've sown what you reaped, my lord, a demesne filled with people who worship you. But all your former good deeds will be forgotten soon if you don't stir yourself to add to your legend."

Listening to her warning, William wished he weren't so scrupulous. That part of him that insisted on equity for others insisted on equity for himself. He wanted to deny the woman's point of view, proclaim his justification for being self-centered and forlorn. Goaded beyond control, he asked, "Have you ever been in despair and in need of a human touch? And those who love you are too afraid of your disability to touch you? As if it would rub off? Haven't you ever been alone in bed at night and felt the walls closing in, felt imprisoned by your own body?"

Saura's throat closed with incipient tears of recognition, but he charged on. "You creak like a woman too old and dried-up inside to understand the weakness of the flesh. Never loved a man, never held a child. The way you talk, I'd think you never sinned."

The legs of his chair thumped heavily as he flung himself into it, and Saura grappled with the surge of unexpected affinity that twisted her heart. She tried to talk, but she couldn't: comfort was nothing more than a whisper, fragmented in her mind and constricted in her breast.

"What are you doing? Praying for me?" William's voice lashed at her, and then softened in a hush of thought. "Praying for me." His fingers tapped an impatient dance on the arm of his chair. "Are you praying for me?"

She remained silent, and was rewarded with his charge.

"You're a nun, aren't you?"

"Oh, dear lord."

"Of course." He snapped his fingers. "I should have realized. It's logical; only a nun could bring this kind of discipline to a household."

Saura gulped and patted her flushed cheeks. "Your father. . . ."

"Swore you to secrecy? Why, madame, are you here to teach me?"

She sighed and smiled, entertained by the evidence of his lively mind, and his faith in his own conclusions. "I'm here to teach you," she acknowledged. "I am a teacher of the blind."

"And you have every reason to sound so sanctimonious. You never have sinned, have you? Never held a man with love, never mothered a child."

"And I never will." She touched her barren womb with the intense pain of one who wants more. "An aging maiden with no hope for tomorrow."

William bit his lip in regret. He'd wanted to bait her a little, but he never meant to probe an open wound. "The choice was not yours, to enter the nunnery?"

"If I'd had my choice, I would have my husband and my family."

Struck by the call of a frustrated kindred spirit, he offered the best comfort he could. "I cannot help you with the husband, madame, but we are your family now."

Touched by the graciousness of the offer, she answered, "Thank you, William."

He grinned. "William? Will you call me by name only when you're pleased with me?"

"My lord," she faltered, embarrassed by her revealing slip of the tongue.

"I like it. It reminds me of my mother."

"Your mother?" Stunned, she grappled with her dissatisfaction. She was nineteen and that poorest of creatures, an unmarried woman, but his *mother?*

"When I vexed her, she called me 'my lord.' In quite a sarcastic manner. I recognize your kinship with her."

She coughed.

"I called you for a reason." He ignored her emotion, recognizing the enigma of a woman's mind. Whatever interpretation he put on her reaction, he would probably be wrong. "As you so tactlessly pointed out to me, I stink. I've not had a bath since last fall, and through the long process of learning to eat I've dropped food on my clothes and in my beard. Do you think . . . ?"

That Woman moved with speed and confidence, he thought sourly as he poured water over his chest. A contingent of female vassals had escorted him to the solar and stripped him while the men wrestled the huge tub in front of the fire. Buckets of water had been hauled up the stairs and kettles of water hung over the fire to boil. In no time he had dipped his big toe in and then settled with a sigh. He waved everyone away with his enormous hand and let the warmth seep into his bones and move his blood. He had endured the cold for too long: the cold without, and the cold within.

Now peace reigned in the chamber, the door shut tight against drafts.

Lady Saura and her handmaid were in consultation over his clothing trunk, and the murmur of their voices washed over him.

"This feels like a fine, light wool tunic."

"Aye, and 'tis dyed a serviceable brown with braid at the sleeves and hem."

The other serving women worked quietly under Saura's direction or settled with their sewing. Their hushed chatter reminded him of a spring bath four years ago, and in his mind's eye he saw the large chamber as it looked then.

Built off the great hall, it was dominated by the polished wooden master's bed, raised on a dais, fitted with a canopy and hung with curtains to keep out the winter winds. The clothing trunks sat against the opposite wall, close enough to the hearth to keep the contents dry but not to catch a stray spark. Blessed with more light than any other room in the castle, the solar contained clusters of stools and benches in the window seat where the women worked. Windows overlooked the fenced garden of the bailey. The iron grille protecting them cast square shadows into the room and the wooden shutters were finished with elaborate carvings.

William chuckled as he remembered how his wife had insisted on first the windows, then the carvings. His father had shouted she would beggar them with these ridiculous ideas, and Anne had shouted back, telling him to fix his own dinner and mend his own clothes and bear his own grandchildren. It had been quite a violent altercation, and in the end Lord Peter had cheerfully ordered the shutters carved and Anne had continued to bear him grandchildren.

Until she died with the last one. William had laid her to rest beside the four tiny graves of their children who had gone before.

He waited for the familiar rush of grief, but there lingered only a sweet melancholy. He missed her: her boisterous laugh, the scent of lavender on her clothes, the plump cushion of her body against his at night. But he no longer mourned her, and if this monstrous handicap had not been visited on him, he would have cast his eye around for a woman to marry and live with.

He didn't like this process of pursuing one woman until she capitulated and then forsaking her and pursuing another. He knew men who did: Arthur, and to a lesser extent, Charles, sought the myth of the perfect woman in every bed. During the years they were fostered by his father, no serving maid beyond her first flowering lay on her pallet alone.

But that particular pattern of male behavior was foreign to him. His energies were better utilized as a warrior, his desires better cared for by a woman who loved him. He had used the serving women around the castle to sate his bodily needs, but he yearned for the one lady who would heal his soul. He sighed and dug the rag out of the bottom of the tub.

A rustle of material caught his ear, and one of the maids stepped up to test the water. William perceived the swirl of her finger by his thigh and smelled the spicy scent of carnation, and grinned. Catching her hand in his, he rubbed the soft skin beneath his thumb and rumbled, "Wench! Is my leg so interesting you yearn to touch it?"

The girl said nothing, only laughing in a startled, breathless way and tugging against his hold.

Emboldened by her laughter—she was obviously not afraid of him or his blindness—he tugged back. "Don't go, I have more I can show you than mere leg!" With a jerk, he pulled her into the tub and onto his lap.

Water rose in a great splash and they were instantly wet from head to toe. The girl gasped and struggled in an inept, careless manner, as if she weren't accustomed to having a man hold her. The quick skim of his hand down her soaking body assured him this couldn't be the case. Any wench blessed with generous bosoms and hips and a tiny waist had been the recipient of many an embrace.

Her amorous struggles grew wilder and less effective and a pleasured smile split his bearded lips. The tiny squeaks she let out were charming, showing spirit but not resistance. This girl knew all the tricks.

His manhood rose in immediate response to such blatant encouragement. Her hips rubbed against him as she kicked out and weakly tried to rise. Her fists pummelled his shoulders as he gathered her to him, turned her sideways and slanted her derriere across his lap. Her head fit into the crook of his elbow, her braid slid over his arm. With a laugh, he captured her flailing fist and tightened the crook of his arm beneath her neck. She was held now, stationary enough for him to find her mouth with his own.

In only a moment, he changed his opinion of her experience. Her mouth yielded, easily opening for his insistent tongue. But she didn't know what to do with it when it surged inside. She didn't meet his thrusts, didn't answer his lures, but she reacted. That mouth was sweet and hungry, amazed and willing. His intentions gentled and turned to guidance.

He relaxed the grip of his arm on her head and supported her back with his huge hand. He massaged up and down her side, petting her, mellowing her. He freed her hand and placed it against his chest, on the flushed skin above his heart. She snatched it back, but he patiently retrieved it and replaced it, still stoking the fires of her innocence with his lips. This time her hand stayed. Her fingers flexed into the curling hair blanketing his skin, trembled and flexed again.

He broke the kiss with a moan. "Sweet thing," he whispered into her ear as he searched the rim with his tongue. A moan of her own puffed across his cheek.

His remaining hand went exploring. Cupping her breast, he circled the nipple, tight with chill and nerves. The heel of his palm kneaded the mound warmly, tenderly, thoroughly, until the woman stretched across his thighs melted into limp pliancy. Gratified with the return for his effort, William bestowed one last fond stroke and searched further. The tuck of her waist confirmed his first hasty diagnosis, and her firm belly quivered as his fingers slid across. The drenched material of her skirt bunched at her knee and his hand eagerly sought the bared skin of her calf. As his fingers made contact, his breath caught and she sighed and tossed, jerked from her lethargy. With the instincts of a magician, William captured her mouth again, delighting her with the return of his lips, and slid his hand up the long, silken pathway of her leg. The pathway to heaven.

And heaven was so close, so close.

A dose of ice cold water splashed his back and brought him crashing to earth. Two powerful hands pushed him backward and grasped the girl by her armpits. She was yanked from him and dragged out of his reach.

He rose to his feet in fury, restrained from attack only by his blindness.

His indignant roar would have frightened lesser women, but Maud was no lesser woman. "Are ye crazy, Lord William? Would ye attack a young damsel in full sight of the maidservants?"

He roared again, inarticulate with wrath, and then as his sense returned, he shouted, "Attack? Attack? All she had to say was 'nay,' and I would have released her. By our sweet Savior, Lady Saura, did you hurl that cold water?"

Saura, soaked and shivering by the fire, answered, "In a manner of speaking."

Liberated from the restraint of silence, her voice sounded quavery, and his temper cooled proportionately. "Give the wench back and I'll forget about it." The group in the window seat released a collective giggle, and he sank back into the water. "Give the wench back and send these she-lackeys away."

Wringing out her full draped sleeve in both her shaking

hands, Saura swiped her hair off her forehead and refused. "I can't do that, my lord. The girl is spoken for."

"Spoken for! She is a serf. I am her lord."

Saura smoothed the rough wool of her garments and cursed her own industry. Her sense of responsibility had demanded she perform the jobs Lord Peter assigned her before she availed herself of the fabric he had offered. The time had come to sew new clothes, clothes marking her as a lady and not a serving maid. "The girl's gone."

"Gone! No one has left this room!" His anger brought him back to his feet. "And I want her now!"

Exasperated beyond her usual self-restraint, Saura shouted back, "I'll speak to your father! We'll make arrangements!" With a swish of her wet skirts, she turned on Maud's arm and went out the door held by a sewing maid who, overcome with nervous humor, bit her hand to stifle her laughter.

"Do ye want me t' warm your bath, Lord William?" asked Linne, one of his late wife's serving women. "I've got more water heated."

"Nay," answered William slowly. "Nay, I think my bath has been sufficiently warmed already. The cold has been vanquished."

In a screened nook off the great hall, Lord Peter wiped his brow on his sleeve and tried to concentrate on the accounting his seneschal was explaining to him. He would rather be out in the bailey, training the young lads Kimball and Clare in swordplay; anything but this everlasting boredom. This had been William's job, keeping track of the year's crop yield and their tenants' rents and whether their stewards had cheated them. He had no head for it, no matter how often or patiently the intelligent young cleric explained it.

"Due to the raids at Fairford," Brother Cedric was saying, "the rents have been down again." He suspended his report, his attention attracted by the commotion coming from the great hall.

Lord Peter looked up, too, interested in anything that would distract him from the agonizing tally. "It has been too long since we've had laughter in the castle," he commented. "The arrival of Lady Saura has set all to rights. The servants are well behaved and cheerful, the meals are well prepared and I believe William is responding at last."

Saura, dripping and angry, appeared in the arched door, one hand on the mastiff's neck, one hand on Maud's arm, and the words died on his lips.

"Lord Peter!" she demanded. "Forgive me for asking, but how long has it been since William fornicated with a woman?"

Stupefied, Lord Peter questioned, "Fornicated? With a woman?"

"His tastes definitely seem to run to female," Saura snapped, gathering her sleeve and wringing it out.

Lord Peter stared at the drenched Madonna before him, at the puddle on the planks around her. "You're wet," he said. "Did you fall in a puddle?"

"Nay, I fell in a bath with your son, and a lusty fellow he is! How long has it been since he was bedded?"

A small sound escaped Brother Cedric, and Lord Peter turned to see him struggling against a chuckle and staring at Saura. The utilitarian wool *cotte* was drenched, the gold undergarment showed through the lacing at the sides. Her violet eyes glittered, her cheeks were flushed a pretty pink. Her lips throbbed full and red and carried the delectable swelling that was the symptom of a thorough kissing.

Maud cleared her throat and Lord Peter's gaze flew to hers. The message that passed from her mind to his was explicit and vehement and he hastily answered, "Ah, I think 'twas before he was blinded."

"Oh, marvelous. It has been months. Well, that must change. Bring a woman to him now. She has to have my shape," Saura measured her waist with her hands, "and have all her teeth. He has intimate experience with my teeth. I'll send out my clothes, she can wear them. And Lord Peter?"

"Aye?" Dazed, Lord Peter tried to put together the sequence of events leading to these extraordinary demands.

"You promised me material from France. I'll get the sewing women started on my new wardrobe at once." She nodded regally and took Maud's arm. Tugging at the dog's neck, she ordered, "To my chamber."

Lord Peter stared after them and repeated with mild astonishment, "Damn! What did I tell you? Lady Saura is setting all to rights."

"Shoo! Ye big dog, go on, ye don't belong in m'lady's chamber."

"Let him in, Maud. He'll just claw at the door if you don't."

The dog's claws created a clipped rhythm on the wooden floor and the bedchamber door closed behind them. Maud scolded, "Every stupid dog in the world worships ye. Get over to the fire and strip out of those clothes. This chilly spring's no time to take a bath."

"I hadn't planned on it!" Saura protested, hands busy with the lacing. "Oh, help, the tie is stuck."

Maud dropped the clothes she was lifting from a trunk and hurried to attend her lady. "Aye, 'tis wet, and it would seem Lord William's busy fingers knotted it tight. If I didn't have reason to know better, m'lady, I'd say your performance in the bathtub smacked of an experienced woman."

"I am an experienced woman—" Saura smiled a lopsided, charmed smile. "Now."

"I've not seen such passion since the first time your mother helped your father with his bath. She was a maiden, too, but not for long."

"I was curious." She lifted her arms and let Maud remove her garments.

"Curiosity, is it?" Maud mused. "Nay, I've seen curiosity before, and that wasn't it."

Goaded by an interest she didn't understand, Saura asked, "What does he look like, Maud?"

"*That's* curiosity." Stepping back, she examined her lady's naked form. "Ah, Lady Saura, ye're beautiful. Ye should have been wedded and bedded at thirteen, like the other women."

"And perhaps dead in childbed at fifteen."

"As God wills, but I long to hold your babes in my arms. 'Tis not too late, ye know. Ye're only nineteen."

Saura hugged the old woman. "Only nineteen? Ha! Well past the age of marriage. Don't open my mind to hope, Maud. I can live with resignation, but if I begin to dream of a man, a man of my own. . . ." She shivered. "I'm chilled."

Maud brought a rough towel and rubbed Saura all over, handed it to her and ordered, "Dry your hair. He's big."

"Who?"

"Who!" Maud snorted.

"William? I *know* he's big! His voice is way up here." Saura leveled her hand above her head.

She plucked the veil from her hair and wrung the water from the long, single braid hanging over her shoulder. "He's a magnificent stallion, and he's tall and well muscled. He has a pleasant voice, very pleasant. I know all that. But what does he look like?"

Maud tossed a dry under-shift over Saura's head and tugged it down. "His face is broad and stern, and he smiles but rarely. But when he does, m'lady! His dimples show even above that scraggly beard. He's so blond, so light, he appears golden in his bath." Maud checked her lady's face.

Enraptured, Saura clung to every word with her lips slightly open and white teeth peeking out. Her hands, employed with the business of unbraiding her hair, froze in midair. Her chest rose and fell with deep inhalations, her eyes shone.

To Maud, Saura's expression and her sudden interest revealed hope for her mistress's future. Maud expanded her description with sly intention. "He's the type of man women gawk at. Whoever they dress up and send in there will be more than willing, I assure ye."

"That relieves my mind," Saura said wryly, her fingers busy with the braid once more.

"Aye, I'm sure it does." Maud chuckled. "This relieves my mind, too."

When the door of the master chamber opened and William walked out on Linne's arm, Lord Peter had to fight back a swell of tears. His son had returned.

William's beard was trimmed close to show the strong chin

held at a determined angle. Cut into a golden fringe above his eyebrows and around his neck, his hair swung in cadence with his stride. He walked upright, his step firm and his shoulders unbending.

He was back again: William was back.

"Father!" Kimball rose from his bench at the head table and tumbled out onto the floor. "Father." He ran to him, catching his hand.

"Aye, son?" William tilted his head down, seeming to look at the boy. "Is everyone seated at the tables? Am I late?"

"We waited for you. Lady Saura said you'd had lots of excitement and you might be taking a nap, but Grandfather said taking a bath is hard work and insisted we wait. So Lady Saura ordered a soup and we've been having some music. Her harp playing reminds me of the angels. But now we're starving!"

"We mustn't have that. Will you take me to the table?" He freed his hand from Linne's arm, leaned down and whispered, "And make sure I don't bang my shins?"

"Aye, sir." Pleased to have his father back, too young to be sentimental, Kimball grinned. "I won't let you trip. Put your hand in my elbow; you want me to sit beside you and cut your meat? The quintain only knocked me off my horse once today and it knocked Clare off four times—here's the bench, Father, lift your leg over—but Grandfather says he's going to be a great jouster if he keeps practicing. He's seven and I told him I didn't do as well at seven and he's not as big as I was even then but Grandfather says he has a good seat. Here's your trencher, feel it?" He took William's hand and put it on the rough wooden plate.

"Aye, thank you, Kimball." A smile tugged at William's mouth. "Have you missed me?"

"Well," the eight-year-old thought about that. "You

haven't been gone, exactly. But you didn't like to hear me talk."

"I know. I'm sorry, it will not happen again." He raised his hand and searched, found the boy's face and then his head, and smoothed the tangled hair back. "But tell me, who is Clare?"

"Why, he's Lady Saura's brother," Kimball said in astonishment. "He's sitting at the end of the head table. He usually shares my trencher."

"Her brother?"

"Grandfather had to take him for fostering or we couldn't have her. He's been here all spring with Lady Saura. She's nice. She's been taking care of us, talking to us and kissing us good night and slopping comfrey salve on our bruises. Except she forced us to take a spring bath. Did she have the servants strip you and throw you in, too?"

A tomblike officiousness hushed the table: every ear strained to hear his answer.

"Nay, son," William rumbled. "There are incentives for adults who agree to bathe without struggling."

A low chuckle rippled around the trestle tables and William's retainers and admirers nodded and murmured to one another.

He was back. Their lord was back.

"Did you enjoy your incentive?" Lord Peter asked at William's left hand.

William smiled pleasantly. "She was a very accomplished young lass, willing and eager to accommodate her lord. She had a lovely shape and pleasant breath. She matched almost perfectly the girl I kissed in the tub."

The page who was dishing out dropped his wooden serving spoon and he danced away from the hot soup as it splattered on the floor. The clank of the wood on the flagstones, the

sound of his feet shuffling, the murmur of his apology rever-
berated through the great hall as the knowing heads swiveled
from Saura to William and back again.

William, of course, didn't know who else they stared at,
but he knew he had everyone's attention as he continued,
"Aye, Father, I am blind. But I'm not simpleminded. The girl
in the bath had an innocent fire no other woman could
duplicate. Her sweet mouth branded me. I don't know who
she was, or what she was, or why I can't have her, but my
bathing companion was unforgettable. And until I can put
my hands on her, I'll not bed a substitute."

three

"William, you have to stop kissing the maids." Saura slapped her leather gloves against her palm.

The girl in William's lap slid off, giggling, as he patted her bottom. "Thank you, dearling, but you're not the one." His voice resounded in the screened cubicle where he worked with Brother Cedric.

William's only fault, in Saura's mind, was his predilection for kissing the maids. The brush of a skirt against his hand brought prompt response. He grabbed and kissed indiscriminately, old and young, single and married, sweet and sour. The women giggled and grabbed back, or giggled and slipped away, but he always pronounced, "You're not the one," as he released them.

It warmed Saura's heart to hear him repudiating them, as much as it burned her gut to listen to the kiss.

The cupbearer slipped past as Saura stood in the doorway, and William complained, "You need to bring in some new girls. How can I find my mystery woman if I'm kissing the same ones day after day?"

"Don't kiss them!" she repeated in exasperation.

"But I like to."

Saura flung her hands into the air. "You're hopeless."

"Just curious."

"Dressed for an outing, Lady Saura?" With conscious design, Brother Cedric supplied the clue William desired.

"Going riding this fine afternoon?" William asked.

Instinctively straightening her new linen bliaud, she agreed. "If I can find the boys to join me. There's trouble at the miller's and Linne's prepared a basket. Would you like to—"

"Aye." William stood up. "I would."

She laughed and blushed and stepped away. "I'd be flattered at your eagerness, my lord, but I suspect the real attraction is the horse." She halted in her tracks. She had detected a note in her voice she had never heard before. A coy note, a shy curl of laughter: the sound of flirtatiousness.

William smacked into her back, almost knocking her down. He grabbed and caught her elbows from behind. "Saura?"

"Excuse me, my lord." She tried to jerk away and his hands tightened briefly, then released. "I stopped in front of you, all unthinking."

"Aye." His voice sounded strained also, she noticed. "You're thinner than I'd believed."

"Did you imagine me stuffed like a palliasse?" She inched across the bare floor, uncertain of her location.

"Nay," he answered flatly as he followed. "I imagined you . . . I've wondered."

" 'Tis natural," she assured him, seeking the role of

teacher. "The blind often wonder how the people around them look."

"Every other face I do remember well. You are a stranger in Burke Castle. Would you let me touch your face?"

Saura drew in a shuddering sigh. She'd love to have him touch her face: and, she suspected, anywhere else he desired. But it was too soon. He'd developed into a recognizable master in the past two weeks. When he discovered the trick they had played on him, he'd be furious, and justifiably so. She cursed Lord Peter and this imaginative deception.

"I don't think that would be a good idea," she told him, a kind and patronizing lilt to her voice. She hated it, but it seemed necessary to discourage his interest.

"Really?"

"The relationship we share is based on mutual respect, and curiosity on your part shouldn't be indulged," she babbled.

"An interesting theory."

His voice advanced toward her and she took a sudden step back. "Lord William?"

"Hmm?"

He was smiling, she could tell, stalking her across the floor of the great hall, and serfs working by the fire chuckled with amusement. "What are you thinking of?" He lunged and she scrambled back. "I wish you wouldn't!"

He lunged again and caught her wrist, and slowly pulled her toward him. She resisted with the halfhearted struggles of a reluctant maiden, freezing when a raucous whistle echoed through the room.

"Still lusty as ever, eh, William?"

The stranger's voice sounded amused and William released her in surprise. "Charles?"

"Of course." The stranger moved into the room. "The way

you chased that wench, I thought you had regained your sight."

"I have eyes in my fingers," he replied, wiggling them. "Raymond, is that you?" he asked when another set of footsteps advanced into the room.

"Well met, William," Raymond said. "We hunted the day away, and rode in to sup with you. We left Arthur in the bailey with his hand up a wench's skirt."

"As always." He laughed. "I bid you welcome. And where is Nicholas?"

He jumped when a quiet voice close to him said, "Here I am."

"God's teeth, I should have known you could still creep up on me." He held out an arm, and Nicholas grasped it at the elbow. "Well met, Nicholas. Lady Saura?"

"At once, my lord." She blundered away and was rescued by Maud's hand on her arm. In silence, the older woman showed her her location. "Put up the trestle tables," Saura ordered as she found her bearings. "Draw ale and wine and bring cheese and bread. Hurry the meal arrangements. Tell the cook to prepare cabbage soup and aforce the stew with barley. And Maud," she lowered her voice, "escort me to a more private spot."

The serving woman led her behind a darkened support arch. "Will these three cause us trouble, m'lady?"

"I don't know," Saura murmured. "Perhaps."

Sandaled feet thumped on the floor as servants scurried to do her bidding and the three guests hauled their own benches to the newly erected tables. She heard the scraping noise as old Bartley dragged William's chair to the center of the table and murmured, "Here ye are, m'lord."

William carefully seated himself in the place of honor, and she tensed; a pewter pitcher clinked and liquid splashed into a goblet. The stream grew thinner as the cup filled. The sound ceased.

"Well done, William," exclaimed Raymond and Saura sighed with silent relief.

Pushing the cup across the wooden table slab, he said, "Take it, and avail yourself of cheese and bread. My father is out in the woods, teaching the lads to ride without hands. We'll send for him. He'll want to display his accomplished knights to the boys."

Nicholas took the ale. "To prove he's dragged many a boy up to manhood?"

"By their hair," Raymond joked, and the three men laughed in unison.

William poured another goblet for Charles. "He swore he'd never again take four lads to foster, all at the same time. You wore him out."

"We wore *him* out?" Charles hooted. "I used to sleep in my trencher after he finished with a day's training. Arthur used to pretend illness when it rained, and Lord Peter would drag him out of his blanket by his toes. Raymond never complained, just followed orders and ate so much the dogs under the table were starving. And remember when Nicholas broke his arm and had to learn to wield a sword with his left hand?"

"Lord Peter never slacked off." Nicholas groaned. "He said every knight should use his sword with either hand."

"Aye, and he made us all practice with both arms." Raymond remembered. "You're lucky, Nicholas, we didn't break your other arm."

"Now he's got some other pages to torment?" Charles asked.

"One is my son," William admitted.

"That's interesting." Nicholas tapped the table with his

fingers. "Will Lord Peter work his own grandson harder, or will he be soft on him?"

William grinned, baring all his teeth. "What do you think?"

"The poor boy." Raymond accepted a brimming cup. "The poor, poor boy."

The men guffawed, their sympathy mixed with humor, and William asked, "What do you hunt, Charles?"

"Boar. But we've had the devil's own luck. We brought you venison instead. Since you can't hunt anymore, we thought your table could use the meat."

Raymond's deep, precise voice corrected, "William's huntsmen won't appreciate such a compliment."

"We're not starving," William agreed, his tone deliberate and bland, and he felt the touch of Raymond's hand on his in brief communication. Of all the men his father had fostered, only Raymond was his close friend, and why, he could not discern. Raymond was younger, and richer, more noble, and so clever it made William's teeth hurt. Prey to dark moods, Raymond had depths William couldn't understand, yet the two of them meshed in some inexplicable rapport. Grateful for his support, both spoken and unspoken, William filled another cup. "What news of our King Stephen and our Queen Matilda?"

"Stephen's on the march again, and Matilda's still licking her wounds across the Channel. Stephen should have killed her while he had her in his hands," Charles said with disgust.

"He's too much of a chevalier," Raymond conceded. "Too much of a fool. And what good would Matilda's death do? 'Tis her son who's making the heads turn now."

"Are the rumors true? Is the boy back in England again?" William asked.

"The *boy*," Raymond emphasized the word drolly, "is at least twenty and ready to pluck the throne from Stephen's unsteady grasp."

"Have you seen Duke Henry?" William asked, interested and intense.

"Nay, not yet," Raymond said, "but he landed in January, and I hear he fights like a man and thinks with the uncanny statesmanship of Matilda, but without her uncertain temper. Nor should we discount the advantage of his marriage to Eleanor last year. She's the duchess of Poitou and Aquitaine and—"

"The queen of France." William grinned.

"The queen no longer." Charles chuckled with the glee of a born gossip. "They say she drove saintly Louis of France to distraction. She accompanied him on crusade, you know, and created a scandal. Last spring they divorced on grounds of consanguinity."

"Are they cousins?" William interrupted.

"Something like that," Charles agreed. "Half the royal marriages are tainted with consanguinity. It's only important when a divorce is needed."

Raymond picked up the knife and with vigorous motions cut slabs of cheese for the men. "All of Eleanor's crying of consanguinity with the king of France, and she and Henry share a blood line, also."

"Of course, her lands in Poitou and Aquitaine make her a vassal of the French king." Charles tore chunks of bread from the loaf and passed them around.

"Just so." Raymond gave a peal of laughter. "She's required to receive his sanction to marry anyone, and she flouted Louis. Henry, too, should have received permission. He'd just paid his vassal's vow of fealty to his overlord for his lands in France. Henry had given him the kiss of peace, and still the wedding was accomplished before Louis heard a breath of it. Eleanor's beautiful lands have gone to fund Louis's greatest rival."

Nicholas crumbled bread between his fingers as he listened, but he could keep silent no longer. "That my vassals would flout my authority to wed and combine themselves against me would stick in my gullet, also."

"Personally, I believe 'twas their marriage not even two months after the divorce that distressed Louis," Charles said. "No matter how holy Louis is, he could hardly wish to believe that the she-devil he couldn't tame leapt gladly into another man's bed. A younger man's bed."

"It sounds as if the wedding were political, but the marriage bed was preference," William observed. "When Eleanor was queen of France, she complained that she'd thought to marry a king and found she'd married a monk."

"The contrary woman bore Louis only daughters," Charles reminded them.

"Poor Louis couldn't even win when he marched into Normandy to crush his former wife and her new husband. Henry charged in from the west and left Louis's army in ruins." Raymond spoke, but all the men were laughing now. It was a bright day for the English when the king of France was discomfited, and the men reveled in it.

"What says Louis about this today?" William asked.

Raymond answered with smug pleasure, "What can he say? Eleanor is going to have a babe this summer, and the stars predict a son."

"Then the young stallion will produce what the old saint could not." William settled back with a grin. "So Henry has the funds to continue his battles until the tide turns his way?"

"He has the funds to buy England, should he desire it,"

Raymond said. "Eleanor's eleven years older than Henry, of course, but she's an attractive woman."

"Age has no bearing on a royal wedding so long as the woman is fecund," William said. "Queen Matilda was fifteen years older than Henry's father, and he's preceded her in death."

" 'Twas a wise marriage for Henry," Nicholas concurred. "It gives him a great deal of power."

"Does Stephen hold him off?" William asked.

Raymond said bitterly, "Stephen wavers in the breeze, as uncertain as ever."

"Stephen's your cousin," Charles pointed out.

"So is Matilda," Raymond agreed. "I'd support either one of our sovereigns, or their sons, if they'd just settle the country."

"There's profit to be made with the chaos," Charles said thoughtfully.

"Profit! What kind of man destroys his honor to cull profit from his country's disaster?" William asked, his scorn palpable as he filled another cup and pushed it toward Nicholas. "A man without honor crawls on his belly like the worms of the earth."

" 'Tis a way to gain lands."

"By theft!"

"Or chicanery," Nicholas interjected smoothly.

"Stephen has plunged the country into disaster with his vacillating." William poured one last cup. "Were he backed against a wall, think you he would declare Henry his rightful heir?"

"That's the question, is it not?" Raymond laughed. "And what will Stephen's sons say about such a dismissal?"

"A new generation of war." Nicholas sighed. "To burn the earth and bring pestilence to the land."

Charles said, "We should have kept our oaths to—"

"To whom?" William flashed. "My only oath of fealty is to the sovereign of England, and I know not who that is."

"Perhaps God has abandoned us," Raymond said with sardonic dismay.

A heavy silence fell as they contemplated the chaos, then Nicholas roused. "That's why I like to fight."

"You, Nicholas?" William queried. "*You* like to fight?" Nicholas was a large man, quiet, jocular when it suited his purposes. He was not an accomplished knight, yet as an administrator none could surpass him. What others did with brawn and might, he did with his clever brain and ability to read others. If William felt a bit of contempt for Nicholas's cowardice, he held it firmly in check. He'd seen Nicholas, as a newly dubbed knight, return to his older brother's home to serve him. He'd seen the brother carried off by the bloody flux almost immediately, seen Nicholas take control of the estates with a steady hand that never faltered.

"Come, William, I'm not so clumsy," Nicholas protested. William took refuge in a sip of ale, and Nicholas's voice smoothed and thinned. "Perhaps I am, but I like to watch. Fighting keeps my mind off these weighty matters over which I have no control. I'm hosting a tournament on Whitsunday, and William, I wish you could participate. No knight in England holds himself in full good honor unless he defeats you."

William's voice filled with eagerness. "A mêlée?"

"Aye," Nicholas said. "Remember the time in Chichester your lance broke in the first charge and your horse was wounded? And you fought on foot and won ransom from five different knights?"

"I just utilized the first rule of combat," William said smoothly, and the others laughed as if they'd been told a marvelous joke. William grinned at their relish. "I equipped myself and my retinue handsomely that day."

"But the span of your shoulders measured so large no hauberk you won could fit you." Charles chuckled, easily turned to reminisce.

A voice called from the doorway. "Remember the time you took that barbarian of Kirkoswald prisoner?"

"Arthur, trust you to avoid the talk of England's welfare and appear only to reminisce." William's tone echoed a disdain for the light-minded man who'd never grown up.

"You look well." Arthur's footsteps pattered across the floor, childlike and frisky, like a puppy greeting his master.

"I thank you."

Over the top of William's head, Arthur spoke to his hunting companions. "Is he still blind?"

"He is," William interrupted. "But he's not deaf."

Impervious to William's frustration, Arthur poured himself a goblet of ale. "The greatest knight in all of England, fallen from glory by a single blow. What a shame."

"A greater shame to dwell on it," Charles suggested. "So shut your mouth, Arthur."

"I will, but I wonder if his liver's turned white?"

William slammed down his cup and rose to his feet, but Raymond grasped his arm and pulled him back down, saying, "Do you no harm to the little coward. 'Tis *his* liver that's white, and his mouth blathers of matters better left to greater men. Apologize, Arthur."

"My liver's not white!" Arthur said.

"Apologize, Arthur." It took only one demand from Nicholas's cool, smooth voice, and Arthur mumbled an apology.

The moment was fraught with unspoken tensions, the apology unacknowledged by the recipient, and Charles broke the silence with a false jolliness. "Do you remember how the barbarian shrieked when you demanded his horse?"

Their voices droned on, recalling events of past glory, and Saura set her jaw and gestured. Bartley stood by her side immediately. "M'lady?"

"Send for young Kimball and Clare at once. They will want to see these good knights, I am sure, and we need pages to serve the head table. Order the panter up here to trim the bread. Summon Lord Peter again. And hurry the meal arrangements."

"Aye, m'lady."

She cocked an ear to the conversation, disliking its flavor. It contained the potential to destroy William's progress. She dated the events at Burke Castle with two labels: prebath and postbath. Prebath William fought against blindness as if his refusal to accept his fate would alter his circumstances. But that day in the bath, William had truly returned. The creed governing his life motivated him once more and he vanquished despondency.

Now Saura understood why his vassals and servants worshiped him. The chair in front of the fire rested bare, no longer the haven of an angry man. What needed to be done was done promptly and with no complaint, and what he required was the guidance to dominate his handicap. In a few short weeks he had learned everything she could teach him, absorbing knowledge as a freed prisoner absorbs sunlight. He ate with knife and spoon, he ordered the work in the stables, he disciplined the boys. Desiring freedom, he'd ordered that ropes be strung from the castle into the woods, providing him with a guide along the path he preferred to walk.

It had been a time of triumph for Saura. Her pupil proved himself to be a *nonpareil*, and she had proved herself in a manner that bemused and flattered her. She was no longer an outsider, no longer a temporary chatelaine or a surrogate to be endured. The churls treated her well, for she had shown she had the ability to capture their lord's attention with her feminity. That was a skill they respected, and it held a power they understood.

Still, it was not the thought of her enhanced prestige that brought a smile to her face when she lay on her bed in the dark, but the memory of a man's strong arms about her and his golden voice saying, "I don't know who she is, but she is unforgettable."

"Your blindness, William, is such a tragedy." Saura jerked back from her dream and clenched her fists, for Arthur's voice throbbed with pity. "What do you do with yourself all day?"

William laughed, a pleasant sound that fooled all but her trained ear. "I rise and dress with the help of my pages."

"Surely your squire lays out your clothes? But, no," Charles recalled. "Sir Guilliame removed his son from your care."

"Young Guilliame complained most sorely, for we were fond of one another. He had been with me for six years. But I urged his withdrawal. I could not complete the boy's training to knighthood without the eyes to direct his progress." Now William's pain echoed for all to hear, but he fought his voice to an even tenor. "I break my fast with a sop in wine and go out to the stables."

"Do you not trip and fall?" Raymond queried, real interest in his tone.

William laughed again, long and heartily, and stuck his leg out from beneath the table. "Beneath these hose, chevaliers, are shins bright with black-and-blue bruises, tokens of encounters with unforgiving wood and stone." He shrugged.

"My years as a squire handed me worse punishment for less reward."

"What reward?" Charles shoved his cup toward William. "More ale."

"I'm free to wander in the bailey. As long as I count my steps and follow my landmarks, I'm never lost." William found the cup with his groping fingers and poured it full. He shoved it back to Charles and refilled his own. "I walk with cane in hand, practicing until the drag of the tip on the ground resembles my own touch. With the help of our cleric, I deal with the estate accounts. And I render judgment in estate court."

"You've found useful occupation then, William," Raymond approved.

"But not pleasant, eh?" Charles joked. "I remember how you hated the dull days of listening to the lies of one villein pitted against another, and deciding the truth."

" 'Tis a fitting duty for me," he answered.

"And my thanks, son, for relieving me of it," Lord Peter said. His spurs clanged on the stone floor as he strode in with the dog and two youths dancing at his heels.

"You ride, too, Father," Kimball shouted.

"Indeed I do," William said warmly, wrapping his arm around the boys who nestled against him. "With the help of these pages and Lady Saura."

"You ride your destrier?" Raymond asked, surprised.

"Nay, I'm not fool enough to try to ride that fighting steed. They've found me a colossal farm horse, big enough to carry me and young enough to retain its spirit."

"And they understand each other," Kimball bragged. "Father and the horse think as one, and we hardly needed to touch the leading rein connected to his bridle."

"A leading rein? Like a woman?" Arthur murmured. "How you must complain about that!"

"Not at all: 'tis necessary," William answered curtly.

Lord Peter stepped forward. "Welcome to our home. My Lord Raymond." Cheeks brushed lightly as they embraced. "Nicholas. Charles. Arthur. I do believe you four have grown!"

Kimball shouted with laughter. "That's what he says to me when he hasn't seen me in a while."

The men guffawed and agreed. "So he always has, to all the lads he's fostered."

"A man's got a choice. If he isn't growing, he is shrinking. I hope you always grow in my eyes, Kimball."

Calling softly for a stool, Saura relaxed in her corner. Lord Peter would direct the conversation, and surely he wasn't such a fool as to speak endlessly of the clash of arms that William longed for.

Bartley approached and announced, "Supper's ready, m'lady, will ye not come t' dine?"

"Nay, Bartley." She smiled at the anxious churl, and petted the head of Bula, who had discovered her in his first circuit of the room and now leaned against her shoulder. "These gentle knights would unintentionally inform Lord William of my blindness. Let me direct the dispensing of the meal from my corner."

"I'll bring ye a saumon coffyn," Bartley said firmly, "an' a goblet of wine. The wine'll warm ye an' that fish pie's tasty today."

"Come, chevaliers," Lord Peter called. "My farrier tells me the mares in the stable bred clean and true this season. Let's go and see the colts."

Without pause, the conversation veered to horses, to

halters, to saddles. The men left the hall, William in their midst, and the serving folk scurried into action.

The serfs swept the head table clean and laid a white cloth and overcloth on the board. The salt was placed in the center while the panter hurried to Saura and asked, "M'lady, how should we arrange th' seatin'? My Lord Raymond is an earl, an' since the death of his brother, Lord Nicholas is a baron. Lord Raymond should sit before th' salt, but Lord Peter insists he is th' lord in his own castle, barrin' a visit from th' king."

"Quite right," Saura nodded. "So Lord Peter and Lord Raymond shall sit before the salt. Lord William shall share a trencher with Nicholas, Lord Peter share a trencher with Raymond, and Charles and Arthur shall share. Do you arrange it that way."

She listened to the preparation for the evening, ever ready with a suggestion or command. She questioned whether the room needed light, and now tall candles flickered on heavy iron stands and torches of resinous wood smoked in wall brackets. She asked about the meal, and was assured the trestle tables sat at right angles to the head table, now set with eating knives and spoons. Two trenchers rested equidistant from the center and another set toward one end. She heard the buzz as men-at-arms, castle watchmen, and subtenants filtered in to jostle one another. For them, she decreed ale to drink as they waited for the nobility to return. The laws of hospitality had provided an unexpected bonus: their evening meal was usually a crust of bread and a thick porridge. The roar of voices echoed deep and full until the rattling of spurs announced the return of the lords.

Brother Cedric said a brief grace and the working men turned their ravenous attention to the food. Peace reigned as they filled the yawning empty spaces of their bellies. Lord

Peter's squire carved the mutton for the head table, Kimball and Clare carried the pie and pasties in on chargers. Servitors raced to satisfy the demands of the lower tables, and Raymond joked, "Have you discovered a miracle pot in your kitchen, Lord Peter? For the first time in many years, the fare of your table is fit for consumption."

Lord Peter laughed, accepting another slice of meat on the tip of his knife. " 'Tis Lady Saura's doing. She bullies us to cleanliness. The cook lives in fear of her visits."

"You mean we'll not go to bed suffering from a flux of the bowels?" Arthur sneered, and then halted with his knife in midair. "Lady Saura?"

Already sorry he had revealed his treasure, Lord Peter chewed and swallowed before saying, "Aye, she's one of my wife's relatives, come to be our housekeeper." He deliberately didn't glance into the corner where Saura huddled, afraid to draw attention to the woman.

"Lady Saura," Arthur murmured. "The only Lady Saura I know of is Saura of Roget. Now there's a treasure. A virtuous maiden and an heiress, but her stepfather hides her away for fear she'll be abducted and married and all those glorious lands taken from his control."

William raised his head and Nicholas examined his alert face with eyes that gleamed with interest.

"How old is she?" William asked.

"Old. She must be . . . twenty-two? And never wed. But she's—"

Clare tripped and spilled the venison stew into Arthur's lap. With a shriek, Arthur leaped up and backhanded the boy into the wall. "Stupid oaf!" Brushing at the thick wine sauce, he lamented the ruin of his best tunic while servants rushed to his assistance. When the hubbub had died down, he turned to chastise the page who had caused him so much grief, but Clare had disappeared.

In Saura's bedroom, she pressed him down on her bed and laid a wet rag on his swollen face. "I thank you. You're a brave boy," she said, hugging him tight. "Mama would be proud of you, defending me like that."

"All of us brothers have to defend you," the young warrior answered stoutly, and then winced at the vigor of his speech. "Rollo said so."

"All of my half brothers are most loyal," she praised.

He stuck his tongue in his cheek and examined the injury. "I don't think that man loosened any teeth."

"Nay, but you'll be bruised in the morning." She smoothed the cowlick waving in his short bangs. "You can sleep here in my bed. It would be better if you didn't return to the hall tonight."

"Aye, please!" He bounced up and down. "This is better than the palliasse I share with Kimball."

Snatching the chance to question her brother, Saura asked, "Clare, do you like it here? At Burke Castle?"

"We're not leaving, are we?" he asked quickly.

"Nay, of course not." Smiling, she positioned her palm on his face. "You were too young to come for fostering, and I wondered if you missed Lord Theobald. If you missed your father."

He gave it consideration. "Well, sometimes I do miss him. I liked it when he taught me things and talked to me. But most of the time, he just drank wine and yelled and threw up. Lord Peter teaches me things and talks to me, too, but he only hits me when I deserve it. I miss Blaise," his voice quivered wistfully.

"And the babies and Lady Blanche?"

"Well, the babies."

Saura skimmed her fingers over his expression of disgust and laughed. "As long as you are happy. Come in, Kimball."

The boy stuck his head in the door. "Can't I ever sneak up on you?" he complained.

"Some people can sneak up on me," she answered reasonably. "But an eight-year-old boy with big feet is not one of them."

"How did you know my feet were big?" Kimball stuck out a sandaled foot and examined it.

"All boys' feet are big. Clare's sleeping in my bed tonight. Do you wish to join him?"

Kimball shouted and leaped up, and Saura moved aside.

"Is the meal over?"

"Aye. Oh, how's your face?" Kimball climbed on the bed and callously pronounced, "That's not as bad as when you fell off the rafter in the barn."

"The barn?" Saura queried.

"Oops." Kimball squirmed and Clare whacked him.

"Does your grandfather know about this?"

" 'Twas his idea to tell you Clare was thrown from his horse," Kimball replied, glad to spread the blame on broader shoulders.

Saura groaned, but couldn't stop a chuckle. The boys sighed in a harmonic whoosh and wrestled as she moved to the door.

A sudden attack of conscience hit Clare. "Where will you sleep this night?"

Pausing in the doorway, she said, "I don't know if I will. It seems to be developing into a long evening."

Hovering by the rail in the gallery, Saura listened to the talk from the tables below and sighed. Her faith in Lord Peter was misplaced. War was the business of the day, and war dominated the conversation. He could not avoid the subject, and she doubted he had tried. Battles, warriors, knights, foot soldiers. Maneuvers, destriers, armor, defence. Lord Peter, Raymond, Nicholas, Arthur and Charles argued and agreed, suggested and refuted, with the vehemence of trained men whose life and honor depended on their ability to fight, which it did.

William said not a word. Only the clink of the pitcher against his goblet indicated his presence.

She crept down the stairs and into her corner where Bula slept. The ominous silence from her pupil weighed her spirits. Maud fetched Saura's hand loom and bent to listen to whispered instructions. Bartley came, too, listened and nodded his understanding. When the chevaliers rose and stretched, maid servants appeared at their elbows immediately to escort them to their rooms. A great deal of groaning ensued, genial groans of weariness and satiety, and Raymond, Nicholas, Charles, and Arthur followed the women to their beds.

Lord Peter followed, and stopped. "Coming, William?"

"Not now." The golden voice contained no emotion.

"You didn't say much tonight."

Saura ground her teeth at the father's oblivion to his son's pain and his clumsy attempt to repair a mistake he didn't know he'd made.

"It didn't bother you, did it, that we discussed things you. . . ." His voice trailed off.

"Nay, Father, I'm fine." William sounded weary, slurring his words slightly.

"We didn't mean to."

Maud rescued the moment. "Come on, ye old fool," she said. "I'll put you to bed."

"But—" Lord Peter sounded amazed.

"Come on!" She jerked him by the elbow and he stumbled

after her, heeding her wisp of an explanation and giving over his protests.

Saura waited and listened. As she had instructed, serfs cleared the tables and left the room, the slow shuffle of their feet indicating their curiosity. She rose from her stool and gestured, and the shuffle transformed into a stampede.

Satisfied that every man and woman would sleep elsewhere this night, she stroked Bula's ears for courage and strolled to the table. Pulling out the bench beside her lord, she asked mildly, "What are you doing?"

"Lady Saura! What a surprise," he mocked. "How amazing that you would be the one to keep me company in my misery."

She was silent. How she hated that cultured modulation of French, that refined accent he affected to convey her lesser status.

"What am I doing? Why, dear madame, dear nun, I am drinking."

"And stinking?"

Now he was silent, releasing at last a very small laugh. "How clever you are. Almost clever enough to be a man."

Her hands clenched the edge of the table until her knuckles cracked. "Cleverer than this man. Smart enough to know getting stinking drunk will never bring a change for the better."

"Ah, but it will. For tonight, I am happy."

"Are you?"

"Indeed," he said, too quickly.

"And in the morning?"

"I have a hard head. I never bring my dinner up. I'll feel fine in the morning."

"But will you still be blind?"

His cup clanged on the table and ale splashed her hand.

"God's glove! Blind drunk tonight, blind in the morning, what difference does it make? I'm only half a man, anyway."

"What do you mean?"

"I can't fight, I can't defend my lands, I can't order the education of my son in the knightly arts, I can't keep a squire, I can't ride a real man's horse."

"What's done is done, and the egg cracked cannot be mended. As you told them earlier, you can keep accounts, you can sit in judgment."

"I'm not a man, I'm just a monk."

The pity, the clogging pity, brought her to her feet. The bench crashed behind her and her fist sent his ale mug flying. Her normal serenity disappeared behind the wave of disappointment and fury, and she roared in a voice that rivalled his own. "You're blind? So? You want to know what trouble is? I'll tell you what trouble is. Athele's a widow and her last son has died, and she carries sixty years. She's got no teeth and no way to support herself and pain twists her joints, and half the village thinks she a witch because she's lonely and her mind wanders and she mutters to herself. That's trouble." She paused, breathing hard. Somewhere in the back of her mind, she was amazed at her temerity, her lack of control, and her rage.

But she didn't want to stop. The anger of all her years roiled in her gut and demanded an outlet, and she shouted, "You want to talk about trouble? Maybe Geoffrey the Miller has an excuse for to pity himself. A band of reavers crept into the mill and stole wheat and tied him to the side of the water wheel. Dear God, they've had to amputate his legs. He's going to live, and he's happy. He's grateful, but he'll live with pain the rest of his life, every day."

Leaning her hands against his chair, she bent and put her face to his. "But the great William is blind. 'Tis so sad, to think a man has his health and his teeth and his legs and his wits and is missing one tiny component."

Now he rose, slowly, like a gigantic tidal wave gathering strength to crash over her indignation and douse it with his resentment.

"You're a nun. You believe resignation and industry will cure all ills, but nothing can bring my sight back. Nothing can give me the view of good English foot soldiers marching into a battle. Nothing can return the satisfaction of laying siege to an enemy and dispossessing him of his castle. Nothing can bring me the pleasure of a tempered sword in my hand and a mêlée before me." Rising from a reasonable rumble, his voice gathered strength as he spoke and he snatched at her, snagging her wrist. "I am a lord. I do the things you praise me for, because 'tis the work I am required to do. But I am also required to fight, to defend my villeins and their crops, to defend my castles, to destroy thieves, and maintain justice. And that's my pleasure, my reward." He shook her wrist. "Do you understand, little nun?"

Bula whined in the corner, unable to decide how to react to such a scene between his master and his mistress.

"Aye."

"You *are* a nun, aren't you?" he sneered. "That display of unholy temper should have been beaten out of you at the convent. What order of nuns are you?"

"I . . . it doesn't matter."

"Are you ashamed of them? At what age were you dedicated to our Savior?"

"Early."

"Was your father unable to supply the dowry for a husband?"

"Nay. I mean, aye."

He cocked his head. "You don't sound very positive about

this. You don't know what order you belong to, when you were dedicated, or if you're a nun by virtue or material needs. And uncertainty drips from your voice." He shook her again. "Are you sure, are you sure you're a bride of Christ?"

"Aye."

"Swear."

"My lord!"

"Swear by your mother's immortal soul you're a nun."

Wrestling her arm away from him, she said, "I am not a nun."

"Not?"

She didn't know what to make of the tone of his voice.

"Not?" he questioned again.

She would warrant it was relief.

"Swear." He reached for her again, but she slid away. "Swear by your mother's immortal soul you are *not* a nun."

"By God, William—"

"Swear!" he insisted, and the odd note of his voice swelled with panic.

"I swear," she said. "By all that I hold holy."

"Not a nun. Well." He collapsed back into his chair and it rocked dangerously back on two legs and then settled with a thump.

Hugging her elbows, Saura waited for his reaction. The guffaw started deep in his chest, growing and amplifying through the rafters until it was a full belly laugh. Her concern changed to indignation, then to animosity. "What's so funny?"

"Are there any other little deceptions you have perpetrated on me?" he wheezed.

She put her hands on her waist, and blurted, "Hundreds of them."

That sent him into fresh paroxysms of mirth. "Get you to bed, Saura."

"Are you going to drink some more?" she asked.

"Nay, no more drinking for me. I just remembered the other thing that makes me a man. Now, get you to bed before 'tis too late."

Stiffly, she moved to the winding stairway and stopped.

"What's wrong?" he asked.

"The boys are sleeping in my bed," she mumbled. "I'm going to sleep on one of the benches."

"Ah." He considered. "Take my bed in the solar. I'll lie out here with the rest of the servants. Where is everyone?"

"I told them to sleep in the barn."

He laughed again. "Get you to bed."

In a dark corner of the gallery, the silent eavesdropper watched as William picked up his cane and took the stairs down to the bailey. He noted the strength William gained from Saura, the affection and mutual respect between them, and in his twisted mind Saura joined William as a target to be eliminated.

four

"June is the month of love. The month when the very air acts as a love philtre, filling my lungs and heating my loins." Exalting in the afternoon breeze that tossed his blond hair across his forehead, William, with a flick of the reins, urged his mount to a trot.

"Father!" Kimball protested, bound to his father by a leading rein and jostled as his horse danced sideways along the woodland path. "You're going to run over me."

"Move that pony along, then," his father replied sharply, tapping his son's mare with the oak cane he held. Undeterred by Kimball's smothered protest, he returned to his musing in a mellow voice. "In June, lambs suckle and life bursts forth with new vigor. Smell the flowers! Smell the new growth! Even the grass transforms itself into a carpet for lovers, offering itself gladly to be bruised by an embrace."

"Hurray, hurray, the end of June, all the folk rut outside soon," Clare quoted.

"Clare!" Saura sounded shocked and distracted. "Where did you learn that verse?"

"Lord Peter taught me," the boy replied tranquilly, holding his sister's leading rein.

"Do you know what it means?"

"Aye. It means the servants will go out in the barn instead of keeping me awake at night."

William exploded with laughter. "Hurray, hurray," he said.

Saura sighed.

"Come," he encouraged. "Plebeian joinings have no impact on us today. Revel in fresh perceptions of the English summer afternoon. Breathe deep the scents of flower and herb. Feel the motion of the horse between your thighs. Listen to the birds mating in the trees!"

"William!"

"Pretend the boys aren't with us."

"My imagination isn't that good," Saura replied repressively.

He considered and asked, "Kimball, where are we?"

Kimball cast an experienced eye around him. "On the south corner of the property, close upon Fyngre Brook."

"That's what I thought," William said with satisfaction. "Why don't you settle Saura and me by the water and you lads can race your horses on the meadow east of here."

"Aye, sir!" they chorused, moving the horses briskly down the forest trail.

"We've ridden a long way today, madame," William explained to Saura. "I'd like to stretch my legs in the wild. It's been too long since I stood in the stillness of the woods."

Saura said nothing. In sooth, she didn't know what to say. The foolish idea appealed to her with a deep tug of yearning. These spring days, riding with William and the boys, had ignited in her a desire for a normal life. The pragmatic woman she had been before she came to Burke Castle was vanquished by the surge of craving. No longer could she resign herself to a barren life, stripped of husband and children. Dreams floated in her mind: dreams of William and his healing passion, dreams of their babies gathered around her skirts, dreams of a long life, igniting candles in their darkness until the light of their love cast a beckoning glow to all.

"Fair friend and sweet, what say you?" William asked in dulcet tones.

Shaking off the remnants of her impossible fantasy, she replied, "I, too, long to dip my feet into the cool water of an English brook. Lead on, my youths."

"You'll have to leave your horses here," Kimball instructed. "The path is too tangled and narrow for them."

With the help of the boys, William and Saura were installed on a tall tumble of boulders beside the stream and left alone.

"Peaceful, isn't it?" William rested his spine against the sun-warmed rock. "This is one of my favorite spots. In my mind, I can still see the great oak trees, spreading their branches abroad. The brook kicks the pebbles with its current. The willow dips its branches for a drink. And 'tis green, green as only England in the springtime can be." Sitting up on his elbow, he queried, "Am I right? Is that how it looks today?"

"Aye," she sighed with pleasure. "That's how it looks today. How lucky you are to have a place such as this to see in your mind."

He considered her remark seriously. "Aye, I suppose I am."

"And I'm lucky to have you to sing me the song of its beauty."

"Madame, I'm known to compose the best *vers* after a banquet. The ladies swoon at my eloquent style."

Chuckling, Saura agreed, "And at your modesty."

"That, too." He lay back again. "Shed your shoes as you desired and wade."

She unlaced her sandals and wondered; should she?

As if he read her thoughts, he stimulated her longing. "This brook runs clean and the rocks at the bottom are round and tender to the unprotected sole."

"As you wish, my lord!" she said, sliding down the rocks and into the water. Its pristine depths reached only her ankles and delighted her toes. "Oh, William." She sighed. "This is all you said, and more."

"Trust me, Saura, I'll never misguide you."

The deep note of meaning in his voice worried her. Whatever demon had plunged William into depression that night was expelled and Saura flattered herself her common sense had turned the tide. Still, in her mind the vaguest inkling of doubt curled and writhed. It almost seemed as if his renewed spirit was linked to her admission of subterfuge. As if he rejoiced to extricate her from the masquerade of nun and awaited with anticipation her final unmasking. It almost seemed as if she had lost control of their relationship during the conversation a week ago, as if he were now the teacher and she the pupil.

Wading cautiously, one foot in front of the other in tiny increments, Saura explored. She slipped in a hole, stubbed her toes on a stone, and yipped.

"What's the matter?" he asked. "Did you see a snake?"

She froze. "A snake?"

"Snakes abound in this pleasing land. Many a time I fished this stream and found hooked to my line a mammoth snake, as big around as—"

"In the water?" She screamed and leaped straight into the

air, disoriented by horror but sure she would somehow reach shore.

"Well, aye, but there are snakes littering the ground."

She screamed again, louder this time, floundering on the slick pebbles, and William could no longer maintain his gravity. He roared with laughter; he rocked from side to side in an excess of mirth. "No snakes," he gasped. "There're no snakes, but I'd give the devil's hooves to see your face."

"Do you tease me again?" she cried.

"No snakes." He cackled and rubbed his face on his cloak.

"Promise?"

"I promise."

"You braying ass." She waded closer to the sound of his amusement. "You dare to make merry of me? You cretin."

"Whoa, my lady!" William sat up. "I've done no different than you've done to me."

"What do you mean?"

"A nun? You told me you were a nun. And," he waved an encompassing hand, "hundreds of other deceptions, you said?"

She didn't answer, for she didn't know what reply to make.

"Is it as bad as I suspect?" he questioned gently.

"Oh, much worse." Wretched, she wondered: confess the truth or continue the lie? And how much to tell? A coward to the end, she thought, grimacing. When she explained this subterfuge, she wanted to be somewhere safe, not alone in the forest and easily abandoned. And, preferably, with someone who would stop him if he decided to hand out a salutary tap. With Lord Peter, perhaps, who would admit to his part in the sham. That decision made, Saura mumbled, in what she hoped was a natural tone, "Oh, I've wet the ends of my sleeves."

William hesitated and then accepted her change of subject

with a voice drooping with disappointment. "You do have trouble keeping your clothes dry, don't you?"

Knotting her skirt at her waist, she agreed, "Aye, I—" and stopped, flummoxed by his observation. "What do you mean?"

"Shh." He cut her off firmly.

"Why so?"

"Quiet!" he insisted.

Cocking an ear to the woodland around, Saura heard what he suspected. "William, there are horses and men all around us," she whispered.

"Aye. Come here." Groping, he located his stout cane and vacated his boulder, tentatively splashing into the brook not far from her. She slid close to his side and he jerked his head up. "Get up on the boulders and stay out of the way." He waited until she had obeyed and asked, "What do you see?"

Dumbfounded, she repeated, "See?"

"How many men? How close?"

"Oh, William," she began sadly, but the crunch of branches beneath many stomping feet interrupted her.

"We've got them, Bronnie," a man said in the uncouth English tongue. "Just like his lordship ordered."

"Are ye sure these are t' uns, Mort?" another questioned.

"Aye, a couple of ducks in th' water waitin' t' be bagged," the first replied.

"Th' big un's blind, ye say?" the second asked. "I'd hate t' tackle that un any other way."

"But th' wench I'd tackle anytime," the first voice leered.

"What did they say?" Saura asked frantically, not understanding the rapid, accented English and not liking the tone.

William moved close, his back against the solid rock, and flexed his fists around his cane. "They said they desired a wetting."

Cowering on the boulders, Saura wished the boys were there to help and hoped they were safe away, all at the same time.

"Stop chatting, you scum, and take them," a new voice ordered in English and then switched to Norman French. "Lord William? You're surrounded by twelve men. Come out of the water and surrender."

"I counted no more than seven men," William replied smoothly.

No one said a word, and then Bronnie protested, "Ye told us he was blind!"

"We are eight men," the leader snapped.

"So he can't count," Bronnie whimpered.

"Devil burn you! He's blind, for God's sake, can't you tell? He's listening, not seeing. Now get them, gently. The lord wants to render his own tender care of them."

"Duck down, little lass," William rumbled, bracing himself for the onslaught.

Feet splashed into the stream and Bronnie whined, "Wait! I haven't got me shoes off, yet." A whack and a shuffle, and Bronnie stumbled into the water with a groan. "Awright, awright, but I ruined me new shoes."

The cane in William's hand began a low, threatening whistle as it swung in rhythmic figure eights. "I got him," one man crowed, leaping at the blind lord.

A resounding thwack, a howl of pain, and Bronnie said, "His jaw's broken."

William laughed, a jubilant thunder of joy.

Another rushed him and Saura heard the breath leave the attacker's body as the tip of the rod drove into his stomach. "Come, knaves, come, knaves," William called, as if they were cats to be lured to him. He parried the charge of one more man with the broad of his oak shaft.

The churls murmured with dismay, backing away until their commander roared, "Take him!"

"A fine leader you are," William said with contempt. "Afraid to get me yourself?"

The men's breathing labored with harsh, angry rigor.

"All right!" The commander splashed into the water, ordering, "I'll grab the stick, you—all of you—tackle him."

A plan destined for failure and success. Men piled up in the stream beneath William's punishing weapon, until, with a mighty splash, William went down. Terrified, Saura heard the cries of the attackers, enthusiastic as the Promethean warrior weakened beneath their blows. She clutched the huge boulder supporting her and discovered a smooth, round stone loose beneath her fingers. It was a good size, heavy enough to require both hands to lift it, yet small enough to fit between her palms. Bronnie shouted, "I'll bring th' woman!" and before clear intention formed in her mind, she turned and smacked his skull.

The lucky blow toppled Bronnie into the midst of the battle below and ended it as his disgruntled compatriots turned on him. Flushed with triumph, Saura leaned out and knocked a few more bobbing heads before the rock was torn from her hands and discarded. "Damn it!" the leader swore as he dragged her into the water.

"This was supposed t' be an easy task," one of the churls complained, and Bronnie groaned, "Why did ye think his lordship ordered eight sturdy men t' capture un blind man an' his woman?"

This bit of logic from one so muddleheaded silenced the grievances. William and Saura were prodded from the brook and forced, one after the other, onto a broad-backed horse. "Tie his wrists together around her waist," the leader ordered, his voice shaking with fury. "He'll not jump and bring her down, too. And hurry, we've tarried too long on Burke land."

"Should we tie th' woman, too?"

"Nay," the leader replied scornfully. "Can't you see what she suffers? She's harmless."

"Huh!" Bronnie snorted. "Me head can't agree."

Unaware of her part in the fight, William queried, "What did you do to our friend Bronnie?"

"Smashed him with a rock."

William laughed softly. "That's my warrior queen. One day I'll teach you to defend yourself as if you were a knight." He grunted as they tightened the ropes around his hands and looped them around her waist.

"Are you hurt?"

"A few cuts," he answered with disdain. "My pride suffered the most damage."

"Not many knights could stave off eight men," she pointed out.

"I could, before." His voice sounded flat and uncompromising, and she believed him.

Their horse on a leading rein jerked to a walk and then a trot. "Can't you hurry that nag?" the leader snarled.

One of his men replied, "Not with Lord William on it. Not with him and the woman."

The leader rode close to their side and warned, "Listen well. We are a troop of mercenaries—"

"Troop? A powerful name for one mercenary commanding a flock of untrained serfs."

"—of eight able-bodied men—"

"Eight?" William mocked.

"At least six," the leader said sourly. "You didn't kill anyone back there, but only broke a couple of bones. You are a wet, blind man, but once you were a warrior, so I caution you now. His lordship wants you alive, but my patience is at an end. Unless you want to ride tied hand and foot and dropped over a horse like a portion of game, don't try to escape."

"Wisdom I will endeavor to follow," William answered ironically.

The leader left to ride to the front of the column. The troop of men thinned to a single file, brushing past branches and bushes in their haste to put ground between themselves and the avenging Lord Peter of Burke. They grumbled and spit, compared bruises and argued.

William and Saura adjusted to the jarring pace, and William wiggled his hands.

"Can you free them?" Saura asked quietly.

"I can loose them from your waist. The knots are so tight my fingers tingle." He worked with silent contortions until he sighed with pleasure. "There." He rubbed his fingers across her flat stomach. "Much better."

Saura jumped and quavered, "What if they see your hands are free?"

"They'll not care. He's right, only a fool would try to escape now, and I'm not that. Nay, the battle was never in doubt, but our miniature squires must have heard the shouting and be on their way to the castle. Let us enjoy the ride until we reach our destination, wherever that might be." His fingers flexed again and hugged her waist. "You're tiny." His breath sighed across her neck and she jumped again. "And high-strung. I never would have suspected a woman of your *elderly* years would be so responsive to the touch of a hand. Have you never married?"

"Nay." Her voice began steadily and rose to a squeak. "William!"

His lips caressed her neck and shoulders, roughening the

skin with his bearded chin. "I love the scent of carnations. Such smooth skin." He smiled. "For a woman of your *elderly* years."

"William. . . ."

"And such high, tight breasts." His hands moved across her bosom, exploring and pressing. "For a woman of your—"

"*Elderly* years." Her hands caught his and positioned them on the saddle. "How long have you known?"

"I told you before I'm not a fool. Clare is seven. A mighty difference in age between an *elderly* woman of forty and her brother."

"It's not impossible!" Saura protested.

"But unlikely. Once I made that connection, it wasn't hard to equate my mystery maid of the bath with the untouchable nun of gentle birth. The unknown relation of my mother, our housekeeper. I gave you every chance to tell me."

Reduced to silence, she could only nod. The movement of her head jogged him and he guessed, "Lady Saura of Roget?"

"Aye," she whispered.

He settled her against his chest to cushion her ride. He tenderly wrapped his mighty arms around her waist, but his mind bubbled with revolt. Had he discovered this woman, his woman, only to be murdered by some anonymous evil that feared to show its face? It would never have been so in the old days, before his sight was stripped from him by ruse or deceit. In the old days, he would have fought for this lady, protected her with sword and shield. Now he was constrained to ride with the enemy to some unforeseen fate. He cursed the inaction that dragged at his spirit and longed for another skull to crush.

They rode until evening and the horse beneath them sagged with their weight. As the birds chirped a weary good night and the breeze cooled and thickened, they stopped to let the animals drink. Saura dismounted gingerly, for her shoes had been abandoned on the banks of Fyngre Brook. Her legs buckled beneath her, protesting the hours in the saddle. William reached for her, but Mort stuck out his leg and William staggered over it.

"Ha! I'll take care of th' pretty lady," Mort chortled, catching her waist.

The others laughed, their grudge against the blind knight fresh. Encouraged, Mort pressed Saura close and made kissing sounds by her ear. "Come with me, m'lady. You'll need help to find your way. Let me show ye th' huge tree trunks that grow in these woods."

"Stumps, more likely," she hissed, dragging her nails across his eyes. Blood sprang up where her nails dug and Mort howled with fury. Jerking free, she stumbled across the clearing. The merriment of the troop rang in her ears; Mort's snarling pursuit propelled her.

She feared, oh God, she feared.

But another joined the hunt: William followed them, trailing the threats that rang in the forest. Saura heard as he snared the unwary Mort and flung him around. She heard Mort gurgle as William wrapped one hand around the man's neck and lifted him into the air. She heard the crunch of bulbous flesh as one mighty fist knocked Mort's curses down his throat; she heard William fling the serf into the group of scrambling mercenaries.

What she couldn't see was Bronnie, stalwart Bronnie, as he swung the shaft of his bow and smashed William in the back of the head.

Saura heard the thwack as it connected, heard the rumble as William keeled over in the dirt.

Then it was silent, only Bronnie's whimpering broke the shocked hush.

The leader walked to William and turned him with a heave of his foot. "Have you killed him, Bronnie?"

"Is there a bed?" The stone beneath her fingertips felt dry and cold, but the winding stairs she had climbed had warmed her, as did the anger surging through her veins. The group of men who had captured them had dispersed when they arrived in this strange household, but Bronnie had been retained to guide them, and his new shoes squeaked from their dunking. One giant of a man carried William, draped over his shoulder.

Who were they? Who was this mysterious lord? How dared he take the master of Burke and his housekeeper from their lands? The distinctive combination of smells that identified each castle assured her she had never visited here before. So where were they? The stair leveled into a landing and they halted as Bronnie swung the creaking door wide and ushered them in. "Where are we? Is there a bed for William?" she insisted, her voice sharp as a slap.

"Aye, m'lady."

His French grated with harsh consonants, but Saura could hear the obsequious whimper in Bronnie's voice. She'd taught him respect with the whiplash of her tongue.

"That's to say, nay, m'lady." He groaned under the sharp jab of her elbow. "There's a palliasse on th' floor. In this room we prepared just for ye."

"You call this prison a room?" She placed one hand on one wall and without moving her feet, simply by leaning, she placed her other hand on the other wall. "But a palliasse is better than nothing. Lay my Lord William on it. *Gently*, you fools!" As she knelt beside the unconscious man, her ear caught the squeak of shoes sneaking out the door. "You cannot leave until you bring me water and bandage material," she enunciated clearly, and the feet stopped.

"Eh, well, I'll have to ask th' lord."

She rose to her feet in a magnificent fury. "Ask him! Aye, and ask him if he wanted Lord William killed by your stupidity, too. Ask him how he feels about a churl who disobeys the commands of a baron's daughter. Ask him—"

"I'll bring th' water," Bronnie answered hastily.

"And the bandaging. And something for us to eat, I'm hungry. And extra blankets."

The large man shuffled out, escaping her authority, while Bronnie bowed and said, "Aye, m'lady. As ye wish, m'lady."

Then he left, too, shutting the door with a solid thunk and leaving Saura standing alone. As quickly as he disappeared, so did her supporting anger. Her chin dropped, her knees folded. She crouched beside William, her fingers frantically combing his head, seeking the cause of his long unconsciousness. A lump rose there on the back of his neck, and it felt angry and hard, full of blood. A goose egg, her mother had called them, painful but not serious. Surely there was some other injury, but her hands could discover nothing else. As far down as she could run her hands beneath his clothes, there was nothing. The top of his head, his face, nothing.

With a groan, she thumped her head beside William's. Her hands clutched her middle, her knees tucked close to her chest, and she lay there, unmoving, in the depths of despair, beyond tears. No thoughts crossed her mind, no ideas lightened her darkness.

She was blind. As useless and repulsive as her stepfather had told her. She couldn't see the attackers for William. She couldn't scout out their surroundings, couldn't seek useful weapons, couldn't do anything of any use to anybody. She couldn't even force respect from that lowborn churl, couldn't even get him to bring water and bandaging and food and blankets, all things they would need to survive the night with comfort. She was nothing more than a worm.

Life seemed brightest just before it was snatched away. Those nebulous dreams of hers had led them to the stream, had distracted her when she should have been listening for the whisper of feet in the woods. When she lived in her stepfather's house, she had always listened. She never slept unless Maud guarded her, she never worked alone, she never walked in the garden or bailey without listening, listening for the scuttling sound of Theobald's shoes. He wanted to lay his hands on her body, breathe his fetid breath on her face, poke himself at her. She shuddered and rubbed the serpent that twisted her insides. How could a man despise someone as much as Theobald despised her and still want to fornicate with her?

Did she dare think she loved William? She squirmed as Theobald's jeering echoed through her head. He'd tormented her ceaselessly, and with no effort she could recall every word. She wasn't worthy of love, he'd said. She couldn't work on a tapestry, she couldn't ride a horse by herself: she was worthless. Her face could turn a man into salt, he'd sneered. Her figure reminded him of a couple of fat dumplings on a short stick. What man, he'd asked, would want a stupid woman in his bed, one who couldn't even see the piss pot if she stepped in it?

She couldn't even help William. His goose egg rated as nothing more than minor, but she knew the truth, although she didn't want to admit it to herself. He might never wake up. Head injuries were tricky, her mother had told her. Especially the kind of head injuries that dealt with a previous wound. Whatever brain lurked inside your head conformed to its own rules. A bruise on the body hurt and could be deadly, but a bruise on the head could reduce the brightest toddler to a drooling idiot. A blow in the right area could replace a grown man with a silent block who lived and breathed but slept like the dead until starvation claimed him.

Sometimes, it seemed to her, God must hate her above all creatures. He'd given her enough to live on the fringes of life, but never become a participant. She was capable, never beautiful. She was a sister, never a wife. She was an aunt, never a mother.

One of her hands crept out from beneath her and stroked William's rough arm. She was a friend, a teacher, a woman: never a lover.

What would she do without William?

Tightly, she clasped his fingers in hers. Each individual muscle and bone and sinew bespoke his strength, yet he lay still in the chilly room, his skin unnaturally cool.

Like a slap in the face, Saura's mother arose before her. "Lying there wallowing in your pity, Saura, when you have enough to eat, and shelter, and the sun to warm you in summer, and a fire in winter. Pay attention to what goes on around you. If there's famine, who starves? Not you. If there's war, who burns? Not you. If there's sickness, it's not you who lies in the mud at the side of the road and dies. So what if your eyes don't work? You have a brain. Get up and use it."

With unseen power, the echo of her mother's voice jerked her erect. "Whining about your fate will not cover him with a blanket," she said aloud, and laughed a little. The voice she heard from her own mouth sounded like her mother's, or-

dering the young Saura to deal with the sick because it was
the job of the chatelaine to do so.

Her clumsy fingers searched the hard pallet beneath William until she found a rough woolen blanket folded at the
foot. She covered him, then changed her mind and slid it off.
Putting her hands beneath him, she heaved, trying to get
him onto his back, and then heaved again.

He didn't budge. He was one large, inert block of meat,
and she was only a mosquito worrying his flesh. "It'll be
easier . . . for you . . . to breathe . . . my lord," she
punctuated her words with her struggles, "if you'll roll . . .
onto your back."

"Nay, m'lady!"

Saura jumped and turned.

"Let me do that. Ye're too slight a lady t' do such heavy
labor." Bronnie hurried into the room, dropping things as
he came. "I can move t' lord."

"Well, be careful with him. That's a vicious blow you gave
him," she scolded.

"I'm sorry. I'm sorry, I am. But see, he was beatin' Mort."

"He's a blind man. How much damage did you think he
could do?"

"Well," Bronnie drawled the word with the profound
doubt of the slow-witted. "He looked like he was doin' a
good job of killin' him t' me. Here, you want him on his
back?"

She nodded and wrung her hands as she listened to the
man move William. God knows what the ham-handed fool
did, but she had no choice. William needed to be turned,
and she couldn't do it.

"There ye are, m'lady. He's on his back now. An' ye know
what? His color looks better t' me."

"Does it?" She reached for the blanket and tucked it under his chin, down his body and around his ankles.

"Aye, just look at him. That sick tinge is gone from around his mouth an'. . . ." Bronnie's chatter faded as she turned her violet eyes on him. "I'm sorry, m'lady, I wasn't thinkin'. Really, 'tis just ye don't seem t' be blind. It took me most o' this day t' realize ye didn't even know where the horse was puttin' his hooves. Ye move around so well an' work like a real person." He nodded, pleased he had cleared that up. "Aye, like a real person, ye are."

"Did you bring more blankets?" Saura asked, the cold of her tone penetrating even Bronnie's thick skull, if not the reason for it.

"Aye. Aye, I brought ye blankets, like ye said, m'lady. Lots of them, because there's no hearth in here an' it gets cold at night. Even in th' summer, it is. I'll put them here, on this table." The squeaky shoes crept across the room, stopping beside each pile he had dropped and carrying it to the table he spoke of. "I brought bandagin' material, all torn up into strips. An' a whole bucket of water. Here, just a minute, I put it outside th' door. I'll place it over here, by th' bed. Just a minute, let me drag a stool over an' put it up there an' it'll be higher for ye. Easier to reach, it will be." The stool scraped over to the palliasse and he thunked the bucket up on it. "There's still a stool for you t' sit on, ye know, over by th' table. Th' food'll be comin' soon. Not that 'tis ever any good, that cook's such a slut, but I'll bring it t' ye meself."

He trailed off, distressed with her silence, and she felt a sudden discomfort. Bronnie, she realized, was a puppy dog. A well meaning, idiotic puppy dog who never meant to hurt anyone, certainly not a lord and a lady. He stood before her now, she knew, anxiously waiting to see if she would beat him or praise him, and she couldn't resist the potent appeal he projected. "You did fine, Bronnie. Thank you."

Those new shoes hopped for a moment, and he eagerly inquired, "If ye need aught else ye'll call me, m'lady?"

"No one but you," she promised. "In fact, you can help me now. The lord needs to have his clothes removed."

"Removed?" Bronnie gasped. "Why? He hasn't outgrown them."

Saura closed her eyes in exasperation. "Nay, but he's wet and might catch a chill. And I need to check him over for any different wounds that may be hurting him."

"Check him over? Ye mean, feel him? I'm confused. They said ye weren't married t' th' lord."

"They are right."

Bronnie's voice rose incredulously. "Not married an' ye want t' touch him? Are ye un of those wicked women th' priest talks about?"

The first arrows of amusement attacked Saura's grief. "That's why I want you to help me. So you can look at him and see any bruises."

"Ohh." Bronnie thought about that. "Ye mean ye want me t' tell ye if he's hurt."

"Exactly."

"But what if he's hurt an' ye have t' touch him?"

Her amusement deepened, and she could almost have smiled. "I will do it with only pure thoughts in my mind," she promised.

"Lord William won't like that."

"He'll like less dying of some untreated wound. Now let's go to work."

She rolled up her sleeves, preparing for hard labor, but Bronnie said, "Nay. I'll do it."

"I can help."

"I'll do it," he insisted. "Ye shouldn't touch him more than necessary. Ye bein' a noble lady an' all."

Saura nodded, bemused by the code of ethics that allowed for murder and kidnapping but balked at a lady touching a lord outside of the state of wedlock. Was it just Bronnie, or did all these Saxons hold such strange beliefs?

"He's a big 'un, isn't he?" Bronnie grunted. "But healthy as far as I can see. Only a few little bruises. Ye goin' to want him dressed again?"

"If you want to. If you don't want to leave him naked in here with me."

"Nay, nay, 'tis awright. 'Tis awright." Bronnie stood, panting. "Ye're a lovely lady, ye'll not be playin' with him when my back's turned."

Saura turned away from him, unable to keep the grin from breaking through. "I'll endeavor to restrain myself."

"An' I'll bring th' food soon. An'. . . ."

Saura could hear him squirm.

"I brought ye a comb."

"A comb?" She reached up and touched her hair. Her veil had gone long ago, the ties of her braids had loosened. She looked, she supposed, like a witch.

"Aye, I thought ye might like t', well, comb your hair. 'Tis on th' table. With a bit of ribbon from me girl. If ye like it. 'Tis a pretty blue color."

"I'm sure it is. Thank you, Bronnie. Thank you very much." She turned and smiled at him, her gracious-lady smile, and she heard the little jig start again, for just a moment. Then the squeaky shoes backed toward the door.

"I'll bring th' food," he promised.

"I know you will. Thank you."

"An' some good wine. An' aught else ye need."

"Thank you."

The door clicked behind him, and Saura chuckled. "Well, I guess I can convince someone of my authority," she told the unconscious William. "Even if it's not you."

But even her authority with Bronnie couldn't convince him to tell her who the lord of this castle was. The man brought dinner, as promised, and wine, and bread for the morning. He remembered her distress when she'd walked barefoot through the muddy bailey, and carried in another bucket of water for her to wash with and a rough towel. But when she tried to question him, he bumbled about, straightening the table, placing an iron candle stand against the wall. When she insisted he take the candle away, it distressed him. At last, he removed the candle and backed out of the door, and left her to the silence.

And it was silent. This keep wasn't the main castle for the lord. The bustle of a large company, of knights and attendants, was conspicuously absent. She alone was responsible for her William.

She ate the dinner, which tasted just as appalling as Bronnie promised. She rattled the door. She explored the room, a narrow, bare cell with two arrow loops to the outside. Two stools, a rickety table, one palliasse, and nothing to make weapons with. She checked William's bandage, covered him with another blanket, and paced. Finally, she sat down on the tiny stool beside the tiny table and took up Bronnie's comb. With trembling fingers, she took apart her braid and began to comb. Her hair hung down to her thighs, a tangled web of fine, soft distraction. It distracted her from the quiet, from the worry, from the loneliness. The tangles diverted her from thoughts of William, so still on the mat, and as she tamed her hair into sleekness, the rhythm of her motion soothed her.

At last she stopped, dropped her aching arms and folded

her hands in her lap. Soon she would crawl onto the palliasse with William and sleep, but for now she just wanted to sit and pray, with a fervor she had never suspected she was capable of.

A sigh from the bed alerted her attention. A sigh, and a groan, and a heave as William turned himself onto his side. Saura flew from her chair to his pallet, touching him with eager fingers until she was satisfied.

He was sleeping. Sleeping! His eyelids twitched when she brushed them, he groaned when she pressed his head, and he snored with the healthy rhythm of a tired man.

Sleeping! Oh, Holy Mary! Her heart filled with thanksgiving as she tried to express to God, to herself, how she felt about this miracle of life. She wasn't thinking of herself, she wasn't thinking of how William's presence filled her and completed her. She only thought about William. He slept, and that meant he would wake, and that meant there was hope! For the first time, Saura felt hope, and she cried. The heavy sobs, the copious tears, cleansed her until she could raise her head and smile once more.

five

Saura had lied to Bronnie.

She hadn't previously suspected it, but she was the kind of woman the priests warned against. Wicked, immoral, a true daughter of Eve.

As the night crept on and the temperature dropped, the pallet and blankets and William seemed more and more inviting. It was, she told herself, the only logical thing to do. No summer penetrated these stones, no fires dulled the hard indifference of cold. She'd suffer, sitting upright wrapped in one puny blanket all night. It would be no sin to sleep with him. Not like a wife or a whore, but simply to share body heat. Didn't that make sense?

Of course it did.

Before she changed her mind, she pulled at the lacing of her cotte and cursed her clumsy fingers. She should have let Bronnie bring the night candle and light it, for now she could have warmed her hands by its steady flame. If she didn't know better, she would have thought her fumbling resulted from a case of nerves.

She wasn't nervous. How could she be? Lady Saura was known for her eternal serenity, her calm disposition in the face of trouble, her common sense. No one of any rationality would suspect her of shaking, of clenching her teeth to keep them from chattering, unless she was cold. She *wasn't* nervous.

Her cotte fell to the floor beneath the weight of its wet hem and she clutched her elbows with her hands. Some lingering modesty made her retain her chainse; because it was linen, she told herself, and because she always slept in it. Actually, she couldn't bring herself to discard the garment with its long sleeves and drawstring neck that could be pulled tight. For the warmth, of course.

Groping down to William's side, she sat on the hard pallet and pulled her hair over one shoulder. Dividing it into three parts, she braided it with quick efficiency and tied it with the pretty blue ribbon. Then she could delay no longer. She slipped beneath the covers. She moved hastily, not wanting to release the body heat to the room, and lay on her side, facing him. She tucked her arm beneath her head and wiggled as a slight thaw set in.

William was healthy. He'd been knocked on the head, and now he hibernated like a peasant after a three-day festival. Flopped onto his back once more, he lay with his head turned to one side, snoring with energy and vigor and enthusiasm. Saura thrilled to the sound. No matter that she could never sleep, no matter that his snoring shook the palliasse, the blankets, and her. He was here, he was alive, and if he woke with no memory of the past or a twitch in his left arm, well, they'd deal with that tomorrow.

It would be warmer if she touched him. She took a breath,

let it out with a gasp, and grinned at her own cowardice. Then she gathered her nerve and extended one big toe, and touched his leg.

One toe, she told herself, wasn't a sin. Her feet were cold. They were always cold, even before the roaring fires of the great hall. No matter that frost no longer nipped the ground outside, the stones of the castle projected cold. Here, in this little room where no hearth burned with fire, the night carried a chill that seeped into her bones. It was ridiculous to suffer.

What would it hurt? That one toe rubbed in a slow pattern up and down his calf, weaving its path through the springy hair that coated him from ankle to knee. His knee, she discovered, warranted closer examination, first with her toe, then with her foot. Her sole was sensitive, and worked in partnership with her toes to sample the rougher, more flexible skin above the joint. Now she had one whole foot on him. This wasn't so difficult. The other foot joined the first, tucking itself between his leg and the mattress, and his marvelous simmer set it tingling.

No sin, she argued with herself, to climb a little closer and melt more than just her feet. Her skin was overrun with goosebumps, and it seemed the closer she inched to his heat the more insistent the chill outside the covers became. Her linen chainse protected her from skin-to-skin contact. Truly, she was only a little wicked. And he was so big and warm. She toasted like a piece of day-old bread before his fire. First her upper leg reached across his thighs, then the other leg pulled up tight against him from thigh to calf. She eased her chest close against his arm, and the sensation endowed her with the courage to close the gap completely.

Then she lay motionless. His snores had diminished in volume if not in regularity. His breath ruffled her hair now, sultry in the frigid air of the room. It seemed pleasant to be so close to him. In fact, it was delectable. She wallowed in this contrast of cold and heat, of pure animal comfort, and hard palliasse below with rough blankets above. It seemed unfair, somehow, that her chainse separated them so completely. She couldn't really feel him, missed the sensation of skin against skin, but when her hand went to the drawstring at her neck, her temerity dissipated. She had to snuggle, she told herself, because he loomed so big he hogged the covers. But she couldn't justify nudity, even to her rationalizing mind, and her hand fell away.

She ran her hands over William with a tentative touch. Tonight was a time of joy, of celebration, of exploration.

She'd never been able to touch him before. She'd never been granted the freedom to read his face and body, and now . . . ah, now.

She pressed her palms against his chest. His heart throbbed there, his chest rose and fell in a wonderful example of robust respiration. Taking her braid in her hand, she pulled it up so it wouldn't tickle him, and laid her head down. Beneath her ear she could hear the rasp of wind and the thu-thump under his skin. Irresistibly, the hair of his chest titillated her cheek, and she turned her nose into it. He smelled like no one else. His dunking in the creek had cleaned away the sweat of the fight, and he smelled golden.

Isn't that the way Maud had described him? Golden. To Saura, golden was the scent of an autumn day, redolent with dry cut hay and crackling leaves. It was the satisfaction of plucking a flower she had planted, the stimulation of velvet beneath her fingertips and the growth of a skein of yarn as she twirled it off the distaff. Golden was the sun caressing her face on an afternoon nap in her garden.

William pulsed below her, and his golden scent rose up in

waves of intoxicating spice. She rubbed her face along his chest, seeking the source of his fragrance, but it seemed his zest lay both defined and elusive.

Leaning herself against him, she explored his face with meticulous care. His neck grew from his shoulders in one decisive column, muscled as surely as his arms. Stubborn resistance sat on the square of his jaw, but he disguised it with his clipped beard. His nose she couldn't read; it had been broken so many times its creator's original intent was undecipherable. His ears she found pleasure in: small and well placed, tight against his head. She swept her fingertip through the whorls and down the lobe, amazed at the existence of such a refined feature on such a virile man.

It seemed her action disturbed him, for he muttered and coughed, his breath coming in a gust, and she jumped back guiltily. She dislodged the covers as she sat up, and she listened to the sounds within the castle. A deep hush saturated the room; only now did it occur to her that he no longer snored with his hearty rhapsody. It had died into normal exhalations as she touched him. Thinking back, it seemed she hadn't heard those snores of exhaustion since she had first inspected his chest.

He settled with a sigh, and she sat without moving until she was sure he drifted deep into slumber. At last, she shivered in the chill draft, and her need for warmth overwhelmed her wariness. With painstaking care, she adjusted the covers until she leaned into him again. She should sleep, she should forget the urge to discover his face, but her hands trembled as she ignored her own strictures. His eyes sat deep below the bone of his forehead, his bushy eyebrows accentuated the contrast. His broad brow elucidated his strength, his hair shifted through her fingers like fine-textured sand.

She knew what he looked like now. Now she could see

him, now she had defined the lines of his face for her mind. Shaped from the workman's chisel, the whole was the sum of the parts: strong, compassionate, refined, determined.

Her curiosity satisfied for the moment, she rested her head against his shoulder and found her hand rubbing his chest in a circular motion. Did he enjoy such tactile stimulation as much as she did? Her lips brushed him, propelled by some primal desire, and her tongue traced the cords of his neck. Savoring his provocative flavor, her mouth traveled down his chest into the jaunty nest.

The tips of his hair thrilled her hands as she delicately pursued its outline up in a triangle to his shoulders. His collarbones extended to a width she had never imagined, and she sat up hastily and compared them to her own. Her collarbone she spanned easily with her fingers: his stretched a full four fingers more. Eagerly, her hands went back and discovered evidence of a break, well healed but still evident to her trained touch. Massaging the breadth of his shoulders from neck to arm, she marvelled. He had so many muscles! They rippled his skin like the grain of a well-honed oak beam. His skin felt smooth as a baby's, until her fingers stumbled across the scars and ridges that celebrated his livelihood. His arms were powerful, his hands huge squares of authority. His fingers surprised her: long, blunt tipped, but sensitive.

Hands were important to her, the mirror of the soul, and his hands told of his kindness and control, his temper and his majesty. She lingered over his hands, pleased by her findings, but at last she could resist no longer.

Following the path she had already taken, she verified her findings. William was big, a mass of muscle and coordination worthy of the title "knight."

But more than that, he was a man, and her seeking fingers

slid down his chest, down his rippling belly, down the line of his hair. A maiden's curiosity drove her; irresistible temptation was not to be resisted.

Saura jumped when her hand connected with his organ. She hadn't expected such a fire and firmness. She thought of all she had been told about the mating of humans, and she shook her head. " 'Tis not possible," she said aloud.

"I assure you, it is," he rumbled beneath her ear.

So startled she forgot to be embarrassed, she jumped, screamed just a little, and released him.

He laid his huge hand on her head. "More than possible, I'd say 'tis mandatory."

"What do you mean?" She held her voice steady.

His hand stroked her hair back from her face. "Just what I said."

"How long have you been awake?" Cautiously, she eased back from him.

"Don't move," he ordered. "This justifies my use as a warming pan."

She froze, so chagrined she blushed to the tips of her toes. "I hoped you hadn't noticed."

Her arm rested against his stomach, and so she felt the convulsion of muscle as he struggled against his laughter. His fingers shook against her forehead and he dropped his arm. "Noticed? That you used me as a warming pan or that your hands were on me?"

"My hands. . . ." She blushed again, for saying something so incredibly stupid.

It was a long moment before he spoke, and then his voice shook and jerked. But he kindly ignored her *bêtise*. "I've been awake since that first dab of your frosty toe against my leg. Every man should wake with a block of ice placed against his leg. 'Tis a great deal of pleasure you've given me, although not," he chuckled, "from your feet."

"Why didn't you speak?"

"You were enjoying yourself."

That made her sit up straight. "And you weren't?"

His hand clasped her shoulder and eased her back down on the palliasse. "So much. Saura. So much."

She lay there stiff, shamed by her previous boldness, and he settled beside her. One muscled arm wrapped under her neck and the other wrapped around her waist, and he cradled her so close against him that his breath regulated hers. He just held her beneath his chin and warmed her.

The tenseness slid away, leaving enormous contentment. When she cuddled her head into his chest, his hands began a slow tugging at her braid.

"What are you doing?" she asked.

"I like the smell of your hair," he rumbled. "I like the silkiness of it, and I want it loose when I love you."

She tried to stiffen again, but his heat had crept into her like a narcotic, and her muscles no longer responded to shock. "You can't love me," she said, but the protest sounded languid.

" 'Tis the reason you came to bed with me," he reasoned.

"I was cold."

"And the reason you woke me with your icy feet."

"I wanted to warm them."

"And the reason you rubbed me when your chill didn't wake me and kissed me when your rubbing didn't wake me. You wanted me awake, and functioning. Weren't you interested in my lips?"

"Your lips?"

"You felt every other part of me."

"Not your legs," she objected indignantly.

"I stopped you before you got that far," he pointed out.

Miserable, she realized she couldn't justify her curiosity about his body with the obvious explanation that she was blind and had never seen him. He still had no inkling. If he thought about it at all, he thought she walked and worked and moved with the confidence of a seeing person. Flattering, but difficult to explain.

"My lips," he prompted.

"Lips are for kissing, that kind of deep kissing that men enjoy, and I didn't want. . . ." Her voice trailed off, lost in the muddle of explanation.

"Who gave you such a low opinion of a man's kiss?"

"Sometimes the visiting gentry would kiss me, in jest, of course, and sometimes my stepfather tried."

"Pigs." He spat the word. "But those are not kisses. We shared a kiss once, don't you remember? Has no one else kissed you correctly?" His hand followed a similar path to her own, petting her brows, sliding down her dainty nose to her two quivering lips. "Has no one taught you the pleasure brought by the meeting of male and female in the nectar of a kiss?" He caressed her cheek with one finger. "Has no one brought the rose of paradise to your cheek with the glowing seal of a kiss? Has no one brought you the taste of delicious strawberry?"

"Sounds like an outdoor pursuit to me," she said with acid emphasis.

He laughed and squeezed her. "What a humbug you are! Resolutely unromantic, truly the character of Lady Saura, sour with the lack of love. But I lay here as an enchanting elf cuddled me, and I remembered the innocent maiden who wrestled me in the bath, and kissed me, and brought the taste of strawberries and roses and nectar to a man lost to the joys of life."

"That kiss was different. You surprised me."

"Ah. Will I never bring you pleasure unless I surprise you? Then I'll sneak up on you." His lips touched her ear and slid around to peck her mouth. "Or swoop on you." He smacked loud kisses on her chin. "Or kiss you like an inexperienced boy." He put his mouth on hers and ground them together, huffing in a parody of passion until she laughed. "And then kiss the smile on your face," he whispered against her lips, "until you open for me willingly."

His intent shifted so subtly that she did as he said. She opened for him willingly, his tongue brushing her teeth, then her tongue. It bore no relation to the attentions of other men, and she wondered, for the first time, if what they had done to her had been less a kiss than a rape. Perhaps William was right, perhaps a kiss between a man and a woman required the correct ingredients to make the dish complete.

She tasted him again, as she had done before, but a different flavor rolled across her tongue. Stronger, more manly, clarified by his breath and emphasized by his tongue. He pressed against her now, body to body, making her aware of his manhood, and she broke the kiss.

"I still don't think," she sucked in air, "that 'tis possible."

"We'll make it possible." He began to rise above her, but she pushed him back.

"But you shouldn't. You were hurt today."

"Aye, my head aches, but not as badly as my—" He stopped short. "Pardon. That word isn't appropriate for a lady's ears."

"You needn't be delicate. I know what you mean, and I promise I have heard every crude word in the Norman language."

"All the more reason to be delicate. I swear, you'll never confuse me with the other men in your life." His breath came lower, whispering across her face. "What happened today cannot impair me. The danger of our circumstance, past and present, can only add flame to our loving."

"Tomorrow might never come." She completed his thought.

Again he rose above her, and as he untied the bow that held her chainse, he promised, "Tomorrow will come. Only hope will greet us tomorrow."

The string slipped through its guide, widening the opening until he slipped the garment off her shoulders and kissed them, first one, then the other. "Such a fragile frame for such a fierce warrior." He raised her hands and held them against his face, rubbing his own beard with them, guiding her to touch his neck and shoulders. "I like that, I like it when you touch me," he said.

Her hands clung to him, but she felt frightened and odd, intrusive, somehow, and the "fierce warrior" couldn't find the strength in her soul to please him as he desired. He chuckled, ever so softly, and adroitly maneuvered her chainse until it rested at her waist. "What a delight you are! Blessed with the ripe sweetness of a woman, yet as green and untutored as any girl."

He made her sound, she realized with bemusement, as charming and pleasing with her cowardice as any courtesan with her wiles.

He gathered a handful of her hair in his fist and raised it to his nose. "Ah," he sighed, "every wine should have such a fine bouquet." His big fingers combed through her hair, and began a deep, marvelous massage at the base of her neck. Her head tilted back, baring her neck to his gentle kiss. She had never imagined such riches. Then he massaged her scalp, feeding her pleasure through his fingertips until he reached her forehead and his touch changed to a wisp of curiosity. She recognized the light touch as he outlined her eyebrows, skimmed her nose, caressed her lips. He was reading her face.

Perhaps she was shy as a green girl, but he disguised his need to see her with a lover's embrace, and his faint reserve endeared him to her as nothing else could. "Do you think I'm pretty?" she asked, encouragement and pleasure in her tones.

His fingers paused, quivered, traced her cheeks. "A lovely bone structure," he muttered and cuffed her lightly on the jaw. "And a willful chin."

Laughing, she stretched as he caressed her shoulders, her arms, her neck. She braced for rough hands that fumbled at her lower body, and his unexpected care left her breathless with pleasure and longing for a more intimate touch, but where?

"I like it when you touch me," he repeated. "Won't you show me where you wish I would touch you?"

Again he raised her hands, but left them hovering in the air between them. She flexed her fingers until her sense of foolishness overcame her timidity and she could reach for the muscles of his chest, and with an astonishing lack of coordination, landed on his shoulders. At once his hands found her shoulders and waited, waited until her palms stroked over the joints. Then his palms stroked over her joints. Her fingers slid down his ribs. His fingers slid down her ribs. Her fingers twitched, rushed, twisted, and in a rush found his chest. His fingers performed none of the convolutions, contained none of the hurry, but they floated to their mark with such smooth precision that she suspected he knew where to search.

Conscious thought left her mind as his hands enfolded her breasts. As pure a sensation as she had ever experienced, the press of flesh to flesh unified them in one crystal moment of communion. Her eyes drifted closed, her breath sang out in one ecstatic cry. One perfect moment, complete in itself and promising treasure.

"More?" his voice murmured in her ear.

She nodded in leisurely agreement, whispering, "Please."

"How?"

Her hands searched for his nipples, buried in the mat of curling hair, and her thumbs rubbed them in a circular motion.

"How straightforward you are," he marveled. "Most women would prefer this." Like the leaves of autumn drifting to the ground, his fingers swept and danced across her skin, cultivating the sensitive underside of her breast, complimenting with unspoken admiration. Sensation swelled within her, the reaction of an inexperienced student to the work of a master. She wanted, desperately wanted, his hands on her nipples, but coherence had fled, coordination had fled.

Then he granted her desire, closing on her and squeezing in a light and steady rhythm, and the thinking part of Saura had fled and in her place writhed this sensual being on the pallet.

"Still more?" he asked.

It took three deep breaths before she could stammer, "What more can there be?"

His mouth took her nipple, and every muscle in her body flew to rigid attention. He suckled as she worked her leg beneath him. Then he licked every inch of her breast until she wrapped her legs around his waist in open supplication, and then he repeated the treatment on the other breast. When he pulled away at last, the chill of the room struck her chest, damp with his loving. It brought a little rationality to her mind, a little organization to her thoughts, and she wanted to speak, to beg him.

He murmured, "Cold, little one? Let me cover you." Slowly, so slowly, he descended on her body, covering first the vulnerable skin of her belly, then her breastbone. Her nipples nestled into the rasp of his hair and the weight of his chest descended on her, flattened her, opened her to the miracle of flesh on flesh for the first time.

Her life usually rumbled along, dull and routine or horrifying and terrifying, broken occasionally by golden moments. This moment she relished the most. Her golden man. His lips floated across her eyelids, his spice teased her nose, and she lifted her head and captured his kiss with her own, as fresh and ardent as any apt pupil's.

Now his lips opened under her probing, now he let her lead them down the path to paradise, and when they came up for air she was gratified to hear the gasp of his breath and feel the heavy thump of his heart, so close to her own.

"Pleasure," he said, his voice out of control and amplified by the bare room. He moderated his tone and repeated, "Pleasure is a marvelous thing. It can be slow and fiery, burning every inhibition in its path." Leaning sideways across her body, his hand glided from its resting place on her ribs and down to her hip. "Our conflagration has ignited everything. Saura, I'm on fire."

Almost inaudible, his eloquence meant less to her than the fine tremble in his arm as he supported himself above her.

"Saura, show me what you want."

She found her fingers shook, too, as she gathered his hand in hers and put it on her pubic bone, but he asked no further urging. It was a honeyed delight when he opened her to his probing. One by one he found, and recognized, the organs of her response, showed her that all that had gone before was a preparation for this. When first one finger, then another, skimmed inside her, her soul began the slow glide to pleasure. Not his whispered warning of pain, not his careful probing, not the slow introduction of his essence into her body could stop the updraft that lifted her.

Her tissues yielded slowly: not all her will could force her body to part for him. Yet the discomfort was nothing compared to the agony of rapture his hands supplied her. His litany of, "I can't wait, I can't wait," meant only that he eased into her in tiny increments, backing off and returning until she clawed at him in frustration. Then he fought his way past her maidenhead and chuckled in choked amusement when she groaned, "At last!"

Her impatience blossomed. She kneaded his waist, pulled at his buttocks, gasped his name. That ignited his spark.

What had been a patient and gentle loving grew to a tumultuous fierceness. Unbearable delight, gratified distress, she'd never been here before. William pulled her into the center of turbulence and propelled her from one extreme to the other until her body could no longer demand, could no longer receive. She captured him in her arms and legs, hugging him, following his dance, and she found that place of color and light.

In this blessed place, there was gold beneath her fingers, gold in the scented air. There were golden sounds for her ears and golden dishes for her taste. The gold ebbed and flowed with William's thrust, grew to be more than gold under his encouragement, and in one glorious revelation they welded themselves into one entity. William and Saura, Saura and William. Together, where the treasures of their bodies transformed into the treasures of their souls, and lodged there past the time of passion.

Perhaps, Saura dreamed, these treasures would never disappear.

She returned to a kind of consciousness when his weight collapsed on her. "Sorry," he groaned and lifted himself from her body. Regret made her hug him close for one last moment, and then she released him. Understanding her with an affinity that dazzled, he settled himself and brushed her hair back from her face. "There'll be more for us," he promised.

"Aye," she said, not because she agreed, but because she hoped. Strength returned to her limbs, and in a surge of activity she shoved the blankets to the foot of the pallet and complained, "I'm so hot."

In the night, she put her feet on him and he woke with a jolt. "Damn, woman, you're freezing again."

"Aye."

"If you'd keep the covers on you—"

"You can warm me," she suggested, snuggling tight under his arm.

"Aye, you wanton, I could. But I won't." He cuddled her close and kissed the top of her head. "You're too inexperienced and I'm—stop that! Where'd you learn that?"

She raised her mouth from his nipple. "From you. Don't you like it?"

"I don't know. 'Tis . . . different. I suppose I like it. *Stop that!*" He caught her under her chin and held her while he shifted so they were face to face. "Wait another night, love, and I'll bring you satisfaction again. There's too great a difference between us for you to be comfortable with further joinings tonight."

"Don't you want me?" Her voice quivered with rejection.

"Not want you? God, woman," he took her hand and wrapped it around his organ, "that's as large a want as I've ever had. But more than that, I love you. You're the most honest woman in the world. And generous and clever."

"I sound like a nun again." She sighed.

"Oh, nay." He laughed and shook his head in an emphatic negative. "You're also stubborn and determined and feisty and I'll never put a rock in your way," he raised her hands and kissed them, "when my head is close and I've made you angry."

"I've never hit anyone before," she protested. "At least, not with stones."

"I'm flattered."

She could hear the smile in his voice.

"Only in my defense do you become an effective fighter. I'll teach you to defend yourself. No woman of mine will be raped or murdered without a struggle."

Woman of mine.

The words stood out and thrilled her, but beneath the thrill rested a cold fear and confusion. Did he really believe any woman was capable of defending herself? Her own defenses were guile and watchfulness, honed by years of danger. Was she deceiving him unnecessarily? Should she tell him, before someone else did, of her blindness? She hated it so much, when one of the slack-witted fools made a game of her, and she feared he would think she had done so with him.

They were easy words to say: "William, I'm blind, too." But those few syllables could destroy the cocoon of trust and passion that surrounded them, and so her innate honesty struggled with her craving to procrastinate, for just one more night. For just a few more hours.

"You've wandered far away from me," he murmured, tugging at a lock of hair. "Come back and sleep in my arms till the morn. Then we'll discover who's made such a torment for us, and after I cure his pretensions we'll be on our way."

Analyzing the emotions from the voices around her had kept Saura from harm more times than she could count, and now she heard the false confidence in his tone, the projection of assurance that he did not feel.

But what could she do? Putting her own assurance in her voice, she murmured, "Of course, William," and drifted off to sleep.

The sun leaked its rosy light through the two arrow loops, illuminating the sorry furnishing of the room, and William stared and wondered. It looked so real. Since his accident, he had dreamed vivid, sighted dreams, but this one looked so real. Since the days of his boyhood, when William had wakened with anticipation, he had never shaken his irrational assurance that each new day would be a landmark day. This morning was no different. The pleasure had been made sharper, perhaps, by the events of the night, but still he had stretched and embraced the morning, and opened his eyes: and seen this.

He closed his eyes again, and the vision disappeared. His remaining senses, the senses he trusted, fed him information. Borne on the wind, early morning air brushed his face with its dewy kiss. Outside, he could hear birds practicing their salute to the sun with increasing vigor. Beside him, Saura still slept. He could hear her even breathing and feel her warmth against his arm. Aye, it was morning.

He opened his eyes. Those damn arrow loops seemed

brighter, the increasing light flattered the grey stones. He flicked his gaze across the narrow room. Table, stools, tall empty candle holder. How odd. Wooden buckets. Cocking his head up, he stared down at the pallet.

Look at that. Two bumps under the brown blanket where his feet should be, and they moved when he moved. This seemed so real.

Look at the woman beside him. God's teeth, now he knew it was a dream. This woman, this dream Saura, was gorgeous. *Vers* sprang to his lips under the influence of her sensuous face. A lovely bone structure, indeed, and a willful chin. And red lips and long black lashes that brushed her cheeks. Long, shiny, black hair artfully placed across her chest, hiding and revealing the proud arch of her breast. Her skin, all over, creamy and clear, unmarred by freckle or blemish. What a dream. *What* a dream.

He shook his head at his own gullibility, and his imaginary scenery rocked back and forth. He lay back, chuckling, and raised his hands to rub his eyes. But before they connected, he stopped. They looked so much like his own hands. Look, there was the scar in the pad of his thumb where he'd broken the skin polishing a helmet in his squire days. And look, his middle finger cocked to the side, just a little, from the broken bone he'd earned in battle five years ago. And look, his hands didn't seem as muscular as they had, just as his hands should appear after months of inactivity. And look, he flexed his whole hand. Look.

Look.

His heart began a slow, hard pounding.

Look. Look at the way his hands obeyed his commands.

He sat up on his elbows.

Look at this room. Look at this place.

Look at the light.

SIX

"Only hope will greet us tomorrow." Was it his own incantation that had healed him? Or was it the love of a good woman, a virgin, that old panacea for every ill?

William stood and peered out the arrow loop. He knew where they were. He'd been in this castle once before on a hunting trip. Below him he could see—dear God, the miracle contained in that simple word!—he could see the wall walk, and that told him this room was located at the top of a tower. Far below the wall curved a river, and he saw a shallow-bottomed boat preparing to tie at the dock and disgorge its single impudent stooge.

He couldn't believe it. Or he didn't want to believe it. The villainy of this whole plan astonished him. The stupidity of it amazed him, too. He'd dressed, then he'd checked out this prison. There were no restrictions here, not for a sighted man. If he wanted to, he could break down the door. If he wanted to, he could rouse Saura, wisk her past those pitiful sentries, steal two horses and ride back to Burke. It would not have been horribly difficult without the use of his eyes, and now that his vision had returned, it was ridiculously simple.

But he wouldn't. He wouldn't. This man who held them, this worm, this misbegotten knave, he would pay. And he would speak. William couldn't think of one thing that could render this *âme damnée* courageous enough to stand against him. A modest man, William knew that in a rage, he was a force no one, certainly not that filthy whoreson who imprisoned them, could withstand.

Walking to the bed, he stood and stared at Saura. Her beauty shocked him. He was a pragmatic man, one who expected no more from life than it gave. But this woman was a prize.

A maid at nineteen. He'd known she was a maid by her amazed reaction to pleasure, but the confirmation of her state made it difficult for him to control himself.

What a reward! The girl became a woman in a burst of flame, burying him in passion, pulling at him with exquisite convulsions. She burned him with her erotic flame, but she credited him with the heat they created, and perhaps she was right. Apart, they functioned as two normal human beings. Together, their fiery union lit the night.

A maid at nineteen. Uneasy, he pulled a stool up to the table and tore off a chunk of bread. Dry, chewy, it tasted like heaven to a man denied both his dinner and his supper the day before. But his attention wandered back to Saura, her eyelids tinted a delicate blue by the tracery of veins beneath sheer skin. Any heiress with her looks should have been married at thirteen. Why wasn't she? The question nagged at him. She seemed perfect. Beautiful, compassionate, accomplished, rich. How had her stepfather kept her from marriage? Of course, a bigger bastard than her stepfather had never existed. The distaste Theobald had given her for kissing was soon vanquished, and she'd shown a remarkable ability to improvise on William's own theme. She'd kissed all the parts of his body until his muscles ached with rigid constraint. The memory of it brought him to his feet again, unable to sit with any kind of serenity beneath the prod of nostalgia. If she weren't so new, if she weren't so tiny, if she were awake and smiling at him. He swore at himself. With a smidgen of encouragement, he'd jump on her in a moment. How had he checked himself last night, when she'd asked for a repeat?

He paced away to the window. Something nagged at him, something one of the servants had said, but he couldn't quite resurrect it. He looked out the window again, down to the river. Where was that little twirp who had imprisoned them? If he didn't come through the door soon, William would have to break out. He couldn't bear being in the same room with her and not slipping the blankets from her body. Clenching his fist, he pounded his forehead and groaned. What a fool he was, to torment himself.

A soft sigh alerted him to her waking. Swinging on one heel, he watched with eager eyes as she stretched like a cat, first one arm, then the other, first one leg, then the other, then the whole long length of her in one sinuous motion. Her skin glowed with health, light against the dark cover over the palliasse. Her long hair concealed and revealed as it shifted over the mounds and valleys of her flesh. She was the loveliest thing he'd seen in—he laughed at himself. She was the loveliest thing he'd ever seen.

A belated desire for drama caught him unaware. He wanted to surprise her, please her with the return of his sight. Hastily, he faced back to the arrow loop, never thinking that in itself would alert a sighted person, for what blind man stares out the window?

"William?" Her word sounded with the musical allure of a flute. When he didn't answer, in a frantic tone, "William?"

"Here, love." He found he couldn't face her yet, and rubbed his palms across his face with boyish glee.

"Are you well?" she asked, concern lacing the clear notes of her voice.

In answer he turned and faced her. Her eyes astonished him. The violets of the spring lost the contest for velvety color, or perhaps the contrast of her black lashes against her white skin created an unfair advantage. Her lips, like petals of carmine peonies, drooped with the worry absent in her slumber. Asleep, her face turned the envious beauties of the world to stone; awake, the compilation of fine bones, delicate muscles, and fragile skin created a classic animation he could study for hours.

But she wasn't really watching him. So he winked at her. And she didn't react. So he grinned at her, a boyish, look-at-me grin. And the worry lines on her face deepened.

"William?" She threw back the covers and rose in one swift, graceful movement. "What is it? Your head?"

She started toward him. His throat closed with appreciation of her body, and his warning remained unuttered. He threw out his hand to her. But she kept coming, not seeming to see his gesture, not seeming to see the bucket until her toes caught around the leg of the stool, her knee whacked the bucket and the whole contrivance, and Saura, went flying.

Jumping after her, his mind buzzing with concern, he was relieved to hear a very normal shout of "Plague take it!" from those petal-soft lips. Wrapping his arms around the fallen beauty, he lifted her with tender concern. He let her stand first one foot down, then the other. "Any broken bones?" he queried.

"Of course not," she answered scornfully. "I've done worse. But you, William, are you healthy?"

"Aye." He stared down at her shins, tracing the redness already beginning above the bone. "T'will be painful." He realized he wasn't looking into her face as he should. A man who wished to surprise his lady with the return of his sight had to alert her somehow to his good news. So why was he afraid?

He froze. Afraid? What was he afraid of? What had he seen, with his new eyes, that he hadn't wanted to admit to?

"What ails you?" she insisted, shaking his shoulder. "You're stiff as if you were paralyzed. Is that it? Are there parts of your body not functioning? You must tell me, trying to keep it from me only makes it worse."

"All my body parts are functioning. All of them." He raised his eyes to her face and saw it there, that gaze that looked through him, that gaze that didn't touch him. His first incredulous thought was that her sight had been taken so his could be restored, but her very natural demeanor relieved him of his suspicion. The whiplash of remorse convinced him. All his scorn and rebellion had been directed at this beautiful, sightless girl. A shiver ran through him. "Saura."

"You're ill," she said. "I knew I shouldn't have let you love me."

She tried to disengage her arm from around his neck, but he stopped her by swinging her up into his arms.

"If you're ill, let me help you," she insisted. "Put me down."

"Aye, I'll put you down." He lowered her all the way to the

palliasse on the floor. He pulled the loose cover around her, tucked her tight in its folds.

She let him, unresisting, not understanding. "William?" she whispered, touching his face as he knelt before her.

An immense guilt swallowed him. "Oh, my God, Saura, you can't see."

Saura sat straight and tall, her legs curved beneath her, hugging the blanket to her bare body until she understood the import of what he'd said. The bleakness of her existence rushed over her, and her mind screamed, *No escape! You'll never escape.*

"And you *can* see." There was flatness to her voice, but it strengthened as the elation in his good fortune took her from herself. "God's blessing on you, William! You can see!" She brought his head close with her palms on his chin and kissed him full on the mouth. Her hands came away wet. "Tears?"

He leaned his cheek against hers, and she wondered at the reverse of their positions. When she had the moment, she would give in to the despair that licked at her existence.

He was crying beside her. The way he cried astonished her. No sobs, no shaking of the shoulders. Just silent tears soaking her neck. It seemed to bring him pain, as if each rare tear ran with his heart's blood.

She found, to her surprise, that his tears caused her pain, too. When had anyone cried for her? Since the death of her mother, nurturing had been a gift she had given to others and almost never received. Now this man, tough and purposeful, a warrior in every sense of the word, cried for her. And it distressed her, more than the evidence of her first selfish reaction. With shaking hands, she stroked his hair back from his forehead and cleared her throat. "Why are you crying?"

He didn't answer, only his hand rubbed her knee, his arm hugged her waist. He tried to crawl into her skin and share her travail.

Her stroking hand grew stronger, tugged at his hair. "Surely I've taught you that blindness limits us only as we let it."

"It's . . . not . . . that."

"What is it?"

"I've been a foul-mouthed knave."

"Well, I don't know."

"A beetle-headed malfeasor."

"Nothing so—"

"A base, proud tottyhead."

He paused, but she said nothing.

"Aren't you going to object?"

"No," she drawled the word. "Humility is so refreshing in a man."

Instant outrage brought him to a half crouch, and then he remembered his harshness and sank back to her. "You have a distressing manner of teaching humility to a man. When I think back to all the times I've mocked Lady Saura, made fun of your age and said you didn't understand my plight, because *you* could see, I want to flog myself."

"Actually, you didn't mock me, you teased me. There's a world of difference. To a woman of advanced years, it would have been flattering. To me. . . ." She thought about all the barren years in Theobald's house, ignored by any eligible men or taunted about her disadvantage. Or being offered a place in some knight's bed with the arrogant assumption she'd be grateful. "To me, your teasing has been a kindness."

To her horror, her voice shook with emotion, and his grip on her tightened. Hoarsely, he said, "I've been cruel to you, yelling at you, being rude."

Surprised, Saura laughed. "So? Why am I so special? You've yelled at every one of your household, and hurt your son's feelings and your father's, too."

His misery abruptly checked. "I have not!"

"And they're the ones you really care about," she continued as if she hadn't heard. "I've been quite flattered."

"Flattered!"

"Aye. It makes me one of the family. If you didn't yell at me, I'd think you didn't like me."

"Woman!" he thundered, rearing back from his position of penitence. "Shut your mouth and listen to me. I do *not* shout and I am *not* rude, and I certainly am not going to be rude to you anymore!"

"Of course not," she chuckled, and with a groan he settled his head onto her bosom.

"You are," he said, "a wicked woman."

"A beetle-headed malfeasor?" she suggested, swallowing the tickle of enchantment that threatened to overwhelm her good sense and reduce her to torrents of merriment.

"At least that," he agreed gloomily.

"I am not. But I am what Bronnie worried about."

Her voice lowered with carnal significance, but his thoughts were elsewhere. "I wish you'd stop trying to hold in your laughter," he said, his voice laced with disgust. He looked up at her. "I can feel it fighting to get out, and that expression of innocence on your face wouldn't fool a friar."

Hastily she rearranged the muscles of her face in a gentle smile, and he snorted. "I've always wondered what Saura, the nun, looked like. Now I know."

"I am not a nun," she protested. "And I'm damned tired of having you compare me to one."

"Believe me, love, I know you're not a nun. No one knows better than I. I'm the expert on your lack of nun-ness."

Saura could feel his face approaching hers.

"Not only do I know you're not a nun, I've ruined your chances to become anything but a penitent nun with the simple act of—" He stopped, so close his breath skimmed her face and her lips were pursed in ready anticipation. "What do you mean, you are what Bronnie worried about?"

"I'm the sort of woman the priests warn of." He drew farther back, and she followed him with her mouth until she realized her behavior rivaled an effervescent bubble chasing the blustery north wind.

"How did he know that?"

She didn't like his tone, and she said, "By my wanton demeanor, I surmise."

"What have you been doing with Bronnie?"

Pulling one hand out of her cover, she shook her finger right beneath his nose. "He was worried when I had him strip you. He thought I wouldn't be able to keep my hands off a naked man, but I assured him my intentions were pure. Do you quarrel with me?"

"Ah." He sighed. He caught the finger that waved too close and folded it among its fellows. "I could never quarrel with you." His hand moved to her wrist, and he pulled her arm out straight, ignoring the jerks she used to regain possession. "But I'm glad to hear you resisted your pure intentions."

She could hear the smile grow in his voice, and it infuriated her. "I may have resisted my pure intentions last night." She jumped with the application of his open mouth to the pit of her elbow. "Stop that!"

"Go on, scold me," he said against the tender skin, and the hairs rose on her arm in blatant reaction. "I'm listening."

"But those intentions are clear this morning!" She flung

her arm back, and he let it go with no struggle, and the blanket swung back to expose more than half her body. "You rogue!" she cried, as he caught her bared waist and tumbled her backwards across the pallet. "Do you think you can insult me and then," she gasped as his body followed her down, "then attack me?"

"Attack is a drastic word." Deftly, he untangled all of her limbs from the blanket. "I'm going to strongly persuade you."

"To do what?" Frost coated her features, and her freed hands bobbed to his chest to protest his encroachment.

"I just want you to kiss me."

"Kiss you? You insinuated—" She put a little pressure against him and grimaced. As easy to lever a boulder with a twig.

"I'm sorry." His fingers brushed her rib cage and pranced away. "I'm sorry. I'm a jealous fool."

"You're a man." Loathing dripped, scorn withered. She was good with nuances of voice.

They were wasted on William, who with abominable cheerfulness admitted, "Guilty as charged. I'm only a man, and you must make allowances for my pigheaded," a daring caress to her stomach, "asinine," a tender squeeze on the lobe of her ear, "positively loathsome doubts about you and that stupid little whine-tit."

He tickled her ribs and her hands flew off his chest and snatched at his hands, which eluded her by spreading out in a Y. She braced herself, but his upper body landed on her gently. "Muscle control," he grunted.

She could ignore him, surrounding her with massive masculinity, but she wondered how to recover her hands, squashed between their bodies. Dignity seemed to elude her under William's influence, and she said, "That stupid little whine-tit, as you call him, brought food and water and bandages. You ought to be grateful."

"Oh, I am," he breathed against her neck.

"Grateful that Bronnie—" His tunic provided a sweep of soft cloth that moved against her. "Bronnie. . . ."

His tongue outlined the rosy shell of her ear, and the wet temptation halted her thought processes.

He whispered, "I'm sorry for my lunacy. I know you too well to seriously suspect you of misdeed. 'Tis my own damaged self-esteem that spoke so rashly."

The warm draft affected her auditory perceptions, creating a loss of crucial resentment. The movement of his lips against her skin felt too good; what could he do with a full attack on her senses? "You base, proud tottyhead," she murmured, and he slid his mouth across her cheek, surprising her with a light kiss, as he had promised the night before. So close to her, she felt his grin stretch his muscles and bathe her with sunshine.

"At last we agree."

His contagious grin affected her mouth and she knew her rancor had lost the battle. She pecked a kiss onto his nose, on his cheek, on his chin, and she heard danger rumble in his chest. His lips coaxed her until she opened and let him in. Shyly, she returned his surge of tongue with quick touches of her own. That seemed to ignite him, for the body above her heated and he wiggled one knee between her. In the cradle of her hips, she encountered his tumescence and it gave her hope for another skirmish. His marvelous vehicle had carried her away last night. She squirmed to accommodate him, hoping to roam with him this morning.

So when he lifted his head, she murmured in protest, and his most unromantic "Sh!" hurt her freshly created confidence. Then she heard it, too: the scrape of a key in the lock.

William leaped up. "Stupid idiot," he complained, and lifted her to a sitting position, swaddling her in the blanket. As he tucked it under her chin, he noticed the trail of a tear down her cheek and wiped it with his thumb. "Not you, love, I was talking about me. Don't cry, my indomitable one, I need you to be strong now."

The door swung open as he spoke, and he twisted toward the man who stood in the doorway. He wanted to speak his name, but the masquerade of blindness suited him now; it gave him a vulnerability that would destroy the inhibitions of the slightly built man who gloated with such humor.

"My dear guests!" said Arthur, his frisky voice grinding on William's nerves. "Lord William of Miraval and," his eyes bugged in open avarice as he surveyed the lady's tumbled state, "Lady Saura."

"Of Roget," she reminded him.

Relieved to see she had gathered her blanket and her invisible cloak of dignity tight around her, William rose to his feet. "Ah. 'Tis Arthur. To what do we owe this unexpected hospitality?" Arthur, he was pleased to see, took one step back in reaction to William's commanding size, and then one step forward in the press of men behind him. Whipping his voice into scorn, he added, "And how many men do you need to help you enforce your hospitality on one blind man and his woman?"

Arthur's stature was always a sore spot to him, and he reacted as William knew he would. "Go, go." He waved his men out the door, glanced back at William, and pulled two armed hulks back in. "There, we're alone now."

"Exactly so," William agreed, cursing his bad luck. He would have laughed at Arthur's cowardice, at his ignorance about what a blind man could know, but the situation reeked of deceit and destruction. The fragile, vivid woman

Arthur ogled with such rapacity depended on him. Of all the people to have kidnapped him, Arthur was the worst. Flighty, vindictive, impossible to question because of his lightness of mind. It would take all his wit and skill to save Saura from ruin. Fixing a vacant gaze in his eyes, he asked, "What do you want?"

"Why, nothing." Arthur simpered in expectant pleasure. "Only your lands and wealth and all those other things."

Arthur smiled at Saura, noting the flush of her cheek, the bright sparkle in her eyes, the rosy blush of her well-kissed lips.

William's hands itched to slap him. "How?" he boomed, and Arthur twitched his attention back. "How do you propose to do that?"

"Well, we were going to do it with your little accident, but I told him it would never work. You're too damned tough. But it did blind you, and that made this whole game a little easier."

"Game?"

"Your kidnapping! He's received my message by now. He'll be so surprised!"

"Aye. When he gets here, he'll be horribly surprised." William stroked his hand over his beard, and wondered who "he" was. And more important: "When do you expect him?"

"Soon, I would think. I got the message from the mercenary yesterday afternoon. It has taken them days and days to get close to you but I sent a message to him immediately. I boarded the boat last night to get here. I couldn't wait to see you. Oh, William, this is so much fun! I've never been in on a plot before, much less actually thought of one."

"Didn't he think of this plan?"

"Nay." Arthur shrugged petulantly, impatient at being interrupted and not wanting to discuss the omnipotent "he." "He wants to think of everything. He thinks I'm stupid, but I showed him."

"Who is he?" William asked.

Arthur waggled his hands. "Nay, I'm not going to tell you. I want to see your face when he gets here. Your expression will almost be payment enough for the hardships you've put me through."

"But I won't know him," Saura interrupted. "What's his name?"

William cursed silently as Arthur's attention switched back to her. "A woman as lovely as yourself shouldn't concern herself with such trivial details."

"As trivial as who's going to kill me?" she asked bluntly.

"He's not going to kill you."

"Well, somebody's got to do it," she snapped. "Is it you?"

"Nay." Arthur took one step closer to the pallet. "I'm sure we'll work something out."

"Soft as butter where women are concerned. And as slippery," William said with contempt. "Be advised, your friend won't be pleased about having you kidnap Lady Saura."

"Well, William, what else could I do?"

"You could have had her left on Burke land." William saw the slide of Arthur's eyes as he contemplated the tousled woman, already naked, already on the palliasse. "Or was it simply the thrill of using my woman?"

Arthur began to laugh, trying to be sophisticated and succeeding only in sounding high-strung. "Could you have done better?"

"I don't know. I've never done anything so dishonorable."

William's flat statement infuriated Arthur, and the soft

laughter stopped. "Of course not. You're so damned honorable it sickens me. We all used to laugh about you behind our hands, about what a fantastic, godly knight you were and how you never stooped to rape or lie and how you never slapped your servants or picked on us squires."

"Actually, I have slapped my servants for good cause, and for not picking on my squires, 'tis not a mistake I'll make again, if this is the result."

"Don't fret, my high and mighty Lord William, you will never have squires again. You're blind, remember? You're going to be dead, remember?"

"Nay, you hadn't told me that part, yet," William rumbled.

"Aye, and as your dear friends, we'll go to comfort your father, and in no time we'll be sitting on your bench, drinking out of your goblet."

"I doubt that." William's voice resounded with confidence. "You haven't the courage to kill me, nor the stalwart strength to take my place."

"Your father will be so distraught."

"My father's not a mewling fool! Do you think he hasn't mourned his failure to implant in you the seeds of chivalry? You'd be the last—"

"You puff your chest like a pigeon, so proud of your puny wit!" Arthur stripped off his surcoat and tossed it into the corner. "I'm going to have that woman you've already warmed for me! You're going to die and the crows will pick at your body."

He flung himself at Saura, knocking her backwards against the wall, and her small cry was engulfed by the roar of rage from William. Arthur dared! Two steps took William to the pallet, two hands seized Arthur and turned him. When Arthur's eyes had widened to the point of terror, William said with harsh conviction, "But I can see. I can see you, you sniveling little worm."

The guards, frozen by the turn of events, rushed them at his words. William grasped Arthur by the neck and the seat, and raised him above his head and heaved him like a dog at the rushing guards. That body, inert with shock, flung them against the wall with a crash of tremendous proportion. It resounded in the little room and brought the slam of guards' armor from outside the door. William was there before them, wedging the spike of the iron candle stand into the wood. One guard inside began to struggle to his feet, but as William raised a stool over his head he prudently dropped back to the floor and played dead.

"Clever man," William approved, and stepped over the bodies to Saura. "How is your head?" Before she could answer, he said, "Here are your clothes. Let me help you." He raised her to her feet and with the impersonal touch of a eunuch. "I'll not make the same mistake again."

He pulled her cotte over her head and she objected, "My chainse!"

"No time." He laced it tightly, trying to cover as much of her bared skin as he could. "I'm the stupid idiot who didn't have you dressed when Arthur arrived. Patience!" he called to the pounding on the door. "I'll not compound that mistake when his accomplice arrives. We must leave before reinforcements come to finish Arthur's pitiable job."

"I'll not argue that." She wiped her hands on her skirt, the hands that still felt the pebbled feel of Arthur's acne-pocked skin. "But how will we leave with the guards at the door? And what's happened to Arthur?"

"He's dead." He answered the last question first. "Broken neck. Didn't you hear it crack? And we'll walk out of here.

Arthur's servants are nothing if not disloyal, they'll scatter like mice freed from a trap. Where are your shoes?"

"Back at Fyngre Brook."

"Then we'll have to have horses," he decided, folding the blankets and tucking them under his arm.

"Aren't you going to do anything for Arthur?" Saura asked, bewildered by William's hurry, by his callous pronouncement of death.

That got his attention. "Do anything for him? God's teeth, I can't kill him more than once, much as I would like to. Do you realize what he was going to do? Besides rape you, which means nothing more than pissing to him? He was going to kill you for making the mistake of associating with me." He stopped tugging the candle stand out of the door and walked back to grasp her shoulders and shake her. "What foolish fancy made you speak to him? I'd tried to keep his attention focused on me, and you blundered into our conversation."

"Making mistakes is more honorable than doing nothing." She broke into his tirade. "You need to know who the other conspirator is, and I thought he might tell *me.*"

"Aye, he'd tell a woman long before he'd tell me, but Saura, don't you ever do anything so foolish again." He spaced the words individually, dealing a warning with them one by one. "I lost ten years when he jumped on you. What if he'd had a knife?"

"It did not improve my outlook, either."

"I'm glad we agree. Now, come." He leaned down and picked up something from the floor beside the mat. "Your ribbon," he said, and she snatched it from him and tucked it in her pocket.

Halfhearted pounding barely shook the door now, and William said, " 'Tis time to leave this accursed place." He pulled the door open and waved the three young men inside.

"He's there," he said, pointing. Tucking Saura's hand in his arm, he waited as they rushed through the door. Then the prisoners strolled out, and William slammed the door behind them.

seven

A twist of the key in the lock, and a quick toss out the arrow loop, and William dusted his fingers with satisfaction. "They're safely confined."

He pulled Saura along the short corridor until they reached the stair winding down the tower. Tucking her hand into his elbow and placing her hand on the wall, he added, "At least until they use that candle stand to break the door. The steps are uneven." He paused while she found her footing and then hurried her down, keeping up a steady pace, easy for her to follow. They neared the level of the great hall, and he slowed. "I'm going in to scavenge some bread."

"William!"

"And I want you to stay on the stair. Stand here on the landing." He placed her firmly against the wall and handed her the blankets. "Wait. I'll be right back."

"You fool," she called. "Let's leave now."

He ignored her, trusting his instincts. The danger didn't

exist in the keep, and a moment's worth of preparation would arm them later.

"Halt! Who—what are ye doin'?"

William gawked. The quavering challenge issued from the only servant in the great hall. Tattered clothes and dirty face couldn't disguise the fair young man. Tall and muscular, he displayed the kind of healthy glow that makes women stare and men snort in jealous disgust. His long brown hair shone with auburn highlights, encasing a face angular in its beauty. His beardless jaw jutted out with authority, his skin displayed the kind of texture that made a woman itch to touch it. He held in his hand a carving knife, and it trembled and tilted as he called again, "How did ye get out?"

William growled in response, but Saura glided out of her hiding place. "Bronnie!"

The rest of what she said was lost in the buzzing of William's ears. *This* was Bronnie? The sniveling coward at the riverbank, Saura's caretaker, was this comely youth?

He turned to look at Saura, and a gracious smile lit her face as she spoke to Bronnie. She liked the idiot! Fondness etched her face in lines of indulgence. He looked down at himself, at his rough warrior hands and his tough warrior body, and realized blindness could indeed be a blessing. He trusted Saura, but good God! This boy could tempt a saint!

"See, m'lady?" Bronnie was saying. "All your worryin' last night was for naught. The lord is fine, just fine."

"And he can see," William warned and watched with disbelief as the youth hopped behind the table.

"Not true!" he protested.

" 'Tis true," Saura affirmed. "A miracle."

"Oh, aye, m'lady." His head bobbed madly. "But what of—" He jerked his head upward.

"Lord Arthur decided to let me go." A pounding echoed

down the stairway, belying his story. "And he suggested I take a horse from the stables."

"And bread and wine, Bronnie," Saura added.

"Oh, aye." Bronnie's eyes had widened so his silky lashes swept his upper lids.

"And a sword, Bronnie," William mocked.

Cowed by William's towering animosity and the outbreak of yelling from above, the boy backed even further around the table. "Lord Arthur would cut off my hands. I dunno aught about swords an' such."

Brushing her sweeping hair back over her shoulders, Saura soothed, "We know you don't. The weapons room is undoubtedly in the undercroft—"

"And we can break down the door," William interrupted.

"There's . . . there's this sword right here on the bench. Lord Arthur dropped it off on his way upstairs, but he should—"

"Thank you." William vaulted across the table and seized the sword in its scabbard. "Very nice," he said.

"But Lord Arthur—"

"Will be glad to loan it to his old friend." William pulled the sword and pointed it with meaning at the trembling servant.

"Put that sword away and stop intimidating him, William," Saura scolded, and he jumped guiltily and sheathed it. "Bread, Bronnie? And wine?"

When at last Saura waved good-bye to the palsied boy, they rode the two finest horses in Arthur's stables and carried their goods in a leather saddle bag. "That's exactly the kind of watchdog I'd expect Arthur to have. Anxious to unload everything to save his neck," William confided as he hurried them across the drawbridge, Saura's leading rein in hand. Pushing their mounts into a gallop, he muttered, "The sooner we're away, the happier I'll be."

Hidden in the trees, the silent watcher observed as they fled. The morning sun illuminated William, his giant body filled with vigor, his hair and beard golden as they flailed in the wind. The joy of sight lit his face, and no one, certainly not the silent watcher, could mistake it for anything else. He observed William and Saura, and cursed them with the most fluid and virulent curses he could bring up from hell. And cursed Arthur, too, for his intervention, and wondered if the stupid fool had spoken his name to William, his dear friend, his deepest enemy.

"We'll stop here," William decided, looking around the tiny copse. A shelf of rock broke the wind and created a fall for the tiny stream where he would water the horses. The mixture of oaks and rangy poplar provided a sort of shelter, giving a protected feel to the hollow.

"But why?" Saura asked in bewilderment. "I thought you wanted to ride to Burke tonight."

He raised his head and sniffed the air. "We're safe enough now, I can feel it. And you're tired." She was more than tired, he knew. He'd watched her squirm on the saddle for the past hour, trying to find a comfortable position. She hadn't complained, but he suspected the riding he'd done the night before had stretched her tender muscles long past the point of comfort. And they *were* safe. That prickling of caution had left him as they rode away from Arthur's castle. He'd keep his trained senses alert and make her rest all the night. Rest and heal, for tomorrow at Burke Castle would be difficult for her.

"Where are we?" she questioned.

"Nowhere," he replied with satisfaction. "I dare not stop at a castle. The explanations would be too tedious, and this episode has taught me a caution I never possessed previously. Now come," he ordered, going to her horse and touching her ankle. She slung her leg over without complaint and slid down into his arms. He held her for a moment, her body no bigger than a will-o'-the-wisp against his muscular chest.

"William?" she said. "My feet are dangling."

"Aye," he breathed. "And you're a bonny woman." He held her one more moment, and then he placed her on the ground and lightly slapped her bottom. "Stop tempting me."

Surprised by his abrupt change of mood, she stepped away, rubbing herself. "I'm not tempting you! How am I tempting you?" she asked indignantly.

"You sit on the horse, riding with such grace and dignity, and all the time I know underneath that lady's camouflage, you're a wanton. Not just any wanton, either. You're mine, gracious to everyone else and waiting for my touch to ignite."

She pulled a face of disbelief. "Can I safely walk to the water?"

"Aye, the ground is smooth, and the pool is that way." He gave her a little push in the right direction and watched her limp toward the water that gathered beneath the tiny waterfall. "And you deny you're tempting me!"

"Not at all," she said. Gathering her skirt high, she tied it with the rope around her waist. As William gaped at the shapely display, she waded into the ankle-high water and sank down with a sigh of delight. "Tempting you is my primary ambition."

Turning to the horses, he muttered, "You've succeeded." He groomed the horses, watered them, pegged them to graze.

He rummaged through the saddlebags and spread the blanket across the soft grass. Then he lay back and watched the clouds form themselves into fluffy representations of feminine calves and thighs and buttocks. When Saura called him at last, he wished he were not a conscientious man. An *âme damnée*, like Arthur, would have eased himself with her with no thought to her misery.

He could not. He rose and caught her hand as she waded from the water, ignoring her dripping flesh. He placed her on the blankets, ordered her to stay and walked upstream to fashion a pole and fling it into the water. By the time he returned, freshwater trout strung on a string of vine, Saura napped in the late afternoon sunshine and reason ruled his body once more.

She woke as he kindled the fire, sitting up with no warning to say, "William?"

"Here." He fed twigs to the fire and watched as she relaxed. "Are you hungry?"

"Aye," she said bluntly. "Did you have luck on your hunting trip?"

"Fishing. And aye, we'll eat well tonight. You're an independent woman, aren't you?"

She raised one eyebrow at the question, coming as it did out of the ether. " Aye, I'm independent."

"And you take pride in doing a woman's duty?"

"I doubt this questioning relates to our activities in the night." She chewed her lip. "But aye, I do a woman's duty."

"Good! Then you can clean the fish." He sat back on his haunches and burst into laughter at the look of fastidious disgust on her classical features.

"I'll tell you what I always tell my brothers. You caught them, you clean them," she said promptly.

The sun said good morning to the gliding clouds with intense hues of gold and orange and pink. It lit the treetops and wakened the birds, but William needed no waking. Like a child before Christmas, he woke early, anticipating the return of the sun, the return of his sight. Would he ever stop marveling at the dawn's light? he wondered. He cuddled Saura closer under his chin, tucking the blanket around her shoulders to ward off the chill. The pine boughs covered by one blanket provided a fragrant, springy mattress for them.

He hadn't let her take off her clothes to sleep, hadn't let her touch him in any way, and she'd cried until he'd made it clear his rejection was only temporary. "Saura," he'd said, "we'll have many days ahead of us."

But she'd only cried harder, shaking her head and clutching at him. He'd rubbed her back, soothing her until she slipped off and then he'd drifted into the light sleep of a warrior. He'd kept one ear tuned to pursuit, but as he expected, none had disturbed them.

Now he quivered with the expectations of a child on Twelfth Night. By the glove of God, today he would feast his eyes on the world, on *his* world. He would view Burke clad all in the glory of summer, see the face of his son, puzzled at first and then overjoyed, see his father break into the manly tears that characterized his deepest emotions. He'd show them Saura, tell them about his plans to marry. He snagged her caressing hand.

"Awake, little girl?"

"Um." She rubbed her head on his chest and strands of her loose hair caught in his beard. As he disentangled it, her other hand crept across his thigh.

Scooping her wandering fingers up and out of the blanket,

he kissed her palm. "You are, indeed, the sort of woman Bronnie worried about."

She laughed, a musical sound that blended with the rustle of the leaves and the ripple of the stream. "And you're too determined."

"Determined to ride home today." Sweeping the cover away, he stood and urged, "Rise." His grip on her wrists tugged her erect on the grass beside the blanket.

She stumbled and swayed, and he supported her until she steadied.

"Wash and prepare yourself," he commanded. "We ride to Burke at once."

Some of the cheer faded from her face. "Of course, William," she said and went to do his bidding.

She performed her ablutions, combed her hair with her fingers and braided it. He glanced at her as he folded the first blanket. Wondering at her sober mien, he kicked the boughs aside, lifted the two corners of the other blanket and said, "Help me fold this." As she found the other corners and placed them together, he studied her. "Saura, what's wrong?"

" 'Tis nothing," she assured him, a weak smile curving her lips.

Folding once more and then flipping the cover to straighten the wrinkles, he grunted disbelievingly.

"Truly, my lord," she assured him as they walked together and she handed him her half of the blanket.

"You're an abominable liar, dearling." Hugging her, he trapped the cover between them. "You don't know how to arrange your features correctly."

She hesitated, fighting it, but at last she burst out, "Oh, couldn't we stay here another hour? One more hour before we go back to reality?"

He searched her upturned face, dewy with unshed tears, and without a word shook out the freshly folded blanket and spread it on the grass. He placed the other blanket, folded, on one edge as a pillow. Sweeping her into his arms, he knelt and laid her in the middle. He tumbled with loose grace at her side, fit his shoulder against hers, and a silence fell between them.

"I should not have asked," she whispered. "But this time with you has been," she didn't know how else to describe it, "golden."

Too few golden times had graced her life, William realized, and his contentment deepened. It was his company, his love that made her happy. Watching the leaves quiver in the light wind, curiosity stirred within him. "If you could change aught about your life, what would it be?"

"My height," Saura answered promptly.

"Your height?" Startled, he turned his head and studied the woman lying beside him. She stared up at the leaves, too. He would have sworn she saw them. "Why your height?"

"I always wanted to be tall and willowy, instead of short and lumpy."

He swept his eyes across her tiny, elegant figure and whistled with amazement at her own warped imagery. "Your lumps are . . . well arranged."

She ignored him. "Tall people have a presence short people don't have. You know that. You get respect for having a greater length between your toes and your nose. 'Tis easier to reach upper shelves, 'tis easier for small children to find you in a crowd." She laughed. "What do you want to change about yourself?"

"It has been changed."

"What?" she asked, puzzled for a moment. "Oh, you mean

your sight. Happy is the man who's totally pleased with himself."

"Isn't *that* something you'd like to change about yourself?"

Saura thought about it. "Nay," she drawled. "Nay, I don't think about it. My lack of sight is simply a part of myself. I've never seen the world, and I don't miss it."

"I had seen the world, and I hungered to see it again," he murmured.

"Aye, I can understand that. You couldn't function as a knight, do your duty, unless you had your sight. I do almost everything a woman of my status is required to do: order the meals, care for my serfs, direct the sewing. I've cared for my younger brothers, raised them to manhood until they were ready to be fostered in another knight's household."

"You just deal with your handicap without thought, neither seeking pity nor expecting it."

"Pity makes me want to spit," she retorted fiercely. "And there are blessings to being blind."

William started, for that was his exact thought of the previous morning. "What blessings?"

"I don't have to feed my eyes on ugliness, and I'm not easily fooled by what people say. I believe people have a great capacity to lie with their faces and hands, but not with their voices. When my mother wanted to know another's thoughts, she'd have me listen to them. I could always gauge their sincerity."

"A useful skill."

"Aye." Sniffing, she rolled her head back and forth and she said, "Mint! Can you smell it?" Eagerly she lifted the blanket, and pawed the grass bent with her hand. "Here!"

Breaking the sprigs, she carried them to his face, and he caught her wrist. Bringing her hand closer to his nose, he breathed the zesty aroma. He looked at the dark green leaves clasped in her delicate fingers, at her short nails with the gloss of shell. He looked beyond that, at her face lit by dappled sunlight and by simple pleasure, and a tenderness welled up in him that quelled his pity. Whatever Saura deserved, it wasn't pity. He transferred her hand to his mouth and carefully bit one of the leaves. As he chewed, the minty flavor refreshed his mouth, and he led her hand back to her own mouth, urging her to sample the herb. The dainty snap of her white teeth, her smile as she chewed and the tang of spring developed on her tongue; they all enchanted him.

Propped on her elbow, her black hair tangled and the cotte slipping off her shoulder, she was an unconscious seductress. What could he do? What he had avoided the night before became, in the light and the fresh air of outdoors, a necessity.

He kissed her fingers, one by one; he kissed the palm of her hand. Placing her hand on his shoulder, he leaned into her, moving with the slow precision of a gem cutter. Slanting his mouth across hers, he lined up their lips, avoided their noses, and pressed with light repetition until his respiration became hers.

The wind dallied with the tendrils of her hair, and could he do less?

He tugged her braid over her shoulder and untied the bit of ribbon that held it.

"My hair's a constant tangle with you around." She chuckled, a little catch in her laugh.

" 'Tis beautiful." He carried a handful to his face and rubbed it across his skin. He wanted to take his time, take her in this natural setting, and so he cupped her face and absorbed her expression of slightly amazed desire.

His hesitation earned him a surprise. Her hand on his shoulder pushed and he tumbled, off balance, onto his back.

"What . . . ?" he sputtered, but she leaned over him and held his face. She found his mouth with an unalterable instinct and his breath caught on an inhale.

She had, he realized, no idea of a woman's proper place. What he had put down as a natural curiosity the night before was, perhaps, more aptly described as feminine aggression.

He didn't know how to deal with it. He'd heard of women who commanded the loving, but he'd dismissed it as the result of inadequate virility on behalf of the man. Without conceit, he respected his own masculinity, and he thought she should, too. He needed to teach her about submission, about how a man appreciates a woman who lies and waits for attention, who's properly grateful.

As her lips caressed his in the exact imitation of his earlier attentions, and mint flavored their kiss, he decided he could teach Saura her proper place later. Later, when she was done teaching him with her eager hands and her subtle mouth.

"Are you comfortable?" She raised her head to ask, and without pausing for an answer, she tucked the blanket tighter. "Let me make you comfortable."

Dragging at his shirt, she raised it to let the sun shine on him. With her nimble fingers, she patted just the tips of the blonde hair on his chest. The contrast between the warmth of the sun and the chill caused by her titillation brought his hips up against hers.

Leg draped over him, stomach to stomach, she slithered down his body.

His hands sprang out to catch her before he thought, but she pushed them away. "Let me serve you. You're my master. Let me make you comfortable." The words were humble, her tone was not.

Untying his hose, she tugged them down. "I never did explore your legs," she laughed throatily. "So many muscles!

I can feel each one." She traced the length of one muscle and then massaged it with a firm touch. "You're so tense."

He grunted, knowing his tension would dissipate under one of her treatments.

She untied the rope at his waist and urged his hips up so she could lower his drawers. The morning glittered like a new coin; embarrassment struck him.

Exposed in the outdoors?

Never. William was reaching for his drawers to pull them up when her hand brushed across him. Creeping up the sensitive skin of his inner leg, she caressed his hips, found the evidence of his arousal.

Light, gentle touches raised his fever and destroyed his perplexity.

Exposed in the outdoors?

God's teeth, he'd assist Saura in every way possible. He flipped his shoes off to expedite her operations and marveled at his own fond illusion of control.

The midnight of her hair caught in the golden curls at his groin, and he admired the erotic effect with pained suspense. How much longer could he hold out, he wondered. How much more of this torture could he withstand? He grasped her under her arms and pulled her up to his face. "Undress," he ordered. "Quickly."

She stood up, her hands reaching for her ties, and as he watched her body emerged from the cotte, gleaming like sweet cream. "Quickly," he urged again. "Quickly."

Still she stood above him, her brow wrinkled in solemn consideration. Then she put one foot over him and stood straddling him. Her face tilted to the sun; her chin jutted out, casting shadows on her chest. Her breasts sat high, casting shadows down her flat stomach. Her long legs glowed in the light.

He braced himself for her descent, prepared to roll onto her, but she surprised him again. Why, he didn't know. Saura of Roget had done nothing that didn't surprise him, but this assumption of hers that she could sit on top of him. Surely she didn't expect to. . . .

She did.

"How did you learn so much?" he asked.

It took her a moment to comprehend the question. "About what?"

"About pleasuring a man." His finger snuck out and tickled her, and she held herself rigid until he paused. "Tell me, Saura," he coaxed.

"What? Oh, do I give you pleasure?" Her teeth gleamed in a brief smile that faded when he touched her again. "I just think what would give me pleasure, and I do it to you."

He returned to his slow glide, back and forth in hedonistic reciprocity.

Tossing her head, she murmured, "Nay. William, nay." Her lids drooped, veiling those violet eyes and lending her an expression of sensuous enjoyment. Her lips opened and glints of her teeth enticed him, enhanced by the tip of her tongue held firmly at the side in intense concentration. Her nipples puckered as a sudden shiver raced from the heart of her gratification up her spine, and those eyes jolted open. In all seriousness now, she said, "Nay!" and stopped him with her hand on his, pushing away his fingers and guiding his erection.

Slowly imprisoned by her body, he stared, fascinated, as her savor of the moment gave way to a new urgency. Her first upward surge caught him by surprise, and unschooled as she was, she almost rose too far. He caught her hips and held her as she readjusted. Then he helped her set a leisurely rhythm, in tune with the morning peace.

He watched the clouds float overhead, looking so close they could catch in the trees and yet so far up they piled in towers above. Spring-green leaves swayed in the light breeze, and one robin hopped from branch to branch, seeking just the right twig. Saura's face, set against that blue sky, was the loveliest thing he'd ever seen: delicate and arousing, sensitive and carnal. Beneath his hands, her thigh muscles bunched and relaxed, riding passion from its careful beginning to the ending of his choice.

Lifting his fingers to her breasts, he brushed the tips with exquisite intent and was rewarded by a sudden agitation inside her body. He smiled, prepared to provide for her satisfaction, when she leaned over him, searching with her mouth. Her teeth bit his nipples gently; she suckled with greedy pleasure.

Shock, like a frenzied aphrodisiac, scrambled his brain. He bucked beneath her, startling her with his new insistence, and she responded with a sharp bounce. Suddenly, what was a leisurely pleasure transformed itself into a race for completion. They grappled for dominance; they struggled for fulfillment, twisting and moving in a primeval beat.

Fighting as one, they strained in agonizing pleasure and she reached her peak first. Her exulting scream rent the air, startling the robin above them. In a flutter of feathers, it sprang into the clouds, and William felt his body go with it. Everything he was, he put into Saura, entrusting her with his seed and receiving her euphoria in return.

Then she collapsed on his chest, moaning, "No more," but still shuddering when he curled into her.

He didn't think he could move, but when she quivered in the aftershocks, he found the strength to pet her head, to rub her back, to press up against her pelvis and agitate her once more. When he could find his voice, he murmured,

"Women are marvelous creatures. What I can do once, they can do many times. Of course," he laughed close to her ear, "I can crawl away afterwards."

"Base, proud tottyhead," she said in a voice tinted with scorn and laden with exhaustion.

"Has no one ever told you what a glorious woman you are?"

"Nay."

"Of course not. No man has discovered it, nor will he. You're mine."

A pause. "Aye."

Picking his words with care, he said, "I've been lonely, looking for a woman with whom I share common interests. I'm not a stupid boy, seeing only the outer shell. I want to laugh, eat, sleep, talk with my woman. I want a woman I like." The lax body draped on his stiffened as he spoke, and he wondered. "I like you. I like to laugh, eat, sleep and talk with you. Your beauty and grace add decoration to our meal, but it affects not the substance or flavor. As you said earlier," humor lit his voice, "you don't have to feed your eyes on ugliness, and my face is of no interest to you."

That stirred her to motion. "You're not ugly. Maud told me so."

"Well, if Maud said so," he/chuckled at her vehemence, then returned to rational discussion. "As for the advantages to you, Lady Saura, I'd like to recommend myself as a knight. If we were doing this correctly, my father would be saying this to your guardian, but we've anticipated the proprieties and I feel the need to point out my usefulness. With all due modesty, of course."

She wasn't responding with the animation he expected; indeed, she seemed to shrink into herself. "I'm a great warrior, competent to command your men and protect your lands." Her lack of reaction, her deadly calm cut his words; he wanted to offer for her in a way she would remember with honor all the days of their lives. But this made her unhappy, he could feel it in the clutch of her hands on his arms. "Therefore, Lady Saura of Roget, we will live together and unite our souls as we've united our bodies."

"Nay!" She struggled up and off him. "I cannot."

She swept her hair back over her shoulders, her hands trembling with a great agitation, and he observed her closely. "Why?" he asked simply.

Groping for her cotte, she pulled it on with haste, hiding her body from his gaze as if the fragile cloth were some armor that would protect her from pain. "You're not thinking, my lord." Tugging the laces, she seized on the least of his concerns. "You've no need to marry me because you deflowered me. 'Tis not necessary, not necessary."

Sitting up, he wrapped his arms around one knee. "Did you not listen to all I've said? What happens to us when our bodies meet is unique, a melding of two souls. Your virginity, or your lack of it, influences me not at all."

"Guilt, your guilt when you woke with your eyes that functioned and saw me."

He made an intensely negative gesture, but she could never see it.

Rubbing the crease between her brows with her knuckles, she continued, "You're euphoric about your sight, you're pleased about our escape, but if you think, you'll realize you don't want an imperfect woman in your bed."

"Imperfect!" He drew breath to shout at her, but the view of one rosy-pink nipple peeking through a rent in her cotte disarmed him. With a gulp, he achieved a moderate tone and asked, "What the hell was I when I struggled in the grey mist? I don't feel any more perfect now than I did a fortnight ago."

"You pity me, and I've already told you what I think of pity." Her lips lifted in a pathetic attempt at a smile.

"Is that what you felt for me two nights ago? Pity? Is that why you gave me your body?"

"Oh, nay. Nay. Two nights ago, I harbored thoughts of . . . well, but that was before you regained your sight. Think, William. What if . . . what if we had children?"

"I could almost assure you we'll have children. Within the year. Do you not like children?"

"What if they were blind?"

The nipple winked at him, sliding behind the veil of cloth. Its shy allure encouraged him to try logic, a unique method to deal with women, but Saura was a unique woman. "As God wills. But what of the other children born of your mother? Is there another child in your family without sight?"

"Nay, but—"

"We'll be the best parents any child every had."

"But I can't marry you," she said wretchedly.

The delicacy of this situation required more strategy than he'd realized. He'd never seen such insecurities, hidden as they were in the confident persona of Lady Saura. But there was more than one way to scrape the chestnuts from the fire. With conscious cruelty, he said, "You should mind your needle and leave such matters of business to the men who are your betters," he snapped.

Immediately, a fiery blush ignited her face. "I thought you meant . . . I thought you were asking me if I desired such a union."

"Whether I marry you or not is none of your concern. A woman goes where she is placed by her guardian. Most ladies of your station are married at thirteen, and perhaps your greater age has made you insensible to a woman's true nature."

Her mouth opened, but nothing came out. She seemed to be grasping for words, unable to decide what to say or how to say it. "My greater age? Is that an impediment to marriage?"

"It could be, for a younger woman is easily taught the ways of her lord and molded to his desires. A younger woman sits at her lord's feet in the evening and forgives him his indiscretions even as he commits them."

"You don't need a wife," she said with exasperation. "You need a puppy."

"A younger woman," he said severely, "hasn't yet developed a saucy tongue."

She didn't quite believe this orthodoxy of him, he could see, and her question rang with a hint of skepticism. "Perhaps you could explain a woman's true nature, my lord?"

Step softly, he cautioned himself. No one believed everything the priests told them about the wicked ways of females and how they should be subservient to their male masters. The reality was too different, and this woman was too intelligent to believe him if he pretended to subscribe to the hard line of the Church. Yet he could soften the traditional stance and say, "Women are incapable of deciding what's best for them. They should pass from the firm hand of their father to the firm hand of their husband with their head bowed in obedience and their minds on only how to create a pleasant home. If I should decide to wed you, Lady Saura, remember, your only part in the proceedings is to assent in the ceremony before the witnesses."

Her face displayed a mixture of frustration and amazement. "That is the usual view of marriage."

"Never forget it," he ordered, and he saw her dreams falling in crushing chunks around her shoulders. The misery on her face wrung his heart, yet to release her would destroy his strategy. Hardening his heart, he asked with assumed casualness, "What would you do if you couldn't stay at Burke?"

"I suppose I would have to return to my stepfather's house."

His restraint ended with an abrupt roar. Her breath caught in her throat as he snagged her wrist in a furious grip.

"My Lady Saura, you'd better search that ridiculous mind of yours for another answer, for I'll never allow you to do such a thing." He flung her hand away from him, and she heard a distant barking. "Never. Now conceal yourself. Someone approaches."

eight

The sepulchral barking grew closer, more menacing, and Saura crouched on her heels behind the rocks where William put her. The dampness of the soil cooled her feet, the feet that wanted to fly away from this place of entrapment. Her heart pounded from fear and residual tension. William's vehemence, her fear of recapture, they were nothing compared to the fears she harbored in her soul.

Now she could hear a man's shouting, mixing with the muffled bark of a large dog. She put her hand to her throat. Perhaps the unknown mastermind of William's murder had no plans for recapture, perhaps death would visit their bit of paradise.

William would never let that happen. The thought popped unbidden into her mind. Without being told, she knew William stood alone, the sword glittering in the sun. Whoever or whatever entered into the clearing had better be primed for a fight.

She heard the barking animal spring clear of the surrounding wood and enter the copse, heard William exclaim, "Ye gads," in disgusted tones.

With a jolt of recognition, she called, "William, it's—" Great paws embraced her shoulders and a worshiping tongue slurped her face. Her heels flew out from under her, her bottom hit the ground with a jolt. "Bula." She pushed at the great dog. "Bula! Down! Bula, stop it!"

The beast lay down immediately and rolled its head in her lap, whimpering and yipping. Her hands were full, trying to deal with his ecstasy, and she only vaguely heard the man's voice as he broke into the hollow.

"Saura, come out," William called. " 'Tis the hunter from Burke."

"I know," she said with irritation. "I could guess."

"M'lady!" Her hand was snatched by Alden, on his knees before her and fighting the dog for her attention. "Praise the good St. Wilfred ye're well."

"I'm well," said Saura in irritation, running her hands along Bula's sides. "But who's been starving this dog? He's nothing but ribs and skin."

"He wouldn't eat, m'lady. Moped around whinin' for ye."

"We've only been gone two days!"

"Aye, an' the castle in turmoil an' no un payin' a bit of attention t' an old soldier an' a besotted dog. So after this old soldier returned from his scoutin'—"

"Scouting?" Saura asked.

"It was the afternoon ye were taken, an' Master Kimball an' Master Clare arrived at the castle, acryin' an' ablamin' themselves."

"They raced to the keep to warn Lord Peter?"

"Aye, but Lord Peter wasn't there an' all was in a flurry wi' the men-at-arms tryin' t' prepare for some attack an' no un followin' ye as they should ha' been. So I went out an' looked for the trail till I stumbled on the mercenaries what took ye off."

"Nay!" Saura cried, reaching out her hands to Alden. She found his head, swaddled in bandages and asked, "Are you seriously hurt?"

"I'm all right, they just knocked me down for sport. They didn't recognize me as bein' from Burke."

Saura massaged Alden's neck and Bula's ears with the same compassion, and they both relaxed under ministrations, at rest for the first time in two days. "William?" she called. "We must—"

"He's over wi' th' horses, m'lady, preparin' them t' go."

"Hm."

She thought about that, and Alden lowered his voice. "Did ye an' th' lord quarrel? He seems kinda stiff, if ye know what I mean."

"It matters not," she said. "I'll care for William, but first I must hear your story."

"Oh." Alden was unconvinced, but obedient. " 'Twas night before I got back t' Burke, an' I tol' 'em what I saw. Lord Peter, he listened close, an' then went flyin' off an' thar' was the dog, pacin' an' whimperin', an' all the garrison organized an' in place, an' I thought, why not let the dog out? He's got more sense than ten of these knights put together. So he an' I went out yestermorn an' we've been dodgin' through the brush an' down t' un castle an' then back t' this place."

"Alden," she said with infinite patience in her voice. "Where is your horse?"

"Horse? Ye never thought I could follow that beast through the green wood on a horse?" Alden chuckled with the patronizing amusement of even the lowest man for a woman's mind.

"You've run all the way to Arthur's castle and back?"

"That's why the dog's so skinny, see?"

"Devil take the stupid dog!" she erupted. "My dear fellow, you've done too much!"

His voice trembled, and he rebuked, "I'm your man, an' your lady mother's before that. I couldn't sit by an' do nothin' t' save ye."

His sensitivity abruptly reminded her Alden no longer sat in the first blush of youth. "No other man could have done more," she soothed. "Have you had any rest?"

"Aye. Even the dog had t' collapse last night, an' he'd run ahead of me an' then sit an' wait an' then take off again. If I was too tired he'd lay beside me an' thump his tail an' whine till I stood again."

"Oh, Alden. You're too good, too good."

Alden shifted on his knees, embarrassed by his lady's concern, and Saura tugged at his shoulders. "Up, you faithful fool, and give me a hand."

William spoke from behind Alden. "Aye. Lady Saura, if you can tear yourself away from your fawning slaves, we should move on to escape any pursuing force. I've readied the horses."

His blatant irritation recalled their quarrel, and she grimaced as Alden hauled her to her feet. "Lucky for me it wasn't far to the ground," she grumbled, brushing at her skirt.

Stepping forward, William ordered, "Alden, your cloak," and wrapped Saura in the swinging folds.

" 'Tis hot," she fretted, but he tucked it closer around her.

"You're not decent. You wear no chainse."

"You hadn't complained before."

"What's fit for my eyes—"

"Your eyes!" Alden exploded. "M'lord, ye can see! What miracle is this?"

" 'Tis a greater tale than we have time for now," William replied kindly. "Save your queries. All will be answered at dinner tonight."

"William," she whispered, tugging at his sleeve. "Alden."

"Alden, the Lady Saura is tired and sore, and she will ride with me," William ordered. "You take her horse. Bula will run after." Without waiting for a reply, he boosted her up with a hand supporting her foot. She settled herself, pleased with the proof of William's thoughtfulness. He might be unhappy with her, but he would never take it out on her guard.

He continued, "In that manner, you can watch our backs. I begin to feel an urgency to reach home."

Alden grunted as he eased himself into the saddle. "Thankee, m'lord. I find my weariness catchin' up wi' me now I've found ye. But I think ye'll find Lord Peter put out a net of vigilance o'er the whole o' Burke an' beyond."

"Are we close, then?" Saura asked.

"Ye're at the headwaters of Fyngre Brook."

"Oh, William!" she bounced a little as he leaped into the saddle. "If you'd known where we were last night, we could have woken this morning at Burke."

"Hm."

William ignored her remark, and with a jolt, she wondered if he *had* known where they were all the time. Perhaps he had wanted another night with her. The thought pleased her, and then worried her. Had he wanted to get his fill, or had he wanted to strengthen his claim on her?

She sat back in the circle of his arms as he gathered the reins and spoke to the horse. She had to take herself in hand. She couldn't marry William, he deserved better than that. Yet if she panicked, she'd never maintain the serenity to refuse both the man and her own profound desire. She had to think. She had to reason. It was, after all, one of her traits that most antagonized Theobald.

Perhaps she fretted for naught. Perhaps William believed what he said about marriage. About how it was a business matter and her part included only obedience and good housekeeping. Perhaps he believed she was too old.

She'd learned to curb her imprudence in Theobald's house, his lash had taught her that; but at Burke the hard-earned lessons had fallen away. With Lord Peter and William, she no longer felt her every word should be examined for boldness before she spoke it. These men seemed so secure in their masculinity the false respect of a female seemed almost an insult to them. Now William demanded she return the bridle to her tongue and she didn't remember how. With a blossoming poise, she assured herself his scathing comments were nothing more than the hurt reaction of a man whose suit has been rejected. Nothing more. Nothing more.

William's chest felt carved in stone, and he held himself erect as if his annoyance were a permanent, solid object. Still, she knew how men cherished their anger and responded to feminine blandishments, and so she snuggled close against him and placed her hand on his thigh, a long length of tempered steel it pleased her to touch. The muscle tightened beneath her palm.

Alden rode abreast of them. "I've been out, an' don't know Lord Peter's plans. Do your woodsmen have a signal?"

"They're an independent clan of people, older than the Saxons, and never conquered by anyone. My father leaves them to go their own way, and they serve us well. If they choose to show themselves, then we'll see them. Until then, let's hasten onto Burke land."

Urging their mounts forward, he set a rapid pace through trees and over rocks, protecting Saura from branches as they slapped at their faces. He avoided the roads, keeping to the thinly marked trails, and Bula trotted at their stirrup.

They moved quickly through the sylvan silence, a silence that was too deep. The sound of their movement echoed in the quiet; they jumped as a stick cracked beneath a hoof.

Puzzled, Saura twisted around to face William, and he stared down at her. Her rosy lips parted to reveal her white teeth. Her minty breath reminded him of the morning, of her body rising above his and all the glorious sounds and sights of love. Her face contained trust and a transparent affection he would nurture into love, but first he must return her safely to Burke. The back of his neck itched, the signal that someone observed them from a hidden post.

"Why aren't the birds singing?" Saura asked in a whisper.

"There are men in the wood." William glanced around, his fighting senses heedful. "But are they my father's men, or the enemy's?"

Both William and Alden had the wary eyes of men on the alert, and when Saura warned, "I hear the pounding of hooves," they pulled up in a wide spot in the path and listened to the far distant sound.

Without warning, a short, dirty man clad in green materialized before them. Bula barked once and then sat in obedience to William's signal. The man spoke the uncouth English of the peasants, and William strained to understand.

"Your father's acomin', Lord William." He watched solemnly as the lord's face lit up, and then spoke the graver news. "We watched over ye last night an' no un followed till this mornin'. Twelve fightin' men grouped together at the edge of our wood. A great man directed them an' they followed your trail till they caught un of my men."

"Is your man dead?"

"Aye," the woodsman said bitterly. "Like a worthless dog, they smashed his skull. He told them nothin', but they pulled back."

"What did the cruel lord look like?"

"All Normans look alike, an' his face was concealed by a helmet."

"What did he sound like?"

"He spoke little, an' what he said, he said quietly."

William nodded to the little man. "Thank you, Aschil, for your information and your protection. Come to the castle. I'll pay a death wage for the man you lost."

The little man faded without a word into the forest, leaving no trace of where he stood.

Saura tugged at William's wrist. "Is the strange man gone?"

Remembering how he'd longed to know the subtleties of the scenes played before his face, but with details not obvious to the blind, he described his woodsman with words that built an image for her. "He never stirred a leaf as he left," he concluded.

The galloping horses sounded closer, and Saura asked, "Is it the knights?"

William shook his head and chuckled. "No one else but my father would ride at such a breakneck speed through this rough terrain."

Bursting around the bend, Lord Peter leaned over his horse's neck, and William shouted a warning. Lord Peter pulled up so abruptly his gelding reared and he slid off the back in one easy motion. Plunging toward them, he yelled, "William!" and his son vaulted off to yell, "Father!"

They met with a collision that rocked the forest, embracing and laughing while Bula pranced around them and barked until the leaves shook in the trees.

"We thought we'd lost you this time," Lord Peter roared, pounding William's back. "Who was it? How'd you get away? Did you kill the bastard? But no, how could you, you're. . . ." His loud delight trailed off as he stared at his son. "You're. . . ." He moved his head back and forth, watching William as William watched him. The fire of his joy died completely, replaced by a slow and fearful hope. "William?"

"Aye, Father," William agreed gently. "I can see."

Lord Peter wrapped a hand around each side of William's jaw. "Is it possible?" he whispered. "How could such a miracle happen? Have you been to paradise?"

"And back, Father. And back."

Lord Peter's hug was restrained this time, not jubilant but thankful in the deep and quiet way of a sire whose deepest prayer has been granted. He spoke a vow, all the more powerful for being spoken in God's wood. "I'll go on a pilgrimage to Compostella and thank the Apostle James for his blessing to you." Father and son stared at each other for one strong, emotional moment, and then Lord Peter broke away and strode toward the horse. "Lady Saura! 'Tis glad I am to see you alive and well."

He reached up to help her down, and she smiled at him in open satisfaction. "Aye, my lord. When you came to me at Pertrade Castle and asked me to help your son, we never foresaw such an ending, did we?"

She slid down, her hands on his shoulders, and he examined her face with care. But whatever miracle had visited William hadn't touched her, and he smiled gently into her beautiful violet eyes. "That we didn't. I have stern instructions not to come back without you."

"Maud?" she guessed.

"Maud has been—"

"In a frenzy?"

"In a pitiful state," he confirmed.

"Then let us return." She grinned in the direction of the exhausted knights straggling onto the path. "Before my maidservant loses any more sleep."

Her hand was wet.

William walked through the village clustered beneath the protective walls of Burke. He led their mount, and she sat alone in the saddle, but the crowd around them slowed their progress to a crawl. So many of the loyal folk had kissed her knuckles in their passionate welcome that it warmed her heart. But her hand was still wet and she still very much wanted to get to her chamber and rest. If she just made it across the drawbridge, she promised herself she could collapse.

William responded to his castle, his people, his home with an unfeigned pleasure. He called to the men by name, kissed the old women and hugged the young ones.

She was happy to hear the joy in William's voice, but her head ached from thinking. Hands reached up and snatched at her, wringing her tender fingers until the bones ached. The horses' hooves created a hollow sound as they clopped over the wooden drawbridge. Her feeling of being exposed to the great open spaces gave way to the more protected feeling she experienced when in the bailey. If she just made it to the stairs, she promised herself she could collapse.

The rumors of the miracle that cured William's sight had raced ahead to the castle folk and it added to the babble that assaulted her ears. Questions shouted from every direction confused her, and she wanted to cringe from the rampant curiosity.

"Father!" Kimball's shout echoed up to the battlements.

William uttered, "Kimball," in a choked voice and dropped the reins.

A hush fell over the pressing humanity, and then the whispers floated up to her.

"See how they hug."

"See the boy's tears."

"See Lord William. He can't stop lookin' at Master Kimball."

"Look at them twirl."

The last was said with such affection, tears pricked at Saura's eyes, and the tension that had held her in its coils for the last two days relaxed its hold. She held herself erect with a combination of good manners and stubbornness, and some of her weariness must have shown in her face. A large warm hand wrapped around her thigh, and William called, "Come down, my dearling." Her arms trembled as he lifted her off the saddle and set her on her feet.

"Saura?" Clare said timidly. "Are you angry?"

Her brother stood next to her, stroking her hand and worrying, just as he used to at Pertrade Castle when Theobald rampaged about in one of his drunken rages.

"Why should I be angry?" With less than her usual grace, she reached out and stroked his cheek.

"Because I didn't save you from those men!"

It was a cry from his sore heart, and for the valiant little boy she could pull herself together for a few more moments. "Didn't you run to Lord Peter at once and tell him we were captured?"

"Aye."

She smiled at him. "Just as you should."

Two skinny arms wrapped tight around her hips and his grubby head dug into her ribs. She hugged his neck and then as his embrace loosened, she rumpled his hair. "My own knight-errant." She chuckled. "Will you wear my token into battle?"

A sunny laugh answered her, and he stepped away as if he were embarrassed to be caught cuddling with a woman.

Her knees wobbled, deprived of his support, and she wondered if this unstructured ceremony would ever cease. If she could just make it up to her room.

"Saura!" Maud's cry cut through the babble. "M'lady!"

Saura plunged toward that beloved voice, and it seemed a path opened for her. Those motherly arms enfolded her, that motherly voice scolded, "What have ye been doing? Ye're white as a ghost, your eyes as big as a full moon."

"She's tired," William said from behind her. "She's not used to such adventure, to playing the part of warrior queen. Take her to her room and put your little lambkin to bed so she'll be fresh for the celebration tonight."

Maud watched him, watched his eyes that crinkled at the edges. He looked at her and nodded, and she backed away from him as if she'd gone mad. Bumping into Saura, she wrapped her sturdy arm around her and led her to the stairway.

William stood staring after them. With a fierce scowl wrinkling his brow, he vowed to Lord Peter, "That is the woman I'm going to marry."

Kimball said, "Oh, good," and Clare crowed like a rooster.

Glancing down at the boys with their identical grins plastered on their dirty faces, William's intense determination broke down into relief. "So you like that, do you?"

They nodded with huge up-and-down motions, their enthusiasm bolstered by the optimism of youth.

"Then make sure you wash before dinner, or Lady Saura will find out water hasn't touched you since we left, and you know what will happen then."

The nods this time were subdued, and Clare groaned, "Horse trough."

"Exactly." Catching Lord Peter's eye on him, William asked, "And what do you think of my mate?"

Lord Peter shrugged and queried with a straight face, "Are you sure she's not too strong for you? She's ordered this household like the Queen of Heaven these last few months, and she'll order you, too."

"Well, she'll think she does, anyway." William guffawed in a superior, masculine way, and Lord Peter slapped his shoulder and joined him.

Climbing the stair, Saura heard them and stiffened.

The dinner that night was splendid. The great hall of Burke shone with the light of torches, and the open fire at the center leaped toward the ceiling. Every trestle table had been pressed into use. The benches were so closely packed with men and women the serving folk had difficulty reaching between them. All the knights sworn to Lord Peter and William attended, worn out with hurried preparation for war or siege. The men-at-arms and villeins who had searched for their lord crowded the benches, their voices loud with relief and speculation. Among them sat Alden, a simple man whose loyalty to Saura had earned him the place of honor. William sat at Lord Peter's right hand, Saura at Lord Peter's left, and beside Saura lay the supine form of Bula, sleeping the slumber of the just. Grinning in mindless jubilation, Clare and Kimball performed their duties as pages, serving the high table with an alacrity seldom seen in such young men.

Mead and ale were served to those below the salt and a cask of red wine tapped for the noble folk. Beneath the harrying rod of Maud, the cook had outdone himself. The breads had been formed into special shapes and made fragrant with herbs. The earliest greens growing around the streams had been plucked and minced and added to the thick *Charlette*, adding the longed-for taste of vegetable to the curded beef soup. Maud's recipe for *farced fesaunt* brought sighs of satisfaction as the birds, stuffed with oats and dried apples, disappeared from the chargers, and *luce* wafers added the dainty flavor of fish to the meal. A sweet pudding sprinkled with gilly flowers completed their repast.

When they had finished, Kimball poured water first over Lord Peter's hands and then over William's and Saura's, and Clare followed after, offering a towel. Glancing at William, Lord Peter received a nod and stood as if this were a prearranged signal. Pounding his fists on the table, he shouted, "Silence!" The song of replete voices calmed as neighbor shushed neighbor and the loudly drunk were quieted with a simple knock against the chin. A hundred curious pairs of eyes strained to see through the smoke, a hundred curious pairs of ears strained to hear the story that promised to be the stuff of legends.

When everyone's attention was focused on him, Lord Peter proclaimed in a booming voice, "My son William, Lord of Miraval and Brunbrook, heir to Burke and Stenton, the greatest knight on the isle of England and the duchy of Normandy, has returned to us unharmed, thanks to the intervention of the saints and the Blessed Virgin on the side of right and honor."

He paused for the cheer that boomed from every throat.

"The tale of his going and his return is one fraught with treachery and warmed with a sign of God's grace. He comes before us tonight to tell us the tale."

Beside him, William rose to his full height, a height emphasized by the dais on which he stood. Lord Peter moved to the other side of Saura, and William stepped to the place before the salt. As the eager crowd transferred their attention, his father sank down and smiled at Saura, an amused, impudent smile that would have disturbed her had she seen it.

"My friends," William began. He pitched his great voice lower than Saura expected; loud enough everyone could hear and low enough they had to strain to capture every syllable. "The tale I will tell you is not so much the story of myself, as the story of my Lady Saura and the miracle worked through her."

Saura's spine sprang straight up, like an arrow shot to the skies. What was William saying?

"An evildoer captured us both, submitting us to the greatest indignities and cruelties, and I found myself stimulated to a fury. In my blinded state, I fought the army of the malefactor, and lost." He sighed in a mighty gust, and all the hall sighed with him. "A giant warrior beat me until I no longer knew my surroundings, and then took us and threw us into a dungeon."

Saura's lips twitched to hear Bronnie characterized as a "giant warrior." But what was William saying?

"If not for my Lady Saura, I would have died. She shamed them with her kindness and amazed them with her beauty, and these outlaws brought her food and drink and blankets. She bandaged my wounds, mending them with her touch. She protected me from the demons of death with the flaming sword of her righteousness. And as she lay in my bed, she healed my eyes with her virtuous kiss."

Like a great weight, Saura felt the attention of the entire room shift from William. Every eye bore into her as she sat with her mouth slightly open and a dazed amazement on her features. What was William saying? What was he insinuating? How were the folk in the great hall understanding his story?

"The night of our captivity, Lady Saura folded me in her arms and roused my passions and became my bride. Although the Church has not yet blessed our union, although I have no bloodied sheets to display as proof, I bear witness now that she was a virgin. My eyes bear witness, for all know of the curative power of a virgin bride."

Well! That spelled it out!

"And I declare now, in front of all witnesses, I will take Lady Saura of Roget as my wife in the eyes of the Church and honor her for the rest of our days together."

A large, firm hand gripped Saura's as she was pulled to her feet, and the mightiest hurrah of all shook the rafters. As the sound ebbed around them, and he held her hand aloft, fingers entwined, William said in her ear, "You'll not escape me easily, dearling."

níne

Lord Peter stood up beside them and shouted, "A toast! A toast to Lady Saura, the wife of my son, Lord William!"

Eager hands grasped the goblets, raised them high, and drank.

"A toast!" Alden shouted. "A toast to Lord William, the greatest warrior in all England!"

Eager hands grasped the goblets, raised them high, and drank.

"A toast!" Maud shouted, and the hall quieted, for women didn't usually propose a toast. "A toast to their churching!"

A roar of laughter greeted her toast, but eager hands grasped the goblets, raised them high, and drank.

Ale and mead sloshed freely from the pitchers to the cups, and satisfied with his ruse, William sat down. The folk of the castle and the tenants from beyond erupted in a spontaneous babble, convinced by his logic, entertained by his wit, overjoyed by the telling of such a love story and its pretty ending. If they had any doubts, they had been firmly squashed by the message from God, the message that cured their master.

Now they sat back to visit with their friends in a rare evening of leisure, to discuss the exciting events of the past few days and to plan for the eminent wedding. They failed to hear the quiet beginnings of the quarrel at the head table.

Watching Saura gather her weapons to assault his resolve, William noted with pleasure that her pale and forlorn delicacy of the afternoon had fled. Maud's cosseting had restored her self-assurance and her color. And if she were still just a little subdued, well, so much the better. Dealing with a woman of Saura's stamina required all the advantages he could obtain. Now he fortified himself with patience, knowing Saura would never let their tale end so conveniently.

She sipped her wine, and turned to William, sitting close against her thigh. "A pretty bit of fable, my lord. Do you not feel a weight on your soul for telling such lies?"

"Not lies, but as much truth as they wanted, or needed. My father knows the whole truth, as do you, as do I. Who else matters?"

"You must reconsider. 'Twas not my body that brought you sight, but the end of Bronnie's stick."

"I'm not going to marry Bronnie," William replied acerbically. "And I am not so bold as to determine which cure God has granted."

"Perhaps you've never slept with a blind woman before, and I'm just a novelty." Saura chewed over that idea and found it unconvincing, and he destroyed its credibility.

"God's teeth, I've never slept with a man before, but I have no desire to sleep with my *father*."

Lord Peter blew a mouthful of ale across the table in surprise. "Damn, 'tis thankful I am to hear that."

"Aye, but that's incest, too," she couldn't resist pointing out.

William grinned. How easily she was misled.

"You'd grow tired of having to be so gentle with me," she said.

The grin disappeared. How promptly she returned to the argument. "Gentle?"

"Aye. You treat me as if I'm some rare form of glass. You'd come to resent me, feeling obligated to treat me with endless courtesy."

William's annoyance faded and a genuine smile wrapped his face. "I hadn't thought of it that way. In my experience, dearling, the early time of tenderness dissipates under the influence of the day-to-day irritations of marriage. Tenderness is simply one of the early stages of love."

Saura mulled that over. "You mean, as you got used to me you'd grow out of the tenderness?"

"Not completely, we hope."

"I am durable."

"Is that supposed to convince me not to wed you?"

"No. I didn't mean it that way, but. . . ." She hesitated, aware her desire to marry warred with her good sense. "I still say 'tis infatuation."

"So you think I'm not astute enough to know whether or not I wish to marry you?"

His voice sounded light and amused to her, but an undercurrent of something she couldn't define made her uneasy. Not uneasy enough to cure her of wanting to help him overcome his odd obsession, but uneasy. "I think you're sagacious enough to do aught. I also think you're feeling grateful to the wrong person for the return of your sight. You should be lighting candles in the chapel."

"I already have."

"Instead of feeling honor bound to marry me. You're doing everything as an honorable knight should, but I tell you, I release you from your obligation."

"You seem to be more than pleased to release me. As my wife used to say, 'love teaches even asses to dance,' " he said even more pleasantly. "Is that what you mean?"

Her hands trembled for just one moment, and she wished he hadn't mentioned his wife. Her surprise at the stab of emotion made her disregard the extraordinary sweetness in his tone when relating such an insolent statement. "I don't know if I'd put it so rudely. Not that your wife was rude," she corrected herself.

"Anne was unerringly rude," Lord Peter interjected, the fondness in his tone belying the insult. "My daughters-in-law, for all their differences, have one thing in common."

Startled, Saura asked, "How many daughters-in-law have you had?"

"Only two," Lord Peter replied promptly. "Anne and you."

"I'm not—"

Lord Peter swept on, ignoring her objection. "Both of you seem to have an unerring penchant for arguing the wrong points for the most idiotic of reasons. Brimful of intelligence and not a drop of horse sense between either one of you."

"Saura," said William, solemn and projecting his voice for the knights to hear. "I love you."

With a wave of her hand, she discounted his declaration. "I certainly don't think 'tis love, and I'm sure with a little distance between us and a little time, your infatuation will fade."

"Do you advise me what I shall do?"

That thing in his tone strengthened, grown from a wisp of warning to a blatant token from this man who refused to take logical advice. As she had told him earlier in the day, she did everything a woman of her status was required to do, and so she proceeded with the pacification of her man. "I would never be so bold, Lord William. 'Tis simply my lowly belief I should not aspire to be the summit of your household."

"The summit of my—"

"Your wife. Yet, in my own way, I believe I could fill a position here, at least until the time comes for you to marry again."

The noise of chatter was fading, distracted by the scene on the dais.

"What kind of position?"

No doubt about it, irritation vibrated in his voice, but Saura had faith in her ability to soothe her savage lord. "I could tend your household and take care of your son and if the evenings stretched too long, you and I might—"

"You want to be my whore." Saura couldn't see his face, but the others in the great hall could. Benches scraped back, grown men picked up their eating knives and migrated in a slow exodus toward the back of the room.

No one left. No one could resist the drama foretold by William's reddening cheeks and clenched fists, and they observed avidly the struggle between the master they adored and the woman he would wed.

"That's not the word I would use," Saura began, hurt by the word, but still seeking to soothe.

" 'Tis the word everyone else will use," he interrupted brutally.

For the first time she labeled that thing in his voice as anger. Belated caution made her suggest, "My lord, perhaps we should discuss this tomorrow."

"A paramour usually has more experience, more talents than you have."

The hurt washed away with a rush of humiliation. "You thought me talented enough this morning."

"Tenderness, of course, has no part in an arrangement between a lord and his harlot. When a lord wants to be served, his meretrix strips down and services him."

Saura felt him start to rise from the table, and the intensity of his fury colored every word with fire. For the first time since she had known William, the fear of him touched her mind. It wasn't the kind of fear her stepfather instilled in her; this was the kind of fear that dampened her palms and made her breath catch and urged her to push back her bench and prepare to flee. She stood slowly, grasping the table for support and hoping she'd misread his tone, but his next blast dispelled her expectation and fed her alarm.

"When a man—a man who is bigger and stronger and obviously smarter than his little, weak, damned stupid woman—demands attention for his body, that woman had better bow her head meekly and say, 'Aye, my lord.'" His feet stomped as he spoke, his voice amplified as he towered over her.

Determined not to be intimidated, Saura straightened her spine, lifted her chin. "I'm not stupid."

"I hadn't thought so previously, but events have proved me wrong." He stripped the veil from her head and tossed it aside, grasped her braid and tilted her head back. "Say it. Say 'Aye, my lord, I'll service you as you demand.'"

The foundation of her determination weakened, undermined by the sheer bulk of him above her and around her. "I won't service you," she faltered. "Not without respect and a mutual regard."

"Respect?" He roared it so loud the rafters trembled and a few of the more cowardly villeins scooted out the doors.

Saura wanted to clasp her hands over her ears, but he held them to her sides with one massive arm around her waist.

"Respect for a harlot? If you want respect, you'll never prosper as my meretrix. My dear, resign yourself. 'Tis marriage for you. But let me reassure you about that tenderness. No need to worry I'll treat you like glass tonight. Tonight I find all my tenderness dissolved in a brew of boiling frustration!" His mouth found hers without the subtlety or care he'd shown before.

A brew of frustration, indeed, as he ground his lips against hers. "Open," he ordered, and when she tried to shake her head, his grip on her braid tightened and he caught her lower lip between his teeth. His nip was quick and almost painless, but the threat of his anger overcame her reluctance. She parted her lips, but only a bit. What had been a tiny concession became, beneath his plundering tongue, a full-fledged surrender. With his mouth he imitated the surge of love, opening her and arousing her for all to see. When her hands were curled into his waist, when her face blushed with the flush that bore no relationship to embarrassment, when her body sought his with the unreasoning urge to mate, then he released her to announce, "You, my Lady Saura, are the woman who's going to purge me of my frustration. Right. Now."

He tossed her over his shoulder as if she were a bundle of reeds, and a cheer from the men washed over her as she hung face down across his back. She found relief by seeking the bare flesh beneath his shirt with her nails. His immediate retaliation brought a mortifying sting to that part of her that sat highest on his shoulder, and again the men cheered. It wasn't his hard hand that convinced her to pull her nails away, but the tremor of rage that developed in the body beneath her. Caution blossomed and grew as he swung around and bounded toward the door of the solar.

Maud spoke in front of them, and William skidded to a halt.

"Ye can't do this, my lord," the maid scolded, standing with solid tenacity before the door. "The Lady Saura is a sweet and gentle woman, and I'm responsible for her reputation. Ye cannot take her to your bed."

"Woman!" William spoke through his teeth, and the tremor in his body grew in intensity. "Get out of my way."

"Damn, Maud, have you lost all your senses?" Lord Peter shouted. He raced from the table to the older woman. "Get out of the way!"

"I won't!" Maud said, and Saura heard a scuffle before them, heard Maud exclaim, "You dare!" and the shouts of the crowd as it surged forward to obtain a view.

William strode forward, slamming the door behind him with a backward kick of his foot.

"Maud?" she insisted as he strode forward.

His hand grasped her thigh under her skirt as he rolled her onto the bed. "My father," William said clearly, "treats his women as they deserve to be treated. As I do."

"You dunce! As if women deserved more obstacles than are already furnished them by simpleminded men!" She sat up on her elbows and he pushed down with one hand on her breastbone.

The hand on her thigh flexed in warning, and her quick inhalation told him of the tingle that burst deep into her body. "You don't know when to shut up, but I'll teach you. I'll teach you a lot of things tonight."

William eased off the bed and stared at the disgracefully satisfied woman asleep on the bed. Asleep! He laughed. A weak word for the total exhaustion that blotted out that too-active brain. He had allayed at least one of her fears tonight, he knew, even as he allayed his own indignation. There were no obstacles to their marriage, except those she erected in her mind. And those, he knew from personal experience with the Lady Saura, were as sturdy as the cliffs that lined the coast of England.

One person could help him tonight, and so with quiet care he slipped into his clothes and opened the door. The fire burned in the center of the great hall, and most of the servants lay in the rushes on the floor, wrapped in their blankets or with their lovers. Stepping over the bodies, William sought the few hardy souls still gathered around one table to drink to the health of their lord. "Here's the bridegroom," they hailed.

He grinned at their mellow intoxication. "Where's Maud?"

"Maud?" One of the women gave an amused, lopsided smile, numb with ale. "Last we saw of Maud, she still lay on your father's shoulder."

"Oh, indeed?" His grin widened. "And which way did my father go?"

"To his chamber, brave soul that he is." One of the men cackled.

"And has anyone come out?"

"Nay, m'lord, he and the woman probably wrestled each other into submission."

The whole group fell about the benches, laughing at the suggestion, and William shook his head and left them, well aware their amusement was mixed with awe. Despite Lord Peter's age, and he was into his forties, he was a vigorous man who enjoyed women both in and out of bed. And Maud had terrified the minions from the day she set foot in Burke Castle. She was a woman not to be trifled with. The combination of Lord Peter and Maud seemed likely to change their establishment in ways they couldn't imagine.

William's firm rap at Lord Peter's chamber brought only the muffled shout of "Go away!" in a disgruntled masculine voice.

Ignoring the directive, he flung the door open and stepped over the threshold. Lord Peter came out of the covers with a roar that diminished abruptly when he saw their visitor. "This had better be important, son," he mumbled in disbelief.

"I swear to you it is."

Maud's head peeked up through the furs on the bed. "And m'Lady Saura had better be in good health."

"Oh, she is." William moved closer to the dais, dragging a stool after him. He sat himself astride, surprised by the bobbing of Maud's head. "She's wonderful. And sleeping very soundly." He peered at her in the feeble light of the night candle. What was the matter with the woman?

Lord Peter sat all the way up, the furs falling away from his bare chest. He shoved at the pile of clothes on the bed and rubbed his eyes with the heel of his hand. "So what is it, boy?"

"I need help with Saura. She's resisting me. She's resisting the idea of marriage, and there's only one person I have to talk to."

Both men turned to stare at Maud, her gray braid set over her shoulder, and she blushed and sank into the pillows.

God's gloves! William thought. The woman is embarrassed. Embarrassed, at her age! How he'd love to poke fun at her, to torment her a little with his teasing. But in Maud rested his key to Saura's consent, and so he tactfully said the one thing guaranteed to distract her. "Saura wants to stay on as my concubine."

Maud clucked her tongue. "That girl doesn't have a bit of sense." Realizing that sounded like a compliment, she hastily added, "Not that marrying you would be so wonderful, but 'tis better than going back to live with her stepfather."

His father stroked his chin. "Well, son, are you sure you want to wed her? After all, there's no reason to own the tree if all you want to do is pluck the apples."

Maud landed a punch in the middle of his chest that rocked him back into pillows and made him wheeze with breathlessness. She folded her arms across her chest and a protective fire flamed in her eyes.

"I was jesting!" he gasped.

William drew two fingers alongside his mouth, pulling the smile off his face. "Jesting or no, my problem remains the same. The lady doesn't wish to marry me, and she has the strength of character to refuse me at the altar."

A short silence greeted him, and then Lord Peter nodded. "Refuse you regardless of the marriage contract."

Maud morosely agreed. "Refuse you in front of a hundred witnesses."

William sighed. "She must be convinced before that time. What do I do?"

Maud shook her head. "Manipulating my mistress is almost impossible. She knows when you lie to her, she knows when you seek to persuade her to do something good for her and bad for you."

William's fist pounded the bedpost with a short, powerful rap. "Bad for me? This marriage will be a blessing on my life. Can't she be convinced it's a sign of God that in her arms I was bequeathed my sight?"

"Aye, God's sign that she stay with you. She wants to stay

with you, I'm sure. But you don't understand how she feels about her eyes, about herself. You don't understand the horrors of living with Theobald, may God curse his name. From the time she could toddle, he kicked at her. He used to tease her by holding her breakfast so she could just smell it, tell her to grab it, and then he'd move it. And laugh, like he was doing something clever."

"What about her mother? What did she do?"

"My mistress, Lady Eleanor, didn't realize when she married him. Not that she had a choice." Maud reached out and dragged her shawl from the tangle of her clothes and wrapped it around her shoulders. Rubbing her arms with a slow kneading motion, she remembered, "Saura's father died so suddenly, like a candle snuffed out, and Lady Eleanor was big with the child, and ill with a rash and fever. She couldn't keep the estates together. The neighbors began to tear the lands apart immediately. Saura was born, and we didn't know there was any problem, the babe was so pretty and fair. So Theobald offered for Lady Eleanor and he seemed like a decent man." She stared back into the past and knit her fingers together. "We knew right away we'd made a mistake. He made her put the child out to a wet nurse and got m'lady pregnant at once."

"When did you discover Saura couldn't see?" William asked.

She hesitated, sad with memories and not sure if she should share them. The two kind faces turned to her convinced her, and she told them, "I knew before Lady Eleanor, and long before Theobald. Saura was so bright. She lifted her head from the moment she was born and laughed out loud when most babes can only smile. At first I thought that unfocused look was just the way of infants. But soon it was obvious to me, and to the wet nurse. When Saura began to creep on her stomach and groped for everything she touched with such amazement, Lady Eleanor knew. That slut of a wet nurse told Theobald, and he wanted to kill the babe."

William sucked in his breath, and Lord Peter muttered something dark and horrified under his breath.

"If m'lady hadn't stepped between them, he'd have broken Saura's neck. If m'lady hadn't been carryin' his child, he'd have thrown her aside. As it was, he threatened her if his heir wasn't perfect. He raged like any weak man faced with a situation he couldn't bend to his contentment. He sent Saura away, to be raised on her properties, and I went with her. M'lady ordered it, ordered I train her to run and play in the sunshine like any child. And I did until her ninth year, when Theobald grew afraid of the disorder around the country and demanded she come back where he could keep an eye on her. Afraid someone would abduct her and demand her properties."

"Was Lady Eleanor happy to have her back?" Lord Peter asked.

"Oh, aye. Started right in training her to be a lady in charge of a household. Didn't allow for any excuses, and between the two of us Lady Saura learned everything a chatelaine needs to know. A good thing, too, for m'lady produced five healthy boys for Theobald and grew old before her time. Trained little Saura to care for them, always suspecting she'd not be there for any of them."

Alerted by the tone of her voice, William asked, "How did Lady Eleanor die?"

"I think he kicked her in the belly when she carried his last babe." A tear trickled down her cheek, and Lord Peter put his arm around her. "Another beautiful boy, stillborn on the wash of his mother's blood."

Recalling the pride and affection in Saura's face as she

spoke of Lady Eleanor, Lord Peter asked, "Does Saura know?"

"Of course," she said flatly. "We've never talked of it, but she knows. I wouldn't be surprised but Theobald has bragged about it to her. He worked her, you know, forced her to run the household and raise the children, and then condemned her efforts. Never let up on her. Would have raped her, but for the whole castle who loved her and interfered for her."

William leaped to his feet and swore. "I'll skewer that whoreson on a spit and roast him over slow coals."

"I'll make the sauce," Maud nodded. "And when he's done to perfection, we'll bake him in pastry and toss him in the dung heap."

They nodded in unison, equally pleased by the picture in their minds, but Lord Peter interrupted their vindictive relish. "That's fine, but unless William weds the woman Theobald has every right to demand her return."

"Possession—" William began.

"—is worth nothing if the lady decides to leave you," Lord Peter said brutally. "Indeed, she'll not get her pennyworth with you as a husband. What sane woman would seek a protector who awaits his death from a knife in the back?"

With grim resolve, William sank back down on his stool. "Have you thought about what I told you this afternoon?"

"What? That Arthur was a traitor? I agree. That we need to discover who has masterminded this outrage? I agree. That you need to sharpen your skills as a knight? On that point there can be no doubt. The brain, the muscles have atrophied. That bit of work you did today convinced me of that. Your swordplay is atrocious, your work with mace and broadax is enough to affright your destrier into ducking."

"All right! I'll practice with the squires until I can challenge even you, my father, but that's the easy part. What of this sly, slinking cur who seeks to destroy me and mine? Who can it be?"

Maud sighed in exaggerated patience and asked, "Have ye a bed robe, m'Lord Peter?"

"Of course." Lord Peter pointed at the trunk where a warm velvet wrap lay flung. "But you're not leaving me? This strategy will take only a moment."

"Men who talk of war and fighting can stretch a moment to its greatest length. If Lord William will hand me the robe, I'll pour us a cup of wine to sharpen our wits and wet our tongues."

"A good woman." Lord Peter hugged her, his eyes glowing with amusement and tenderness.

"A sensible woman." William tossed her the robe and turned his back as she struggled into it. "But how could she be less, to have helped raise up such a woman as my Saura?"

Maud lifted the pitcher of wine left for the night thirst of the lord. Deliberately she clattered the pewter cup to signal William he could face them once more, and brought him his wine with a puckish grimace. "Flattery will win ye no allies ye haven't already earned, and expediency buy ye the rest."

She flipped her braid behind her as she turned to serve her lover and returned to the bed with her own goblet in hand.

"Thank you," William said gravely. "Both for the wine and the advice. Both are good and necessary, and we're still faced with an unpleasant discussion of serpents and weaklings."

"Our choices are limited." Lord Peter stared right at William, and their thoughts meshed with identical links.

"Aye. Arthur was fostered with Charles and Nicholas."

"And Raymond of Avraché," Lord Peter reminded him.

"Not Raymond. He's one of the richest nobles in the land, one of the highest placed."

"Son, men are not always what they should be. Raymond was an unhappy boy when he came to us. His parents cared nothing for him. They were only interested in him as heir, as a political being who could help advance the Avraché cause. Sometimes, such an upbringing can never be cured."

"Do you believe that?"

Lord Peter weighed the facts against his instincts, and shook his head. "Nay."

"Raymond is my friend," William declared, and for him that ended the discussion. "Let us check, instead, the other two and how they influenced Arthur."

"Nicholas." Lord Peter massaged his forehead and then his brow as if the failure of his own fostering drove a pain into him no wine could cure. "Nicholas is quiet, deep, with little to say. He never confided in me, not even as a boy. If there's rot in him, I'd never know it."

"Nor I. Did he influence Arthur?"

"Arthur had no mind of his own, he blew with the breeze and relished the different currents. Nicholas could have influenced him, but why? Nicholas's elder brother held the title, but he died three years ago, not long after Nicholas returned to the family holdings. Now Nicholas is lord, and one of the wealthy men of Suth Sexena."

"We have left only Charles."

"Charles." Lord Peter took a swig of his wine and lay back against the pillows.

"What of Charles," Maud interposed sharply, "that you two should look so thoughtful when you mention his name? Is he not lord to some powerful estate?"

"He's lord," William agreed. "But the estate is not powerful."

"When Charles came to his inheritance, the fine castles he should have received had dwindled to a mere one. Only one estate, and 'tis ridden with debt and dishonesty. His father was ever a wastrel, letting the fortifications decay while he followed old King Henry around the courts. Charles is not much better, bragging about his prowess and afraid to joust for fear of losing his horse and armor. And with this wicked disorder that governs us, I fear. . . ."

"Aye, and I." William massaged his forehead and eye in such natural imitation of his father Maud chuckled as she carried the pitcher to refill their cups. "If 'tis Charles, how can we trap him before he does us harm?"

"Invite him to the wedding," Lord Peter answered promptly. "In such a festive setting, he's bound to betray his intentions. We'll watch him like a hawk, keep witnesses nearby."

William rubbed his hands in glee. "What a marvelous persuasion for Saura. Surely she'll wed me if her consent frees me from such a threat."

"I wouldn't depend on that," Maud said.

"Well, 'tis the best idea we've uncovered yet," William retorted, rising from his stool and thumping his cup on its wooden seat.

He strode from the room, invigorated by the discussion and the plan, and Maud watched him with a dry approval. "I would have never thought a loud, blunt man such as Charles would be capable of such underhand treachery," she mused.

"Nor I," Lord Peter said. "Still, one can never be sure."

"I'm sure of one thing. Saura will never marry Lord William unless we take the steps necessary. You, m'Lord Fox, will never betray our plan, ye're far too wily for that. And I'm too wise a woman to tip our hand." She cuddled beneath the covers and grinned at him, baring strong, white teeth and a considerable glee. "He'll play his part with conviction if we don't tell, and will never alert Saura by his voice that we've tricked her. Come closer," she beckoned. Waiting until he draped an affectionate arm around her, she tumbled backward and took him with her. "And listen to my plan."

ten

Saura floundered out of the deep well of exhaustion, urged by the scolding sound of Maud's voice and a strong conviction she was late for morning Mass.

". . . leaps out of bed to selfishly break his fast after he uses you half the night so you're too tired to rise like a decent woman to greet the dawn. Half the castle is sniggering, sure you've been shown your proper place and you'll marry Lord William with no more fuss. But don't you worry, Lady Saura!" Maud's strong hands grasped her shoulders and lifted her to a sitting position. "I'll help you escape. I'll not let any bullyboy push you into something you don't want."

To Saura's groggy mind, Maud sounded gruesomely cheerful. "I don't think—"

"Rape! 'Tis rape!"

"Nay, nay." Saura pushed her loosened hair from her eyes and massaged her temples as if they hurt.

"Like a savage, he carried ye off over his shoulder."

"Maud, it wasn't rape."

Maud shoved Saura's hands away and kneaded with deep and knowing fingers. "What else would ye call it?"

"It would have been rape if I hadn't. . . ."

"Hadn't?"

"Hadn't enjoyed it so much!" Saura flounced off the bed.

"Oh, isn't that just like a man," Maud complained. "Never thinking of you, never thinking of your reputation. I'm supposing you'll be producing a babe in nine months."

"A babe?" She paused in midstep, and her maidservant caught her long enough to drop her chainse over her head.

"Oh, aye. Everyone knows when a woman enjoys her man, a babe's not far behind. But don't you worry, we can handle such a wee problem." She never stopped talking, never paused long enough for Saura to think. She shoved Saura's arms into the sleeves and said, "However, I'm not sure I'll have to help you escape. Lord Peter stopped me last night and asked me to have you come and talk to him first thing in the morning."

"What for?" Saura rubbed her mouth and Maud handed her a cup of fresh-brewed ale.

"That'll give you strength to face Lord Peter. That man didn't look pleased at all. Gruff and rude, grumbling about a marriage between you and his son and how he hadn't been consulted."

"He doesn't want me?" Saura asked, dazed by the hurt she felt.

"Ye hurt his consequence, I'd say. Well, I told him he hadn't looked so stern with William's eye on him, and he snorted. So maybe we'll walk out of here with our bags packed by Lord Peter. That'll make you happy, won't it, m'lady?"

Saura nodded, and Maud pushed her to her feet and briskly finished dressing her. "Of course, we'll have to go back to your stepfather, a happening I had hoped to avoid, but we cannot stay here with Lord William so determined to marry you. T'would be cruel torture to him. So 'tis back to Theobald the whoreson, I guess." Loathing dripped from Maud's voice, and Saura clenched her fist as she thought, really thought, about living with her stepfather again. That busy voice kept talking, kept filling in the picture for her. "Pertrade Castle will seem like a small, dirty hole after living at Burke. Ye can't ride there, and Clare'll stay here as a page, so you'll have no companionship. We'll have to start watchin' out for the men again, since they never give you a bit of respect. Still, maybe by now that snip of a girl ol' Theobald married has learned how to manage her own household and won't have to depend on you so. I imagine by now the servants are used to runnin' to her for instruction." Maud twitched the skirt of Saura's cotte and smoothed her sleeves. "There, now, you look very pretty, just right to meet with Lord Peter after Mass."

Lord Peter didn't want her? The thought haunted Saura as she stood through Mass, and broke bread with the servants in the great hall. With a very human reaction, Saura was distressed. The man she thought so much of didn't want her in his family. She prepared imaginary dialogues between Lord Peter and herself, dialogues in which she pointed out all the reasons she was worthy of his son. Sometimes the dialogues disintegrated into arguments, for Maud had planted two very unpleasant seeds in Saura's mind. The first seed, of unworthiness, she could deal with, for she had dealt with it her whole life. But the other, much less agreeable seed, Saura stored away to fester in horror. She didn't want to go back to her stepfather's house to be a useless dependent, shunned and despised, a charge on her brothers, and always in fear of her life.

Making her way to the little cubicle off the great hall where the priest worked on the accounts, she found Lord Peter loudly shuffling papers and muttering. "Sit, Lady Saura," he ordered. "There's a chair for you."

He didn't rise to assist her, and she didn't expect it. His gruffness she understood; he was protecting his son from a match he considered below him. Yet Lady Saura of Roget embodied advantages he couldn't imagine, and she would explain them.

"You understand, girl, I'm not quite as thrilled as my son. You have proved to me you're a capable housekeeper, and my grandson worships the ground you walk on. William is completely besotted, of course, and unable to see there are other considerations. I don't want you to feel I'm ungrateful; I am very pleased you could help restore William's sight, but . . . exactly what is your dowry? Will you bring any properties into the family?"

Leaning forward eagerly, Saura didn't realize how conveniently Lord Peter had zeroed in on her strongest argument. She only thought how lucky she was to be so rich. "I am sole heir to all my father's properties."

"That must be a sizable amount of land." Lord Peter pondered, tapping his fingers together in indecision. Then in a different tone he said, "I knew your father."

"My lord?" Startled, for this was a connection she had never heard of, Saura listened with a still and anxious air.

"We were fostered by the same family. He was younger than I, a page at the same time I was a squire. Elwin assisted in my dubbing, bless him, and wished me well when I returned to my lands. I liked him. He was a good man, an honorable man—and a very rich man." Returning to business, he said, "Women, of course, know nothing about such things, but do you happen to remember any of the names of the properties or their locations?"

She straightened her shoulders and recited the place names and sizes of her lands. This list he didn't dare question, for her clear, certain voice conveyed her pride and sense of possession. Maud hadn't steered him wrong; this lever would move Saura to matrimony.

Finished, she waited with peaceful certainty until he gained control of his amusement to ask, "Are you aware of how is the land entailed?"

"Sir?"

"Are there any other claims to it?"

"There are no other living relatives; my father was the last of his line, except for me."

"When do you take possession?"

"It is my guardian's until I marry."

"Are you sure? On your marriage to William, you will be heir to—"

"All of it," she confirmed.

"Has your stepfather any claim to it?"

"None of it," she said firmly.

Settling back in his chair, Lord Peter had a smile on his face she could hear. "Women are always so flighty, but if this information is correct—"

"I swear it is."

"Then you will bring a sizable chunk of land to our holdings, and we would be willing to waive most of the dowry that should be paid in coin. Do you know how the lands are being run under Theobald's hand?"

Her face clouded. "He wrings them dry and lets the stronger neighbors take what they please. I've spoken to him, but all that got me was a blow and an order to mind my needle. My brothers help where they can, but—"

"So there will be work to get your lands in shape."

"Aye, I'm sorry."

"And that will keep William away from real combat until we are sure he's healthy, with no return of his blindness."

"Oh."

"Aye, indeed. This will be a most profitable union for my family. I'll contact Theobald at once to start contract negotiations. Personally, I see no problem at all. You are living in my house already, and 'tis acknowledged you were a virgin, recently deflowered by my son."

Recalled to her misgivings by his rush to secure her, Saura objected, "I don't want you to think I've taken advantage of your hospitality by trapping William into marriage."

"My dear girl, I've got warts on my thistle older than you, and with more guile. I can't think of one reason to repudiate you."

"I'm blind!"

" 'Tis not a disadvantage, to my mind. There is perhaps an impediment to the wedding, however. Did you know William's blood is not pure?"

"Not pure? What do you mean, my lord?"

"I'm a Norman. My père fought beside William the Conqueror when he came from Normandy and defeated Harold at Hastings. My mother was Norman, but my eye roved over my lands and discovered the Saxon daughter of the previous lord was fair and young. The young lady wanted none of me." My father, a stern man, wanted none of her. He laughed softly at his far distant memories. "She wed me when she carried our babe, and my mother welcomed her in feminine sympathy."

"Your father?"

Lord Peter shrewdly watched as Saura stroked her own flat stomach. "William picked up a stick the day he walked and brandished it like a sword, and then sat with a thump on his padded bottom and howled in frustration. He was my father's pride from that moment, and my wife was honored as William's mother. You're daughter of a proud Norman house. The marriage of Norman and Saxon is not a blot; but perhaps you should consider whether you feel prejudice against William's lines."

"What nonsense!" She swept his logic aside with a sweep of her arm.

"Think carefully. Your children would carry the blood of a conquered race."

"My lord, the Saxons fought until the streams ran red with their blood. Conquered they may be, but their courage could never be questioned, and it seems the greatest warrior in England is a result of the mix of blood."

"You speak of William?"

"Of course," she said proudly. "All else is myth and madness."

"I agree." He paused to let that sink in, and asked, "Other than your blindness, you have no mark on you, I assume?"

"None."

"There is no history of blindness in your family, I know, and God has compensated for your lack of sight with the gifts of intelligence and beauty. In these times of trouble, the marriage needs to be witnessed at once. In all modesty I must admit we are one of the great families in the district. Everyone must be invited, or offense will breed offense and I'll have a war on my hands. It will be a huge wedding. Can you handle such an undertaking?"

"Of course!" She sounded just as insulted as he'd hoped. "With Maud's help, we'll make ready."

"There'll be hundreds of folk in the castle, nobles and their servants, and much work for you. William and I will handle the entertainment, if that would help, but you will have to organize all the sleeping arrangements and the feeding of such a throng."

"I can do it," she said stiffly.

"Good. I've turned away suits from other fathers who will be here. Fathers who would attain William for their daughters. Lazy sluts, women without grace or talent, bores and nags. You'll be doing me a favor by taking William off the marriage market. Your mother was a remarkably fertile woman. I would prefer to obtain additional grandchildren from this union, of course, but should there prove to be no issue, William has a healthy son whom we can marry off in the next—"

"Why are you questioning my woman?" William's roar from the passage interrupted them, and Saura jumped guiltily, as if she and Lord Peter had been plotting against him.

"Now, William," Lord Peter soothed. Pleased with the timely distraction, he wondered, with strong justification, if Maud hadn't seen the need to end discussion before Saura grew suspicious. William's advent came after he had covered all the important points, after he had assured Saura of her suitability, after he had whetted her taste for her own lands.

"I can't believe you have the gall to question the woman of my choice," William said huffily.

"Now, son, there's no need to—"

"She'll bend to my will."

"William, stop yelling!" Peter raised his voice in a shout that rivalled his son's. "I couldn't have arranged a better union for you if I had tried!"

"Saura and I—what?"

"I said, this girl is rich. Did you know she is her father's only heir? And she takes control of her inheritance on her marriage, free and clear? God's teeth, Elwin of Roget had as much land as I do, it will double our holdings. No wonder that worthless fart, Theobald, never married Saura off. Take her away!" Peter waved his arms vigorously as Saura rose and walked toward William. "And send me Brother Cedric. We will begin to work on the contract at once. We'll have a huge party to celebrate this union, invite every neighbor and friend. I only wish I could see the look on Theobald's face when he receives the contract." Peter gave a great burst of enthusiastic laughter, a laughter Saura softly echoed. "I bet he has fits."

As William led Saura out of earshot, Peter grinned in triumph. "This will be wed*lock*, indeed."

Out in the great hall, William took Saura's arm awkwardly. "I apologize for my father's, um, great enthusiasm for your holdings. I assure you 'twas not your lands that attracted me to, that convinced me to. . . ."

Still smiling, her face shining with pleasure, she answered, "Nay, William, I realize that and I'm very grateful. But just think, my own lands will be mine, to manage as I see fit."

"Does that mean," William asked slowly, "you will marry me?"

"Aye, your father has convinced me. 'Tis the right thing to do. I am blind, but he assures me I'm beautiful."

"And you believe him?"

His tone was a mystery to her, completely neutral and delivering a fleeting blow to her newfound confidence. "Am I not beautiful?"

"Very beautiful," he confirmed. "I've told you so many times."

Her brow cleared of its pucker. "Aye, and your father convinced me. Also, he says my personality is pleasing."

"Pleasing?"

"Is it not?"

"Aye."

"And I'm competent to manage a household."

"My *father* convinced you of that, too?"

"Nay, I always knew that. Your father forfeited most of my dowry. A good thing, since I doubt Theobald can pay even a paltry sum. Lord Peter also reminded me of the good I'll be doing by attaining command of my lands."

"Am I permitted to share in the stewardship of these lands?" William asked sarcastically.

Waving her hand with airy grace, Saura conceded, "You know more about administration than I could ever know, but don't you understand? At last the people I remember from my youth will be protected, the country I roamed as a child will be handled correctly. 'Tis perfect, William. You get a great amount of land in compensation for marrying me, and I get my lands. Not the least of the matter, the profit is taken from Theobald. Isn't it glorious?"

Piqued by her capitulation and the reasons for it, William questioned, "Is this all we get with our marriage?"

Her puzzled face turned up to his. "What do you mean?"

Picking her up, William showed her with his mouth and his body what he meant, and then he stood her with spine-jarring suddenness on the floor.

His sword called him, his lance, and his broadax. His weapons promised relief from the consternation and disbelief that boiled in him.

She didn't love him.

He had taken her to his bed, showed her in the bluntest manner possible he worshiped her, and she would have nothing of him until his father convinced her to wed.

By bribing her with her own lands.

It tasted bitter on his tongue. The gall of that woman!

He knew where he could work off his rage, and he strode down the stair to the bailey. There the hands led the horses out to be groomed and exercised, maidservants plucked the weeds from the herb garden, and Kimball and Clare practiced their mock battles.

Glaring around him, he stopped by the stables. His hands worked, his muscles begged for action, and a fiery promise lit his eye. Activity melted away as all around him recognized the signs. The stable boys working with the horses skipped out of the way and Kimball and Clare skinned up a tree, hiding in the leaves. William barely noticed, so concentrated was he on relieving his temper. Leaning down, he hefted the long rod the boys used as a lance and shouted for his chief man-at-arms. The soldier came running down the steep stairs that led to the wall walk, and William ordered, "Channing, I want a message sent to Sir Guilliame, telling him to return his son to my care. I need a squire. I need one at once."

"An' if the thane has entrusted his son t' another knight?"

"Then see if he has another son. But I doubt that young Guilliame has gone to fostering yet. The family will keep him home for an extended visit." Channing nodded. William twirled the stick in a slow design, and tucked it under his arm to heft the weight. "I'll need many messengers prepared to go to all the neighbors and my vassals and castellans with an invitation. I am," grimness bracketed his mouth, "to be married."

The boy-laden tree whooped with approval.

"Ye have persuaded the lady, m'lord?" The man-at-arms was eager, smiling with pleasure, and William sourly wondered how Saura had extended her influence to his fighting force.

"What does it matter who persuaded her?" William

growled, jabbing the makeshift lance into the ground. "It is done. At the end of this moon, I'll need a troop of men ready to ride with me to Pertrade Castle to 'persuade,'" his mouth tilted with pleasure, "Lord Theobald to sign the marriage contract."

Channing's face glowed with his own pleasure. "Gladly, m'lord. Lord Theobald has an ill fame in these parts that owes t' his treatment of his peasants an' his servants, an' I'll have no problem fillin' a troop."

Nodding dismissal, William stepped into the open stable doors. "Bring my destrier!" he shouted with a volume that blew a great explosion of dust and hay into the air. Stable boys raced to do his bidding, and he rapped the tree trunk with the rod. "If you want to see some practice with the quintain, come at once."

He could hear the lads scrambling to get down as he warmed his muscles with a measured run out to the outer bailey and around its perimeter.

The quintain had never changed in all the days of his life. It sat at the center of a jousting course, challenging the untrained to combat. At one end of a timber, a weighted dummy sat dressed in a discarded knight's robe and sporting a scarred shield. At the other end hung a bag of sand, and the post in the middle acted as a pivot for the revolving crosspiece. Many boys had tilted at Sir Quintain; many boys had eaten dust when they failed to gallop past after striking the shield with their lance. The sandbag would swing behind them and knock them off their horse, and the next time they tilted at Sir Quintain the painful lesson prompted their flawlessness. It was better, as Lord Peter explained to the bruised boys, to be knocked breathless by a sandbag than to be dead of a lance that pierces your chain hauberk in battle.

The destrier came prancing out, dragging three grooms by the bridle, and William measured the distance with his eyes. Taking a running start, he leaped into the saddle without touching the stirrups. It was the test of maturity, that show-off bit of bravado every newly dubbed knight performed for his sponsors. Now he performed it for the children and for the men whose loyalty had never wavered, and they expressed their approval with a roar.

He steadied the horse as the grooms fled away from the animal's fury. The destrier reared, twirled, and William fought it to a stop. The familiar feel of a saddle, the smell of horseflesh between his thighs made the world return to its state of rightness. It made him whole again, mended his torn pride and returned him to the confident persona of Lord William.

He gave a bellow of pure joy as one of the men-at-arms handed him an ashwood lance, and without pausing he kicked the horse into a gallop. The lance settled into his hand like an outgrowth of his own strength, his eyes estimated the distance, and with a shock he smacked the center of the shield and galloped past. The quintain swung in rapid rotations as his audience cheered.

Turning and saluting the gallery, William directed his mount back to the starting line and held him against the wooden barrier while one of the stable boys straightened the quintain. He still had the ability to control his destrier with his knees, still had the timing and the balance to deal with the challenges of jousting. If the skills of combat had never left him, surely the guile to deal with one young woman lingered in his brain. He could plan an attack, prolong a siege; those abilities could be trained to deal with the female mind. She considered him her passionate lover. She consented to marry him as the protector of her lands. Yet there had to be a stratagem that directed Saura's thoughts away from the practicalities of body and property and toward this melding of minds that William labeled love.

Restlessly, the destrier pranced as he settled in the saddle and took a firm grip on the lance once again. Leaning forward, he kicked the horse again, braced himself, and struck the shield again. But in that moment of impact, an appalling thought distracted him. What if her wretched stepfather refused to yield her lands? Would she then refuse to marry him?

Like the thought which knocked him from his complacency, the quintain swung with solid force and knocked him square in the back. Unprepared, he tumbled out of the saddle and end over end until he came to rest in the grass at the side of the wall. With a groan, he rolled onto his back and stared at the white clouds drifting through the summer-blue sky, and wondered how long this woman would destroy his equilibrium.

Perhaps, if he were lucky, forever.

William weighed the contract in his gloved hands and stared with level intent at Theobald, seated before him, his elbow resting on the same tiny table that held his cup. "Do you insinuate I would cheat you?" he asked.

"Nay, nay," Theobald insisted, wiping a drop of sweat off his temple with his wrist. "Only, won't you sit and have a cup of wine? After the ride you've had this July day, wine would refresh you and liven your mind."

"Do you insinuate I would cheat you?" William repeated, his voice slow and deep and demanding. The lord of the

Pertrade sat on a chair while William stood. Dressed in comfortable furs, the lord sipped wine, but William dripped from the rain on his hauberk. Yet William stood with one foot on the floor, the other foot planted firmly on the dais. His imposing presence reduced the lord before him to a trembling jelly, the outstretched document creating a demand of its own. "I bring you a marriage contract to take your blind, useless stepdaughter off your hands."

"I never said she was blind and useless," Theobald protested, his reddened eyes squinting from the effort of thinking. "She's . . . she's actually quite capable and we've missed her sweet presence here at Pertrade."

"A worthless stone hanging around your neck, you told my father."

William's select men-at-arms stirred restlessly, transmitting anger by their stance. Their menace overwhelmed the larger group of sloppy fighters who posed in various corners of the room.

"You told my father no one would have her. I'm asking for a reasonable dowry. You should be grateful to me for removing her from your hospitality." William rattled the contract again for the joy of seeing Theobald wince.

"I'm her guardian. She has no right to wed without my permission," Theobald mumbled.

"This marriage contract frees you from the unwanted responsibility of Lady Saura and of the heavy duty of protecting her lands."

"And of the income from her lands." Theobald lurched to his feet in a drunken show of bravado. "What makes you think you have the right to demand her lands from me?"

William never moved, but his back grew straighter and he became, in some indefinable way, dangerous. "I not only demand her lands from you, I demand an accounting of every kernel of grain you've received and every measure you've taken to ensure the safety of the properties."

"An accounting?" The flame that glowed in William's eye and the unexpected demand for an accounting spun Theobald around. He looked helplessly at his men, and they looked away. He looked at his girl-wife, and she stared back at him with no expression. He looked at the hardened faces of William's warriors, and in them he read his defeat. He sank back down into his chair, picked up his cup in his trembling hand and drained it. "I'll get my records. From my priest. But he's, uh, not here. And the records are not . . . well, the priest is stupid. He drinks too much ale."

William stood like a stone, immovable, hard.

"The records are incomplete. But if you want to stay the night?"

"Nay." With distaste, William gazed around at the hall where children and dogs rolled in the filthy rushes. "Nay. Sign this contract and I will await the accounting."

His words were stark, unconciliatory, offering only one choice and expecting to be obeyed. Theobald's gaze roamed the disorderly room again, and his weak attempt at deception died aborning. "Give it to me," he muttered. "I'll make my mark."

William reached up and dragged the little table close to Theobald's knee. A snapping of William's fingers brought one of his men rushing to his side, producing a quill and a stoppered bottle of ink from a pouch at his belt. The mark was made, shaky and blotted, and William's man sprinkled sand over it and handed it to his lord. A smile passed over William's face, the kind of smile that made Theobald shrink into his chair, and then he rolled the parchment. With no word of farewell, William strode across the room.

Clutching the signed contract close in his fist, William

turned at the door of the great hall. With a critical eye, he observed the smoky fire that sputtered in the center of the room, the slatternly maids who stood about, the insolent knights, the dirty, stained tablecloth. He raised a blond eyebrow in demand. "Of course you'll attend the wedding, Lord Theobald. We will expect your blessing on our union. We'll expect all our guests to hear your pleasure in the wedding. You'll be there?"

"Of course," Theobald muttered sullenly.

His eyes shifted away from William's forthright gaze, and William declared, "I shall send my men to ensure your safety on the road."

"Not necessary," the scurvy lord protested.

"I would have it no other way." William smiled with all his teeth, and left with the clang of spurs on stone.

eleven

The great hall smelled good, clean, and scented with herbs mixed with fresh-cut rushes spread on the floor. William scuffled his foot and brought the aroma of mint to his nose. Embroidered cushions lay scattered on the hard wooden chairs; serving women hustled between the solar and the first floor of the castle with braziers and blankets. The fire leaped toward the ceiling with a clean, bright flame and torches hung in the sconces. The influence of a hard day in the saddle and a loathsome confrontation faded as he recognized the managing hand of his dearling. He could hear, from a distance, the voice of Saura, and it came clearer and closer as he stared in appreciation at his home.

"Thank you for the suggestion, Lord Nicholas. The undercroft will serve perfectly for the servants of our guests to sleep."

William stiffened with surprise as his betrothed climbed out of the stairwell that led to the storage area beneath the floor. A plain white veil hid her hair, and a streak of dirt crossed her cheek. A brown, rough-weave dress of no shape covered her from head to toe, and the wooden shoes she wore clomped as she walked. She was dressed for work, and William thought she looked charming. Charming, except for the appendage that trailed her into the room.

Nicholas followed closely behind her, his eyes fixed appreciatively on Saura's derriere. " 'Tis my pleasure to assist you, Lady Saura," he murmured, as he took her hand and carried it to his lips. "Still, I know you would have thought of it. A woman as intelligent and well organized as yourself."

An enigmatic smile graced her lips, and William didn't like the way the charmed guest fed on her beauty.

"Saura, I am home," he said, and his woman spun on her heel.

"William?" Her tilting smile blossomed into open-faced pleasure, and she stepped toward him, her hand outflung.

In a rush, he crossed the floor and lifted her in a hug. Spinning in a circle, he kissed her face while she laughed.

"Stop, William, we have company," she protested weakly. This made no impression on his celebration, and so she cried, "Stop, William. Now that you're home, I'll have to order the evening meal."

His twirling slowed and he slid her down his body. " 'Tis late," he said. "The sun has long set. Has supper not yet been served?"

"Nay, I held it for you." Her hands lingered on his shoulders and then she tucked them in a demure clasp before her waist. "Are you hungry?" Unconscious of her womanly wiles —for how could she know those universal lures without observing them in others?—she flirted with him. Her dark lashes fluttered, revealing and concealing her shining eyes.

Her smile slipped on and off her mouth as if her joy at his return couldn't be hidden.

His gaze lingered on her creamy skin, made irresistible by the pink of her cheek, and he wanted to lick her like cool custard. "Famished," he assured her, his voice choked with a meaning that had nothing to do with food.

"I'm hungry, too." Nicholas's reproachful voice broke into their *tête-à-tête*, and Saura jumped with surprise. In her absorption, she had forgotten their guest.

Blessed with better control than she, William turned to his friend with a smile. "Welcome, Nicholas. Did she make you wait, too?"

With a charming bow, Nicholas said, "The lady has such a pleasant way of making one wait, one does not even notice the pangs of hunger."

Saura laughed at his eloquence. "A polite way of saying I've starved you. Everyone will have an appetite, then." She clapped her hands and like a wild boar rush, the serfs flew from their other duties and began supper preparations. " 'Twill be a simple meal tonight," she assured him. "Pottage and clabber."

"My favorite." He watched the stampeding servants with astonishment. "Have you fed them nothing since dinner?"

"They made a foolish mistake." Saura smiled with her mouth, but her body stiffened in grim concern. Turning toward him, she projected her voice over and said, "Your churls, Lord William, believed my authority over them no longer existed. With insolence they reacted to my orders with disbelief and ignorance. The battle fought over my rule many months ago had to be fought over again this day. So I ask you, my lord, to what extent does my power exist?"

William stared at her and then raised his head and stared at his servants. They had slowed their rush to hear his answer and stood staring at him. His own displeasure was at fault, he realized. The sight of Saura hanging over his shoulder had shaken their good will. They didn't know whether he would marry such a quick-tongued woman, and because of that, Saura existed in a vacuum of position and authority.

Nothing he'd done this last moon had eased their speculation. Those last days of May had slipped into June, and the roses bloomed and faded. He had practiced his knightly skills; he had ridden with his father to hunt; he had closeted himself with Brother Cedric, drawing up the marriage contract. He'd been restrained, he thought, and not shown his pique at Saura. He'd not played the dedicated lover, true, but that was his own misguided attempt to assure her his love was no hot flame, quickly burned out. He'd tamped down the tenderness that welled within him and treated her like an established wife.

Occasionally, he'd ignored Saura, ignored her meals, and in the evening ignored her seductions. His failure to fornicate with her was nothing more than his insistent haste to complete the marriage contract, but the retainers hadn't understood. A contract such as theirs, involving lands and moneys, took weeks of hard work to draw up. Like a fool, he'd never thought to check to see how his casual treatment acted on the churls. He'd only been pleased as Saura slowly relaxed and slipped back into her role as chatelaine.

He'd left her sleeping in the night, riding to Pertrade with the haste of a maniac to secure her lands, and the churls thought he'd abandoned her. She had paid the price for his desire. Like a lazy, sly flock of vultures, his servants had picked at his lady all day, and now they waited to hear what he would say.

"My lady Saura." He gathered both her hands in his and carried them to his chest. "Forgive me for presenting myself to you with the dirt of the roads clinging to my boots. My mission today was with your stepfather, Lord Theobald. In this pouch on my belt I hold our marriage contract. Your guardian freely made his mark on it today. The arrangements for our wedding must proceed at once. All that I own is yours, in jurisdiction and in fact. Let anyone who disputes that speak to me." His gaze lingered on her upturned face, and then swept the room and its uncomfortable serfs. No one spoke, and then with the quick and quiet demeanor of a flock of trained mice, the serving folk returned to their duties. The trestle tables appeared, the cloth laid, the trenchers set out.

"I detect Hawisa's brazen hand in this rebellion," he said quietly.

"Aye," Saura agreed. "Dismissed to the kitchen to be a turnspit, she still creates misery with her venom. We have a good lot of servants in this keep, yet their ready response to such agitation troubles me. Could she not be married to one outside the manor?"

"I'll see what I can do," he answered. "I'll have to find some poor man to take her, and I don't know whom I dislike enough."

"Hawisa?" Nicholas inquired. "Isn't she that slut you've always had here?"

"Aye." William shrugged. "She's not worth our attention. I'll do something with her later. Saura can use every helping hand until the wedding is over."

"But only until the wedding is over," Saura agreed. Turning to Nicholas, she invited him to take his place at the table. "Help yourself to cheese and ale. I'll help relieve Lord William of his armor and assist him with his washing, and we'll join you directly."

"Where is my father?" William questioned as they moved away.

"He took the lads out to get some fresh meat."

"In the rain?" he asked incredulously.

"It wasn't raining this morning," she reminded him. "I imagine they found shelter among your folk, and have built a fire and are telling stories of bloody battle. Your father said he took the boys to train them in the art of the hunt, but I think," she snapped her fingers at the handmaidens as they entered the solar, "he does it because he heard Clare say how much brighter the stars were under Burke skies."

He chuckled. "Aye, that would do it. Father always spoiled the children if he could. Perhaps he considered them well out of your hair?"

"No doubt." She grinned in sudden amusement. "Maud went bumping along behind on some old nag. Your father has become attached to her."

"Ah, aye. I've noticed." He also noticed how efficiently the handmaidens worked. One drew clean clothing from a trunk and laid it across the bed. Two others lifted his hauberk from over his shoulders.

"Give that to the armorer to be oiled," Saura ordered, and one of them slipped from the room with the chain mail. "Linne, you strip him and wash the rust from his skin." As Linne removed his wet and muddy clothes, the other wenches dragged the wooden tub out of the corner. Standing on a stool, Linne gestured him in and sluiced warm water over his shoulders and head while he soaped his hands and scrubbed himself quickly.

Rinsed and cleansed, he ordered, "Give my lady Saura the towel. She can dry me."

A giggle broke the silence, but Saura snapped her fingers again and the sound was swiftly muffled. The length of linen was thrust into her hands and the maids fled the room. "Leave the door open," William ordered sharply, and the closing door swung back to reveal the lord and lady to any walking past. Saura's raised brow questioned him, and he explained, "You're to be my wife, and as such I'll not dishonor you before company. No matter how difficult that may prove." His teeth snapped together with irritation, and she made soothing noises as she wrapped him in the towel.

"Are you laughing at me?" He raised her face to his, and she grinned with companionable empathy.

"Aye, but I don't think you'll suffer more than I."

"Aye, I will, for I'll have to give up my bed and sleep in the great hall on a palliasse."

"I will, for I can't sleep without you."

"I will." He grimaced with painful amusement as she rubbed him with brisk motions. "For I no longer fit in my drawers."

Her brisk motions slowed and gentled, and he said, "None of that!" Taking the towel from her, he turned his back to the door and finished drying. She lifted his shirt and started toward him, but he shook his head, saying, "No. I will dress myself."

"Then why did you send the women out?" she asked, puzzled.

"I wanted to talk to you without the constraint of listening ears." He stared at the flower of her face, and thought, *Because I'm mad with love for you, and must woo you at every moment.* But he said only, "Will my intervention heal your problems with the churls?"

"For the most part, the servants are good folk. They need a firm and steady influence, and your support was more than I could hope. Thank you, William." She bobbed a quick curtsey. "How could you force Theobald to sign the marriage contract so quickly?"

He put on his shirt before he answered. " 'Twas my good looks and the charm of my personality."

Saura laughed out loud, and William quirked a brow toward his lady. "You don't believe it?"

"Of course I believe it. Your good looks, your charming personality—and the presence of your sword—would have an irresistible influence on Theobald."

"How well you know him," he marveled, tugging on the rest of his clothes with an efficiency that belied his need for a squire.

"Aye, I do. Will he come and give me to you freely?"

"He'll come. And by God's glove, he'll give you to me with a smile."

"I suspect he will, if only for the chance to visit a keep as great as yours. We must keep the wine away from him until after the ceremony, however. He is a vicious drunk."

"Swilling wine will rot the strongest man."

"He was never that. I hoped you would keep a watch on him, make sure he doesn't fall in with the wrong influences." She smiled a lopsided smile, as if afraid to call his attention to potential trouble.

"I'll watch them all," he agreed easily, if not truthfully. "Our enemy won't be a threat at our wedding. With all the folk around, and the failure of two attempts on my life, I'd say whoever it is will be cowering. Don't worry, my girl. I shall care for you."

"I know that, William. I've always known that. I thought that August would be an ideal time for the joining. We can't assemble the guests any sooner," Saura suggested.

"August," he agreed. "We will need help from the villagers to prepare for our company, and that we cannot have until

August. Then the heaviest work of summer will be over and the first rush of harvest barely begun. Thirty days to assemble the guests, thirty days to plan and provide, and by then your authority will be pounded into my serfs with my heavy hand."

"Not all of them betrayed, only a few questioned my authority. Don't use them hardly. 'Tis my responsibility to bind them with loyalty, and this day was a shock to my conceit." As she begged pity for the pack of squawking minions, Saura's smile clung with a tremor on her lips.

Damning the open door he caught her in his arms. "Don't fret, dearling. The wedding will be an ordeal, I know, but the vows before our villeins are necessary. We'll have Brother Cedric to bless us, and your father will be here, if he must be dragged by his . . . neck."

She giggled, for quite clearly he wished to drag him by some other appendage. "You cherish the thought," she accused.

"Nay," he protested with sarcastic innocence. "Perish the thought. The wedding day will be a good chance to renew the vows of my castellans to me, for all will be here to witness and the priest will ratify their word. 'Twill be a chance for us to see which of your vassals have defected, too, and need to be brought to heel."

The pleasure fled her face. "A chance for you to see who you must fight."

"Aye," he said with relish. "It has been a long time since I've lifted my sword in battle."

She twined her arms about his shoulders as if she would shield him. "You'll take your father, will you not?"

"For a few minor skirmishes? Perhaps a siege or two?" He reared back in amazement. "Whatever for?"

"You're unused to warfare."

"Too true." He nodded. "And practice with lance and broadsword cannot replace the conditions of actual battle. Perhaps a mêlée at our wedding would sharpen my skills. 'Tis a good thought. I'll discuss it with Nicholas. Thank you, my love." He hugged her, kissed her with brief inattention, and dove toward the great hall.

Saura followed more slowly, and seated herself on the bench William held out. Nicholas sat at her left. Bula lay behind her, waiting for scraps to fall. William shared her bench and her trencher and served her most tenderly.

A quiet permeated the hall as the minions served and ate their meal with concentrated subservience. The supper proceeded smoothly. Saura urged the conversation into innocuous channels: hunting, riding, the problems of managing an estate. She never gave William the chance to discuss the mêlée, but she did take the opportunity to interrogate their guest, for a vague misgiving gnawed at her.

"My Lord Nicholas, you've never told us what prompted this welcome visit."

"Didn't I?" William noticed how Nicholas softened his voice when he spoke to her. "How remiss of me. I had heard rumors, curious rumors of changes in the household at Burke, and my curiosity could no longer be contained."

"What sort of rumors?" Saura persisted.

"The truth, apparently. That William's sight had returned, that he would marry the mysterious heiress from Pertrade."

William wondered, "How does the news travel so quickly? The messengers have not even been sent out yet."

"So that's the reason you weren't bewildered when William arrived," Saura mused. "I anticipated a scene when you realized his vision had returned."

"What disappointment in her tone!" William said. "Women thrive on scenes that touch the heart, eh?"

"We mustn't disappoint the lady." Nicholas's voice filled with laughter, and he rose from the bench. "William!" he cried with mock animation.

"Nicholas!" William rose and met him behind her back, and Bula whined to come between them.

They embraced, murmuring soothing nonsense words until she chuckled and told them, "Sit, you fools."

"Look at your stupid dog," Nicholas said.

William laughed, and Saura asked, "What's he doing?"

"Sitting, of course. Didn't you tell the fools to sit?" Bula whined, and William murmured, "Does that feel good, boy?"

Saura knew that sound. The dog wasn't complaining; he was in ecstacy. "Does he like it when you pet him?"

"He likes it when Nicholas pets him, too." William thrust his long legs close beside hers and sat. "I thought you didn't like dogs, Nicholas."

"This is Lady Saura's dog," Nicholas answered.

"Ah, I see." William found it a strain to smile, but advised, "You'll have a friend for life if you continue to scratch his ears like that."

"He's so big, you'd think he was vicious," Nicholas said.

" 'Tis all for show." William showed a cordial contempt for the animal. "We can't even hunt with him, he's such a coward."

"Hush," Saura chided. "You'll hurt his feelings."

"The only thing that would hurt that dog's feelings is if you didn't feed him," William answered with irritation. "I don't know why we keep him around."

"Because you're soft," Nicholas said.

"Because you love him." Saura put her hand on William's knee, and William patted it.

"No doubt you are both right," he replied.

"Actually," said Nicholas as he resumed his seat, "I wasn't

terribly surprised about William's vision returning. It was obvious as his health came back, so would his sight. The rumors of his marriage drew me."

"Where did you hear all these rumors?" Saura asked.

"Oh, did I not tell you? 'Twas Charles who told me. I assumed by the way he spoke he'd been here when it happened."

"When what happened?" William said sharply.

"When your vision returned. Nay?" William shook his head and Nicholas shrugged. "He was drinking, you know how he gets. Drinking and riding around, just staggering with, I don't know, some burden weighing on his soul. And confused. The whole story was mixed up with you and Arthur and some foolishness about how Arthur tried to ambush you." He paused, but William said nothing. Nicholas shook his head. "I do wonder about Arthur. He's just an easily influenced boy. Never seemed like a man."

"Aye," William agreed heavily. "He was just a boy."

"Was?" Nicholas jumped at William's slip. "By God, William, what do you know?"

Sorry he'd revealed the information, William could see no way to deny it. "Charles is right. Arthur's dead."

"Not . . . not that ridiculous story Charles was spouting?"

"It was fairly ridiculous," William acknowledged. He took a swallow of ale and then pushed it away. He couldn't afford another slip like that one. He'd forgotten how astute Nicholas was. Nicholas's broad-cheeked face, nubby with a new beard, hid a powerful intelligence. His smooth, cool personality expressed itself in an occasional burst of sham heartiness, but his demeanor was that of an older man.

Nicholas's body excluded him from any feats of arms. His shoulders seemed no wider than his hips and his belly attested to his fondness for food. Bald except for a sandy fringe around the back of his head and his ears, his head was smooth, a fact he checked with a constant nervous stroking. His fair complexion burned and peeled with regularity, leaving his nose a rough crimson that owed nothing to intoxication. Indeed, he kept his indulgence to a minimum, retaining his secrets and his passions with iron control. Only his eyes, burning with some inner fire, hinted at his intense personality. They were hazel, a bland color, and surrounded by short blond lashes, and red-rimmed from the smoke of the fire, but when William remembered them he never thought of their unremarkable color. He only remembered the conflagration that lit them.

Doubt filled William. Doubt about Nicholas's motives, doubt about the information that fell too easily into his hands. He felt a reluctance to tell Nicholas all Arthur's confessions, and Saura seemed to agree. "Arthur was crazed with jealousy," she told Nicholas. "He bragged about how clever he was to have ambushed William and me."

Nicholas said nothing, waiting with nerve-racking skill for her to continue, but the silence stretched out. Impervious to such tactics, Saura sat with her hands resting in her lap. Nicholas grimaced at William, and William relaxed at the sight of his astute friend baffled by his dearling.

Nicholas said, "He kidnapped you, too?"

"No one said he kidnapped anyone," she observed. "The word was ambushed."

"I'm sorry. I understood from what your serving folk said today you'd been gone and I assumed. . . ."

Now he trailed off, dangling his words like a bait, but he'd made a mistake and he knew it. "Are you safe now?" he asked bluntly, paving his way to withdraw from the conversation. "A great lady such as yourself is always a target to scoundrels. You're lovely to look on and a great marriage prize."

"My Lord William will take care of that in August."

William laughed, trying to relax the unusual tension that sprang to life between his woman and his friend.

"You make it sound, Saura, as if I'll cure your beauty on our wedding day."

"Nay," she said with great seriousness. "But I'll no longer be a marriage prize when I'm wed to you, and you'll be responsible for my welfare. That will cure *you* of recklessness."

"Pity me, my friend," William mocked. "She nags me already."

"A womanly trait. She nags you because she loves you." Nicholas glanced away from Saura's marvelous face to see William stir uncomfortably. "But forgive her, for you'll never cure a beauty as great as hers."

William stared down at his hands, clenched in fists on the table. She *was* beauty, pure beauty. She transformed ordinary men into towering heroes, and she never realized how the look of her called forth chivalry in the roughest peasants. He wondered if he would ever cease to marvel when he saw that Madonna face lit by her unwavering courage. He looked up at her, and he was caught again. Had he really had her? Had he really brought her to an amorous lassitude? She looked so innocent, so untouched, like a child, like a woman.

She trusted him implicitly, believed everything he said to her. Yet he had portrayed a false confidence to her. Whoever had tried to kill them would be at the wedding. He could take care of himself, but she was a woman, fragile, delicate, and he knew a sense of possessiveness he'd never dreamed of. His own well-being was never in doubt, but this villain would know she constituted his weak spot. The thought of Saura, kidnapped, alone, blind, afraid, made him sweat and fear as no other threat could. He would keep her safe, he resolved. Somehow he would keep her safe.

twelve

Rubbing her arms against the chill, Saura pulled off her *cotte*. Clad in her shift to protect against the chill, she slipped between the sheets of the bed in the solar. They were comfortable; someone had brought in the warming pan and prepared the bed for her use.

The serving folk had had their doubts answered. In the weeks since William's return with her signed marriage contract, she'd been treated with respect, as befits the mistress of the castle.

Saura touched her lips with her fingertips. They retained the brief savor of familiarity, a deliberately passionless kiss left by William as he escorted her to her chamber door and then deserted her there. It tasted sweet, a pleasure of longing and respect. He wouldn't sleep with her, nor work his magic on her body, not as long as they had company in the keep.

Nicholas had remained with them through the end of July and the first weeks of August.

She spat out a brief, violent expletive, and buried her head in her pillow. Damn him for being there, and damn William for being so honorable.

In some odd way, she wished William was not her betrothed. No other man could command her respect and her affections as he did. No other man could make her feel guilty for being the woman she was.

Unworthy. Inferior.

If she were to marry William—and she would, for it was the right thing to do, never mind that it fulfilled her heart's desire—she must conquer these feelings and become the woman William believed she was.

Determinedly, she fluffed the pillow and lay on her back with the covers arranged over her chest. She sighed and closed her eyes. A draft touched her cheek, and she pulled the blankets up higher, up around her neck. She'd forgotten to shut the bed curtains. Scrambling up, she pulled the curtains from their loops and tucked them close together. The chill sent her back under the covers, and she settled herself again.

Sleep would not come. For a month, sleep had eluded her, and like a churning mill wheel, her thoughts whirled in a disruptive cycle.

The servants. Her ability to efficiently run her household was the one support she had to offer William. William's authority had kept them in order temporarily; she controlled them in the long run.

The wedding. This had been her first chance to prove herself as chatelaine. Ordering the meals, supervising the preparation of food, and arranging the sleeping quarters had kept her up from dawn to dusk, but she had done it.

The mêlée. That much heralded mock battle wherein all the knights present chose sides like boys playing at ball, and then proceeded to smite each other with swords. Men were killed in mêlées. Fighting terrified her; still, William was right. He should practice with his friends before confronting his enemies. She'd never undermine his confidence by suggesting she feared for his life; she knew the value of confidence better than most.

So all her worries were settled. She could sleep. Sleep.

How could something so ardently pursued evade her? She was tired. Surely she could sleep. She turned on her side, hunched her shoulders and drew the covers up to cover her ears. The summer rain brought a dampness into the keep no fire could dispel. A dampness, a chill. William was lying to her. Lying with his voice, not telling her all the truth, trying to protect her. She wanted to let him lie to her, protect her, but she couldn't ignore her surging instincts. He worried about this fiend who menaced them. He told her all was well, but he didn't believe his own words. Whoever this enemy was, he presented a real threat. He could slip among the guests at their wedding, promoting havoc. He could murder or kidnap, and how could they pinpoint the culprit?

William would protect her with the ways of a warrior, but she must defend him with the ways of a woman. She'd poke and pry, she'd listen to every voice. She'd seek those lies that fell so easily from men's mouths and she'd find their friends and determine who were their enemies. And she'd warn William of every potential risk.

Admitting her real worry eased her. Planning a defense helped her relax. With one final big sigh, she pulled the extra pillow from the empty side of the bed. She tucked it under her chin, embraced it close to her bosom, slipped one leg beneath and threw one leg over the top. Now she could sleep.

"I count four," Channing observed.

William squinted through the bright August sunlight to the riders on the road. "Five altogether. See, one of them, a female, I think, is held by a leading rein, and one rider holds a child."

"No danger, then." The older man leaned against a battlement with a sigh.

"We'll have many riders coming up that road to the castle in the next few weeks." William clapped a hand to Channing's shoulder. "But I didn't expect them so soon. 'Twas only eighteen days ago we took the contract to Theobald, and only ten days ago we sent out the messengers."

"An' only seven days till the ceremony." His man-at-arms beamed at him.

"God speed the day. Who could have arranged to come so soon? Are they guests, or do they bear news?"

"Guests carryin' news?" Channing guessed.

"Aye. Watch for Lord Peter and the boys, but keep the drawbridge up, and let all who desire entrance call out their names and business until we have a steady stream of visitors."

"Will that not cause offense?" Channing frowned, at home with the workings of war but not the workings of society.

"In these times of turbulence, none will question our wariness. Keep a suspicious eye on all visitors entering the gatehouse when we open it to traffic, and call me at once if you smell trouble."

"Aye, my lord."

"I'm putting responsibility on your shoulders, I know, but I must stay in the keep with my lady and greet our guests."

Channing opened his mouth as if he wanted to say something, and then exhaled as if he didn't dare. Long familiar with his man's traits, William encouraged, "Say it."

"Ye needn't worry about the lady an' the servin' folk again, m'lord." Channing scraped his toe in the rubble on the wall walk. "There's talk, an' even I've heard it."

"Talk?"

"The whole castle an' the village is buzzin' with it."

"What?" William encouraged.

"I'm tellin' ye! No one'll question the lady's authority again. They're sayin' they made a mistake, they were stupid."

"Aye, that they were." William's chin firmed to a clean granite line as he thought of the churls' insolence.

"Well, no one needs to hang on her all the time. The serfs'll do as they're told now." His voice held the contempt of an armed man for the house minions, but it held something more, too.

William stepped back and examined the scarred warrior. Channing refused to meet his eye, looking over the battlements instead and saying, "They're gettin' close."

"I haven't been hanging on her," William observed mildly.

"Oh nay, m'lord. You've let her alone to do her womanly work."

William pondered, then queried, "Who's hanging on her?"

" 'Tis just that . . . perhaps Lord Nicholas could help you with the preparations for the mêlée. Or maybe with the stable preparations."

His bland suggestion told William more than he wanted to know. "Is there gossip?"

Channing was saved by a hail from below. " 'Tis your guests, m'lord." He started away at a run. "I must approve their entrance."

William ran right beside him. "And I."

The calls from below floated up to the men at the gatehouse, and William leaned out to hear. No sooner had he made sense of the shouts than he roared, "Let them in. Let them in at once." Turning to Channing, he said, " 'Tis my lady's brothers. Send someone out to search for Clare. I'll fetch Saura."

As William raced down the stairway on the inner face of the wall, Channing shouted the order to open the draw-bridge. It lowered with the creaking of wood and the clatter of chains, and a fresh breeze blew through the wide-mouthed door as the brothers rode in. William went among them at once to relieve one young man of the boy he held.

Dudley nodded pleasantly as he handed the three-year-old down. He rubbed his arm and groaned, "He gets heavy after so many miles."

William looked into the child's face and saw a muted beauty that looked like Saura. "This is Blaise," he pro-nounced. "And you're Dudley, who studies for the Church. Rollo, the eldest." He received a curt greeting from the eigh-teen-year-old. "And his young wife." Very young, he thought privately, as he surveyed the gangling girl whose horse pressed as close as possible to Rollo. He grinned at the youth dismounting with painful care. "You're John, who is being fostered, and we already have Clare."

Four pairs of violet eyes stared at him with various expres-sions, and William reeled from the shock of seeing his Saura stare at him from so many different, masculine faces. "I am William, your new brother. Welcome to our home. Wel-come."

Dudley slithered off the horse and smiled in return. "Thank you, William. It has been a long ride from the monastery, and I'm glad to get here."

"And I." John rubbed his behind and nodded permission as the stable boy took the reins of his horse to lead it away.

" 'Tis good to meet our new and mysterious brother. Theobald sent Rollo such a garbled message, we knew not what to expect. And fathoming our esteemed father's mind as we do, we wondered if you'd be hunchbacked and one hundred years old."

William laughed with such full-bellied enjoyment Blaise clapped his hands and even Rollo couldn't restrain a chuckle. "The truth," he sputtered, patting the baby on the back, "is even more incredible than that." Blaise patted William's cheeks in return, fascinated by the man with the big rumble. William hugged him and then handed him to John. Walking to the side of Rollo's wife, he held up one hand. "May I assist you, my lady?"

The girl checked Rollo with a quick glance, and when he nodded she placed her hand in his and slid off her saddle. "What is your name?" William asked kindly.

"Alice, my lord." Then, with a troubled look at her husband, she corrected herself. "Alice of Montreg, my lord."

"You are welcome. You'll be glad to see Saura again."

"Oh, I've never met her, my lord. Lord Theobald never let her come to my wedding."

"Alice." Rollo spoke firmly as he dismounted.

The girl jumped and blushed, hanging her head like a rebuked child.

Rollo put his arm around his bride. "Alice, we all know how contemptible my father is, but let us not chat about it in the bailey with the stable boys standing about." He hugged her tight for a moment, and then released her. Standing straight and strong, Rollo reached out a hand to William. "As my brother said, you are indeed a relief."

"I am flattered," William said ironically.

"Nay, you're not. To prefer you to a hunchbacked old man is no compliment." Rollo smiled, and it was Saura's smile.

William's gaze swept the assembled boys, noting their black hair and clear, pale skins. "None of you resemble Theobald."

"Nay." Dudley fixed his clear eyes on William. "Our father's a weak man, and he passed none of himself on to any of us. We all look like our mother."

"Perhaps your father married her for reasons other than just her lands."

"Oh, aye," Rollo agreed. "He loved her. And he hated her. Just as he does our half sister."

"Rollo!" Everyone turned at the shout to see Clare fling himself from the horse he shared with Kimball. Clare flew over the drawbridge with winged feet. "John! Dudley! Oh, here's Blaise!" The brothers surrounded him like a clutch of enraptured black birds with a new hatchling. As the sounds of joyful reunion filled the bailey, Clare took the heavy babe from John, hugging him with homesick intensity. His brothers ruffled his hair and hugged his thin shoulders and smacked him on the back, and when they parted to let him draw breath, he was laughing and crying at the same time.

Dirty and disheveled from a foray in the woods, Kimball walked to his father's side and tugged his sleeve. Without taking his eyes from the male fraternity, he said, "Those are all Saura's brothers, aren't they?" It wasn't really a question, more an incredulous statement.

William nodded his head at his son. "Half brothers. An amazing resemblance, isn't it?"

Peter rode in, with Maud riding pillion, and handed his reins to one of the stable boys. Dismounting, he helped ease Maud down and steadied her as she shook her legs out. They strolled over, and William smiled at the older woman who held his father's arm. "Are these your young ones?"

"Aye," Maud agreed, her eyes sparkling with pleasure. "I've changed the swaddling clothes on every one of them."

In a surge, the boys surrounded Maud with loud enthusiasm, hugging and teasing her as she lashed them with her acidic affection. "Does my Lady Saura know ye're here, yet?"

They muttered and shuffled, and she patted their behinds with vigor. "Get ye up there, then."

"Can we sneak up and surprise her?" Dudley asked.

"You jest," Rollo snapped. "Have you ever sneaked up on our sister?"

"Never," Dudley admitted. "But think how pleased she'd be!"

They stood and thought, and William suggested, "I'll go get her and bring her down to the herb garden. If you stand still and I place her in the midst of your circle. . . ."

"Aye, and if we can keep Blaise quiet." John's eyes shone with delight.

"Go bring her," Maud directed. "I will position them."

When William strode into the great hall, there sat Saura at the table with the cook and the baker, discussing every meal and subtlety to be served to their company. And there lay Nicholas on a bench, propped on one elbow and watching her with those intense eyes.

She turned at his step, calling, "William, these clods say you don't like cold lamprey pie!"

She looked so indignant he knew his love had discovered a major stumbling block to their marriage. He put his foot on the bench next to her and leaned against his upthrust knee. "The way I like lamprey best is poached and drained, wrapped in pastry, and given to the dogs."

"William!"

"Lampreys are long, slimy things that live in the mud. Hot

lamprey, prepared any way, is a horrible prospect. Cold, it doesn't bear contemplating."

"With extra lamprey syrup?"

"Please!" He put his hand on his stomach. "Grievous illness comes upon me when I consider it."

"Oh, William!" She sounded disappointed as he pulled her to her feet.

"Come for a walk," he invited.

"I can't." She pointed back at the table. "I've got too much to do."

"I've got something to show you."

"But the cook—"

"Take care at the stair." He slowed down while she located the first step with her toe.

"If I don't organize—"

"Here's the bottom. Here's the doorway."

"I can't walk as quickly as you do!"

Deliberately, he kept his steps long and hurried. "Warm day."

"William." She planted herself in the grass of the bailey. "I won't walk another step!"

He picked her up with a mighty swing and strode on. "God's teeth, woman! Come on. What a slow lass you are!"

She didn't say anything, thinking hard, and then she touched his face. "William, are we going to be alone?"

"Nay, love." He dropped a quick kiss on her upturned countenance and stopped. "Definitely not alone. Do you know where we are?"

She sniffed. "The herb garden." He lowered her to the ground, and she sniffed again.

"Saura, Saura." The wee boy raced over to her and embraced her knees and she snatched him up.

"Blaise?" She touched his face and then hugged him tight.

"Oh, Blaise, you've grown so much! How did you get here?"
The light glimmered on her face and she flung out her hand.
It was taken at once, and she worked her way up the arm to
John. He caught her in a crushing hug, interrupted only by
Blaise's indignant wail.

"You'll have to share her, lad," John told him, and turned
her.

"Dudley!" Their embrace was tender and sweet, two people too long apart.

"Look here," Dudley directed, and as she found herself in
Rollo's arms her emotions gave way and she burst into tears.
The brothers grinned and gulped, pleased that their calm,
efficient sister should cry over them, and embarrassed by her
womanly weakness. They patted her shoulders and hugged
any part they could capture and helped her settle Blaise securely on her hip.

William watched the scene through a rosy glow of sentiment, and looked around to see if others were affected. Alice, the child bride, was rubbing her nose with her palm as if
she didn't want to admit to tears, and he walked over to
stand beside her. "Isn't it sweet?" the girl asked.

"It makes me wish I'd had siblings," he agreed, glaring at
his father who stood shoulder to shoulder with Maud.

"Oh, I had them," Alice said. "Mostly they just pull your
hair and spit at you during dinner."

True to her words, Dudley reached under Saura's veil and
pulled her braid. "You can't cry all day. We brought someone
to meet you."

"Ouch!" She grabbed her hair. "You mean, there's a
stranger here?"

"Aye, watching you blubber," John said with fraternal
kindness.

"My wife," Rollo smiled with tender concern at the forgotten girl.

"Your wife! You brought your wife and you forgot to tell me, you fool!" Saura caught Rollo's beard and tugged hard.

"Hey!" he yelped. "She doesn't mind."

"That you've been married only a year and forget her existence? You're a bigger fool than I thought." She put Blaise down on the ground and reached around her brothers.

Alice hesitated, but William pushed her gently into Saura's arms. Saura threw her arms around her with familial enthusiasm. "Alice, how I've longed to meet my sister-in-law!"

Alice mumbled, stuttered, stood stiff in Saura's arms and seemed to have reverted to uneasy childhood. William stared, surprised by the girl's inadequacy, and Saura froze, pain etched in fleeting discomfort. She eased her embrace and stepped back. "How tall you are. You're so lucky." She smiled, projecting kindness and warmth. "Welcome to Burke Castle. If you should want for anything, please let me know."

William stared at Saura, amazed at the brief greeting. What was wrong with his dearling? Was she jealous of Rollo's wife? Surely not; Saura's eternal compassion for the less gifted attracted him as nothing else did. This was something else, and for an uneasy moment, he knew he'd run into Alice's attitude before, in the dark time of his life. Brow wrinkled, he couldn't quite remember.

Then Rollo stepped forward and caught Alice's neck in the loose trap of his elbow. "She's terribly young, sister. She's only thirteen."

Switching his gaze to Alice, William understood. The girl was afraid of Saura, of the difference between them. Perhaps she was repulsed by Saura's blindness, perhaps she was simply frightened of making a blunder. But her rigid body and her wary eyes that never wavered from Saura told their own story. Saura, with her acute sensitivity to atmosphere, could not fail to notice.

" 'Tis goodish, brother," she told Rollo. "I understand." She reached out to William, close against them, and he reeled her in with firm hands.

Rollo tightened his arm around Alice's neck and then released her in censure. The girl stood bewildered, too immature to realize she'd given herself away.

"Rollo, you be nice to her," Saura instructed, just as if she knew what he was doing. "She's in a strange place."

"Saura." Like a ragtag beggar, Clare tugged at her skirt. "Saura, you never greeted me."

Saura laughed with husky pleasure and swept her little brother in her arms. "So I didn't. Forgive me?"

"I suppose so." The boy sniffed with mock sadness. "Kimball is feeling left out, too."

Kimball released a heartrending wail in a blatant bid for sympathy, and she flung an arm around him, too. To William, she asked, "What shall we do to soothe two such obviously agitated boys?"

"Oh, I can think of something." The note in William's voice warned Kimball, and he tried to wiggle away from Saura's restraining arm, but she held him securely until William grabbed him by the scruff of the neck. He lifted them off their feet and carried them, tucked under his arms, out the gate and into the bailey.

"Nay! Father, nay!"

"Please, Lord William, nay!"

Everyone in the herb garden strained to hear as the boys' yells increased in intensity. The splash sounded loud and satisfying, and their screams shivered with chill.

"Where did he dump them, sister?" Dudley asked with a grin.

"Horse trough." Saura smirked with renewed spirits and hooked her arm through Dudley's. "Come up to the keep, and I'll get you some refreshments."

"You're a uniquely efficient woman."

Nicholas had learned, Saura thought. He no longer praised her beauty. He praised her for those things she considered important. Efficiency, ability, coordination. The man's voice soothed her ear: bland, with the nasal reverberations of Norman French plain in his aristocratic accent.

"Because I can throw together a quick meal for my brothers while they wash?" she asked lightly. "With the food we're assembling for the wedding, this little meal is certainly no problem."

"You're wonderful. Think of what you could accomplish if you were sighted."

Turning away, she said, "If I were sighted, I'd have the liberty to be inefficient. I assure you, Lord Nicholas, I am not wonderful."

"Nay, my lord, she's only human."

She smiled at the deep-toned baritone from her closest brother, calling down from the gallery. "I thank thee, Sir Rollo. With compliments like that, 'tis a miracle I've kept my modesty."

"You are welcome, sister." With a clatter, he flew down the spiral stairs and bounded into the room. "My Lord Nicholas, you're early for the wedding celebration."

Surprised, Saura wondered what prompted Rollo's abrupt, almost rude greeting. "Do you know Lord Nicholas from another place?"

"Until William introduced us, we'd never met, but he must

be a good friend of the family to arrive so early." Again he emphasized the "early," and Nicholas responded with an affable politeness.

"So I am. I'm one of Lord Peter's fosterings." He rose from the bench. "And I've not had a chance to speak with Peter. Do you know where I would find him?"

"He's down in the bailey, inspecting the stables with William. He'll be glad to see you, I'm sure." Rollo's relief was obvious, and Saura reached around and pinched him on the arm. He flinched, but didn't move until Nicholas left the room. "What's he doing here all alone with you?" he asked in a hard voice.

"He's strange, but Rollo, he's a guest."

"Not my guest."

"Nay, he's William's guest and you have no right to offend him."

He spoke not at all, and then he slowly agreed, "You're right. But I didn't like the way he looked at you."

She winced, and he asked, "Has he bothered you?"

"Nay, nay, he's been useful. He assisted when I counted the barrels of meat and wine in the undercroft. He provided shrewd suggestions about brewing the vast amounts of ale necessary for the wedding. He seemed surprisingly knowledgeable about housekeeping chores."

"But why? Why doesn't he help William?"

"William says he doesn't like knightly chores."

"You're right, he is strange." Her manly brother's enthusiastic agreement made her laugh. "Don't worry that I offended him, though. When I was rude, he got that very superior look of forbearance that mature adults get when youths such as I are bombastic."

Saura laughed at his emphasis. "He would."

Rollo threw his arm around her neck and gave her a loud,

smacking kiss on the cheek. "What's to eat, you wonderful lass? I'm starving."

Embarrassed by his sarcasm, Saura pointed at the loaded table. "If you're going to catch me off guard, you'll have to do with a cold meal." She slapped his hand when he lunged. "Wait until the other boys come in, you pig!"

"Aye, I will, but not for the sake of good manners. I need to talk to you about something else."

It sounded as if he squirmed, and Saura took his hand and led him to the bench by the hearth. "Of course, tell me about it."

The hand in hers trembled, and she tightened her grip in surprise.

"You were always there, weren't you? My older sister who could eternally be depended upon. Kind, generous, free with her time and her understanding." He paused, and asked in the hopeful tones of someone postponing the inevitable, "What did you do with Blaise?"

"Maud's fed him and put him down for a nap," she answered patiently.

"Why should he need a nap? All he did was waller us from the time we snatched him from Pertrade until we got here."

Saura chuckled, as she was supposed to, and then insisted, "Rollo? What trouble are you in, now?"

"I'm not the one that's in trouble. 'Tis . . . my wife."

Saura dropped his hand.

He sighed. "I was afraid you'd feel that way. I'm sorry, dear, I should have realized, but I just assumed she'd follow my lead. I just assumed she'd love you as I do. She's malleable, easily led, and I could have talked to her."

She said nothing, and he tried again. "God, Saura, she's so young. She's afraid of the servants. If I didn't have old Lufu to help, I don't know what would happen in that household.

She's afraid to talk to the matrons, as a married woman should, for fear they'll laugh at her." Saura sat stiff and still, her face still turned away from him, and in desperation, he begged, "Saura, listen to me. Alice still plays with her dolls."

She sighed, and dropped her head. "All right. I'll not hurt her."

He hugged her, kissed the top of her head. "I never thought you would. I just wanted to explain, perhaps ease your offense. We'll teach her, sister, to appreciate you."

"Teach her?" She laughed, a tiny touch of bitterness in the sound. "Why should we have to teach her? Why can't she give me the same chance she'd give anyone else? I have two hands that serve, a mind that reasons, a heart that loves. Am I less than another woman? If I were old and blind and sat in a chair, people would pat me on the head and croon. Instead, they ignore me or talk over my head as if I'm not there or treat me like an idiot."

"They're afraid. They're afraid you have magic powers, for you know them by their smell and the sound of their walk. They're afraid you can see into their souls, because you can catch them in a lie."

" 'Tis so stupid! Don't they realize I must use ears and nose and touch to see the world around me? Would they do any less?"

"They just don't think. Alice, especially. But she's a nice girl, eager to please, pathetically unsure. If you could only see her, you'd understand. She's like a puppy, all legs and arms and big feet and big hands. My wife's so immature, she's not even formed yet."

Something in his voice alerted Saura. "Your wife? Is she really?"

He laughed, briefly and with irony. "You've guessed, haven't you?"

" 'Tis my magic powers," she retorted. "That, and your frustration."

"Is it so obvious? That she's not yet my wife?"

"Only to me. I know you so well. How do you handle it?"

He stood and paced across the floor and back. "It isn't a problem, normally. I've not yet been knighted, and I'll live with Lord Jennings until I've completed my training. Alice lives at my main holding of Penbridge and learns what she should have learned from her mother. When I'm home, we sleep in separate rooms. The only problem comes when. . . ."

"When what, dear boy?"

"When we must visit and the hostess thoughtfully beds us together."

"And?"

"Alice likes it very much. She says I'm warmer and more comfortable than her dolls."

He sounded so desolate, she couldn't help it, she burst into laughter. "Oh, poor Rollo. Poor, poor Rollo."

He pulled her braid in disgust and stomped over to the table, snatching a wedge of bread and stuffing it into his mouth.

"That merriment's a pleasant sound," Dudley called from the doorway.

"Aye, and it makes me want to strangle her." Rollo stared at his chortling sister with unbrotherly irritation.

"I wonder if her laughter has the same effect on William?"

Her brothers contemplated that in silence, until Saura choked, "Not yet."

"Hmm." John sounded thoughtful, and then perturbed. "Couldn't you have kept that pig out of the food until we got here?"

"Nay, 'twas beyond me," Saura said, and went into another gale of laughter. "Many thanks to you, Rollo. I've sorely missed your humor and sorely needed a joke."

Over her head, her brothers exchanged a long look and Dudley began to juggle two pasties with a casual skill. "I'm juggling your meat pies," he warned.

"Well, stop it!" she said sobering. "You'll drop them on the floor."

"First, tell me why you needed a joke."

"Dudley, the rushes were fresh last week!"

"The dogs are drooling."

"Better tell him, sister," John suggested. "The meat's coming out."

She snapped, "I can afford to lose some pies."

"I'll juggle drumsticks next."

"Beast! Stop! My whole life's changed and I'm to be married and the groom is more than I'd ever hoped or dreamed or deserved. Surely I have the right to some tension!"

The juggling slowed and stopped.

"And you'll never be a good monk with such dreadful habits of blackmail."

"On the contrary." Dudley stuffed one pasty in his mouth and flipped the other to Bula. "Used judiciously, it forces confessions from stubborn women who would otherwise never say a word."

"You're satisfied with little," she commented.

"I listen with my heart," he answered.

Unease touched her, but she was distracted by the pounding of feet up the outside stair. She rose as the boys tumbled into the room. "I'll tell her," Kimball shouted.

Clare shouted back, "Your father told *me* to tell her."

"I'll not listen to either of you if you don't know a more mannerly way to enter a room."

Clare stumbled, clumsy perhaps, or Kimball shoved him,

she could not tell, and she ordered, "Stand right here in front of me, both of you."

"You're in trouble," John crooned, "when she gets that tone in her voice."

"She can still make me tremble," Dudley agreed.

"That's enough," she told them, and then to the boys she said, "All right. Lord William sent me a message. To whom did he give it?"

"Me!" Clare said fiercely.

"I'm older!" Kimball complained.

"And capable of more responsibility," she agreed. "So we must teach Clare that same responsibility, and this is how we do it." Kimball said nothing, and she smoothed his hair on the back of his head. "Isn't that right?"

"Aye, my lady."

"Spoken like a true knight," she praised. "Now, Clare, what is the message?"

"Lord William thought you'd like to be alerted," the boy said. "Sir Charles and his party have arrived in the bailey and there's more dust in the distance. The guests are arriving early."

"Oh, my." Saura sank back down on her bench. "Three days early. Praise God I've done so much of the preparations in advance. But nothing can cure a cold meal on the table, and the beds not ready."

In her mind, the truth brought a shiver. The danger crept closer as the guests flocked to the castle. Who now would keep William safe from danger?

thirteen

Looking up from his appraisal of the young stallion, William noticed the young men observing him. They stood in a row outside the stall: Rollo and Dudley on the ends, John and Clare holding Blaise's hand in the middle. The golden afternoon sun touched their fair complexions with color and lit their solemn expressions for his study. Even Blaise, all unknowing of their mission, stared at him with unblinking intensity.

Loosed of his rigid restraint, the destrier reared and bucked. William vaulted to the top of the gate and said, "I'll come out, shall I?" Lowering his feet to the ground, he motioned to the boys to follow him. In the hay-strewn corner beside the stack, he pulled benches into a semicircle and waved them to their seats. They sat two to a bench and William willingly took a stool in the middle. Blaise rolled on the floor in the straw between them.

Resting his great hands one on each knee, William peered

directly at each brother in turn. "You wished to speak to me?"

Given permission, they exchanged glances and Rollo agreed. "About several things, my lord. The first, and perhaps the most important, is the tale John brings us."

William transferred his attention, and John straightened beneath the weight of so many sober eyes. "I don't want you to think I'm trying to increase my own importance by repeating tales, but this is such a fantastic story, I feel I must warn you. I'm fostered with Sir Hutton of Gent. Not a rich landholder, and unable to provide well for the knights he hires." His background given, he took a deep breath; the news he brought rested heavy on his shoulders. "One of those knights left Gent eight days ago to seek his fortune in London and arrived back in only four days."

"He rode like the wind," William commented.

"Aye, for he brought great news. Eustace is dead."

"Eustace?" William puzzled briefly, and then straightened his spine with a snap. "King Stephen's son?"

John nodded. "His heir and eldest son. Is this God's judgment on King Stephen for usurping the throne of England?"

"Perhaps. If 'tis true. Such tales are too often rumors that seep from place to place by unseen channels."

John assured him, "The man is honorable, my lord, and saw enough to convince him."

Sadly, William shook his head. "Stephen has another son, and Matilda's son Henry presses claim—with more right, some believe, than any of Stephen's spawn. What a dreadful maelstrom we find ourselves in! Thank you for alerting me. Had a guest brought the news, I might not have been able to guide the conversation with any intelligence. God knows, with such an occurrence, there'll be fighting among the landholders, the knights, the women."

The boys nodded in unison, even Blaise, who watched them with great wondering eyes. William laughed at the serious imitation on the little boy's face, and ruffled his hair. "But that's not why you came to me. What else preys on your minds?"

Again that brief exchange of glances, and again John was elected to speak. "When our father sent word Saura was to be married, we each took the fastest road to Pertrade and found him wringing his hands and mourning the loss of her lands, but we could gather no more information from that pitiful—" He pulled up short. "We don't know yet why you wish to marry her."

A small smile touched William's mouth. "Is it so strange I should wish to wed a beautiful young woman?"

"Who is blind."

"Damn it!" William had heard that one too many times. "Is that so important?"

Astonished, then pleased, the brothers shifted and settled themselves, now comfortable with his attitude. "Not at all," John said. "But she's more vulnerable than other women. Are you prepared to protect her?"

William's face lost all expression, and his eyes glittered with an intense concentration. "What have you heard?" he asked softly.

"Naught, but she's a woman who needs more than the usual protection. We just—" John stopped short. "Wait. What should we have heard?"

"It's their kidnapping," Clare blurted. All his brothers stared at him. He reddened, and then cringed as William cleared his throat noisily.

"They were kidnapped?" Rollo said with heavy forbearance.

Clare nodded, glancing at William and then at his eldest brother.

"Tell us about it, Clare, lad," Rollo instructed.

William watched Clare steadily, waiting for the boy to decide where his loyalties lay: with his brothers or with the knight who fostered him. At last Clare said to Rollo, "If my Lord William believes you should be informed, he will do so." Then he dropped his head, embarrassed and not at all sure he'd made the right choice.

Rollo patted his hand and John hugged him around the shoulders. William watched them and decided the duty that required him to love his wife's brothers could stretch to hold respect and liking. "There's more to the story than Clare could tell you, and I'd be glad of your helpful surveillance." With an efficient lack of detail, he filled them in on the accident that had blinded him, the kidnapping, the continued threat from a mysterious source. They listened incredulously, saying nothing until he concluded, "I'll not tell you who my primary suspects are. I fear to direct your attention. Watch them all."

"Well!" Rollo exploded. "An incredible tale."

"Do you still approve of my plan to marry your sister?"

To William's surprise, the brothers laughed with various degrees of irony and amazement. "Oh, there's no question about our approval. What good would it do if we disapproved? Saura's made up her mind to have you, and have you she will. She'd never thank us for our interference."

"Then why doesn't she want to wed?" William demanded.

Rollo asked sharply, "Why do you say so, my lord?"

"Oh, she'll do it, but with reluctance. She'd rather live in the shadows, accepting bits of my attention and depending upon my goodwill." His bitterness rang out, and one by one the brothers dropped their gazes from his. William deduced more from their lack of response than they desired. "So you know why. Explain this puzzle to me, please, for I ache with the blow to my . . . my pride."

The boys looked to Dudley, expecting him to speak for them. "That's her legacy from my father," he said gently.

"How can you say that?" William asked. "He gave her nothing."

"Like the evil fairy at the christening, my father gifted us all with something vile."

William stared at them. They no longer sat with negligent grace, but shifted as if the benches had developed splinters. Dudley explained, "We are men, unscarred, outwardly perfect. But inside ourselves, Theobald has affected us." Dudley touched the simple crucifix that hung around his neck, the first sign of nervousness William had seen him make. "John will not drink wine, in any amount. He fears the monster who dwells inside every man and waits for a lack of control to pounce. Rollo would never beat his wife, no matter how richly she deserved it. He abhors cruelty to women. I, well, I thank God my vocation frees me from the complexities of family, for I bear a great fear of hurting someone with word or deed."

"What about me?" Clare asked with innocent trust.

Dudley smiled at him. "You're perfect." Clare still stared up at him, waiting, and he said, "Sometimes I think you're just the slightest bit timid."

With the sudden appearance of a summer storm, Clare's eyes filled with tears.

"In sooth, you think he's timid?" William remarked. "I hadn't noticed."

The boy's smile appeared as suddenly as his tears, and Dudley winked at William.

"I understand," William said soberly. "Must this little one carry a scar, also?"

Blaise piped up in clear tones, "I have a scab on my knee and one on each elbow, but Mama says they won't scar."

William stared, astonished.

John chuckled. "Is that the first time you've heard him speak?"

"Aye." His gaze roved over the brothers, stiff with pride and amusement. "Does he understand all?"

"And says little," John agreed. "But when he talks, he'll be our diplomat, he will. Our father's afraid of him, our little stepmother protects him. She's worthless as a chatelaine, but fiercely protective as a mother."

Rubbing his hands across his eyes, William said, "Tell me then, what is Saura's scar?"

"A feeling of unworthiness."

Remembering the stories Maud had told of Theobald's abuse, William understood. "But I am no great prize."

"False modesty, my lord. You're very rich, the sole heir of a great family. You are the greatest warrior in England, and much admired."

"I've got a roaring temper, I'm rough and uncultured, I'm not interested in politics or life in the court. I sit before a warm fire in the winter and ride the woods in the summer. I like to fight and rut and eat. Do I seem like a great marriage prize?"

"You seem like a simple man."

William shrugged in disclaimer. "Just a man, and one who can hardly believe that Saura struggles with the demons in her depths. She is the most restful woman I know."

"Except when she makes you long to murder her," Rollo complained.

"There's that," William agreed. "Stubborn, outspoken."

"Determined, intelligent." John continued.

"Bossy." Clare put a wealth of disgust in that one word, and everyone laughed.

Dudley folded his hands on his lap and said rapidly, "This does bring up the one subject it's my sworn duty to discuss with you."

As if raised by a spring, Rollo bounded up and dusted his seat. "Time to leave!"

John rose in agreement. "Past time. It has been a pleasure, my lord."

William watched, amazed, as the two brothers fled toward the open door.

"Cowards, come back and sit down," Dudley called. The men stopped at the entrance, pulled by the authority in his voice but reluctant to return. "You know this should be said. You'd be ashamed if ill fell from your reluctance to interfere between man and wife. Lord William will forgive us our intrusion, and mark it down to brotherly concern."

Moving with a creaking reluctance, they dragged themselves back. John seated himself on the corner of the bench and Rollo stood behind, shifting from one foot to the other. Clare stared at his brothers, wondering about their uneasiness, and Blaise tasted a handful of dirt and chewed with obvious enjoyment.

"That's no good for you, my lad. Stand up."

Blaise stood, and William looked him up and down. "How old are you?"

"I have four years, sir," the boy answered promptly.

"Why do you eat dirt?"

"Because it tastes good."

William didn't laugh, a restraint he was pleased with. "Any lad who is old enough to learn to ride a horse is too old to eat dirt."

"Ride a horse?" Blaise lit up, and then asked suspiciously, "Who will teach me?"

"I will," William leaned down so his gaze and the boy's met, "and I never break my promise."

Blaise thought about it. "As you wish, sir, I'll not eat any more dirt. And I never break my promise, either." He wiped his black-rimmed mouth and sat down at William's feet, his arms crossed.

William brushed the boy's black bangs off his forehead. "His hair's too long."

"He's a demon when faced with the shears," John excused.

"I'll take care of it." William sifted a handful of straw over Blaise, and the boy grabbed it and tossed it back. "Now, what bothers you, Dudley?"

The young monk refolded his hands, arranging his fingers with fussy precision, and cleared his throat. "Mother Church teaches us many things about women. They're the descendants of Eve, temptresses all, and for their sin they are subservient to their fathers and then their husbands. They're frivolous and light-minded, and 'tis a husband's duty to discipline his wife. A wife who's undisciplined is a wife who rules the home, to the detriment of all. Women shouldn't be beaten too vigorously, nor with a cane any bigger than the width of a man's thumb." Dudley held up his thumb as illustration, then shifted his gaze from William to his hand and held it there. "Our sister Saura is at times a difficult woman. As we've commented, she is determined and outspoken. She's honest to a fault and, worst of all, she's intelligent."

"I have noticed," William said, heavy with sarcasm.

"Still, she's our sister, and we love her. When our father would strike her, she could not dodge or run and 'twas always a nasty blow. It seems an act of cowardice to strike someone who cannot see."

"What he's trying to say," Rollo interrupted impatiently, "is that if you beat Saura, you'll have to answer to us."

William stopped sprinkling hay over Blaise's head and examined them all. "Because she has no father to advise me, you lads take it on yourselves to do so?"

"Aye, sir." John stared at him, a worried frown wrinkling his brow. "That is, nay, sir. Not to advise you, but to explain that in the absence of a father's defense, Saura has her brothers to stand behind her."

"You're good men," William said, and the brothers relaxed. "Let me reassure you. I seldom even strike my servants. They must display a consistent cruelty to merit such attention, and even then, 'twill not cure an evil temperament." He thought of Hawisa, still stirring up trouble in the kitchen, and sighed. " 'Tis a weak man who must resort to physical discipline. 'Tis necessary your servants respect you for what you do and not just what you are. And I never beat my women, regardless of how much they deserve it."

The boys grinned and stood, shuffling their feet.

"If there's any assistance we can render to prepare for this celebration, my lord? Preparing the games or the stables?" Rollo sounded anxious. "If we stay within the keep, Saura will have us doing women's work."

"My thanks. I can keep you busy with the preparations for the boar hunt two days hence, and for the *mêlée* on the eve before the wedding. Indeed, your work outside would free me to watch over Saura in the keep. When a man gets old, as I am, he'd rather stay within and help with the woman's work than pitch manure outside."

"Oh, ho!" John disagreed. "You wish to keep an eye on the guests, more likely."

"Aye," William sighed. "This rumor of Eustace's death worries me, I cannot lie. What will happen to my poor England now?"

"The way I see it, things will either get better or they will get worse." Charles waved his tankard with drunken emphasis, and stared with innocent surprise at the spreading stain of ale on the cloth.

Outside, the bright summer sun stood high in the sky and warmed the servitors as they finished the preparations for the mêlée, but in the great hall men squabbled and Lord Peter looked grim and forbidding. "If the rumors are correct, and Stephen no longer has a trained heir, by God, who will rule England on Stephen's death? These last black years of disorder will be a mere pittance compared to the horror of England without a king."

"There's Henry, Queen Matilda's son, who demands the throne, and if he doesn't get it, there'll be two armies marching over our lands again." Nicholas swore with delicate precision. "When my churls have to spend their time rebuilding their burned-out huts and the harvest is trampled by the horses, my accounts fall on evil days."

"All you ever care about is the money," Charles sneered. "Like a damn merchant."

Nicholas rose, his face flushed by the insult. " 'Tis better than you! Drunk before the noon meal, and you with not a pot to piss in or a window to throw it out of."

The guests in the great hall, two hundred strong, broke out in a babble of conflicting optimism and pessimism. William stood and pounded on the table with his fist. "Quiet!" he roared. He wished, with all his heart, this tale of Eustace and

Henry hadn't come on the heels of his wedding announcement. The gentry gathered in his hall had marveled at the tidings that Lord William of Miraval would marry, and prepared with all haste to attend. Then the rumor of death and confusion swept the country, and their haste had turned into a flurry. Before the consequences of Stephen's heirless state could take effect, they galloped to Burke to exchange gossip and opinion. They brought their outriders to protect them on the road, they brought their servants, and they all came early to feast and sleep and argue.

The noise slowly faded under William's towering authority, but the sibilant whispers couldn't be completely hushed. "Speculation will avail us nothing. Less than one hundred years ago, William the Conqueror vanquished this island and divided it among his followers, and this bastion will not fall."

"Well spoken." From the stairwell came the cheerful voice of a travel-stained lord. "I come from London this day, riding at all speed to attend your wedding, and I leave great happenings behind."

"Raymond!" William leaped over the bench and strode to his friend. Embracing him, he murmured, "I've been worrying."

"All is well," Raymond murmured back, and then raised his voice. "All's well, and better than it has been these last years of darkness. Stephen will acknowledge Henry as the future king of England."

Frozen with surprise, not a servant moved, not a lord breathed. Total silence descended at last.

"The Angevin pup?" Lord Peter lowered his goblet from his lips. "Have you seen him?"

"Aye, and a grand man he is, too." Raymond strode in. His spurs jingled, his mud-spattered squire limped at his heels, and an excitement lit his cool eyes. "He's everything Stephen is not: decisive, energetic, vigorous. He's an easy man to talk to, but one never presumes on his geniality, for an air of majesty surrounds him like a cloak." Raymond's voice rang with conviction, his hands waved with fervor. "The clerks and the priests are working out the terms of his succession right now. Stephen speaks of adopting Henry as his heir."

"His heir?" Lord Peter said. "Is Eustace really dead, then?"

"Quite dead. He left court in a pique. He realized his father would be forced to give up the throne to Henry, and it didn't sit well with him. They say Eustace plundered Bury St. Edmunds Abbey in the morning, sat at noon for his meal, and choked on a dish of eels."

William meditated on the news with grim intentness. "A fitting end to the impious Eustace *and* the eels."

"Stephen has another son. What about him?" Lord Peter asked.

"His other son will be satisfied with the lands his father ruled before he became king of England, and Stephen saves face with this adoption. He says Henry's succeeding him by designation. I say Henry's succeeding him through his mother, the rightful queen of England. He's collecting his birthright."

"What terms are they discussing?" Lord Peter asked.

"That's the sting. Henry will not recognize the lands Stephen granted his followers, for Henry considers Stephen a usurper." There was a gasp in the room, and Raymond's gaze swept them all, bright and amused. "Oh, yes, good people. There will be changes in England."

William watched him and judged him to be drunk with the narcotic of power. "Bring Lord Raymond a cup of ale to quench his thirst and escort him to the head table where," he glanced and smiled, "where my lady has already ordered a place set. Can you eat and talk at the same time, Raymond?"

"I can't bring my dirt to table." Raymond laughed. "I carry half of England on my boots."

Saura came forward from where she stood. "I've ordered warm water taken to the solar, and there you can wash with all speed and return to these waiting ears."

With a nod of acceptance, Raymond followed her as she led him to her room. Every eye in the hall followed them, eager for the tales of monarchy from one who knew the truth.

Saura waved at the steaming bowls, the handmaidens and towels, and apologized, "Forgive me if I don't help you bathe, my lord, but I'm needed in the hall. I leave you my competent maid, and if you desire anything, please command her."

"Wait." Raymond stepped up to her and tilted her chin up. "So you're Lady Saura. We haven't officially met."

A tiny smile tilted her mouth. "Aye, I'd forgotten. Events have rushed at me with such scrambled speed I neglect the courtesies."

"You're beautiful," Raymond breathed. "I hadn't expected that."

"Beautiful?" She froze with a kind of horror. Beautiful. She didn't want to hear "beautiful." Just last night as she hurried across the bailey from the kitchen, she'd thought she heard a hoarse voice call her beautiful. She'd thought she'd heard footsteps beside her, just out of reach. She'd thought a menace stalked her, but when she turned to confront it, nothing was there.

"You *are* beautiful," Raymond said again, bringing her back from her imaginings.

"And you're tired," Saura answered. "For the controlled

and quiet Lord Raymond has loosened the bonds of his restraint." She pushed his hand away from her chin, and both his hands immediately fastened on her shoulders, halting her before she could step away.

"I told Lord Peter about you."

"What?" she asked, dumbfounded. "When?"

"All those moons ago, when William had been blinded and needed someone to help him, I told Lord Peter about Saura of Roget."

She searched her mind. "Had you been a visitor at Pertrade?"

"Nay." His hands kneaded her shoulders and she thought he smiled. "But I'd heard stories from a knight who had. Fantastic stories about the beautiful blind girl who knew everything, who walked without help and kept house for her miserly stepfather. When Lord Peter was desperate, I passed the stories on. I am responsible for your marriage."

"Oh, so you're the man to blame." She ignored the stroking fingers and put frost into her voice. "Why didn't you address me when last you visited?"

"Address the mysterious Lady Saura who improved the cooking at Burke? If you chose not to show yourself, who was I to speak?"

Her thoughts whirled. He'd known about her, but never told his friends the truth. There were depths to Raymond, depths she didn't understand. Should she trust him?

He teased, "Were you hiding in the corner?"

" 'Twas easier," she excused herself.

"And now, poor thing, William has forced you to perform for all."

"I pay the price for marriage," she said calmly.

"The marriage every woman insists on."

"Not my woman." William strolled in, blocking the view

from the great hall. With great deliberation, he removed Raymond's hands from her shoulders. "She'd rather be my meretrix."

"But William is forever honorable," Raymond mocked. "He insists on marriage." He rolled his neck in weariness, and a faint regret tinged his voice. "God, I must be tired."

William wrapped an arm around Saura's waist and turned her away, but Raymond called, "Stop!" Stepping in front of her, he examined her, then ordered the maid, "Wet me a cloth." With gentle hands, he took the rag and wiped at Saura's chin. "I dirtied your face."

She laughed, a pure, musical sound of pleasure, and he stared with an air of enchantment. "Welcome to my heart, Lady Saura." He leaned down and touched her cheek with his lips.

"Many thanks, my lord." She curtsied.

Gruffly, William ordered, "Wipe the dirt off her cheek, Raymond, so we can go out and finish our meal." Grinning, Raymond did as William ordered. William picked up her hand and played with her fingers, observing her creamy skin and the slight flush that underlay it. She *was* beautiful, and he couldn't fault Raymond for seeing it. But he preferred those past days when she was his to look on, and his alone.

Had she ever been his? It seemed so long ago, he could hardly remember. She looked like a princess, untouched, pure; and wanton with the curves of her body to tempt him. He pulled her a step closer and she came willingly, her hip pressing against his thigh. The touch liberated the thought from his inner mind; kiss her and show Raymond whose lady she was. He pulled her closer again, put his hand on her waist, brought her flush against him. Her hands clasped his arms to keep her balance and she raised her face with sweet readiness. A sudden rosy pleasure at the warmth of their two bodies filled him, and he raised her onto her toes. In a voice as smooth and golden as honey, he murmured, "You're short for me, but I like it. I like lifting you to me, I like towering above you. It makes me feel that only I can protect you and keep you from all harm."

It was heaven and hell. He shut his eyes, blotting out the world, and with searching instinct found her lips. They were open slightly, encouraging him to feats of madness, enticing him to plunge in and create fantasies for them both. He did not. He brushed her with his lips, dragged the grain of his beard across her mouth, and drove her to cling to him in spasms of joy. He wanted to fling her on the bed that sat close at hand, but remnants of his conscience refused for reasons he couldn't remember.

His inner mind, the one that first suggested this madness, kept insisting he should pleasure her now, but he nobly ignored it and dragged himself back out of this pit.

Saura clung to him, whimpering deep in her throat, and held him to her with one hand at his waist. He shut out the world for one more moment, savoring the sound and the feel of her, and then he set her down and opened his eyes. That was almost a mistake. Her head tilted back, still begging for attention. Her lips were swollen, her cheeks flushed a fiery red, and tendrils of dark hair etched her forehead.

By our Lady of the Fountain, could he wait another day?

"A convincing demonstration."

A voice interrupted William's intense scrutiny and brought his gaze up to stare blankly at the speaker.

"The priests say 'tis better to marry than to burn, but it seems you will do both."

William cleared his head. This was Raymond who teased them, Raymond who watched with kind interest as he slavered over his woman. Glancing toward the open door, he saw the craning heads of the too-curious servants and the grinning folk at the head table. Reaching out, William took Saura by the back of the head and brought her close to him once more, to bury her head in his shirt and hide her face. He stroked her hair, soothing her, and answered Raymond with rough humor, "If this be hellfire, the sinners would jump into the coals."

Raymond laughed, his gaze on Saura. "Trust you to steal the beautiful heiress before any of the rest of us has a chance."

The sharp agony of unfulfilled desire made William want to strike his dearest friend for gazing at her in appreciation. Instead he turned the subject with admirable composure. "There'll be a mêlée after we've eaten. Will you be too tired to participate?"

Raymond tossed his filthy cloak to his squire and stretched his arms toward the ceiling. "Today I could kill a boar bare-handed."

"We hunted boar yesterday," William answered drily.

"Do we eat it today?"

"Aye. Come out and have a slice."

"I could eat the whole boar."

Saura broke into their sparring, turning her face out of William's chest. "Hurry then, my lord. We await you in the great hall." She withdrew from William's grasp and tucked her hand into his arm.

"You look well kissed," he told her. "Are you ready to face them all?"

"I'm proud that all know my lord desires me." She tossed her head in disdain of opinion, and privately thought she was glad that all would know he'd protect her. Again she remembered that ghoulish whisper in the yard, and she

pressed closer to William. He led her back toward the room
filled with gossiping folk.

He had watched the embrace, watched as his friend swept
that woman off her feet and kissed her until both were senseless, and he raged and he lusted. Raged at William, powerful
lord of all he desired. Lusted after Saura, delicate and misguided enough to want William. When he had first seen her,
he'd only wanted to crush her, stomp her into the earth for
reviving William's appetite for life. Now he wanted her as
William wanted her, wanted her because she was William's;
wanted her to savor her beauty; wanted her because William
wanted her.

He clenched his fists. He'd woo her, be her unseen ad-
mirer, assure her of her beauty when no one else could hear.
He'd touch her, too, soothe the fears she'd felt when he
called her beautiful. He'd take her from William before he
killed him. Then he'd be satisfied. When William was humbled and then murdered, he'd surely be satisfied.

fourteen

Raymond seated himself, and answered the shouted questions between mouthfuls of food. Admiration for Henry colored his every word. "Henry's twenty-one, young enough to be energetic. He wears out his associates with his breakneck vigor. He seldom sits, his senses are always alert. But he rules his lands in France with wisdom."

"To be a duke is not to be the king," William objected.

"Between the inheritance he received from his father, the counties he rules for his mother, and the counties he acquired from his marriage with Eleanor, he rules a greater area of France than his overlord, King Louis. He can handle the mantle of royalty for England."

"Stephen?" Lord Peter asked.

Shaking his head, Raymond delicately discouraged any hopes about the current king's health. "Stephen's a broken man. The death of his son put the final period on his hopes.

The useless campaigns, the treachery of the barons—he could never solidify his claims to the throne."

" 'Tis treason you speak," Nicholas suggested, and Raymond turned and considered him.

"I don't even know what treason is anymore. If my words encourage the growth of a healthy England, then let those words spring forth." He grinned at Nicholas, showing all his teeth. "If any lord wishes to steal and kill and plunder, he'd better do it now, and do it well. Law will return to the land. Henry will bring it, and woe betide the man who gets in his way." He swung to look at Charles, then back at Nicholas, and a message passed from Raymond to his friends.

Saura shivered at the tone of his voice. As she'd promised herself, she'd listened to the speeches and they left her troubled and confused.

Raymond meant more than he said, Nicholas said too little, and Charles mumbled in the excess of drink. Or was it guilt? She didn't know, she couldn't tell. Her usual sharp instincts were clouded by fear for William, and since last night, fear for herself.

It seemed so odd, but her unease had been growing during the past week. Some instinct warned her of treachery and stealth. She hadn't really even been surprised when that voice hoarsely declared her beautiful, but she had been frightened. And doubtful. Her fancies had conjured a menace; now her fancies conjured a voice and a presence. And her perplexity grew, for she still felt that menace. She felt it right now. She flinched; someone was staring at her. Even when he didn't speak, even when she couldn't hear that hoarse whisper, she could feel those eyes on her, and it made her want to squirm.

"Saura?" William spoke close in her ear, interrupting her discomfort and patting balm on her fears. " 'Tis time."

Blank for a moment, she remembered and grimaced. "For the *mêlée*? Of course."

He helped her away from the table, and she retained his hand. "I'll help arm you," she informed him.

"My squire is here for that," he said.

"As if I didn't know." She tugged at him. "Come, you'll find no better help than I."

"I'm too easily persuaded by you, my lady," he rumbled, following her like a lamb.

"You're a fraud," she scoffed. "You tell me I am in charge, when you only do as I suggest if it follows your own convenience."

"That I should be reduced to such chicanery," he mourned with false sadness. He checked behind; young Guilliame followed on their heels. The three of them entered the solar and he saw his clothes laid out on the bed. "Are you both to be my squires?"

"You're not the first man I've dressed for battle," Saura answered, shutting the door. She found the stool that waited beside the bed and dragged it to the center of the room where William waited. Climbing up, she pulled his embroidered surcoat off and carefully passed it to Guilliame. Guilliame folded it, placed it in the open chest and returned with the padding William wore beneath his hauberk. With a smooth teamwork, Saura and the squire stripped him and reclothed him, then hefted the hauberk over his head and buckled his sword on. The hauberk shone, free from rust, and his sword was honed to a fine edge. The leather of his boots gleamed with oil and the leather of his gloves moved with supple ease. His gilded spurs clanked as he strode around the room, pleased with his return to the world of the knight.

"But I have no helmet." He frowned. "My own was crushed in the accident. Didn't the armorer send one up?"

"We thought you could try this one first," Saura replied calmly. From her own chest, she pulled a fine helmet, banded with iron and protected by a nose guard. "It was my father's. 'Tis the only memento of him I have retained. How my mother saved it, I'll never know. He was a large man, too, they tell me, and perhaps this will fit you. If not, there's another waiting."

She held it out to him with both hands, and he took it, handling it with care. She said, "The armorer inspected it. He says it's in good condition, although old-fashioned. The conical shape is called a basinet, I believe?"

He examined her face, and she looked serene, waiting only for his approval. Red and lush as an apple in the fall, her lips curved in a gentle smile. Like a prayer, her hands rested before her, and she waited in delicate expectancy. Trying the helmet on, he was surprised to find it fit. Big hands, big feet, big head, his father teased him, but it seemed Saura's father fit the description also. "Thank you, my lady. I am honored to wear your father's helmet."

"You're sure it fits properly?" she questioned. " 'Tis not so large it slips, not so small it binds?"

" 'Tis perfect," he assured her.

"In that case, it is my wedding present to you." A smile broke across her face like sunshine. "Wear it as my token."

He stepped close and caught her in his arms, and her hands flew up around his neck in a desperate hug. The links of his armor pricked at her, but she clenched him in a fervor and then broke away. "I'll be waiting for you to bring me the prizes." She smiled at him again, and her mouth trembled. He leaned down to kiss away her silliness. The kiss, of necessity, was light and insignificant. The nose guard bumped her cheek, and they were aware of Guilliame waiting in the room. But as William strode out, she touched her lips with her fingers, treasuring the token he left her in return.

Maud entered the room almost before William had left. "Come, m'lady, I'll take ye to your seat in the gallery. As the bride, ye have the place of honor."

"Where everyone can watch me, I suppose," Saura said glumly. "I'll have to appear confident and at ease."

"William's a great warrior," Maud soothed. "Ye *can* be confident and at ease. He'll not disappoint ye."

"He has enemies." She bit her lip. Should she tell Maud about the feeling that had been creeping up on her these last few days? The feeling that grew as the crowd around them swelled? The feeling of malevolence, the sound of a whisper in the dark?

"He has more friends. Ye're being ridiculous."

Maud scolded her, and the worry slipped away. Her maid's common sense helped persuade her she deceived herself, and she listened to Maud and was comforted.

"Lord Peter's fighting, and he assured me he'd never let his son out of his sight. Not even a fool would harm Lord William in his own bailey surrounded by his own family and friends."

"Not a fool," she said soberly. "But a madman."

Maud grasped Saura's shoulders and shook her firmly. "Give Lord William credit. He'll not widow ye before ye're a wife." She brushed Saura's gown with her hand, straightened her belt, resettled her veil. "Ye are worthy to be the center of all eyes. Ye're gorgeous in these clothes Lord Peter gifted ye with. Now go out and make him proud. Ye're the hostess. Ye're the bride. Ye're the guest of honor. Remember who ye are, and never lower your chin."

As the stern encouragement sank in, Saura nodded and took Maud's arm. "I'm ready."

She made her way outside to the gallery where the ladies watched the mêlée, and she did look like a queen. More than one guest envied her the blue linen bliaut that turned her eyes to the color of hyacinths. The scarlet cotte accented the black wing of her hair and the belt, woven with scarlet and blue and precious gold thread, focused the gaze of all on the slender sway of her hips. Young and beautiful—and blind— she had stolen a great marriage prize. She settled herself in the chair on the little raised dais as if she could see the fighting, and she appeared to have her nose in the air, for she neither smiled nor greeted anyone.

She had no friends among these neighbors. The anarchy of the past fourteen years had limited travel. Bandits ruled the road and dishonorable lords laid waste and took what they wanted. It took a major event to bring the people out, and then they rode quickly, surrounded by bodyguards and bristling with armament. No respectable lady would visit Theobald's infamous castle, ruled by a cowardly lord and rife with licentiousness.

Saura's years of isolation had effectively placed her away from noble society, and many who attended William's wedding were of the highest nobility. Earls rubbed shoulders with landed barons. Their wives knew one another from other weddings, other funerals. They traded their sons for fostering. Saura felt the great gap when the women called greetings with the comradery of old acquaintanceship. All around her buzzed the news of babes newborn and pregnancies just begun, of grandparents who ailed and husbands who strayed. She wished she knew someone, just one person, to whom she could speak and smile and not feel as if she were breaking in like a bold-faced hussy.

She'd never felt so unsure. She was failing as hostess. She knew how to feed a hungry army, how to provision a castle, but never had she been forced to mingle with a group of strange women. Her hands were clumsy and she tucked her feet far beneath her skirt.

Why did it have to be now? She desperately needed someone to tell her what was happening on the field in front of her. She squeezed her fingers tightly in her lap. She didn't think she could bear to sit there like some marble statue while her love fought to recover his skill and his pride and she was not to know what happened.

Anxiety wrapped itself around her as she heard the teams lining up on opposite sides of the bailey. The clank of spears and the muffled snort of horses, the smell of the sunshine on the grass and the slowly rising dust marked the preparations of the knights. The gallery sat against the outer stone curtain wall, out of the sun and out of the way, and she knew a wooden wall protected the rows of benches from the accidental incursions of horse and knight. Mêlées were dangerous, dangerous enough that the Church strove to control them with bans, but for the knights who fought for prizes and glory and practice, they were a glorious imitation when battles were too few.

Lord Peter shouted for quiet, and announced the prize. A war-horse, an unbroken destrier from his own stables, would be presented to the warrior who was judged most deserving. The destrier snorted and pranced, displaying his fierce temperament. Amid jeers and laughter, Lord Peter assured them he would take himself and his son out of the running, for all knew no one could vanquish such knights as they. Saura heard the panting of the stable boys as they fought the destrier back into the stable. She heard Lord Peter ride to his end of the field, and then someone thrust a handkerchief into her hand and whispered, "Hold it aloft, then drop it!" She did, and with a roar of hooves and the war shouts of the men, the mêlée began. She heard the first clashes as lance met shield and heard the ring of the swords as those un-horsed fought on foot. Women stood around her, calling the names of their men in encouragement.

"Wilfred, get up and beat that blackguard!"

"A fine stroke, Jourdain!"

"Did you see Philip's lance shatter! Oh, he's angry now."

No one mentioned William's name, and Saura's muscles contracted, winding her in coils of fearful imagination. When the ladies' shouting suddenly stopped, halted by some extraordinary circumstance, Saura blenched and begged, "What is it?"

The woman next to her, the wife of an earl and daughter of an earl, and outspoken with the privilege of rank, told her, "I've never seen this before. Lord Nicholas does not fight today, and he's coming to sit with the ladies!" The horror in Lady Jane's voice made clear the indecency of such an action.

"He says he doesn't ride well or fight well," Saura said timidly, unsure how to respond to such outrage.

"Then he should go out on the field and get knocked off his horse," the lady next to her snapped. "Do you think all of these knights before us are warriors? Some of them are already so drunk they can hardly sit a horse, like Sir Charles. God's teeth, he's down already! Some of them would do better if their wives wore their armor."

Saura laughed in relief. "Are they so awful? Then perhaps I shouldn't fret, for my William is a great warrior."

The ring of pride made Lady Jane look at her sharply, but before she could speak, Nicholas's soft voice interrupted. "May I sit with you, Lady Saura?" He sounded polite and

urbane, but he failed to wait for her consent as he squeezed
onto the end of the bench, pushing Lady Jane aside. Saura
could hear Lady Jane sputtering, and she wished with all her
heart Nicholas hadn't made her the cynosure of all eyes.
Then he gathered her hand in his. "You looked so alone,
sitting here, and my heart twisted with pity. I knew how you
must be worried. I wished to tell you about the dangers William
is encountering. I thought it would be better than leaving
you to your imagining."

She cried, "Aye, oh aye! Thank you!" Her hand tightened
on his; she was ridiculously grateful to him, forgetting the
negative reactions of the women, forgetting everything but
the opportunity to "see" her beloved in action.

He watched in silence for a moment, and then clicked his
tongue in distress. "He fights so carelessly, and his skill has
grown rusty with disuse. He'll be killed for sure. Overconfidence,
dear lady, overconfidence."

He patted her hand with his damp palm, and she drew a
deep breath. "If that's all you're going to tell me, you can—"

Painfully, his fingers tightened on hers, and he leapt to his
feet. "Beware, William! Watch the swordsman behind you!"

On the field, William surveyed the six opposing knights
galloping toward him, and he bellowed with laughter. Gripping
his sword, he wondered how he could have ever
doubted his fighting ability. Some of his friends had engaged
him cautiously, granting him time to warm to his sword
work, but they soon learned their lesson. They lay on the
ground, spitting out dust and swearing.

Wheeling his destrier to meet the oncoming charge, he
disarmed one knight while his horse lashed out behind and

threw another down. He ducked beneath the wild swing of the youngest and pushed him off his saddle with a slam of his shield. Then he turned to thrust and dance away. His long reach held them at bay, while the grace of his large body enabled him to escape their swings by a hair's breadth. The knights challenging him faded beneath his strokes like blades of grass in a whirlwind. Time after time he disarmed his challengers until even the few remaining on the field avoided him in hopes of retaining their reputations.

All in vain. Drunk with the joy of fighting, he sought them out and vanquished them. At last he alone remained, and he raised his sword and howled in triumph. His erstwhile enemies flocked on the field, congratulating him, pounding his back and shouting insults that sounded like admiration. He dragged off his helmet, his sweaty hair sticking to his forehead, and tore off his gloves. Young Guilliame appeared to take the accoutrements in charge, grinning with reflected glory.

William loved it. He revelled in the praise and adulation he had scorned and then missed without realizing it. He lingered until he glanced toward the gallery and saw Saura, standing alone on the dais with the still expression that bespoke intense listening. Breaking away from the men, he strode toward his lady, glancing neither left nor right, and as he neared, Lady Jane took his bride by the hand and led her to him. Saura dragged at first, but when Lady Jane spoke to her she brightened and hurried. She ran the last few feet, rocking him back with the impact of her small body against his. Pleased by her frantic embrace, he picked her up with one arm beneath her knees and one behind her shoulders and swung her around. "I've beaten them all! All!" he exulted, and she shrieked with equal parts of exasperation and pleasure.

At last he slowed his wild cavorting, and she grabbed his ears. "By the Virgin, William, never frighten me so again. My heart stopped with every battle you fought. I don't know whether to slap you or love you," she told him.

"Oh, love me," he said with naughty intent, and she swept her hands over his face.

"Your dimples are showing, and there's not one sign of regret for the worry you've caused me," she pronounced. "Why should I love a scoundrel such as you?"

Beneath her hand, he rearranged his features into a parody of distress and she took hold of his neck and shook as hard as she could. It was like trying to rattle a rock column, its only effect to bring his face closer and closer until his breath was hers. More than she could stand, less than she wanted, she kissed him greedily.

That kiss didn't taste as if she wanted him only so she could have her land. It didn't taste like lust or mild affection. It tasted like a deep and desperate fear for his life, and for the first time he hoped for everything. She slanted her mouth, as if she wanted to absorb his essence; her hands tangled in his beard and tugged him closer. Carried away by her passion, he let her legs slide down his body and held her like a child; one arm clasped around her back, one arm held her thighs. Her feet dangled, her little body trembled, and power swept through him, unequalled by the pleasure of fighting. Raising his head with the intention of finding the nearest bed, he discovered with a jolt that he stood on the field of battle. The sun shone with a westerly slant, the dust from the mêlée had settled, and he still wore his hauberk and boots. The quiet bound the air, and all around them people stared with unabashed curiosity or appetite. As his gaze swept them, the men whistled lasciviously, nudging each other and chuckling, amused to find such a mighty warrior vanquished by such a gentle weapon. With a cool assessment, the ladies of the gallery stared at them.

"Son!" Lord Peter called, and William suspected he'd been saying it for a long time. "Son, if you'll put Lady Saura down, we'll award the destrier and everyone can prepare for the evening meal."

William blinked at his father.

"We have more guests to greet." Lord Peter enunciated every word as if he knew how slowly William's mind was working. "Saura's vassals arrived during the fight and were greatly impressed with your prowess in the saddle."

He gestured, and William found three men standing not too far away, dressed in traveling clothes and watching him with a staid disapproval. Saura's head lifted from its spot on his shoulder, and he looked down at her dazed face with its swollen lips and rosy skin. She distracted him, pulling him back with the sensual promise she projected, but Lord Peter whacked him on the back and said, "Let us present the award *now*."

Signs of cognizance appeared in Saura's face, and reluctantly William let her slide all the way down to her feet. He steadied her with one hand under her arm until she no longer swayed, and thanked God for the hauberk that protected his form from exploring eyes. "Who wins the prize of the destrier?" he asked.

Lord Peter suggested, "Sir Osbert of Carraville must surely claim the prize, don't you agree, Lady Saura?"

She nodded. "All the praise I heard was for Sir Osbert of Carraville, so there can be no doubt. Sir Osbert of Carraville it is."

Osbert whooped, and William grinned at the man's unrestrained glee. The prize enriched his penniless state and created new markets for his knightly services. No matter that he was clearly second in the mêlée; to be second to William was no shame at all.

As the other knights and ladies flocked onto the field to congratulate the champion, William beckoned to Saura's vassals. They presented themselves at once, bowing to the lord and then one by one taking Saura's hand.

"Do you remember me, my lady? Sir Francis of Wace."

"Sir Francis. Of course, I remember. I'll never forget playing with your daughter Elly. She was just my age. I trust she fares well?"

"Married, with three little ones herself," Sir Francis bragged.

"Do you remember me, my lady? Sir Denton of Belworth."

"Sir Denton!" She took his hand and squeezed and twisted it.

"My lady!" he objected. "I can't wrestle with you now!"

"Why not?"

"You're my lady! 'Tis not respectful!"

She sighed and relaxed her grip. "Indeed I do remember you, but you weren't *Sir* Denton when last we met."

Before William's eyes, the young man's dignity slipped, and he grinned adoringly at Saura. "I've been knighted."

"I'm proud of you. 'Twas your greatest dream." She turned to William. "This knight used to let me tag along after him when I was but a child. He'd tease me and laugh at me, and he taught me to arm wrestle."

Denton's ruddy complexion blushed a deeper red, and with an alarmed glance at William he protested, "Now let's not carry tales, my lady!"

"Of course not." She smiled. "Perhaps we can meet and talk later. May I enquire about your father?"

"We lost him, my lady, in the bloody disorder two winters ago."

"I'm sorry to hear it. He was a good man and a true servant." Saura patted his hand and then released it.

The last man took her hand hesitantly. "I'm Sir Gilbert of Hartleburgh."

"Of Hartleburgh?" She looked startled. "Where is Sir Vachel?"

"He died and Lord Theobald replaced him with my humble self."

No one said a word. It was an affront to Saura that she'd not heard of the change, but an overture of friendship that Sir Gilbert had come to her wedding. She had the power to replace him, if she chose, or the power to retain him, and his appearance before her was a gesture of faith on his part. Just because her stepfather had appointed him didn't mean he was incompetent or cruel. Saura knew that; knew, too, that the lands around Hartleburgh would be better off under the steady maintenance of one man. "I welcome you, Sir Gilbert. I look forward to receiving your pledge of faith and hearing an accounting of the harvest."

"Aye, my lady, and I look forward to giving it."

She turned back to the castellan of Wace. "Where is Sir Frazer? Does he come behind you?"

Clearly, this question he didn't relish. "Not exactly, my lady. Sir Frazer. . . ."

She raised an eyebrow at his hesitation.

"Sir Frazer refused the invitation."

"Refused?" William negligently lifted a curl from Saura's shoulder and tucked it beneath her veil, seeming to pay only a bit of attention to the conversation. "He was too sick to travel, then?"

"Nay, Lord William."

"His wife was in childbed, his children languished with a fever, and he'll arrive as soon as they're cured?"

"Nay, my lord."

"He refuses to pay fealty to his lady?" William lifted his eyes, but they were not casual. His gaze bore into the uncomfortable vassals, and they shifted from one foot to the other with uneasy attention. "Sir Frazer refuses my Lady Saura, my wife, what is due her?"

"Aye, my lord."

The blue of William's eyes chilled with frost. "Then let him prepare for siege."

fifteen

"I have a poem, dedicated to my lady of love."

The servants cleared the last of the cold meal from the table and refilled the tankards of ale and filled pitchers of wine. The afternoon's combatants compared bruises and lacerations. They listened to tales of combat and laughed at the defeated, and ignored Nicholas as he stood on his bench at the head table and babbled about a poem. He persisted until Lady Jane tapped for silence, and under her commanding presence the head table quieted in exasperated courtesy. Then he cleared his throat and began a series of verses aimed at the bride's heart.

Everyone listened politely. Could they do less with Lady Jane's eye severely affixed to their faces? William listened politely. Could he do less for his guest? Love for a lady was a fashionable commodity, newly arrived from the courts of love in Aquitaine. A knight chose a lady and dedicated his songs to her, languished after her, wore her token into battle. They said that Henry's wife, Eleanor, encouraged the troubadours with her love of poetry.

These paltry verses didn't mean anything, 'twas just a young man's affection. Nicholas had never made a fool of himself over a woman; William should feel amused and proud of the way he worshipped Saura.

These poor verses didn't mean anything. Just because William wanted to keep Saura for himself, he had no reason to grow violent. If he stood up and cracked Nicholas's skull as he longed to, his guests would laugh their guts out and then tease him forever.

These clichéd verses didn't mean anything; so why was he afraid to turn and look at Saura and see the glow of pleasure on her sweet face?

"Describe Lady Jane, please."

The matter-of-fact interest in his dearling's voice struck to the heart of his agony. She didn't sound overcome with admiration, she sounded preoccupied. Turning his head, he stared at his lady. Lord Peter's squire leaned over her shoulder, and she was whispering instructions to him. The boy bowed and backed away, and Saura took William's sleeve and tugged it. "Describe Lady Jane, please." Saura had an advantage over her guests, he realized. She couldn't see Jane's strict gaze. She listened to Nicholas until her boredom conquered her good manners, and then she returned to directing the servants unobtrusively and seeking information in her soft voice.

"Lady Jane?" His eyes sought the woman down the table, and his voice sharpened as he flipped crumbs from the tablecloth. "Why? Was she rude to you?"

"Not at all. She's the sort of woman who wants to do the correct thing for me, but doesn't know how."

"She'd never ask, either," William said with exasperation.

He spoke through clenched teeth, annoyed beyond reason by this ridiculous passion Nicholas displayed for his bride, but he controlled himself and continued, "All the niceties of etiquette are at her fingertips and she'd never admit to being unsure in any situation."

"You don't like her," she observed.

By not looking directly at the proclaiming Nicholas, he could study the lady in question. "Nay, 'tis not that. She's a little older than I, just old enough to remember the time before good King Henry had died, and she never lets me forget it. All she longs for is the peace so she can command her position at court." His fists clenched tight around his goblet as Nicholas developed his fantasy.

"It doesn't sound as if you like her," she said dubiously, misinterpreting his anger.

"Nay, nay. I like her. She's rigid with manners and she never wavers from them." He drank a gulp of wine, and his attention skipped away from Nicholas, directed by the sharp poke of painful memory. "She's got a good heart. When a young man does something cruel or stupid, she'll roast him over an open pit until he screams with contrition. Then she binds his wounds and hides the evidence and no other word is spoken."

With intuitive understanding, she guessed, "She saved you from a bad mistake."

"When I was a squire and far from home. Too young to be on my own, with the cocky arrogance of a new-minted man." Moving his lips close to her ear, he whispered, "There's nothing worse than a woman who's always right. Especially when she really *is* always right."

Saura laughed out loud, pleased that the tension in his voice had diminished under her prodding. That voice of his was a seduction: warm, golden, with a manly rumble that vibrated her deep within. She didn't like to hear the higher notes of stress sneak in; with a shock, she discovered she preferred the job of pleasing William over any other. When had that happened?

She put her hand up to his chin to keep him close, knowing she should be directing the servants but unable to resist the draw of his skin. The proximity of his big body warmed her with more than an outer heat, and as they approached the wedding day, the day of their last mating moved farther back in time. It was hard to wait patiently for tomorrow night when her body was chanting, "Now, now." Pressing herself down on the hard bench, hoping for its distraction, she asked, "Did you love her?"

"Jane?" He jumped and then chuckled with astonishment. He rubbed his eyes between his thumb and forefinger to clear his gaze and then studied the lady. "Nay. She's tall and spare, with a waterfall of sagging chins beneath the primary one that recedes into her face. Her face is bony and her veil would never let one wisp of hair escape for fear of retribution. Her household walks in fear of a frown and her husband's so henpecked he doesn't even know it."

"You adore her."

"Aye." He slid one arm around her waist and pulled Saura closer, until the fur trim at his shoulder tickled her cheek. As her body contacted his, he seemed to relax that strange tautness that held him in thrall. "I was fostered in her household until I made plans to run away with her daughter."

"William!" She reared back, awestruck.

"Her stepdaughter, really," he hastened to assure her. "Lady Jane was the young bride when I came to the household. Lord Nevil taught me war, and she taught me deportment."

"Running away with the daughter of your lord is deportment?"

"God's teeth!" He covered her mouth with his palm. "No one knows except Lady Jane and me, and that's not a story I'd want noised abroad."

"Then tell me," she threatened from behind his hand. "Or I'll stand on the bench and shout it out."

"That 'tis time to take me to your chamber?"

She kissed his palm, her tongue bathing the calluses, and he jerked his hand away. "I'd shout it out if you'd do it."

"Scandalmonger."

She leaned into his mouth and brushed it softly with hers. "If you'd not insisted on marriage, I'd be in your bed at this moment."

"Your brothers warned me about you." His lips moved with his words, his breath tickled her. "Dudley said. . . ."

Her kiss travelled to his neck, and he froze with anticipation.

"Dudley?" she encouraged.

"Dudley said you were Eve."

Tired of the oft-repeated slur, she pulled her face away from him. "Not that again." Then in a different tone, "Not this again." Whistles of encouragement from their guests brought her back from her personal heaven; although why she considered a conversation with a thick-headed male to be heaven, she didn't know. It must be a female quirk that her mother had never warned her about.

Beside her, William withdrew from their embrace with slow emphasis. "Don't leap away," he warned her with a growl. "Make it clear we stop because we want to, not because of their foolery."

"Slow down, son," his father mocked. "You'll have her soon. Only one more day."

"Only one more night," William retorted with a mock heaviness, turning to pick up his abandoned wine.

"Stop enticing him, Saura," Lady Jane said. "He becomes desperate if not fed."

"He's not the only one facing desperation," Saura answered, seeking her own cup. William brought his to her lips, whispering, "Here, love," and held it while she drank. As she finished, he leaned forward and licked the pungent red wine from her lips and the corners of her mouth while their audience laughed their appreciation.

"Your poetry inspires the lovebirds, Nicholas," Charles mocked.

The jerk of William's arm beneath her hand surprised her, and with a finely honed instinct she kneaded those stiff muscles, seeking to ease him. He ignored her ministrations, but at the same time relaxed enough to joke, "I need no inspiration. Saura's presence is enough to bring me to culmination."

"Make your own *vers*, William," Nicholas said. He strove for a teasing tone, but the seriousness of his demand seeped through. "Let Saura hear how you feel about her."

"William's *vers* is magnificent," Saura boasted. "He has no need to prove himself to me."

William swiveled around and stared at his bride. "Where did you hear that?" he sputtered.

"You told me." She rubbed her hand up to his shoulder. "Remember, that day at Fyngre Brook? You told me you made the best *vers*."

"I lied," he confessed with blunt honesty.

In a mighty swell, the merriment of the guests overwhelmed them. With carefully honed timing, Saura waited until the noise died, and then she said, "Thank God. I was afraid I'd have to be polite about your poetry."

Freshly warmed from their laughter, the guests slipped back into their hilarity and laughed until the tears ran and all memory of Nicholas's dreadful poem and his inappropriate dedication faded.

He leaned her over a table so her face pressed against the rough wood and tossed her skirt over her head. With no preparation, he spread her cheeks and drove into her. It was not such a great thing as to cause discomfort, for the bastard children she'd borne had stretched her and his member was not large. Not large like Lord William's; God knew she'd looked at that thistle and wished it would tickle her.

Still, this seigneur's careless disregard made her angry, and each time his legs slapped her thighs she whispered a new invective about that woman. In only a moment, he finished, pulled out and wiped himself on her smock.

"Get up now." He smacked her buttock with the flat of his hand. "Get out there and help your mistress."

Hawisa stood and swung around. "She's not me mistress anymore."

"You do as she orders."

"That bitch—"

His hand swung out and slapped her cheek, knocking her against the table. "Don't you ever talk that way." He lowered his head until his eyes were on her level. They steamed with their intensity. "She's a lady and you're not worthy to speak her name."

Recovering herself, she bunched her fists at her side. "She's not so wonderful. Ye come t' me for *that.*" She jerked her head toward the table, and he smiled unpleasantly.

"But I place you so I can't see your face. You're nothing

more than a dog I can fornicate with. All the time I imagine 'tis *her*, but she'd be better."

With compressed lips, Hawisa whirled and fled the room, his semen dribbling down her legs and her face stinging with his blow.

❦

"Did you see the way he looks at her?" The words hissed through the early morning air as the huddled group of ladies went to prepare Saura for her wedding.

"Did you see the way she held his hand during the mêlée?" A knowing brow cocked, laden with insinuation.

"I think 'tis awful. Her future husband—and her bedmate, if the gossip is true—fights out on the field, and she clings to another man and listens only to him."

"Did you see how she behaved? Mark my words, William doesn't realize the perfidy of that woman."

"His father should have never refused our daughter for William. He'll be sorry now."

Squeezed in the midst of the women, Lady Jane listened and observed. Sarcastic, outspoken, full of common sense, she cultivated her crusty image and kept her kindnesses well hidden. Now she was torn; Saura *had* encouraged a man by her dependency on him. A faint sense of guilt had haunted Lady Jane as she listened to Nicholas's lurid portrayal of the fighting. According to Nicholas and his nimble tongue, William had almost been crushed time and time again, barely rising from the ashes to fight again. Now Lady Jane wondered what intrigue he plotted with his well-worded misinformation.

"Have you seen how Nicholas stares at her, like an adoring

puppy? Has she ensorcelled him? He's not even interested in women."

"Do you think she's a witch? 'Tis her fault that Nicholas loves her."

"Nay, she's like Eve. Leading men down the paths of sin with her body and her face."

That was too much for Lady Jane. "What nonsense!" she exploded. "Sir Nicholas is naught but a wart on the complexion of honor. If she's been unaware of the scandal they created, surely Nicholas wasn't."

Lady Bertha placed her fists on her ample hips and stopped, and the women straggled to a halt, strung out in the great hall. "How can you say that? Why should she pant after his conversation?"

"Because she couldn't see what happened on the field, and he told her. She hung on his every word, and no wonder— the tale he wove put William into horrible danger. Did you offer to describe the action to her?"

"I didn't." Lady Bertha snapped her mouth shut and looked thoughtful.

Sweeping her gaze over the assembled women, Lady Jane said, "Lady Saura has been our gracious hostess, and you pay her back in the stink of spoiled fish. She's a bride, and no one should cast a shadow on her joy."

She started forward with a regal sweep, and a nasty whisper appeared from nowhere. "Lady Saura couldn't see a shadow anyway."

Jane ignored it, allowing the hovering maid to open the door and entering the solar, all the women on her heels. Saura sat enthroned on a chair with bread and wine on a tray before her. A robe of brown wool overwhelmed her with its size; obviously, it belonged to William and the rolled-up sleeves and drooping shoulders made her look petite, like a child. With an inquiring lift to her eyebrow, she asked, "How may I assist you?"

"We come to help you prepare for your wedding," Jane said. Mindful of her failings the day before, she introduced the women by name. "Lady Bertha's here, Lady Edina and Lady Duana, Mary, Earlene, Isolde, Loretta, Valerie, Melbia, and Juletta. I'm Lady Jane."

"I remember you," Saura said. "Welcome, ladies."

"Has your maid laid out your clothes?"

"On the bed, m'lady." Maud curtseyed, her jaw clamped firmly over the words she wanted to say.

Jane turned at Maud's tone and examined the serving woman. A faithful retainer, she decided, jealous of having her place usurped on this most important day. With a patience only few suspected, she explained, " 'Tis a tradition for the ladies to dress the bride. It distracts her mind from the ordeal ahead. For some reason, the thought of a wedding and the night following causes a trembling in the limbs," she lifted Saura's shaking hand, "and a lack of appetite. Have you finished eating?"

"As much as I can choke down," Saura admitted, biting her lip.

"Come then." Lady Jane whisked away the tray. "Has the priest been in? Good. If you've confessed and eaten, we'll proceed." Saura's color faded before her eyes, and Jane cast around for a distraction and found one in her blunt and honest friend. "Do you remember, Bertha, how frightened you were at your first wedding?"

"I was twelve and my husband was eleven. God knows why I was worried about that little thing." Bertha laughed with boisterous amusement, and the other women relaxed. A few chuckled at the well-worn story, and Saura smiled slightly.

Jane lifted her to her feet. " 'Tis nerve-racking to stand

before hundreds of witnesses and swear to submit your properties and your self to a man, but at least Williar 's no stranger."

"I met your stepfather last night," Bertha said. "You must be dancing at the thought of leaving him."

"Theobald?" Saura asked. "Theobald's here?"

"He came in late, escorted by Lord Peter's men. What a turd!" Bertha clicked her tongue. "He must be here to legalize your union, but how any woman could live with such cruelty."

"You've seen him once and you know he's cruel?" Lady Duana asked, a twist of incredulity distorting her face

"He reminds me of my second husband," Bertha answered flatly. "You recognize them after a while. Bullies who drink too much wine and beat their women for sport. Did you see that bruise on his wife's cheek?"

"Where's my stepmother, Lady Blanche?" Saura asked. "Didn't she want to come in?"

"I know not," Jane replied. "Theobald wouldn't let her out from beneath him. They lay in the great hall, wrapped in a blanket, and he puffs and groans like a bull to prove his manhood to any that listen."

"Oo, I'm impressed," Bertha said. "Aren't you, ladies?"

"Oo," the women hummed, and one voice spoke from the crowd. "I'm especially impressed by his speed. He's so quick!"

"Oo," they hummed again, and then they laughed.

Jane stripped the robe from Saura and she stood as bare as a babe. Gaping, the women crowded around her in a circle. "Well!" Jane pronounced briskly. "Now we see why William insists on marrying you."

Bertha sighed. "Ah, well, we all looked like that once."

"At nineteen?" Jane snapped.

"I had three children by nineteen," Bertha returned, "by two husbands."

"Please, ladies," Saura begged. "I'm damp from my wedding bath and the chill of the morning air."

"Dress the child before she freezes," Bertha advised, and one of the others lifted the blue bliaut and slipped it over Saura's head.

Jane reached out and touched the rose wool cotte, as fine a weave as she had ever seen, and sighed. "How lucky you are, Lady Saura, to be able to wear such jeweled colors."

Saura smiled and let them tighten the front lace of the cotte. "Pull it tight," Bertha ordered, "and I'll make sure I keep my eye on my husband. He hasn't seen a waist that size in years."

"Old Frederick wouldn't dare look at anyone else," said Lady Duana. "He's too afraid of your wicked tongue."

This began a quarrel well honed by time, and Bertha swung on Duana with a vengeance. "Old Frederick—"

A pounding at the door interrupted them, and Jane nodded at Maud. She opened the door and accepted two bundles swaddled in canvas.

"Bride gift!" Jane said.

"Bride gift?" Saura asked, puzzled. Then she brightened. "A present?"

"From William. Would you like me to open it for you?" Jane asked.

"Oh, nay. Put it on the bed. I'll open it." With greedy hands, she stripped the rough cloth from the oblong package while she chatted, "I've not had a gift since my mother died." A bolt of cloth appeared, and she found the end and unrolled it carefully. Under her fingers bloomed a royal cloth.

Purple rippled in the light, gleaming and glowing and drawing forth sighs and groans of delight.

Saura wasn't looking toward it at all, which broke the illusion of sight she fostered with her competent ways and graceful movements. Her head was up, a frown of concentration knit her brow, and her fingertips stroked with the grain, against the grain, back and forth. "Silk." She raised it to her cheek, stroked it across her skin with the sensuous enjoyment of a cat. "I've never felt it in my life, but I know it. Silk."

"Your mother never had as fine," Maud breathed.

"Not many women do," Jane said ironically. "That color's reserved for princes, and for the very few who have the wealth to buy. God knows how William found that. There can't be another bolt of such material on this isle. It shows his worth, and how much he treasures you."

"Look, it matches her eyes." Bertha pointed where the shimmering purple met Saura's face, and the cloth did deepen the violet to a purple, bringing its rich shimmer to her eyes.

"She'd be a fool to listen to poems when she can have that," Duana said, her voice clear and sharp with envy.

"Poetry bores me. 'Tis too often the result of hard work, contrived efforts and no talent." Saura raised her head from the shining stuff and those purple eyes seemed to gaze directly at Duana. " 'Tis nothing but a song without music."

Duana's mouth dropped open, and Jane laughed with triumphant amusement. "Duana's eaten with envy that no man addresses poetry to her, and you dismiss it as a bore. Now she has something else to envy." Jane's hand sneaked out and touched the silk as if she couldn't resist. "But there's another package."

"More?" Saura's hands fluttered over the blanket until she

found the second bundle. Its surface sank as she pressed it, but it was stitched together with twine and didn't yield its secrets easily. Jane drew her knife and cut the basting, and the canvas sprang loose, propelled by the release of the contents.

"Dear Holy Mother of Jesus," Jane breathed.

Rich ebony furs caught the light and Saura's hands. She plunged her fingers into the pelts, scattering them across the silk. "So soft," she sighed. "Feel." She swung on her heel and thrust one close to Jane's face, and Jane, in her astonishment, laid her cheek against it.

" 'Tis gorgeous," she choked, overwhelmed by the fierce joy on Saura's face, the pleasure of a child given an unexpected treat.

"Tell me about them," Saura demanded, holding it out for the next lady.

Bertha came to exclaim and pet the fur, and the other women crowded around, waiting their turn as Jane said lamely, "They're black."

Bertha rolled her eyes at her friend, and Jane realized how little she saw with her blessed sight. Steadying herself, she considered what the blind girl would want to know and described, "The pelts are small, but the fur is luxurious. They're sable, and they match your hair in sheen and color. With a gown of the purple silk trimmed with the ebony furs, you'll be the most beautiful woman in the new court."

"There are twenty-four pelts here," Duana said in disgust, sorting through the furs with the avarice of a miser. "Does he want to drape her in fur?"

From the great hall, the ladies could hear William roaring, "Does she like them?"

Bertha jerked her head toward the sound. "Apparently he does want to drape her in them. He could have sent her gold or jewels to display his regard to the folk, but he sent the presents she could enjoy. I'd never have suspected the thoughtfulness of that scarred warrior."

Saura clasped the pelt to her chest and flushed with gratitude. "He's the gentlest man I know."

The women remembered the shambles on the field the day before and raised collective eyebrows.

She continued, "And he owes it to Lady Jane. She taught him deportment."

Jane brayed with laughter. "He was always thoughtful, but a bit complacent with his position. You've been good for him, Lady Saura, you have shaken him from his composure."

William's voice blared from the great hall. "Is she ready?" And more quietly, but they could hear him, "Damn it, what are those women doing in there?"

The ladies exchanged grins and Bertha lifted the hose from the bed. Jane waved her away and asked, "Lady Saura, are you warm enough?"

"Aye," Saura answered, startled and never suspecting the ploy.

"In that case, we'll leave off the hose and put you in only your shoes. After the ceremony, let William know you're naked beneath your gown, and your first mating tonight will not be your last."

"Why, Jane," Bertha cackled. "You've grown quite wicked."

"Married women have to be inventive," Jane retorted. "It piques the male interest. Besides, the ladies will have the pleasure of watching him squirm."

"As you say," Saura answered. "Still, I would not be happy if the other men should discover my state."

"They won't." Bertha reached one arm over and pinched Duana's ear between beefy fingers. "Will they, Duana?"

"Nay, nay." Duana squirmed, trying to get away. "I'll not tell a soul."

The other women hastily agreed, and Saura stepped into her slippers.

"By God, where is the woman?" William's bellow had a sharper tone to it, and the ladies laughed out loud.

"We'd better get out there before he starts pounding on the door," Jane said.

"Aye, and you know what he'd be pounding with." Bertha dropped a slow, wicked wink and sauntered toward the door. As Maud opened it the women spilled out into the great hall, blocking William's view of his bride.

"Leave her hair down." Giving one last order to Maud, Jane backed out. "William stopped me and insisted that Saura's hair be left loose. He says he doesn't care that she's not a virgin on her wedding bed—'twas him that picked the flower, and she'll not be denied her honor."

"Aye, m'lady." Maud curtseyed and shut the door behind them. Lifting a brush, she sat Saura on a stool in front of her and brushed the gleaming locks. "She's not so bad, once ye know her. And your lord William is a bonny man. Beautiful to the eye and with a sweetness to his soul. Marriage to him will be your rescue. He'll keep ye safe and give ye babes and ye'll lead the life of a fine lady. Perhaps if this Prince Henry they're talking about brings the peace, ye'll go to court and make your curtsey before the king. God speed the day!" Arranging two tendrils artistically over Saura's shoulders, Maud said, "There now, your hair's almost dry, with a curl to it that can't be tamed. Stand up and go out there and fulfill my fondest desire."

Saura didn't move, and Maud put an arm around her and hugged her. "Go on, now. No time for wedding nerves."

"I can't," Saura said in a small voice.

Maud checked in her tracks. "Of course ye can!"

"I can't." Saura's voice strengthened as the curl of panic ate at her courage. "How did I ever think I could?"

" 'Tis not a question of can or can't, m'lady. Ye have a bridegroom and a priest and your stepfather and a cartload of folk standing out there waitin' for ye. Ye have to."

"All those people sneering at me for dreaming I could marry and be happy," Saura said wretchedly. She gripped the seat of the stool so tightly her knuckles stained white. "I'm sorry, but how can an ugly blind girl wed a wealthy lord like William? You said go to court? Where I could fall on my face and shame him? I'm not a fine lady. I can't marry him."

"Ye've proved ye can handle yourself with these titled folk. Why, ye have those ladies eating out of your hand. The meals have been planned to perfection, ye've handled all the attention with grace and dignity."

"I'll just have to explain to William," Saura decided, not listening to Maud's reassurances. "We can be like you and Lord Peter. Just share a bed and not be married."

"Lord William must have a wife, m'lady. Where would ye go when she arrived?"

"I just have to go out there and tell him." She gripped the stool harder, frozen in place.

Provoked by her lady's stubborn fear, Maud snapped, "I'm a serving woman and Peter's a lord. 'Tis happy I am to share his bed; he's given me pleasure I thought I'd never see again. But ye're a lady, the daughter of a baron, a pure-blooded Norman. There's no comparison between ye and me. Ye can't stay here in William's bed like some lowborn tart."

"I can't marry him," she repeated.

"There's another difference between us, Saura. I'm old and past the time of my moon cycles. Ye're young, regular, fecund. Ye could be carrying a babe right now."

"I'm not."

"Then ye'll do so next month, or the next. Will ye condemn your child to a life as bastard because their mother is a coward?"

"Oh, Maud, I don't know what's right anymore." Saura put her head in her palms and groaned.

Maud took Saura's hands and held them in her own. "Well, I know what's right. Keeping that wonderful man waiting while ye stew over nonsense, making him wonder if ye'll shame him in front of half the country by refusing him—that's wrong. 'Tis a poor way to repay his gifts of silk and fur and kindness." Pinching Saura's cheeks to bring up the color, Maud straightened the bridal clothes and drew her to her feet. She soothed, "Ye're the most beautiful woman here. Go out and marry him."

"Are you ready, Saura?" William stood in the doorway, his golden voice encouraging. "Our guests await. Will you come out and wed me now?"

síxteen

Without a word, Saura stepped forward and put out her hand, and William carried it to his lips. Tucking it into his arm, he led her out to the place on the dais where the priest stood. Their fathers flanked them, and Maud checked to confirm that her Saura retained a determined look on her face. Then she sank down on the abandoned stool and wiped the perspiration from her face.

Saura and William swore before all witnesses and in the presence of Brother Cedric to be man and wife. Theobald gave Saura away without a quiver. His good grace was fueled, perhaps, by the sight of Lord Peter's steady hand on his sword. Maud crept out of the solar halfway through the ceremony and stood with her hand on her heart. No one produced any objections to the union when asked, and when the vows were finished the company cheered. They broke into little groups who took turns kissing the bride and slapping the bridegroom across the shoulder.

The feast that followed was the best yet, for the kitchen servants no longer wavered in their loyalties. With this marriage, William and Saura joined themselves into one.

William helped Saura to her feet and led her around to speak to the guests.

As the couple moved toward him, Theobald raised his goblet to his lips and drank, never taking his hungry eyes off his stepdaughter. "Saura is Eve," he murmured. "A temptress who leads men to disaster."

"Eve!" Saura stood behind them. Her keen hearing had picked up his words and she ignited at last at the slur she'd heard too many times. For herself and for her sex, she retorted, "Eve! By God, the world should be glad 'twas Eve who first took the apple. Had it been Adam, he would have clung to his sin with such dedication and stubbornness mankind would never be saved."

She flounced away, leaving a stunned silence behind her that slowly filled with the crackle of women's laughter.

Standing on the fringe of the group, William grinned to see the gaping amazement on his father-in-law's face. "You've not improved that vixen you married," Theobald complained. "In my house, she would have never said a word against a man. She respected her betters."

"She does so in my house, also," William said with amusement. "Dudley, the young men are congregating in the bailey for some sword practice. Won't you join them?"

Eagerly, Dudley pushed away from the table. "Aye, sir, thank you."

"You're a monk," his father shouted after him, and then muttered, "Fool boy."

William bowed in his direction and walked away, hearing Duana complain, "I tell you, she's enchanted him."

With a light step, he caught Saura around the waist and swung her close to him. "And so you have."

"Have what?" She tilted her head up and he could see tears no longer threatened. What his tenderness could not do, her anger accomplished. She no longer drooped with melancholy and uncertainty.

"You've enchanted me." He swung her in a pirouette.

"Be careful!" She snatched at the hem of her skirt and tugged it down. "Do you want me to catch cold?"

"Catch cold?" He stopped his exuberant dance.

"Aye, that sends a breeze right up my legs."

His eyes narrowed as he examined her too-innocent face. "What have you done?"

"Done?" Her voice squeaked with sincerity. "Nothing. Why do you ask?"

"Saura. . . ."

"Where's everyone going?"

"Outside for some games. Saura?"

"The sun's shining, let's go out, my lord." She tucked her hand in his and smiled up at him, and he'd taken two steps toward their marriage bed before Rollo and Clare grabbed his elbows and cried, "William's on our team!"

The other members of the team crowded around him, propelling him forward and away from Saura. Sanity prevailed as he moved away from her; he couldn't bed her when the day was new and their guests begged for entertainment. "What are we playing?"

"Football. Dudley brought the ball, and he knows the rules. You must kick it or butt it but never touch it with your hands. 'Tis a exhilarating brawl. We must make merry on your wedding day."

"So it is." William smiled with gentle sarcasm. "I'd forgotten."

The guests surrounding them snickered and teased as they bore him down to the bailey. Glancing behind him, he saw Saura coming in the midst of the women, and when he reached the bottom of the winding stair he broke away, muttering about an untied garter. Stepping into the shadows, he positioned himself and waited. His reward appeared above him. Her hand against one wall, Saura walked down the stairs, and William had a clear view all the way up her legs.

"God's teeth, Saura!" He surged to the bottom of the stair. "What game do you think you're playing?"

" 'Tis not football," Jane answered him cheerfully.

He stood with his fists planted on his hips, his chin thrust out. "You can't go out there like that. You go right upstairs and clothe yourself."

In a diversionary maneuver he could only admire, the women pulled Saura past him and left him confronting Lady Jane. "We're going to go for a walk," she told him. "We'll watch the game and pick some flowers, and Saura wants to show us her herb garden."

"Her herb garden? That's not what she's likely to show."

Jane slipped around him while he was protesting. "No other man knows to look," she said blithely. "Don't worry, we'll bring her in if the wind starts blowing."

That didn't reassure him at all.

He didn't play a good game of football, the women told her with glee. He kept licking his finger and checking the breeze and the big, hard ball knocked his feet out from underneath him more than once. She laughed softly as they peered from the gate of the herb garden and described the action, but she could feel their impatience. They wanted to watch the games rather than chaperone her, and so she suggested, "Your men would play better if you went out and cheered them on."

"Do you want to come and see William," Jane hesitated, and then asked, "Damn, what word do you use?"

"See," Saura said firmly.

"Do you want to come and see William play football?"

"Nay. If you kind ladies don't mind, I'd like to be alone. For just a few moments." No one said anything, and she added, "To think."

" 'Tis too late for thinking," Bertha advised, only half teasing. "The deed's done."

"I know." For the first time in many days, Saura considered her own feelings, and she discovered she did want to be alone. A great desire filled her, wanting the peace to deal with the changes in her life. "I'd just like a moment to rest."

The women seemed to understand. One by one, they slipped from the garden and left her alone. She groped her way to the bench in the sun. It was warm and hard, a sleek stone propped in a horizontal level. The breeze didn't blow into the herb garden, protected as it was by the tall wooden fence and the roses that climbed the wall. Silence permeated the area; not a real silence, for she could hear the voices beyond shouting in unbridled glee. But it was the kind of comfortable silence she'd heard too seldom lately. Alone and at peace, with nothing pressing to do and no one demanding her attention, Saura put her back against the fence and closed her eyes. Smelling the roses and the marjoram, absorbing the light through her pores, she sank into a kind of somnolence. Her mind emptied, her muscles relaxed their subtle tension, and she drifted.

A tightness in her shoulders brought her back to the garden, and she wondered, in a vague way, what had alarmed her. Lifting her head from its spot against the wall, she listened. A slight frown broke the serenity of her brow and made her frown more. She had let the lazy afternoon carry her away. Why should she be disturbed now?

No one was there. She listened, but nothing moved, no one spoke. She almost asked, but felt foolish. She hadn't really heard anything; there was just a chill up her spine and that uncomfortable prickle of awareness.

Relaxing back down, she eased her muscles until she had returned to the light sleep, and then she felt it. A vagrant wind touched her cheek, a rough whisper echoed through the air. She came up with a spring, reaching out for the phantom, but nothing was there. She listened, listened with all her might, and she heard it. The light footfall of slippered feet, the forced and even breathing of a demon bent on cruelty. She had heard those sounds before, knew who played such evil games. "Theobald, you whoreson, stop this at once."

She stopped speaking, hearing only the breathing. It sounded louder now, at odds with the breeze that rattled the climbing roses and carried the scent on its wings. His silence infuriated her. "Theobald, my cook's meals have given you a bellyache before. They can do it again."

Nothing. No answer, and so she shouted the ultimate threat. "Theobald, I'll tell William what you're doing, and he'll beat you to death!"

Only a soft chuckle answered her, and goose bumps raised on her arms. It had to be Theobald, it had to be. Yet Theobald would never laugh at the threat of violence to his person. Slowly she stood, a light sweat beading on her forehead, and her voice quavered, "Theobald?"

"Fear not, fair lady." The voice sounded muffled, almost inaudible, familiar yet disguised. "I love you."

Her heart skipped a beat and began a pounding that almost deafened her. She took long, slow breaths, trying to calm herself enough to think, to trap him, to really hear the voice. "You're not Theobald," she said positively.

"Nay." The answer blew on the wind.

"Who are you?"

"One who loves."

The voice was bland, expressionless, terrifying in its control and lack of intonation. She had to bring emotion to him, to raise the inflections that divulge identity. "How can you say that? You frighten me with your tricks."

"As long as William lives, your fear—"

The voice broke off, and Saura heard Jane calling, ladies approaching. She cursed and plunged toward the molester, but she was no match for him. A patter of feet and he was gone, leaving the disheveled Saura to face the women.

"Did you see him?" she demanded.

"See who?" Jane asked, puzzled.

"You must have seen him," Saura insisted. "A man here talking to me."

"Oh, ho!" Bertha said. "Dreaming of your man?"

"There was a man here, and he said terrible things. He said he loved me and called me fair lady."

"No one left the garden." Duana snickered. "All this poetry has gone to your head."

"Nay. Nay, I tell you."

Jane laid a soothing hand on Saura's arm. "Duana's right. No one left the garden as we approached the gate."

"There must be another way."

"You were dreaming."

"Impossible."

"You were asleep and alone when last we checked you. I promise you, you were dreaming." Jane's hand tightened on her, and she gave a little tug. "Come, let's go up to the solar where you can rest properly."

Hearing them, Saura despaired. They'd never believe her, they believed only the evidence of their own eyes. How could she convince them? She could hardly believe it herself.

In her room alone, she climbed up onto the bed, obeying Jane's injunction to relax. Bare between the sheets, she thought about the strange incident in the garden. It couldn't have really happened. The incident had such a strange, otherworldly feel to it. If only she could convince herself, convince herself she wasn't going mad. Reassure herself about her panic of the morning.

It was nothing, she assured herself. Bridal jitters. Why, she'd heard of brides who sobbed through the entire ceremony. She wasn't really unsure of herself. So what if William should fornicate with a serving maid and bring in a poor relation to be housekeeper and replace her totally? 'Twas her he wanted, her he cherished. He said so and he was a man of honor. So what if he were to discover a new love as she swelled with a babe? All men kept a woman for amusement and a wife for children. She wouldn't care, would she?

A noise at the foot of the bed made her raise her head, like a rabbit on the alert. Fear sprang into full bloom. Memories raced through her mind: the echo of footsteps, a hoarse laugh, a murmured expression of love. She wanted to speak, but found her voice frozen in her throat. She lifted her hand slowly, cautiously, afraid someone watched her, afraid of . . . of what? She didn't know, and that was the worst. With trembling fingers, she massaged her neck until the tendons relaxed. "Who's there?" she whispered. Then louder, "Who's there?"

No one answered, and her heart gave a bound, threatening to beat out of her chest. It was him again, she knew it was.

Somehow that man had gotten into her room. Whoever it was coughed, and she relaxed. It wasn't him. It wasn't even a man, and now she could deal with the intruder with some sense.

Calmly, she said, "You can't fool me. I'm trained to listen, and I know you're there."

Footsteps dragged around the floor, and she sat up and pulled the covers under her arms. Cocking her head toward the sound, she tensed as she recognized the culprit. "Hawisa, how did you get in here?"

"Ye think ye're so cunnin', wi' your good hearin' what knows all, an' your good looks, an' all th' men sniffin' after your tail."

Saura said nothing, trying to judge the depth of Hawisa's mood by the hostility in her tone.

"Ye think ye can hide your wickedness, but folk are talkin'. They're sayin' ye're a witch. They're sayin' your blindness is a punishment. They're sayin'—"

"A lot of nonsense, it seems," Saura interrupted. "Hawisa, you didn't come in here to tell me what some mean-spirited people are saying. How did you get in here?"

"I hid behind th' tapestry when th' ladies brought ye in."

"What were you doing in our solar?" Saura insisted.

"*Our* solar," the girl mocked. "*Our* solar. Aren't we important? Aren't we sure of ourselves? Married this very morn an' already ye own th' castle."

"What were you doing?"

"Puttin' poison in your wine!" Hawisa exploded. "Ye got rid of me, didn't ye? Like offal ye toss in th' dung heap. Lord William's talkin' about givin' me away t' anyone who'll take me, but I grew up here, me roots are here. I'll be leavin' everythin' I know. I'll be at th' bottom of th' group wherever he stashes me, an outsider."

Alarmed by the half-hysterical note of violence in her voice, Saura soothed, "I'm sure Lord William will do his best for you."

"He don't care about me. He only cares for ye. If ye'd never come, I'd not be leavin'. I'd still be top of th' pile, wi' them little flunkies t' wait on me an' first tastin's from th' kitchen an' me own tap for th' ale. 'Tis all your fault."

As Hawisa's voice rose, Saura's cooled and quieted. "Those things are not your right."

"I earned 'em," the woman shouted. "Til ye came an' changed th' lock I had th' key for th' wine cellar because I earned it. The cook offered me food because I earned it."

"Earned it?" Saura asked with scorn.

"On me back, just like one important lady who earned her husband on her back. Don't ye know that's what everyone's sayin'? Talkin' about how William follows ye like he's caught th' scent of a bitch in heat. Talkin' about how good ye must be between th' covers t' have him marry such a useless, blind—"

The heavy pewter pitcher smacked the wall behind Hawisa and water splattered across the room. The woman jumped aside, her shout dying of shock. Trembling, suddenly aware of her great transgression, she whispered, "How'd ye do that? How'd ye see where t' throw it?"

Saura crawled out of the blankets and balanced on all fours on the bed. Her hair curled wildly about her head, her lips drew back in a snarl, her body was magnificently, unconsciously, nude. "I'm not blind, I've forsworn myself. I know every nasty move you've made. I know every time you dragged one of your paramours to this bed. I know every sneer you've directed at me and at William. I'll keep you here and you'll never get away and you'll wish—"

The door slammed open and Maud burst in. "M'lady, what—" She gasped at the scene before her eyes.

Lady Jane followed, saying, "We heard the shouting," but her comments faded, too.

Hawisa backed toward them, chanting, "She's a witch, she can see, she's crazy, I'm afraid of her." Saura raised her hands, formed into claws, and growled, and Hawisa turned and bolted, screaming, "She's a witch, she can see, she's a witch."

"What did she do with your silk?" Jane asked, and Saura flew off the bed.

"Where is it?" she said fiercely, and the sound of her anger carried clear into the great hall. "What did she do to it? I'll kill her, that shrew."

" 'Tis out of the trunk, M'lady, and the knife. . . ."

"I'll kill her."

Lady Jane slammed the door. "You've displayed yourself for everyone, and that should wait for the bedding." Saura stalked across the room, and Jane caught her arm. "Let your maid look first." Saura tugged, but Lady Jane gripped her elbow and shook it. "Calm down. Your maid can see what's been done, and then you can check."

The silk rustled and the bolt thumped, and then Maud reassured them. "She cut a chunk of one end off and she snipped a few threads in a fringe, but the largest portion is intact. 'Tis nothing a little creative sewing won't fix, m'lady."

"Let me see." Saura jerked away, and this time Jane let her go. Maud guided her hands to the destruction and Saura felt the swell of heat beneath her skin. "That she-wolf," she hissed. "Thank the Virgin you brought me in to rest when you did, or who knows what she would have done. That half-wit."

Curious and amazed, Jane queried, "What did she say to you?"

In her fury, Saura could only remember one thing. "She said the only reason William married me was because I'm good in bed."

"Well!" Humor lit Jane's voice. "Someone should so insult me."

Saura's mouth worked until she burst into laughter. "I'm losing my sense of proportion," she mourned, and then she laughed again. "I'm screeching like a fishwife over her comments when I should be ordering her whipped for destroying property." She rubbed her forehead with her palm. "I'll never sleep now. Dress me, Maud, and I'll prepare for the swearing."

One by one William's men knelt before him and put their hands between his and gave their oath of loyalty. They had done it before, and it was a reiteration of those oaths, a repetition made poignant by their concern for William. Sir Merwyn had tears running down his wrinkled cheeks as he swore, Sir Raoul grinned the whole time, Sir Egide and Sir Dillan shook with eagerness; but they all spoke their allegiance proudly, so their words were heard in every corner of the giant room.

Next, Saura's men knelt before her. One by one they placed their palms together in her hands and swore before God they would hold her lands for her. Their words, too, were clear and loud, but they didn't rise when they finished.

As the eldest knight, Sir Francis of Wace spoke for them. Seriously, for the matter required much thought and concern, he said, "We give our allegiance to Lady Saura of Roget with pleasure. Still, we have a query we must know the answer to, for our protection and the protection of Lady Saura's lands. Lord William was blind for an extended time. Will this blindness return?"

Saura's chest filled with a kind of hurt rancor. "Is blindness so important?"

William's hand touched hers. "In a warrior, it is. They must know whether or not I can rescue them in case of siege."

"Aye, my lady, we mean no disrespect, but if Lord William is having lapses in sight or mind we must know," Sir Denton explained.

"I understand," William reassured them. "I'd think less of you if you feared to ask. But I assure you, my noble knights, I've had no problems since Lady Saura rescued me with her healing touch. I'll prove it to you when we go to subdue Sir Frazer in rebellion."

Sir Francis rose and the others followed, murmuring their approval. "Then we'll be proud to follow you, my lord. Do we go soon?"

Saura ground her teeth at the pleasure in their voices, and even more as William readily agreed. "Very soon. We'd be fools to let him settle in for siege."

The men stepped back and William nudged Saura. "Isn't it time for supper?"

"Oh." She jumped, her thoughts far away. "Of course, my lord." A coolness frosted her features as she turned away and ordered the tables put up. William let her go, and had she but known it, he understood her concern. Hadn't his Anne been the same way about fighting? For some inexplicable reason, women worried about a little bit of weapon wielding stealing their husbands. You'd think they'd worry about all the whores of the world instead. He didn't understand it, but he no longer tried to explain their foolishness.

Instead he braced himself for another assault on his ears. Nicholas, he could see, was consulting a parchment scribbled with notes. 'Twas his wedding day, and he deserved a respite from this unrelenting rhyming. He tried to be fair to Nicholas. The man had undoubtedly fallen in love for the first time in his life. He understood, for how could any man not love Saura? But when he heard Nicholas declaring his devotion to Saura, to his wife, to his *woman*, he wanted to beat him to a bloody pulp. He had trouble remembering friendship and generosity when faced with a poacher on his grounds. In fact, Nicholas's worship created enough gossip that he considered speaking to the man. He knew Saura wasn't impressed; indeed, everyone with half an eye could see Saura wasn't impressed. Still, there were always folk eager to spread rumors and malign their betters, and Saura's marriage had put her in the precarious position of eminence. So he was faced with the choice; should he forbid Nicholas to dedicate *vers* to Saura and have folks gossiping about his lack of faith in his lady? Or should he assure himself Nicholas would leave soon and take with him his distressing affections? Either way could accelerate the rumors of a rift between William and his friend, between William and his wife. As a fighter, his first instinct was to action; as a thinker, he suspected a bland show of boredom served the purpose better.

Seating himself beside Saura at the head table, he listened to the ribbing of his friends about the wedding night and grinned in the appropriate spots. The suggestive humor of the ladies brought a blush to Saura's cheek and made her forget her pique with William, and for that William was grateful. But all the while he kept checking Nicholas. Nicholas ate heartily. Nicholas always ate heartily, not even unrequited love could change that, but as soon as he finished, William knew the time had come to decide. Should he stand and make a declaration, or should he suffer through one more night?

The decision was temporarily taken from him. On the other side of Lord Peter, Raymond stood up. He had the presence few men possessed; William had it, and Lord Peter, and those men could bring a silence to a noisy room. Now as the great hall quieted, Raymond bowed to the married couple and then again to Saura. Hoisting himself up on his bench, he placed one foot on the table and leaned against his knee. His squire brought forth a lute, and as Raymond accepted it, he said, "The bride is the queen of the day, the wife is the queen of the night, and I have a song that declares how I feel about the loveliest queen of all. Saura, our Saura, queen of sunrise and dusk."

So saying he launched into a song of breathtaking sweetness. A real musician, he produced a ballad about Saura that brought tears to the eye. Even Saura listened, ignoring the demands of hostess for a few moments as she drifted with the melody.

Alarmed at first, William slowly relaxed. This wasn't the betrayal by yet another comrade; this was a lyric that placed Nicholas's pathetic *vers* under harsh scrutiny. William couldn't understand his own exaltation at this turn of events; why should Raymond's declaration of devotion ease his fears? Yet it did, and looking out over the lords and ladies, over the servants and churls, he knew why. They were confused. How could they say Saura encouraged Nicholas *and* Raymond? They could, of course, but as the accusations widened their reliability vanished. Nicholas had arrived before any of them, and they could speculate about what had happened before they came. But what of Raymond? He'd come long after the last guest, and no one had caught him skulking in a corner with Saura.

The song ended as William smiled, lost in his own satisfaction, and on the heels of the applause another knight rose. "I, too, have *vers* for Lady Saura, the loveliest woman to be snatched from under my nose." He waited for nothing, launching into a poem about the unfair pathways of fate that led him to Saura too late. Her beauty alone put her above his reach; that, and the fact she was married to the biggest, toughest warrior in England.

After the laughter died down, another knight rose, inspired to spontaneous song. Another rose, and another, all singing the praises of Saura with varying talents and messages. Soon it became more than a chance to show off, it became a way of keeping William and Saura at the table as host and hostess. William put up with their foolishness until he decided the most harm had been done to the rumors about Nicholas and his love. Then he rose and swept Saura up in his arms. "Bedtime," he said definitely.

That brought the loudest laugh of the evening, and Lady Jane stood up and the other women followed her. "We'll prepare her, my lord."

William weighed her firmness against his own desire and let Saura slide to her feet. "As you wish. But don't be long."

This recommendation generated such gales of humor Saura suspected everyone had overindulged in ale and wine. She hastened into the solar with the ladies, stood obediently still while they stripped her and placed her hair in strategic locations; not for modesty, for they would display her as a guarantee of physical perfection, but as a tease. The men crowded in, carrying William as if he were unwilling, rather than fighting to proceed. They stood him on his feet and dragged his clothes from him with no craft, and stood him before Saura.

The women, with enticing slowness, lifted Saura's hair away from her shoulders. The men whistled and shuffled, cackling at William's look of painful anticipation, and Lord Peter called, "If you wield that lance as well as you wielded your lance at the mêlée, Saura will be dead by morning."

"Nay," Jane assured him. "She'll vanquish his lance. Women always win that battle."

"Until the lance is resurrected," Lord Peter said agreeably.

"We do so pray," Bertha shouted.

Performing his duty, Brother Cedric said, "Lady Saura is physically perfect, except for her eyes. Will Lord William disavow her for her disability?"

"Never," William testified. "She's the savior of my sight, the wife of my heart."

"But how can she view William's body?" Jane puzzled. "She has the right to see him and verify her willingness to remain in wedlock with him."

Saura stepped forward and placed her hands on William's arms. "I can solve that. All I have to do is. . . ." She trailed her fingertips across his chest in a way that brought forth sighs of pleasure from the men. Her actions carried an immediate reward as William swept her up and carried her toward the bed.

"We'll ask her in the morning if she's satisfied," Lady Jane decided, leading the push into the great hall.

Saura's light laugh floated on the air, and the heavy door slammed shut. William dropped her on the bed with a thump and turned away. "William!" She pushed herself up on her elbows, pushed her hair out of her face. "Let me see you."

"Wait," he growled. "I'll secure us permanent privacy."

The wooden bench scraped the floor as he moved it. The sewing table from the window seat followed it.

"Do you foresee a visitation?" she asked with interest.

"Foresee is too strong a word." He grunted as he shoved the heavy furniture close against the door. "Suspect. There have been times when I led the interruption of an intimate moment, and I *suspect* my friends may have nefarious plans."

"You'd better push the chest over there, too," she advised.

Chuckling, he pushed her trunk over until its weight held the barrier in place. He began to walk back to her and changed his mind. He knelt and opened her chest, and she strained to hear what he was doing, but he closed it almost immediately and she remembered his presents. "I haven't thanked you for the bride gifts. Bless you for making me important in everyone's eyes."

"You make yourself important in everyone's eyes," he replied. "I simply signify my regard for you." The bed depressed beneath his weight.

She laced her fingers together, suddenly aware of the quiet in the room, of their privacy for the first time in too many weeks. "I have great regard for you, also." *Clumsy*, she thought, embarrassed by her lack of eloquence. Sitting there, bare, she felt a creeping consciousness. She raised the covers and crawled under, pulling the sheets over her knees, her waist, her chest, her shoulders. She kept wondering if he would stop her, but he didn't.

She began to speak several times, but could think of no scintillating conversation. He said nothing, and she wondered if he was offended. Had her trick with the lack of hose so thoroughly distressed him he wanted nothing to do with her? Then he cleared his throat, and she knew that wasn't true.

For the first time in a whole moon they were really alone,

and they felt foolish. All their other joinings had been spur of the moment, lusty fallings from the vertical to the horizontal. This night required no hurried disrobings, no secretive plotting or special seductions. They were man and wife. They had every right to lie on the bed together.

"Did I tell you how lovely you looked today?" he asked in a soft bass rumble.

"Thank you." She smiled rather stiffly and cast around for something else to say. "Even without my undergarments?" Immediately she wondered why she reminded him of that.

"Oh." He shifted on the bed. "Well, aye. The lack of aught under your gown kept reminding me of . . . I liked it. Aye."

The silence fell again, until she remembered to ask, "Did you win your ball game?"

"Aye. Aye, my team won by a bit. We started out behind, but after you went in I played well and we won." He shifted again, a little bit closer, and a small bubble of relief was born in her.

"I enjoyed meeting your friends," she offered.

He laughed softly. "All of them?"

"Most of them," she compromised, her eyes solemn.

"They enjoyed meeting you." Lifting the covers he slid beneath them, close against her.

She sat, he sat, their thighs pressed together, their arms touching.

Should she move aside? Would he think she avoided him, or would he think she made room for him?

He wiggled his hips and without her having to decide, she was moved aside. "Did you like the furs?" His hands dragged something under the blankets with them.

"They felt intriguing." Trying to be cordial, she overcompensated and purred her reply.

"I hoped you'd think that." Those big hands moved closer to her, and a plush touch stroked over her knee. "Those furs can all be made into a cape for you. All except one, and guess what we're going to do with that?"

She sat very still, unable to analyze the rich tingle that titillated her leg. It wasn't his hand. The plush caress slid up her thigh and she reached out to identify it.

Pushing her hand away, he breathed, "Nay. This is my part of the bride gift."

That rich smoothness swept over her torso, and a violent sensation of pleasure forced her stomach muscles to collapse. Her nipples peaked, goose bumps covered her. "William," she choked. "Is that one of the sables?"

"Aye." He rubbed the fur across her neck.

"What are you doing with it?"

He pushed against her shoulder. "Lie down," he urged. "And I'll show you."

A scratch at the door pulled her from her sleep. She didn't want to get up. God, after last night she didn't ever want to get up, and especially not in the chilly predawn. But the scratch came again, a long, mournful scrape, and duty, and the knowledge Bula would never give up, dragged her from her warm nest against William's chest.

"Aye, Bula," she whispered, pulling on her brown work dress. "I'm coming, you stupid dog. Why did I ever let you start this?" With soft grunts and moans, she shoved the chest, the sewing table, the bench to the side. She stopped and listened to William's breathing; if she'd wakened him, he was faking sleep with the dedication of a well-served man.

She opened the door to his enthusiastic welcome, and she

scratched his ears. "Shh." She listened to the sounds in the great hall. No one moved in awareness. A few bodies shifted on the floor, rolling over in the rushes or groaning in a nightmare. "Take me out, dog." Clinging to the fur on his ruff, she followed him as he led her through the maze of sleeping bodies and to the stairway on the far side of the room. She pulled the bar back from the door and opened it to the creak of hinges. She found her guiding wall and began to descend. The air got fresher and cooler, and Bula trotted ahead, sniffing enthusiastically. He got farther and farther ahead of her, claws tapping, until he reached the bottom. Then he stopped, and Saura expected to hear him scratch against the outer door. He didn't; a deep, loud sniffing reached her, and then a short, distressed bark.

Saura hurried down, wondering at Bula's change of routine. An obstacle on the last two steps caught her toes, a heavy obstacle that yielded slightly but never moved. Crying out, Saura tripped over the top of it, falling and landing head first with a jarring impact on the paving stones. One cheek cracked down hard. One hand slipped and she landed with all her weight on one elbow. Her knees met the rock last, scraping the skin away.

The pain broke her; her mind shut down, yet when she woke she heard her scream still echoing up the stairwell. Her elbow hummed with the impact, and her face, as she raised herself, expanded against her skin. "God," she moaned. "What was it?" Bula snuffled at her, whining in distress.

Groping back to the stairs, she reached out to touch that obstacle. Coarse homespun met her questing hands, and then a warm body wrapped in a serving maid's clothing. Her fingers skimmed in increasingly frantic circles, trying to find a spark of life in the woman. There was nothing, no movement at all, and when she found the agonized face she discovered why. The woman's neck was broken, knocked at an odd angle.

Above her, footsteps and then more footsteps clattered down the stairs and she looked up in horror. Voices she couldn't identify, voices she should recognize assaulted her buzzing ears. She cried, "Who is it? Tell me who it is!"

The voices fell silent, and then Charles said with cold deliberation, " 'Tis Hawisa. Hawisa, the slut who called you a witch. Hawisa, the serving maid you threatened to kill yesterday."

seventeen

" 'Tis Charles."

" 'Tis not, I tell you."

"Then who is it?" William asked. "You insist it's not Charles, but who is it?"

Wretched, Saura paced back and forth, her hand on the table for guidance. "I don't know," she admitted. "But the voice isn't right."

"Isn't right!" William pounded the board with his cup. "God's teeth, he as much as accused you of murdering Hawisa when he reminded our guests of your threat to her!"

Saura opened her mouth and shut it.

In the waning days of summer, the guests had left. They scuttled away, babbling of the extraordinary events of the wedding celebration and storing up the tales for the winter ahead.

Saura and William had wished them Godspeed, waved until they were out of sight, and then turned to each other and laughed in blatant relief. William had been content to pay court to his bride, assisting her with her chores, walking with her in the woods, loving her every chance he got. But now the time of honey vanished as William stirred and spoke of seige and battle.

In this past fortnight of enchantment, she'd never told William of the threat in her garden, of the muffled speaker who had touched her and declared his love. She feared to infuriate William; she could imagine him stomping out, declaring he would find the bastard who dared approach his wife.

More than that, she feared he wouldn't believe her. The ladies certainly hadn't, not even Lady Jane. They had dismissed it as a dream, and with good cause. They had checked on her, they said, and seen her asleep and alone. They'd seen the gate to the garden as they approached, and no one had left that way. Even Saura agreed her phantom hadn't left that way, but she didn't know how he *had* left. After the guests had gone, Saura had visited the garden and, feeling foolish, had groped all around the walls. All she got for her curiosity was a handful of rose thorns.

Still, she should tell William. She *would* tell William. Turning, she faced him and bravely said, "What do you want for supper?" She blinked. That was not what she'd wanted to say at all, and William knew it.

"What is it, love?" He stood and paced around the table to take her shoulders and draw her to him. "Tell me."

"Oh, William." She dropped her head onto his chest. "I'm such a coward."

"You?" She felt the rumble of his laughter beneath her cheek. "You're the bravest woman I know. Banging heads with a rock, confronting Arthur, forcing those noble ladies to respect you, marrying me. I wish I had the courage you contain in one small finger." He held up one of her hands and kissed that one small finger.

"You're the bravest knight in all Christendom." She drew their entwined hands back down to her face and kissed the back of his. "You're kind and generous and a great fighter. You're clever as a fox."

"And I must go deal with Charles. We can't live with this threat hanging over our heads."

"Nay! Nay." Reaching up, she caught his beard and tugged it until his face was level with hers. "Nay."

"Then I'll go take your fief back from Sir Frazier," he offered.

Her chin dropped.

"It must be done," he said.

"I know," she agreed reluctantly. "But you can't go yet. You promised to teach me to defend myself."

"To defend yourself?" He was startled. "Why should you need to?" They both knew it was a foolish question. "Aye, I did promise, didn't I? But the teaching won't take as long as you hope, dearling." Grasping her by the hand, he led her to the chairs by the fire and seated her. He pulled his seat close, so their knees touched, and said, "Listen to me. My father teaches this first rule of combat to his fosterings, and it applies to all fighting situations."

She sat straighter. "The first rule of combat? I've heard you say that before."

"Only a fool forgets it. Listen closely. There's no such thing as a fair battle. *Battles are fought to win.* I've engaged in wars with the punishment for failure the confiscation of my estates, the death of my son. I've been in clashes where a score of men surrounded me, seeking my death with the edge of their blades. 'Tis not strength that succeeds in such combat, but a combination of skill and cunning. If your opponent expects you to charge, retreat. If your opponent believes you're weak, crush him with your boldness. You, Saura, have a great advantage."

She raised her eyebrows in disbelief.

"Oh, yes, dearling. You're a woman. Women are all idiots. You're beautiful. Beautiful women have even less wit than average women. You're tiny. A man can overpower you with the muscle contained in his little finger. And you're blind."

Raising her hand to his face, she traced his mouth with her fingertips. He was grinning, and she grinned back.

"Any man who engages you in a skirmish expects to crush you with impunity. Use your weaknesses to confound him."

She nodded slowly. "I understand. To be a good knight, you must have strength and skill. To be a great knight, you must be intelligent and contrary."

He laughed. "You're good for my pride."

"You're a great knight, but if you must go to besiege my fief, I require a pledge you'll not be hurt."

"The greatest knight in Christendom? Hurt?" He laughed and kissed her cheek. "This 'kind, generous, great' fighter? Hurt?"

"William," she faltered as his tongue flicked the sensitive skin over her chin. "William, you haven't given me your pledge."

He nudged her chin aside with his nose and kissed her neck. "This clever fox? *Hurt?*"

"William?" she murmured as he nuzzled her collarbone. "Your pledge." The sharp edge of his teeth nipped her shoulder through the material that swathed it. "William." She gulped, and lost the thread of her thought. "William, the churls."

"Curse them."

"Supper. Your father and the boys will howl if 'tis late

again." She sighed as he lifted her off her chair and into his lap, and lightly bit her ear.

"Curse the supper."

"We can retire right after supper."

"And do what?" he whispered.

"I'll show you," she whispered back, pressing her nose to his.

He grunted and eased her onto her feet. "We have the supplies ready for a siege." He supported her as she regained her balance. "I'll take the men out tomorrow morning. You don't need to get up and see me off."

Catching his sleeve, she asked, "Have I been manipulated? Has my clever knight retired from the field with all he sought?"

"Not everything," he assured her. "You still don't trust me enough to tell me what worries you." He waited, but she said nothing. "I'll always be here, sweeting, when you're ready to speak."

She sat in the herb garden, rich with mature plants that awaited their harvest. She waited in the cool of the early evening for William to come to her and tell her he would go and fight once more.

He'd recovered from the wound received at the siege of her fief. She hadn't recovered from the guilt. All those weeks of illness, just to take back a castle she didn't care about. It hadn't been much of a wound, everyone had assured her, but with typical male irresponsibility he hadn't cleaned it, hadn't cared for it. He'd arrived back at Burke, delirious, dragged on a litter of branches.

Frightened, Saura had helped Maud care for him, applying

a steady application of smelly poultices and bathing him when his fever rose. She hadn't thought of the future then, only of bringing him back to life. She thought about it now, bitterly, unceasingly. Was this her reward? Cure him to send him out to fight again?

She shouldn't have let him go, although how she could have stopped him, she didn't know.

Leaning against the wall on her favorite stone seat, she bubbled with a fury and a discontent. He'd come through that gate beside her and stand before her and explain, in that deep and golden voice of his, that he had to go throw himself in harm's way once more. And she'd listen and make the proper discontented noises and then, like a good wife, she'd let him go again.

Gritting her teeth, she listened to the tromp of his boots at the back of the garden. Here he came, striding around the walls to open the gate.

But he didn't. One moment he was outside the far wall, the next he stood cursing inside, complaining of the thorns.

Saura stood up and cried, "How did you do that?" She heard him turn as if bewildered, and then turn back.

"Do what?"

"How did you come through the wall?"

"What? Oh, that?" He laughed, a golden sunshine that never failed to warm her. "There's a miniature gate in the back wall. 'Tis hidden under the roses and well protected by the thorns, I assure you. I used it as a child, but 'tis a squeeze now."

"Who knows about it?" she demanded.

"Every wee one in the castle, I suppose. 'Tisn't a secret." He strode towards her, through the rows of plants. "Why?"

"There was someone in here on our wedding day, but the ladies insisted I'd been dreaming, for they never saw him leave." Excited, Saura caught his arm and shook it. "I thought I must be mad, but he was here. He was really here!"

"Aye, I'm sure he was. What did he do?"

"Touched me, I think. And spoke to me." Remembering those words of love, hissed through a wrap of cloth, she shuddered.

"Why didn't you tell me sooner?"

"That feeling of menace, of eyes, following my every move, vanished with the guests. I don't hear that hungry whisper." Remembering, her voice dropped. "I no longer hear the tread of soft-clad feet."

"Why didn't you tell me sooner?" he demanded again.

She squirmed. William sounded dangerously neutral, and she wondered at his thoughts. "I felt like a fool. No one else believed me. So many people think that because I'm blind, I'm stupid."

"And you group me in with those?" The arm beneath her hand stiffened perceptibly.

"Nay. Nay, of course not." She bit her lip. "I just. . . ."

He sighed. She knew he was disappointed, but he lifted her face and dropped a light kiss. "A chance, Saura. That's all I ask. A chance. I believe you when you say someone was here with you." William's hand covered hers, and he reached around her in a hug. "That's why I must go and confront him."

Her excitement faded, returning her cold fear. "Who?"

"Charles. It has to be Charles," he said with sad certainty, as he urged her down onto the bench.

"Why does it have to be Charles? Why not Nicholas? Or Raymond? Or even someone we don't suspect?"

Propping his foot beside her, he leaned on his knee and said, "Logically, it must be Charles."

"Oh, logically!" she said with a fine scorn.

He ignored her contempt and in an even tone agreed, "Aye, logically. Charles is the only one who needs the profit my death could bring him. Nicholas already owns half of Hampshire. Raymond doesn't need the land. His family owns lands scattered on the Continent and all over England."

"Does Raymond?"

"What?"

"Does Raymond own any of this land?"

"Nay." He snorted with disdain. "His parents wouldn't give up an acre of ground before their deaths. They keep Raymond dependent on their good nature, keep him hungry so they can control him."

"So it could be Raymond."

"Nay," he stated firmly. "Nay. Raymond is my friend."

In some strange way, that made Saura feel better. William was wrong about Charles, of that she felt sure. She'd heard the jealousy in Charles's voice, heard his unhappiness about his station, but she could never discern in it anything beyond pettiness and a longing to hide from his troubles.

Raymond. Raymond was not so easy for her. Layers of complexity colored his speech. He, too, was jealous of William, not of his wealth but of his contentment. Raymond was a man driven by his ambition and his family, cynical and wary.

So that left only Nicholas. Nicholas, her odd friend.

"Nicholas," she breathed.

William hesitated. "I did consider him. Except for one thing. Nicholas would never have killed Hawisa."

"Why not?"

Easing her to one side, he sat beside her and leaned an arm around her shoulders. "He offered to take her off our hands, and I had given her to him. She was his property, and he would never, never destroy anything of value he owned. He still owns the first penny he was given on Christmas morn."

"Hawisa enraged me."

"Nay, dearling, I'm sorry, but I know Nicholas. He maintains his peasants with food and wine so they'll not sicken and fail to work for him. He keeps his accounts meticulously. He never trusts a steward or bailiff." He hugged her. "He'd have to be mad to have killed Hawisa."

" 'Twas no accident, you're sure."

She sought the opposite reassurance, but he couldn't give it to her. "She fought the man who pushed her. She had bruises on her neck in the shape of fingertips."

"No one truly believed I did it?"

"Don't be ridiculous. Not even Theobald thought you did it. As Lady Jane pointed out, you couldn't have knocked her down the stairs. She stood head and shoulders above you and outweighed you by three stone."

She leaned against him, and he shifted her sideways so she lay across his lap. "Does your wound bother you?" she asked.

"Nay. Even your dragon of a Maud pronounces me cured." He tightened his hold. "But I do still have a sickness, a sickness only you could cure." He lifted his knee and levered her head close to his, and her eyelids drooped as his mouth settled on hers. He explored her with the delicacy of a musician, but that wasn't what she wanted.

Before their marriage, she'd been a fallen woman, reveling in dissipation, and then to ensure her respect, he'd deprived her of himself. They'd wed, and once again she reveled in the marriage bed, blessed by contract and the Church.

And he had left, only to return wounded and insensate. When they brought William home, babbling with fever from the infection of his wound, Saura wanted nothing more than to cure him. She wanted to bring him back to consciousness, bring him back to life, and then wrap her hands around his throat and choke him until he promised never to fight again.

They'd had no loving since the day he'd ridden away to siege, and now he came to her to declare he'd go again. In Saura's breast boiled a mixture of frustration and anger at him, at circumstances, at herself. A plague be upon him! He was leaving again, to fight this invisible threat that stalked them. And she couldn't stop him. She wanted to spread a protective cloak over William, for with some dreadful illogic she felt his misfortune was her fault. It wasn't true, of course. He'd been blinded before she arrived and cured during her sojourn. But he was still leaving her.

Tearing her lips away, she said urgently, "Maud says you are healthy?"

"Aye." He followed her mouth with his, seeking her sweetness.

She put her hand against his shoulder and pushed. "Lie down on the bench. I wish to verify."

"Dear heart," he caught her hand and kissed the palm, "this garden is protected by only a gate. I can't lie down here."

Giving in to her fury, she trapped his face in her hands and ordered, "Lie down."

"The servants—"

"Need no instruction on how to knock. I've taught them this is my private place, so we'll take advantage of it *now.*"

Taken aback by the passion in her voice and the fierce insistence of her gestures, he gaped with the amazement of one never ordered. "At least let me—"

"Nay!" Snatching her hand back, she pushed him again. "I will know your body beneath mine before I let you go."

He examined her face in the light of the setting sun. Her skin was tinted pink; perhaps the light caressed her, perhaps she was flushed. Her lips set firmly, her eyes burned with fervor. She was thinner with worry and firm with determination, and he yielded to her. He slid down on the bench as she shifted over him, his back resting on the stone, his feet planted on the ground. She swung her leg over him and her hands raced over him frantically, seeking a confirmation of health. He realized how she missed the comfort of *looking* at him to check his progress, a comfort most wives took for granted. He grunted as she jerked at the laces of his shirt and she slowed to trace the rupture of skin that had felled so great a warrior.

" 'Tisn't much, is it?" she said. "I've not touched it, I feared to hurt you, but I thought they might be lying to me, telling me falsehoods to ease my worry."

" 'Tis only a slight wound," he answered hoarsely. Her fingers were less nimble than usual, probing the still-red flesh around the wound, but he withstood the pain as he comprehended why she did it. She had to reassure herself, and her frantic concern cheered him.

Did she love? Perhaps what he witnessed was the birth of love, and the thought brought a slow, steady burn of desire in his heart. Not just desire for her body, but a real desire for her, for all of her. Her years of struggle and worry and pain with Theobald were behind her, but those years had built a wall of mistrust he wanted to smash. He wanted to demand her trust, force her to give it, force her to tell him her mind. Words and rigor had no power against this wall; only the slow, steady proving of worthiness would prevail. He understood while he railed against the necessity. The only thing that kept his purpose steady was her pleasure in his company and in his body. Perhaps, when he'd proved himself to her, he'd also see the birth of the pure trust that would signal his victory.

He felt the pressure as she settled her weight on him. She rode him like a horse, her skirt tucked beneath her with no consciousness yet of his willingness to stud. She wanted union, he knew, but her need to explore him obviously took precedence. Demanding without words, she kneaded his shoulders, still covered by his shirt. She ran her hands down to his hands, examining each finger, each nail, each line of his palm, and her sure touch pulled his attention from her. Focused with painful intensity on his own senses, he shut his eyes and reveled in the garden of scents and feelings she constructed around him.

Saura would have smiled when she felt him relax beneath her, but it seemed so long since she had smiled her lips felt stiff and unpracticed. Anger held her in its grip, anger and the fervor to know him once more. When she raised his hands to her face, she petted the skin on the backs, nuzzled his palm, tasted one finger. She sought reassurance, but his groan encouraged her to pursue sensuality for his sake. Levering herself up, she unlaced his shirt all the way and pressed her hands to his abdomen. He liked that; he bucked beneath her and suddenly the unpracticed smile broke across her face. If William had been looking at her, he would have been worried, for it was no smile of happiness, but the sweet curl of revenge.

She'd pay him back for the worry, the anger, the painful maturity he was forcing on her. It would be a temporary revenge, but revenge nevertheless. Her hands skipped to the laces at his breeches and with a slow, steady pull she opened the tie and spread the rope to its greatest width. She slid her fingers into the gap, then slipped away, caressing back up to his breastbone where his heart thumped in a heavy beat. And she smiled.

"I can't stand," he began, and reached for her.

"Aye, you can." She raised up, and the evening coolness struck them for the first time. It must be getting dark, she realized, and she had no time to indulge him. "Give me your hands," she ordered, and he submitted them meekly. Placing them on her waist, she said with stern authority, "Don't move them."

She trembled with the effort this slow and steady assault cost her. She wanted to pillage him, satisfy the burning inside her, take him with no care for his pleasure, yet know his pleasure met hers irresistibly. She simply wanted him to realize he could no more deny her than she could him. As he had done once before, she now taunted him. "You, my Lord William, are the man who's going to purge me of my frustration. Right. Now."

He laughed and groaned. Prepared, she caught his hands as they flew away from her waist and returned them with firm emphasis. "You've had your turn, William, now yield me mine."

He groaned again. Her purpose was now clear, but he was a fair man and he let her have her way.

She touched his mouth with her open lips, mixing their breath, and he tried to capture her with his tongue, but she'd have no part of it. Pulling back, she laughed, a slow, mocking chuckle.

"Witch." He accused her with less heat than he intended.

She heard his torment and responded with the slow slide of her body down his. Standing, she untied his garters and hooked her thumbs in his waistband. He lifted his hips in response to her unspoken demand, and she pulled his clothing away, all of it.

She didn't know what prompted her, pure curiosity perhaps, but she leaned into him and tasted him. His writhings stopped; every respiration, every indication of life, every motion of enjoyment failed him. Alarmed, she pulled her mouth away. "Are you well? William?"

A huge sigh answered her.

Never had William been tormented in such a sweet way. He wanted to move, to shout, to keep Saura where she was and to tear her away. He held his breath, gritted his teeth, held the bench as if it would buck him off, and when he could stand no more, he muttered, "Saura!"

Smiling her vengeful smile, she rose to her feet and lifted her skirt, asking, "Is this what you want?"

"Damn you, Saura, come to me if you value your own pleasure."

She didn't question, simply brought herself over him, skirt held high. She wedged one knee against the wall, keeping one foot on the ground, and found him with unerring instinct. She wanted to plunge on him, satisfy herself with one swift race to completion, but more than that she wanted to torture him. Controlling herself, she eased up, using her extended leg for guidance. Experimenting, she swiveled her hips on the way down. He gasped and strained up against her, and she quickened with excitement. Oh, he liked that! She rose again, and swiveled back down, and rose.

His hands clamped on her waist, and he jerked her straight down, lifted her.

With her hands and her body, she fought William; not enough to destroy their union, but enough that he grunted, "Stop, you little wanton."

Of course, if he'd wanted to stop her, he could; he could easily have overpowered her at any moment. It spoke volumes for his patience that he could listen to her curse him, maintain their rhythm and still encourage her with his ever-increasing gusto.

She panted, she struggled; she found little screams escaping from her throat with no volition of her own. And when she rose above him one last time and the feeling burst within, he was with her. He relished the shudders that drove her to the brink of insanity and when she finished, his back arched off the bench and he forced her back to the brink with his own mighty explosion.

She wilted down onto him, no longer stiff with passion and resolve. Lifting one of her wrists, he released it and chuckled as it dropped. He raised her, adjusting their positions for warmth and comfort. She did as his hands instructed, limp in the sweet aftermath of passion. With an insight that surprised her, he waited until he had settled her securely under his chin to inquire, "Still angry?"

"Aye," she answered with a slow drawl that owed everything to gratification. "But I lack the fortitude to express it."

"I'll remember this pleasurable way to subdue you," he promised.

A bit of fight sprang to life and she began to rear up, but his hand on her head forced her back down. Indignant, she said, "You hardly seem frisky now."

"My powers of recovery are remarkable," he reminded.

Sullen, she refused to admit it, and he continued, "You were ready for me. Did teasing me arouse you?"

Her breath fanned his neck. "Aye, of course. When you enjoy it so much, my whole body releases the love I feel."

"Love?" he asked idly, combing her hair with his fingers.

"The love an obedient wife feels for her husband."

"The love the Church ordains." He nodded against her head as if he understood.

"Aye." Her voice trailed off to uncertainty. She could feel the restraint that molded him into a firm board beneath her, and she thought she knew why. "I'd be an ungrateful fool if I didn't thank you for returning that love."

"What makes you think I return it?"

She laughed soft in her throat. "You're kind to me. You're patient with my ignorance. You never remind me I'm a burden or beat me when I deserve it."

"God's teeth! You call that love?"

He sat up, dislodging her from her nest under his chin. Bewildered by his sudden rigid fury, she struggled on his lap, but he wouldn't let her go.

Holding her chest to chest, he growled, "You are a fool if you think that's love! Are you so unworthy you're satisfied with that whey-water version of love?"

" 'Tis what everyone else has."

"Everyone else? We can do better than everyone else."

Amazed at his vehemence and perturbed by their abrupt return from satiation to reality, she demanded, "What do you mean?"

"I'll tell you what love is. 'Tis standing arm in arm against the world and knowing together you could rule the country. 'Tis fighting with each other with tooth and nail and never fearing sly or brutal reprisals. 'Tis going to war against the whole world, yet knowing that peace resides in the bed between us."

Trying to deny him, she said, "You speak of fight and ruling and war, and try to tell me about love?"

"I am a knight. How do you want me to say it?" He put his hands around her shoulders and held her still. The darkness wrapped them around, no one could see him making such an idiot of himself, and his warrior's heart swelled. Dredging the words from some hidden part of his soul, he explained, " 'Tis knowing God created Eve from Adam's rib, the spot that protected his heart. 'Tis knowing without that rib to protect him, a man is vulnerable. 'Tis knowing you're created to be at my side, not under my feet. 'Tis knowing we're one body, one mind."

Angry again, and fearing his eloquence, Saura jumped away from him and he let her go. She tugged her skirt down, flicking it into place, pulling her protection about her. "That's ridiculous. The poets sing of such nonsense, but this is reality. Do you expect me to believe that any man doesn't appreciate gratitude?"

"Gratitude?" He stood up, towering over her and trapping her with his emotion. "For not beating you? Damn, how can you be so intelligent and so stupid? 'Tis not gratitude I want from you. I want you to be happy with me."

"I am happy."

"With me!" His words ran out, and he returned to the plain, unadorned French he used everyday. "When we began, you and I were equal. You were my teacher, I was a warrior. Now you want me to be your father, to protect you and be satisfied with gratitude."

"I don't want a father," she faltered.

"Oh, don't you! The loving father you never had. But for that I endow you my own father."

She wrapped her arms around her stomach, in pain and at a loss. "I don't know what you want."

It was a cry of bewilderment, and his voice gentled. "I want a wife, Saura. I want a woman who loves me, who glories in my love for her, who values my judgment enough to know I'd not love an unworthy vessel. Anne was the wife chosen for me by my father, and we formed ourselves into a marriage and we were happy. Yet I speak no treason to Anne when I say you're the wife chosen by me for me. There's no need to file away rough edges; we already fit. We always fit. We could have the kind of love that shines like a light for all to see, but you're afraid."

"What do you mean, afraid?"

"Afraid to trust me with your confidence. Afraid that I'll be like Theobald and the others, and laugh at you. Afraid to look into my soul and see the kind of man I am. I'm open to you, and you're afraid to *see.*"

He struck at the very heart of her anxiety. He was in her mind, and for the first time she realized what a coward she was. She didn't want him to know her so well, she didn't want to know him as if he were the other half of her. She couldn't maintain her anger in the face of his sadness, and when she spoke she found her voice thickened with tears. "You don't believe me about Charles."

"You haven't given me a logical reason to believe you. You haven't given me someone else to suspect. For God's sake, tell me what's in your mind."

Crying in earnest now, she muttered, "I can't. I just can't."

He was silent, accepting her words, and then he walked away from her. Kneeling on the ground, he cursed. "I can find my breeches, but not my hose. That'll have to do."

She heard him struggling to dress, readying himself to walk away from her, and her sobs overwhelmed her. She remembered crying in front of Theobald, back when he could still hurt her. She remembered his scorn, remembered hearing him say, "Don't play that game with me. Sniveling won't win my sympathies." Stuffing her skirt into her mouth to muffle her sounds, she stood desolate while William prepared to walk away, and flayed herself for cowardice. He was dressed, he was going.

But he came to her and wrapped his big arms around her. "Don't cry, sweeting. You're breaking my heart. Please don't cry."

That made it worse. Kindness when she expected scorn,

caring when she deserved a shaking. The sobs shook her in earnest and he held her and crooned.

When the storm subsided, he petted her and said, "Let's go in now. 'Tis dark out here. 'Tis getting chill."

"Nay! Nay." She shook her head against him and mopped her face on the skirt of her cotte. "I want to stay out here and think." He began to deny her, but she begged, "Please, William, I have so much to consider. Leave me alone, just for a while."

Surprisingly, he did as she implored. He left her standing in the dark, in the damp, in a garden that was no longer a refuge from herself. When she knew he had gone in, she said to the empty air, "I just want to be the right kind of wife. I just want to be a normal wife."

"Bula!" Saura tossed aside the handful of dry leaves she was shredding and called him. Listening, she could hear the distant snuffling noises as Bula sought to scare up another squirrel, and called firmly, "Bula, come."

He snorted in protest, but galloped to her, bringing his ready affection and need for constant attention. She fended off the attack of his tongue on her face. Scrubbing under his chin, she listened to his ecstatic whine and crooned, "Aye, you're a sweet boy, you are." She used his collar to lever herself off the bench and groped for the rope tacked from tree to tree, marking her path.

She didn't want to be alone, for it left her mind open to the fears and regrets, but today the pain had chased her from the castle. She'd had to promise Maud she wouldn't wander far. She'd promised to take Bula for security. When Maud snorted and pointed out that the dog was nothing but an overgrown puppy, Saura had had to agree. Still, his mere size discouraged most, and his unrestrained friendliness acted as a protection in itself. Maud had snorted again, but reluctantly consented to let Saura go. Maud saw the torment that trapped her mistress, and she trusted Lord Peter's woodsmen to keep her darling safe.

Saura followed her fingertips from the castle wall into the forest where she could sit in solitude and think. And think. And curse herself and her inhibitions and wish she had William back.

William had stayed for three days after their night in the garden, hugging her, touching her, preparing to leave.

He'd been kind and encouraging, praising her good sense and helpful hands. He'd done everything to mend the rift between them. He'd given her every chance to tell him what he wanted to hear. Time and again she opened her mouth to tell him; tell him she'd be his wife, give her whole self, hold nothing back. But her intrinsic truthfulness restrained her. She couldn't surrender herself so completely, and she ached with the knowing.

Why couldn't she? What led her to keep her heart safe? She couldn't understand her own mind. She'd never believed she was a coward, she'd never believed she'd be satisfied with less than complete union. So why did she step away from her heart's desire?

They'd fooled the servants, they'd fooled everyone. They'd seemed easy with each other, and only the two of them had heard the dreadful silences between them when conversation had lagged.

And he'd left.

Housework hadn't filled the gap. She'd attacked all the duties of the chatelaine with vicious determination. She'd ordered the undercroft scrubbed, rotting fruit from the previous year discarded, and a thorough cleaning performed. Last year's salted meat had been placed in the front to be used first, and the pickling barrels awaited the first cold snap and the butchering that would fill them. Eating apples were packed in wooden boxes, cushioned by straw, and the tiny apples were pressed for cider. Herbs were hung to dry from the ceiling.

It had all been in vain, worthless distractions that couldn't keep her mind from wandering. Now she walked with Bula, seeking a solution to the ache that plagued her. Together they proceeded down the path, the crisp air wrapping them round.

Saura wanted to reach the large oak. She'd turn back there, she promised herself. It wasn't far, but she wanted to explore the flaking bark with the palm of her hand. She wanted to feel the carving William had made for them one day as they walked the path in their honey month, a *W* entwined with an *S*, he'd explained, guiding her fingers through the loops of the letters. She wanted to find the marks, wedged in between the reminders of other sweethearts, and trace them lovingly. Like a fool, she wanted to hug the tree that kept the remembrance of their happiness.

For the first time since William left, she descended into the depths of pathos. The whole world was unfair. Her brothers didn't need her. Pertrade Castle still stood without her. Her husband was gone, her faithful serving maid had found a love. She tripped on a rock in the path and sobbed out loud. A branch smacked her in the face and she knocked it aside. She wrapped her hand around Bula's collar and urged him forward.

Bula tried to veer off, away from the rope that directed her, and Saura admonished, "Nay, boy, this way. We're almost there."

He insisted they should go into the trees, and she found the rope with her hands again. "The squirrels must be allowed to gather their nuts, and we must go to the tree. We're not getting there very quickly, between your frolicking and my laziness. Come on." She tightened her grip on his collar and tugged.

He came, whining insistently and leaning sideways against her guidance. His weight created an ache in her arm and she pulled him sharply. "Come *on!*" He yelped as if she had hurt him, and she scolded, "You fool dog. You're the biggest baby. Don't you want to go to the tree with me? We'll be there straightaway."

Obediently, he trotted along beside her for another moment and then began his sideways pull. He stopped and sniffed the ground, tangling beneath her feet, and she let him go in exasperation. Released, he didn't run off, as she expected, but stood in her path and barked.

His bark puzzled her. He wasn't sounding an alarm, yet he seemed unwillingly to let her go on. He seemed uncertain, in doubt.

Putting her fists at her waist, she asked, "Bula, are you mad?"

For answer, he bumped her hard with his big head, and the tears that threatened overflowed.

"I can't go back yet." She stopped to suck in her breath and stifle the sobs that broke her voice. "I've got to be alone."

He nudged her away from the rope, but she found it and gripped it with her fist.

"I can't leave the path. I'd be lost in the forest."

He didn't understand, insistent that he wanted her to go away from the cable. He pushed her, and when she wouldn't leave, he trotted a few feet away and whined with entreaty.

"I can't." Even the dog was abandoning her. Her emotions broke, and she cried with unstifled sadness. She turned away from him and groped unsteadily down the path, and when he sprang in front of her and tripped her once more, it was too much. "Go away!" She smacked him with the side of her hand, hurting her bones and his feelings. "Go on and leave me. I don't need you!"

He whined and ducked, tried to insist and whined when she swung at him and deliberately missed. Then he sat in the middle of the path behind her and complained as she followed the cord around the bend—and stopped in midflight, in midsob.

This wasn't right.

She trusted that dog. Not even her own battered emotions could shake her faith. He was her eyes, and if he tried to stop her from going where she wished, there had to be a reason.

Sniffling, she dug her handkerchief out of her sleeve. Wiping her nose, she listened. The woods sounded quieter today. Deeper. With a subdued hush. Shuffling her feet, she found deep leaves, leaves so deep it seemed they hadn't been disturbed by feet tramping a worn path. Odd. And jagged stones, lots of stones. Lifting her hands out, she swung around. Trees hung their shaggy branches thick about her and broke the ground with their untamed roots.

She stiffened; she clasped her fist to her chest. Her fingers kneaded the handkerchief and her teeth chewed her lip.

It almost seemed as if she were in a part of the forest where she'd never been before.

It was impossible.

Unless the ropes had been moved.

"Bula," she called uncertainly.

He barked in reply and scuffled in the leaves.

Raising her head, she sniffed and smelled it: the sour smell of men who had spent many hours in the woods.

Whirling, she grasped the rope in her fingers and ran back toward her dog. "Bula!" She heard his bark of recognition, but he wasn't barking at her. She ran faster, stumbling in an agony of dread, and she heard heavy footsteps racing toward her. She heard Bula growl, deep in his chest, and heard it grow to a full, hostile snarl. Men yelled warnings. A human being screamed. From Bula came the noise of desperation.

She gasped at the sound of a heavy thump, like a rock against a hollow log. Abruptly, the agonized canine noises stopped, and she called Bula again, but he didn't answer her.

As her panic rose up to choke her, she heard a man speaking the same words she'd heard before, but now his voice was unmuffled and recognizable.

"Fear not, fair lady. I love you."

eighteen

William was a man who prided himself on his logic. The world would have been shocked to hear he didn't believe in witches or wizards or imps. He'd been a skeptic since the day he'd captured a squeaking goblin. The goblin had turned out to be nothing more than a stained and frightened man, a charcoal burner who lived deep in the woods. Nothing in his later life had changed William's firm conviction that men feared the unknown for no reason. No one, be they magician or juggler, had displayed powers he couldn't understand, and so he dealt with logic and found it a convincing substitute for humbug.

He'd used logic to decide Charles was the bastard who sought his downfall, but there lodged in his mind a tiny niggling doubt.

Something was missing from his logic.

Staring at the stronghold where Charles lived, William tapped his fingers on his saddle and wished he knew what to do. Somehow, as he'd ridden farther from Saura and closer to Charles, he'd convinced himself she spoke the truth. Slower and slower he'd ridden, the burden of his uncertainty growing heavy. The trip that should have taken three days took seven as he debated the wisdom of his move. He ached to turn around and ride back to Saura, to tell her she was right and he was wrong. But perhaps he simply felt guilty.

He'd thought he could slowly teach her to love him as he loved her. He'd thought the patience he possessed was sufficient to lay siege to her restraints. He'd found, to his own amazement, that it was not. How could he have demanded so much of her? Saura's brothers had told him of her legacy from Theobald; he'd been prepared for years of slow and steady support to wean her from her *idée fixe*. Instead he'd discovered he couldn't tolerate her gratitude, offered him at the end of a halcyon interlude.

Gratitude: It made him want to spit. How could she cheapen their matrimony by offering nothing more than what other women gave? How could she demand less than he was willing to give?

Shaking his head in disbelief, he stared again at the battlements before him. Was he ignoring Saura's conviction from vindictiveness or good sense? She swore it wasn't Charles, but offered no other candidates. With feminine illogic, she'd deemed Charles innocent, but could offer no other suspects.

She couldn't be correct.

Like a well-oiled wheel running in a well-worn track, he again reviewed the facts. Charles needed the money. Charles was weak-willed and envious. Charles was always at the right place, at the right time for the attacks. Charles . . . Charles was all that was logical. And unlikely.

Damn! Saura had affected him more than he realized. Raising his hand to his band of soldiers, he signaled them to dismount. His squire lowered his banner and together they slid to the ground to rest and prepare for battle the following morning.

"How could you kill my dog?"

"I didn't kill him. My men killed him. I just got him to sit still long enough so they could tether him."

"Bula knew you," Saura said in misery. "He knew you were a friend of William's. When he should have attacked you, he didn't because he knew his master let you in his house."

"When I ran after you, he didn't trust me any longer. He mauled one of my men so badly I had to leave him there to enrich the soil. So you see, I didn't kill that dog. I couldn't kill him and subdue you at the same time."

"You're mad." Saura sat before Nicholas in the saddle, her knees on either side of his horse and her skirt tucked up beneath her. He held her with his arm, leaning her back against his chest. She hated it, she hated to touch him and she shuddered when he touched her, but she had no choice. The battle to subdue her had been swift and brutal and lonely. There had been no one in the forest to help her, no one to save her when he had wrestled her to the ground. Her frenzied use of her fingernails and her eating knife had only earned her marks on her face and a swollen wrist, and a grudging respect for her captor's ability to wield his strength. Everyone had a contempt for his knightly skills, but she now held a healthy respect for his cunning and brutality. And a healthy fear of his obsessions.

"I'm not mad," he assured her. "I'm brilliant. The normal run of mankind isn't worthy to receive my foot on their neck."

"This is despicable."

"Dishonorable." She felt him nod in agreement. "So sly and sneaky and clever it's hard to believe one man could have planned it."

"Aren't you ashamed?" she asked desperately. "You're soiling the very men who fostered you."

He laughed in genuine amusement and dropped a light kiss on her neck. "Lord Peter of Burke is nothing but a pious old windbag. Always blathering on about knights and the sanctity of your sworn word and the contracts of loyalty."

"He means it."

"Of course he does. More than that, he lives it. 'Twas so easy to fool him, 'twas pathetic." He grunted. "William wasn't so easy—that's why I've enjoyed it so. William worships at the altar of logic, and so I planned very carefully. You see, he doesn't believe I'm the logical blackguard."

"You *aren't* the logical blackguard. Why are you doing this?"

" 'Tis no mystery." His hand began a slow slide up and down her arm. "I was the fourth son of my father. Did you know that?"

"Nay, I thought you had one brother, your eldest."

"Aye, that was Lance. But there were two others ahead of me, and my father used to exult at his good fortune. Three healthy boys before me. I didn't stand a chance to inherit, and he was glad."

Nervously, Saura urged him to continue. "Didn't he like you?"

"My father. . . ." His hand dropped to the reins again and his voice developed a nasty sneer. "My father was a man like William. Big and fierce. He lived for fighting. And my brothers acted like brawling gods, always propping themselves on a horse and going at the quintain. They didn't understand me, understand how I could increase the property by using my brains. Only my mother understood me."

"Your mother? She understood you and your brothers?"

"The other boys betrayed her, leaving her alone in the castle while they fought and got wounded and worried her into illness. I held her hand as she coughed and wheezed when they came home with bruises and broken bones. She used to get so sick she couldn't care for them. She had to leave them to the nursemaid."

"She left her sick children in the hands of a nursemaid?"

"Mama was too delicate to care for such rambunctious boys," he said piously.

"Hm." Saura withheld judgment.

"The boys always said they were sorry, but they went out and did it again. I watched her cry when my brothers left for fostering, and I swore I'd never make her cry like that. God, how I hated them."

She felt the muscles of his chest tighten, as if he would explode into violence, and asked timidly, "Did they beat you?"

"Oh, nay. Nay. Just treated me with a kind of contempt that lashed at my bones." He laughed with an unpleasant snarl. "Beat me? Nay, they tried to make a man out of me. Tried to make me enjoy getting my head smashed in. My father used to say he didn't understand how he could have sired such a sneaky little wheyface." The horse jolted forward as his hands struggled with the reins. "He sent me to Lord Peter to be fostered because Lord Peter was the best knight in all England." He puffed out his chest and lowered his voice in imitation of his father. "Lord Peter had *bred* the best fighter in all Christendom."

A return of her normal spirit made her protest, "You can't tell me Lord Peter and William were cruel to you!"

"Nay, indeed. The only reason I became a knight was because of Lord Peter's constant coddling. I hardly ever saw his contempt. William wasn't so clever at hiding his."

She didn't answer; she knew that was true. He fell into a brooding silence, but soon they climbed and broke into the sunshine and Saura knew they'd reached the road. Both Nicholas and the horse perked up and his hands began their slow wandering on her belly. Desperate to divert him, she asked, "Where are we going?"

"To Cran Castle. 'Tis my finest keep. It sits high above the sea on the great white cliffs. The great hall is drafty with the wind off the ocean, but the solar is better than Burke's." He laid his stubbly cheek close against hers in a parody of affection. "I picked it especially for you."

Never the fool, she twisted aside, saying shrewdly, "And for its defensibility?"

He chuckled, that low and breathy sound that had haunted her at Burke and now raised goose bumps on her skin. "That's one of the reasons I love you. You're so pragmatic."

When he'd had her down on the ground in the woods, his knees in her back and her wrists twisted up and behind, he'd spoken in that rasping voice chill with intent. "I could take you right now," he'd said, "but I'll teach you to love me first."

The memory made her want to pull her knees together over the horse's neck in convulsive fear, but she was afraid to move and call his attention to her open position. Instead, she argued, "This is silly. You can't love a blind woman. You might love my lands, but never me."

"Your lands are indeed attractive, but you're wrong. I do love you. At first I only coveted you, as I covet all of William's possessions. But as I watched you with William, in my heart bloomed a great longing to be the object of your loving attentions. When I saw how enamored of you he is, that greed turned to love."

"You mean you love me because William wants me."

"Nay," he corrected. "I love you because William loves you. He's devoted to you. He lives for you."

"He doesn't love me, not really." Despondent tears unexpectedly filled her eyes as she remembered his restrained courtesy before he'd left.

"Oh, he loves you. I recognize all the signs," Nicholas said in the singsong voice of a gossip. "He loved his other wife, too, you know, but I think he loves you more."

"What do you mean?" She felt stifled; she knew she shouldn't encourage this conversation, yet she couldn't resist hearing his analysis of her William.

"With Anne, he was content, pleasant, happy. With you, he's not content, he's desperate for you all the time. He's happy when you're happy, always looking for ways to please you. He wants to kill the men who look at you. He dotes on you at mealtimes, as if you were some dish fixed just for him."

Wanting to believe, yet afraid, she laughed unsteadily. "Oh come, Nicholas."

With evil intent, he added, "He'll come after you."

The blood froze in her veins. "He's not at Burke. He'll not realize I'm gone."

"I know. I saw him go haring off toward Charles's castle. I've been watching since the last full moon."

"Since the last full moon." Her statement no longer contained surprise.

"After the wedding, I had to go to Cran and prepare it for you and give my orders. Then I came back and lived in the woods, but you never came out. You were all I was waiting for," he explained intensely.

"Am I so important?"

"Fair lady, you are the center of my whole plan! With your capture, I'm assured of you and assured of William!"

Her hands curled at her waist. "He's gone, I tell you. He'll not know where I am."

"He'll know. He'll know soon if he doesn't know already. I've made sure of that."

Feeling like a complete idiot, William stood below the walls of Charles's castle and roared, "You can't surrender, plague take you! This is a siege!"

Charles leaned out one of the crenels in the battlements and shouted back, "You'll win, what the hell difference does it make? I don't even know why you're besieging me!"

"You jest!"

"Jest! I stand here in ignoble nudity, shivering in the cold air, a beautiful damsel left unsatisfied in my bed, and you say I jest? You are mad," Charles said with heavy conviction.

"*I'm* not mad," William denied.

"You are if you stand out there when the drawbridge is open and a healthy fire burning on my hearth. But do as you like." Charles turned away and cried over his shoulder, "I'm too cold to argue with you."

William shifted from one foot to the other. His forces had waited until the early morn to attack, waited in the first cold snap of the year for the sun to rise. Now the men-at-arms crouched on their haunches or leaned against trees and observed their breath as it steamed in the frigid air. They didn't look at William, standing alone and furious, or at the castle, where the drawbridge lowered with majestic slowness.

William stared at the beckoning gate and then at his men. A trap? "God's teeth," he muttered. Adjusting his belt, freeing his sword, he strode forward over the bridge and into the bailey.

Trained to think with their master's brain, half of his force followed on his heels, and the other half remained outside on alert. The knot of men who walked into the clear area inside the walls stared around them with bright eyes. The partially dressed soldiers inside stared back in disgust, yawning, shivering. They were in such a state of unreadiness William reeled with horror. "God's teeth," he muttered to Channing. "Didn't my father train Charles better than this? He'd be destroyed in a siege."

"Perhaps he doesn't think he's got anything worth fighting for," the man-at-arms suggested.

William whipped around and glared, and Channing shrugged. Turning back, William paced up to the door of the keep and peered in. Nothing. No hidden soldiers, no boiling tar to fling on him. He drew his sword and climbed the stairs to the great hall. Nothing. Just servants scurrying back and forth placing clothes on the trestle table and the smell of fresh-baked bread rising from baskets on the sideboards. He edged into the room, keeping his back to the wall and feeling absurd, and his men imitated him. By the grimaces on their faces, he suspected they felt even more absurd, and he straightened and said, "God's teeth," one more time.

This time he said it loudly, and Charles answered as he pushed aside the screen that hid his bed. "I don't know what you're up to, William, but you're a dunce to think you can get anything out of me. Blood out of a stone would be easier." He tucked his shirt into his breeches as he spoke, and

William could see a very pretty serving maid peeking at him from beneath the covers on the bed.

"I didn't come to take your lands," William protested. "I'm not so dishonorable. I came to kill you."

Charles stopped, his hand still caught in the material, and stared at William as if he had taken leave of his senses. "Kill me! Does your father know about this?"

"Aye." William floundered beneath the hurt in Charles's eyes. "You were the logical choice, you see, to be trying to kill *me*."

"Holy Mary and all the saints." Charles walked to the bench at the head table and sat down heavily, his back to William. Placing his hands on his knees, he shook his head in amazed disbelief. "What in the name of heaven makes you think I'd try to kill you?"

"You need the money," William explained simply.

"The money?"

"Well, we can't figure out why someone would try to kill me unless 'twas for my lands and my—"

"Maybe," Charles interrupted, rising to his feet and facing William. "Maybe 'tis because you're a pompous stew head who deserves a good beating! I've changed my mind. Take your men and get the hell out of my hall and we'll fight. You dullard! You lout, you addlepated—"

William held out his hands and shouted above Charles's roar. "You've convinced me."

"Convinced you? Curse you to hell. Get out of my castle, you yellow-bellied lickspittle!"

"Charles, I need your help."

Charles stopped short, his tirade suspended by disbelief. "You've never needed my help in your whole life," he accused.

"I need it now. Someone is threatening my wife and me."

"I thought you took care of that when you killed Arthur."

William jerked. "How did you know that I killed Arthur?"

"Everyone knows you killed Arthur. Think, you dunderhead! At your wedding, no one mentioned it to you, but does that mean no one gossiped about it? Nay. 'Tis generally acknowledged you killed Arthur when you discovered he'd been the one to blind you."

"Good God," William said blankly. "I never thought."

"I suspected that," Charles said, but without his previous harshness. "Well, bring your men in and we'll break our fast and talk."

"Aye, I need that. I need that very much."

"William said you would never have killed Hawisa." The wind blew off the ocean now, tossing the tendrils that had escaped her braid and making her shiver with the chill. As they'd ridden, they'd been joined by more and more of his men, riding up and dropping in line behind them. Saura felt surrounded, out of control and panicked. "That once you owned Hawisa you would have maintained her."

"I had to kill her. She threatened you."

He said it with such simple menace her breath caught in anguish. "If you want me because William wants me," she said carefully, "if you love me because William loves me, will you still love me when William is dead?"

He didn't say a word, lax with surprise. Then he mused, "I hadn't thought about it like that. William has been in the way for so long, I can't imagine a time when he's not here. Will I still love you?" They rode for so long in silence, Saura almost jumped from the horse in desperation. When he spoke, that breathy lust had settled into his voice. "You know, I believe I will. I really believe I will. I don't think I'll ever tire of you." His arm tightened on her waist and placed a kiss on her neck, moist and repulsive.

She wished she hadn't asked, for what good answer was there? He would kill her or he would keep her, and the choice between an unshriven death and life under his hands seemed difficult and depressing. Difficult and depressing. She laughed harshly. An understatement indeed.

His mouth wandered up to her cheek, fueling the fever of curiosity that seized her, and she couldn't control her question. "What happened to your two middle brothers?"

"They died while I stayed at Burke, quite beyond my control, I assure you. My father died, too." Nicholas sounded replete with satisfaction. "Thus when I returned home, I had only my eldest brother ahead of me in line for the inheritance. Lance was so honorable, just like William, and so gullible, just like Lord Peter, and killing him was so easy."

"You killed your own brother?" She'd begun to suspect it, but even so she recoiled. "How?"

"Nothing so crude as fighting." He laughed as if he were pleased with himself, and added matter-of-factly, "I poisoned him."

"Holy Saint Wilfred."

"He called on Saint Wilfred. He called on all the saints before he died. Do you know his convulsions made him look like a puppet on a string?" He sounded analytical, and her gorge rose in her throat. "It took him three days to die. Three days! I was in an agony of suspense, fearing he'd recover and rob me of the position I'd worked so hard to obtain."

"Please. . . ."

Protesting, she swayed in the saddle, but he misinterpreted her pain. "Oh, don't worry. He did die, and without any more help from me. But next time I'll give a larger dose of the herbs. I beat the witch who gave them to me. She knows her duty now."

With a jolt, she realized the hopelessness of pleading for William's life; any man who spoke of killing his own flesh and blood with such casual contentment could hardly be moved by words of mercy and kindness. No longer did she fear the rape and horror that threatened; that fear was overthrown by the conviction she must save William from this fiend. For the first time on this dreadful ride, she began to plot.

⚜

"Whoever it is killed Hawisa," William reminded him.

"Then it can't be Nicholas." Charles wiped his chin with his napkin. "He'd never destroy anything that could make a penny for him."

"That's what I said," William agreed. "But who's left?"

"You?"

"What?"

"Somebody killed that slut. Saura was the logical choice." Charles laughed. "Listen to me. I've been with you too much."

William pounded one fist on the table. "Saura didn't kill her."

"Nay. If Saura'd tried to kill that big, hulking maid, Saura's neck would be broken. Still, she threatened Saura and Saura threatened her in return. Thus, I can't help but suspect you."

"I've never killed a woman in my life," William said without emotion. Charles said nothing, looking steadily at his friend, and William shrugged. "Yes, if I'd wanted to, Hawisa would have been the one. Remember how she would sneak into my bed and try to tempt me?"

"Until the time Anne caught her, and then the wench avoided you like the plague."

They laughed together, but returned to their serious contemplation.

Charles explained, "Anne outweighed Hawisa by two stone. Lady Saura wasn't big enough to scare Hawisa, so I thought that you—"

"No. Whoever killed her is our hellhound." William peered at Charles. "It couldn't be Raymond."

Charles snorted. "Marriage has scrambled your brain. Raymond loves you."

Hearing what he wanted to hear, William sighed with relief, then straightened with consternation.

"And he loves your lady. Hell, I think half the men at the wedding were in love with your lady. Raymond brooded about her, I sighed over her, and you never even noticed. You had eyes for no one save her. All her attention bent to you. Even Nicholas lusted after her, and you know how he feels about women." Charles finished his second mug of ale and belched. "Those stupid poems and all those innuendos he spread around. And he kept looking at her with those red eyes, like the devil who'd seen an angel land on earth."

William turned his cup and gazed at the ale as if somewhere inside he'd find the answer. "It had to be someone at the wedding. It had to be someone who knew Burke Castle. Whoever it was kept sneaking up on Saura, scaring her and whispering to her. He even came into the garden through that little back gate, remember it? And touched her."

Charles growled in disgust. "That sounds like Nicholas. He always liked to sneak around and frighten the folk who couldn't get back at him."

"I didn't know that."

Shrugging, Charles explained, "You were four years older. You were a squire when we were pages and a knight when we were squires. When you came home to visit, you were the object of our hero worship. God, for years we looked up to you. Especially Nicholas. He kept his corruptions well hidden from you."

A fear burgeoned within William, a fear he kept at bay with his logic. "What else did he do?"

"The usual mean little-boy things. He liked to tie his dog too tight and watch it gag. He'd 'accidentally' knock the squires down with his lance. And he only rutted with women who were unwilling. Or girls."

William quivered, on the edge of discovery. "But he didn't kill Hawisa."

"Nay." Charles rinsed his hands in the fingerbowl and nodded to his squire to take it away. "He'd have to be mad to have killed that maid."

"That's it!" William stood up and shouted. "That's it! That's what's wrong with my logic. There's no logic in madness, and Nicholas is mad. Totally insane. Come on." He smacked Charles on the arm and leaped over the bench. "We've got to go. If he hasn't got Saura yet, he soon will have."

nineteen

"I used to worship him," Nicholas said plaintively. "Did you know that?"

"Who?" Saura crouched, shivering before the fire in the great hall of Cran Castle.

"William. I used to worship his footsteps."

"What changed your mind?"

"Nothing." He stepped closer to the fire and she edged aside, tucking her skirt around her ankles. "I never changed my mind as much as realized I could be him."

"Be him?" she asked stupidly. "Be William?"

"Aye, don't you see? That's the beauty of it. After I kill William, I'll be Lord Peter's son."

Astounded and confused, she blurted, "What about Kimball?"

"Kimball?" He sounded almost absentminded.

"Kimball, William's son. The heir to all Lord Peter's lands."

"Oh, Kimball." He brushed him aside with no concern. "I'll have to kill Kimball."

Closing her eyes in anguish, Saura prayed for guidance. "Don't you want to be . . . William . . . to Kimball?"

"Be a father?" Nicholas considered it. "Nay, children are too much trouble. He can remain until he becomes of some consequence, and then he'll have to die. I'll be his chief mourner, as William would be. Does that make you happy?"

In all sincerity, he was offering her a boon, and that was worse than what had gone before. His idea of kindness was the murder of a boy, followed by a monstrous lie. Her control slipped. She could hear her blood throbbing in her ears. He was evil, and she wanted to send him back home, back to the devil. She rose; she wanted to rip his eyes out, strike him, make him bleed.

The sound of shod feet running up the stairs stopped her. Cocking her head, she listened. The slap of shoes and the whistling gasps reminded her of someone, and when the panting messenger spoke, her fury dissolved in shock.

"I tol' Lord William ye had her, m'lord."

"Dreadful rogue!" Saura exploded. "Bronnie, what are you doing here?"

"Oh, m'lady, I hoped ye wouldn't know me." Sounding more wretched than he had when she'd left him in Arthur's castle, Bronnie shuffled his feet. "Lord Nicholas became my thane when Lord Arthur died an' I'm just doin' what he tells me."

"How could you!"

"I'm not likin' it," he assured her. "I tried t' tell Lord Nicholas not t' do it, but for some reason no un ever listens t' me."

"I've heard too much from you," Nicholas said frostily. "You're not here to chat with my wife, but to report—"

"Your wife? I thought ye said she was Lord William's wife!"

"Fool!"

The sharp crack of hand against face and Bronnie's groan made Saura wince.

"Mind the business you're told to. Now what did Lord William say?"

"I didn't exactly see Lord William." Bronnie danced back and Saura assumed he'd dodged another blow. " 'Twasn't possible! I found Lord Charles's castle just where you tol' me, an' I walks right up an' knocks at th' gate, but they say th' whole throng inside is gettin' ready t' ride out, an' I asks where, an' they say t' save Lady Saura, an' I says who's got her? An' they say Lord Nicholas, an' I says that's right."

Saura didn't want to laugh. She knew hysteria loomed close. But try as she would, she couldn't dislodge her grin. Bronnie's obvious cowardice was too much. With a gasp, she began to giggle and continued until Nicholas laughed, too.

"That's fine, Bronnie," he assured the serf with assumed geniality. "As long as William knows where she is."

"That's not all, Lord," Bronnie said eagerly. "Lord William's comin' by hisself."

"What!" Saura's laughter stopped and she sank down on a bench, clasping the sides with rigid fingers. "By himself?"

"Aye, I went into th' castle for a bite t' eat. Th' kitchen maid seemed t' take a fancy to me."

"Resting?" Nicholas snorted.

"A man can't run so far an' not need t' rest, m'lord."

"Oh, of course not."

Nicholas's sarcasm flew over Bronnie's head, and the man sighed with relief. "Aye, I knew ye'd agree. I heard him talkin'. Arguin', actually."

"Lord William?" Nicholas tapped his toe.

"Aye, Lord William! Who else? They were at dinner an' I

heard him. Tellin' his friend that th' scurvy beast who had his lady would never let an army in, but he might let just him in by hisself. Lord William, I mean."

"Scurvy beast, eh? We'll see who's the beast. Could a beast have trapped the fabulous Lord William? Could a beast have planned such an operation? Who else but Lord Nicholas of Walham could have brought William of Miraval to his knees?"

"Not quite to his knees. Not yet." Saura grunted when Nicholas reached over and pressed his fingers into her shoulder, leaving a bruise, she was sure.

"What would Charles do while William comes to me, by *hisself?*" he mocked. His voice never wavered from her direction, but the query was for Bronnie.

"Oh, he was goin' for Lord Peter."

"Going to Lord Peter," Nicholas said thoughtfully. "Interesting. How long ago was this?"

"Yesterday. I ran like th' wind back here."

"That's what you're good for," Nicholas said. "When were they leaving?"

"Lord William, he was chomping at th' bit, but Charles needed help organizing th' men an' preparing for war. Today at dawn, they said."

"Did you hear that, my love? Luck is with me." Nicholas stroked his hands over her injured shoulder.

"Lord Peter will never accept you," she said casually. "You said yourself he hides his contempt of you."

"He'll be devastated by the death of his son." Nicholas paced away from her and then returned. " 'Tis time for bed."

"Of course he'll be devastated, but I doubt he'll lose his mind. Don't you think he'll be just a mite suspicious when you appear with William's kidnapped wife in tow?"

"True." He considered and then decided, "I'll just have to imprison you here until Lord Peter's death. Come." He caught her wrists. "Let's use the bed in the solar. I've dreamed of you there."

The casual way he tossed away her freedom whetted the edge of her courage, his intense desire drove her to desperation. "What about your mother?" Saura threw the question at him like a dart. "What did she think when you killed your brother?"

He stopped propelling her toward his bed, and she felt a tremor go through him. "My mother was a saint."

"Didn't she love your brother, too? 'Tis an unnatural mother who doesn't love all her sons."

Turning her around to face him, he grabbed her shoulders and shook her. "She loved us all! She doted on us. We were her flowers, her little jewels."

The pain of the bruise, the humiliation of her position made her insist, "What did she say when you killed him?"

"She didn't want me to leave her, but they forced me."

She snapped at the clue. "Did she cry when you left?"

He ignored her. "My father had removed the other boys from her early, but she kept me until I was eight. She told me she'd never let me go and I swore I'd stay with her forever."

"Did she cry when you left?"

"My inheritance came too late for her. She's dead."

"She cried, didn't she? She cried because you betrayed her like all the rest."

"I didn't betray her."

He spoke without opening his teeth, and the muffled bitterness in his voice made her quiver and then straighten. "Your poor mother. Waiting here alone with only her memories, waiting for her baby son to return. Waiting and waiting, while you're out learning to be a knight and japing with the other lads and tossing the women's skirts up over their heads."

"I didn't have fun. 'Twas work, all the time work. 'Twas work to be a knight and 'twas work to train Arthur to follow me like a dog. And I didn't toss the women's skirts unless. . . ."

"Unless?"

"Unless they fought me and 'twas work."

"You didn't want to enjoy yourself while your mother suffered alone."

"Exactly." She could hear the smile in his voice. "You understand. I knew you would."

She lashed him with her contempt. "I understand you're lying to me. I understand you enjoyed training Arthur to follow you with unthinking devotion. I understand you enjoyed watching him be destroyed by his foolish plans for William. I understand you enjoyed fighting those women, hurting those women, making them do what you wanted."

"How could you understand that?"

"Because you're doing the same thing to me. You enjoy forcing yourself on the helpless. You're holding me, watching me squirm like a moth caught by a careless boy. What would your mother think about that? All this pleasure you get from manipulating people? Is that what she taught you?"

"My mother was a saint!"

"Nay, she wasn't. No wonder your father removed you from her care. She was a nasty, perfidious woman who couldn't stand to let her sons go."

Like an asp striking, he grabbed her by the throat. Panicked, her hands flew to his wrists, but the tendons in his hands stood rigid with fury. She lashed out with her foot, but his arms were too long for her to reach him. His thumbs pressed into her windpipe, and instantly her aggression faltered. Her breath swelled in her chest, unable to escape, and she clawed at him frantically. Tossing her like a rag doll, he swung her around and leaned over her, and in some corner of her mind she heard William instruct, "Do the unexpected."

Her knees collapsed beneath her and she dropped all her body to the ground. Her weight shifted and his fingers slipped. She sucked in a breath before he caught her again, but he rewrapped his hands around her throat with great deliberation, like a man prepared to do his duty and enjoy it.

He said nothing, she couldn't speak. She knew she was dying, for she heard a sharp whine fill the air. Did the flap of angel wings sound like the whine of a mosquito?

Nicholas released her, and she fell to the floor, gagging. As the throbbing in her head diminished, she thought perhaps he was toying with her, waiting to move in for the kill. Still, the whine grew louder and resolved itself into words.

"Ye can't, m'lord. She's a noble lady. Ye can't kill a lady."

"You stupid oaf." Nicholas said it as if it were a revelation. "I can do anything I want."

"Lord William's comin' for her. He'll want t' see her." Bronnie sounded anguished and uncertain, arguing with his betters yet afraid to stop.

"William's coming alone. I'll let him see her corpse and then—"

"Ah, nay." Bronnie gasped with loud astonishment. "No man could hold Lord William if he saw her corpse. No man would try." Doubtfully, he added, "An' even if ye managed to kill him, I'd not want those two ghosts haunting *my* castle."

Breathing heavily, Nicholas paced back and forth, back and forth, using small and rapid steps. Coming to stand next to Saura, he rolled her onto her back using his toe. She flopped back, only half exaggerating her exhaustion and her fear. "Get her up," he ordered. "Let's see how clever she is when she's cold and hungry and the damp of the dungeon creeps into her bones."

"Ye can't throw her into that hole," Bronnie protested. "She's a lady."

"She's a vixen, and deserves what she receives. Get her up!" Nicholas's fury waxed cold and pure. "Or I will."

Saura raised a pleading hand to Bronnie and he shuffled to her side. "I'm sorry, m'lady, so sorry, but I have t' touch ye." His big hands grasped her shoulders and withdrew at her gasp of pain. "Grant pardon, my lady," he murmured again, and she motioned for him to help her.

In cautious increments he eased his arms around her until Nicholas barked, "Bring her now!"

Bronnie hefted her all the way off the ground in one swift movement. "Sorry," he muttered, carrying her after Nicholas. They descended the privy stairs into the undercroft and he apologized again, "I'd never touch a lady."

Saura didn't care. Wishing to reserve her strength for her last bout with Nicholas, she was glad of Bronnie's warmth and support. She hoped her voice would work; her voice had to work. It was her only weapon in this unequal war. That, and her brain; and her brain seemed to be operating slowly, dazed with pain and shock.

Wine soaking into wood, herbs, meat kept too long; the odors of the storeroom enveloped her. Here they would find the trap door built into the floor of every castle. The trap door that led straight down to agony and death.

She had to speak now, she had to talk to him. Testing, she croaked, "Nicholas."

Bronnie checked his stride, but Nicholas didn't answer. Perhaps he hadn't heard; perhaps he ignored her. "Nicholas," she tried again, and her voice came out with strength. Still it grated, rusty with pain. "I want you to promise me something."

They stopped, the three of them, and she heard the scrape of the metal handle and the creak of unoiled hinges. Then the door slammed back against the floor and musty air rushed out. It carried a whiff of damp and horror, of mildew and suffering.

Saura jerked back. Satisfied with her reaction, Nicholas said, "I can promise you a living tomb."

"Is it dark down there?" Sarcasm colored her words and he cursed her. Undaunted, she insisted, "I want you to promise you'll not put William down with me." Her throat hurt and she placed her hand on it for support. It had to last through this one final stratagem. "I hate him. I'll kill him if you put him in with me."

"What trick is this?" he questioned skeptically.

"No trick. We fought. We fought before he left. Don't you remember my tears in the woods?"

"In the woods where I caught you? Aye, you were crying."

"I cried until my eyes bled."

Scorn bit through his tone. "He adores you."

"He wants more than I can give. He wants me to pledge to give myself wholly. He wants my soul as well as my mind. He wants me to depend on him for everything, while he needs me for nothing. *You* know William. You know what he expects."

Her bitterness caught him by surprise. "Aye." Eyeing her, he paced again, slowly, across the room and back.

"Please don't put him in with me. I cannot bear his demands and he swore—"

"To make you yield?" Nicholas released an angry cackle, and she could hear him rub his hands up and down his leather riding breeches. "Very good. Very, very good. Put the rope down, Bronnie, and make her go."

Bronnie blubbered with terror. "My lord, please, Lord Nicholas. She's a lady."

"The rats can get mother's milk from her. Make her go!"

Placing her on her feet, well away from the hole, he assured her, Bronnie fetched the rope. She heard him tie the ends to a beam while Nicholas chatted, "Dear little Bronnie worries about you being a lady, but you're actually getting privileged treatment. Most prisoners are thrown down. If they're lucky, 'tis wet and the floor's oozing mud. If 'tis summertime and dry, or wintertime and frozen, they can lie there with their broken bones, groaning in agony, until they die."

Trying not to listen, she leaned against a barrel of wine, but his mocking voice wove spells around her. He continued, "You, Lady Saura, you get a rope ladder that reaches almost to the bottom, and Bronnie to tie the knots that hold it. But do watch for rotting flesh and bones beneath your feet. We haven't cleaned it out for months."

She shuddered, the kind of chill that started at the base of her spine and vibrated up to the top of her skull, and he laughed. "It shouldn't be so bad for you." He crept up beside her and put his hands on her waist. He drew her close against him and liked the shudder that shook her again. "Unless you'd rather stay in my bed?"

She closed her eyes and sighed as if weary. " 'Tis a hard choice." Her voice creaked, and she cleared her throat. "But I must prefer the rats to the snakes."

He shoved her away from him and she stumbled forward. Her slipper caught on the edge of the trap door. She pitched forward as Bronnie cried out. She fell; she knew the hole in the floor would gobble her, but Bronnie caught her. She landed in his arms, astride the door to the dungeon. Out loud, she thanked God for his intervention.

Before she could thank Bronnie, Nicholas ordered, "Bronnie, I don't care how you do it, but put her down that hole and shut the door and leave her. Leave her." He stepped closer, and she cringed away. "Leave her until she's joined by her husband and they can die together in everlasting love."

"You promised you wouldn't put him in with me," she cried.

"I promised you nothing. Nothing!" He stormed away, crossing the store room, climbing the stairs, and leaving them together.

As soon as the sound of his footsteps faded, Bronnie said fearfully, "Lady, I'll take ye an' hide ye."

"Nay!" She grasped his shoulders and rolled off him. "Nay, I don't want you to get in trouble. He'd kill you."

She felt the tremor run through him, but he denied, "Better me than you. I'd run off an' live in th' forest."

"And be hung for a poacher. Nay, Bronnie, I thank you. I must go down."

But she didn't move, and he asked, "Are ye sure?"

His relief leaked into his voice, and she repeated, "I must go down."

"Bronnie!" A roar thundered down the stairs, and he rolled away.

"I'd better climb down before trouble finds you." Still she hesitated, until he picked up her hand and placed it on one of the knots.

"See? I tied it tight."

"Aye." She felt down the rope until she found a step and then she felt up the other rope. She brightened. " 'Tis just like a real ladder!"

"Aye, m'lady. Do ye want me t' get ye started?"

"You'd better."

"Then put un foot there . . . aye . . . an' th' other down with it. Good." He touched her tentatively, but her fears had dissolved in a rush of resolution. She placed one foot on the unsubstantial rope step and then another. Drawing one fortifying breath, she reached out with her foot, but couldn't find the next rung.

" 'Tis a bit further, m'lady," Bronnie said, leaning out over the sill. "I can just see it."

Extending her leg, she found the next step, far down the rope. Sliding her hands, moving slowly, she put both her feet on it. She was inside the dungeon now, and she lifted her head to ask, "Are all the rungs so far apart?"

"They were made for a man, m'lady," Bronnie said apologetically.

There was nothing else to say. Soon she was descending with halting regularity. As she moved deeper into the pit, the rope swayed wider with each of her steps. Her teeth clenched in agony as she felt cobwebs sweeping her face. Her hands clutched the cord. All her concentration centered on the next step. Nicholas would have thought it a fitting torture; descending endlessly, wanting only to reach the floor of her prison. At last, she groped with her foot and found nothing. She strained her toes down: nothing. Nicholas hadn't lied; the cord was too short. She was hanging in midair, held by only a flimsy rope, and all around her was a void with no relief.

"Bronnie." Her voice creaked, weak with terror. "Bronnie, can I jump to the bottom?"

"Don't know, m'lady," he called. " 'Tis so dark in there, I can't see past th' first step."

Her arms shook with nerves. Moving like a caterpillar, she undulated down the final length of support. She hooked her knees around the rung, cursing her skirts, then she inched her hands all the way down, down to the last bit of rope. Taking a breath, she loosened her feet and swung her body out and away, to hang dangling in the chill ether of the abyss.

TWENTY

Saura hung there for days, through a season, until she was old, until her arms trembled with the strain. Then she let go. She fell, she landed. The shock jarred her ankles; the ground was much closer than she'd braced for. She sat there in the dirt and rubbed her feet and laughed and cried.

Bronnie heard her and hollered, "M'lady, m'lady, are ye hurt?"

Collecting herself, she hoarsely called back, "I'm well. But Bronnie, can't you wave a torch and tell me where the bodies are?"

"Th' bodies?" He sounded dumbfounded, then relieved. "Nay, 'tis not all as bad as he tol' ye, m'lady."

She snorted. "I'm surprised."

"This isn't his main castle an' he doesn't keep any prisoners here, an' if he did, he sure wouldn't let them die, just like that. He'd work 'em t' death, he would."

Irresistibly amused by his succinct reading of Nicholas's character, she queried, "No bodies?"

"Nay. But there's rats, for sure, an' 'tis coolish. I want ye t' take me jerkin." He tossed it down, and it fluttered onto her head. "Did ye get it?"

"Aye, thank you. Is there any more—" A dull roaring echoed down from above, and Saura winced. Even in the dungeon, she recognized Nicholas and his wrath. "Hurry up to him, Bronnie. I'll be fine now that I know I'm alone. Except for the rats."

"Oh, m'lady . . . ooo, I hate t' leave you there. A noble lady an' all."

"Shoo." She waved her arms even though he couldn't see her. "I don't want him having second thoughts about me."

"Aye. Aye." She heard him pick up the door. "Are ye sure?"

"I'm fine."

The opening almost closed above her, and then he swung it back once more. "M'lady?"

"Go, Bronnie." She spoke firmly, and he obeyed.

The thump of the door above her sounded so final. The jerkin clutched in her hands retained his warmth and she drew comfort from the evidence she wasn't totally alone. Wrapping her arms around her knees, she hugged them and laid her cheek down and wondered at herself. Being shut in a dark cave shouldn't bother her. What difference did the absence of light make? Nothing was different in this space than in any other. Until she discovered the parameters of any room, she was bewildered.

Still, it seemed the air pressed down on her head, weighted by the closed door. The ceiling, which she knew to be as high as the sky, seemed too close; she fancied she would hit her head on it if she stood up. The walls closed in; the floor seemed to tilt beneath her. The odor of mold suffocated her, and she panted. Digging her fingers into the dirt, she clenched a fistful in dispair.

How had she come to this?

Just yesterday she had approved the repair of roof thatch on the village homes of Burke. She had ridden with the steward as he called for an accounting of the tenants' harvest, and she had recited the figures to Brother Cedric as he wrote them down. Perhaps Peter had only given her the responsibility of the autumn accounting to take her mind off William, but he'd said he would gladly let her do it, and she believed him.

Every night he'd come in from hunting, mud-spattered and jovial, presenting a hart or boar to be salted and stored for winter. Saura understood this display of manly gifts wasn't for her. It was for his Maud, standing at Saura's side and properly impressed with the bloody haunches he tossed at their feet. The love between the master and the maid had blossomed into a steady fire, glowing with the constant warmth of embers and blazing with occasional displays of wrath. Peter and Maud were wrapped up in each other, and Saura felt jealous and abandoned and ashamed.

She'd lost the everlasting attentions of Maud, Peter paid her no more than absentminded attention, the boys kept busy with the duties of young warriors, and William was gone.

Only Bula had kept his vigil at her side, plopping his huge head in her lap when she sat and tangling himself under her feet when she walked. The servants joked about his devotion as they scurried to finish the work of autumn before the first freeze.

Her mind sprang back to Bula's extraordinary behavior on the path. Stupid, she chastised herself. Stupid, stupid wench.

So wrapped in your own desolation you didn't realize what the dog was trying to tell you. If she'd paid attention to the dog, she'd be home at Burke right now, hugging the fire and not a jerkin that jumped with fleas.

Home, smiling about Maud and Peter; home, waiting for William to return.

Home, waiting for Bula to bound in and bestow on her his devoted affection. Scolding him for being underfoot. Laughing as she rubbed his ribs and his foot thumped in ecstasy.

If she'd paid attention to the dog, he'd be alive today, not worm bait in the forest. She wanted to cry for him, but the tears wouldn't come. Her guilt was too deep, her pain too fresh. Her dilemma required reason, not emotion. She'd already betrayed Bula once; she wouldn't betray him again by failing to escape and avenge his death.

Restlessly, she shook her head. Nicholas wanted her to become an ineffective weakling. He wanted her to die down here, afraid and begging for release, and she wasn't giving him anything he desired. Not anything.

'Twasn't dripping wet down here; the dirt was loose powder that sifted through her fingers. Chalk, probably, for the castle sat high above the ocean and this section of England was famed for its white cliffs. Even if they threw William in, he'd probably be uninjured.

Please God, Nicholas would let him come down the ladder. Please God, Nicholas would send William down any way possible.

Even if William were hurt when he arrived in her prison, at least she'd know he wasn't dead. Even if he were injured in the fall, he'd still be William, mighty enough to vanquish all their enemies.

In those appalling moments when Nicholas was choking her and she'd thought her life was over, she'd realized William could save her. While her breath had threatened to explode her chest, she'd decided that together, she and William could destroy this demon.

If only Nicholas would just take the bait and bring William to her. Begging him not to put William in the prison with her was a feeble device, but the best she could think of in her frazzled state. She'd complained William expected too much of her, and in that argument resided just enough truth for Nicholas to believe her. If only he didn't think too deeply on it. If only he believed himself to be in such an invulnerable position that he dared unite them.

Nicholas was just dreadful enough. She laughed at herself. How she skidded around the truth. Nicholas was crazed. Everything about him shouted it. How could she have been unsuspecting? It was as if two people lived in his mind, both diabolically clever. The child in him sought love, the parent protected the child.

Was he crazed enough to put William and Saura together? Perhaps. Crazed enough to kill them and expect to get away with it? No doubt. That was what frightened her, that was what raised her from her despair. To escape from this trap, she and William would have to combine their strengths and become as powerful as the storms that swept the sea. Now as she sat on the floor of her prison, an illogical hope burgeoned in her bosom.

She had found in herself a great desire to live, to prosper, to find a resolution to the problem she faced with William. When William arrived, he'd be calm, commanding, decisive. He'd know just what to do and they'd do it. He'd not find a quivering wreck of a woman who prayed for a man to rescue her. He'd find Saura, his calm, quick-thinking, thorough wife.

What should she do first? Explore. Find weapons. Find

some way to construct a ladder. Prepare herself to help William and be gratified with his amazement at her capabilities. Nodding, she stood and brushed the dust from her skirt.

The door above slammed back with a kind of triumph. She woke from her half-sleep and knew William had arrived. Just by the crack of sound, she knew that Nicholas had seized him, that Nicholas was happy, and that Nicholas was putting them together. She shut her eyes thankfully, but they sprang open at William's words.

"I won't go down there."

Huddled on the ground where she'd spent the night, her skirt tucked about her legs for warmth, she pulled Bronnie's jerkin closer. The vigor of William's speaking voice was heightened by some element she couldn't understand. Cocking her head, she listened, trying to identify it.

"You won't go?" Nicholas mocked. "Very well. We'll leave your wife down there alone."

"Saura's down there? Why, you filthy—"

"She feels safe down there," Nicholas protested with genteel satisfaction. "Safe, away from the nasty man who offered her his heart."

"Who? Oh, you." William sounded so patently uninterested Nicholas sputtered. William listened to the madman's complaints and said, "Well really, my friend, you didn't expect her to lust after you when she's had me, did you?"

Like a worm that eats at the core of a good apple, Nicholas sneered, "She's none too happy with you, either, my friend. She specifically asked I keep you away from her. Aye, that surprises you, doesn't it? That your intense goodness is something to be avoided. That not every woman wants to share herself, body and soul, with you."

"You bastard."

"Oh, I know all about the rot in your marriage. Your wife's quite loquacious after she's been crying."

Saura heard him lunge, and Nicholas laughed in a high tone, marred with ripples of frenzy. "You're tied, William. You're a captive. You walked into my castle alone, armed only with your pride. Struggle all you want, those bindings on your arms will never come free."

"Why was she crying?"

"Crying in the woods. Weeping buckets of water. What could I do? I took her under my wing and brought her here. For safekeeping."

Saura could imagine how Nicholas smirked, and she cringed at this twisting of events.

William said nothing for a very long moment, and then burst out, "If my wife doesn't want me to join her in prison, if she'd rather have the rats for company, then I don't want to go down."

She knew he'd comprehended her ploy. She knew by the sham conviction in his voice; it rang so clear she worried that Nicholas would hear it. Even more than that, she worried about the note of dread. What was wrong with William?

"You don't want to go down. She doesn't want you with her," Nicholas purred. "What more could I ask? And what more could you ask, but a chance to iron out your marital problems before you die."

"She's probably not even down there." William stalled, scuffling with the men holding him. "She hasn't said a word."

Saura stood and walked directly below the hole. "Nicholas, you promised me."

Nicholas laughed, and William roared, "Move!"

A thumping and scraping ensued and she scrambled back just in time. He fell like a wounded eagle at her feet. Dirt flew, she leaped for him. He wheezed, gagged, and she knelt, coughing, at his side. "Are you well? William? Answer me!" She groped over him and tugged at the cord that bound his wrists in front of him.

"One moment . . . woman." He sucked in a big breath of air mixed with dust and coughed like a man bleeding from the lungs.

"Will he live?" Nicholas called.

"My eating knife," William said in a low voice.

Her hands flew to his belt and flipped open the sheath. "He let you keep it?" she whispered back.

"He thinks it's no weapon." He held his arms up for her as she sawed through the binding. "He underestimates me."

"Will he live?" Nicholas demanded loudly.

"Aye, I'll live." William's voice strengthened as he spoke, and he jerked his hands free and rubbed his wrists. "No thanks to you or your henchmen."

"Good. No matter how satisfying that was, I'd hate to deprive myself of the privilege of killing you properly."

The door began to creak shut, and William struggled up on one elbow "Wait, Nicholas!" His burst of noise brought on another fit of coughing and he boosted Saura to her feet with a hand on her behind.

"Wait, Nicholas," she summoned obediently, and paused, unsure what William had wanted. But she knew what she wanted. "I'm hungry. I've been in here overnight with nary a crumb nor a drop."

Smooth as cream, Nicholas answered, "I'll send my personal servants down for your requirements, my lady."

William regained his breath and called, "Drop a torch

down here and let me see Saura. I want to see what you've done to her."

"Nothing." Nicholas leaned into the hole. "I barely touched her."

She touched her tender throat and grimaced.

"I'll come for you soon," Nicholas assured them. "When you've been properly subdued."

He pulled away and as the door creaked again Saura shouted, "I'm thirsty! You can't starve us to death, you know." The door banged shut, and she said to the ceiling, "Although I don't know why not." Kneeling beside William, she groped for his body and found him trembling. "You're hurt," she breathed. More strongly, she said, "You're hurt."

"Nay." But still he shuddered beneath her hands and he sounded frightened.

"William?" Her palms smoothed over his shoulders. "William?"

"I'm well," he said, but she didn't believe him.

"This is no time to be foolhardy. If you—" She stopped. His hands came up onto her elbows and pulled at her, and her arms went around him. He burrowed his head into her stomach and wrapped himself around her. "William?"

From the depths of his soul came a cry of terror. " 'Tis dark."

She didn't know what to say; she didn't understand, she just smoothed his hair on the back of his head.

" 'Tis dark," he said again. "I can't see."

Then she knew. Only a man who had lost his sight for months and regained it again could feel the terror that trapped William. He shook with a palsy, he crept close into her lap. A stab of panic jolted her and she asked, "Could you see after they threw you in?"

"Aye." He nodded against her.

"What could you see?"

"The light of the trap door shining from above."

"What else?"

"Nicholas and his wicked face peering down at us."

"Was he alone?"

"Surrounded by servants and mercenaries." He gulped.

"And is that bastard going to win?"

"Saura," he said desperately, ignoring her plea for strength. "I can't see."

She rubbed her hands in a long, slow circle around his back and wondered what to tell him. She understood; she felt an empathy no one else could feel. She'd been trapped by Theobold's power and then released, by Lord Peter's plea for help. Now her freedom was threatened by the lunatic designs of one man. She'd almost been choked to death for her objections, and in her heart and soul she understood the agony William was experiencing.

Also, she knew the dark. She knew how it felt to have no concept of the spaces around her, of the monsters who lay hidden in the night. She knew just how much William had indulged in the pleasure of sight, using it for his duties as knight and seigneur. She could only guess how many candles he had lit when his vision had returned, how many alms he had distributed.

Now he lay like a child in her lap, cold and still. "William, be logical," she said, using his magic word. "You know you're not blind."

"I know that. I know it with my mind. But I open my eyes and there's nothing there, no matter how I squint and strain." He raised his head, turning it from side to side, and buried it back at her waist. "My heart pounds, my hands sweat, inside my heart I fear."

Holding him, bending over him, she made soothing noises.

"Nicholas knew how to torment me, didn't he?" he asked. "That whoreson knew what would torture me."

"Nay," she denied instantly. "Nicholas had no idea how this would affect you. He'd have done more with it if he had. Even I had no idea how this would affect you. I never thought. I'm sorry."

He laughed, a half-hysterical whistle in his throat. "A grown man afraid of the dark. God, what a fool I am."

"Nay, never that. You're a grown man who faces the challenges that would destroy a lesser man and treats them as mountains to be climbed. You take misfortune and make good fortune. You take the rocks in your road and use them to smooth the road for others."

Uncomforted, he snuggled closer. His face pressed against her and he shuddered in a terror too deep for tears.

The prison buried them in silence. Only the whistle of the wind through the cracks made a noise. They were alone as they'd hadn't been since their wedding, and Saura wondered if she had the courage to say what would ease him. She drew a breath and said, "Do you know what my life was like before I came to Burke Castle?"

She paused, but he said nothing. She didn't even know if he listened to her. For a moment, she wondered if she could raise him from his dread. Determination came swiftly on the heels of her doubt; she had to try, one sentence at a time. She wanted to comfort him, but first she had to talk about that time before she came to him. "I never told you about living with my stepfather, did I?" She didn't wait for an answer, but continued in a flat tone, "When I look back on my time at Pertrade, my predominant memory is of cold. It seemed 'twas always cold there. I lived with the danger of becoming stale and old, someone's boring aunt who skulked in the shadows."

"Your brothers didn't agree."

The words whispered out of her lap and she relaxed. He was listening. "How could my brothers know? They never had to live with hate and distrust every moment of their lives. It warped me. The contempt was pounding me into a new shape—a different Saura. Theobald was winning."

He shook his head in denial, his face rubbing against her belly.

She sighed with quivering sadness. "I promise you, William—where a burst of violence couldn't succeed, the slow wearing of malice would conquer. Then your father came along and offered me a chance to escape. And I took it, for I only existed there." Her hand moved in a slow, firm circle on his back, rubbing him between the shoulder blades, easing the tension in his shoulders. In the mellow voice of a mother crooning to a babe, she said, "I arrived at your house, and right away I was warmed. The fires burned with a pure heat, the servants were kinder, the work was interesting. And you, you were like sunshine on a summer day."

"Sunshine?" He turned his head and spoke up toward her face. "That's not what you said at the time. You said I smelled and was lazy and overflowing with pity for myself."

Her hand tugged at his hair. "So you were. But you had that fascinating voice, all smooth and rich and—"

"Messy?" A note of amusement slipped into his tone, and his grip loosened a bit. One of his hands imitated her, rubbing her back.

"You were that. And obstinate and bullheaded. I liked the challenge of you, I liked the way you made me feel, the way you welcomed me. I could hardly believe you would treat an old woman as if she were a young, vital girl, but you did. I wondered . . . I wondered how you would handle me, if you knew, and I found out. Remember, in the bath?"

He grunted, but she thought he smiled. She stroked his cheek, checking for dimples, and the cheek crept out from her protective embrace. "From that moment on, I had a direction. I had a goal. I wanted you."

"Why would you want me? I'm childish."

"Less than most men." His hand skidded down her back and pinched her backside. She jumped and laughed, and wished she didn't have to say it, but she did. In a low voice, she told him, "You've forced me to face myself, and I haven't liked that. You've made me see what a coward I am. I was afraid to love you, really love you, because. . . ."

"Because the ones you love keep growing up and leaving you to fend for yourself." He pulled himself away and sat up, facing her in the dark. His knee pushed against hers; his chest loomed close and warm. He smoothed his tender fingers over her face.

Straightening her spine, she answered stiffly, "I was going to say it was Theobald and his cruelties."

"I thought so for a long time, too. After all, living with a man who despises you and wishes you harm must cause scars. But you're so resilient, so sure of your worth, that Theobald did little actual damage. Once you came into my household, those scratches he made in your confidence were quickly healed." In a low, coaxing voice, he asked, "Are you so sure you can be loved?"

"What do you mean?" She heard the hostility in her voice and cursed it, but couldn't call it back.

"I don't think you ever cared about Theobald or what he thought." She digested that, and he said thoughtfully, "You know, I blame Maud for our current difficulties."

Indignant, she said, "What do you mean? She couldn't wait for us to marry. She was so happy."

"Aye, happy to have her chick well settled so she could pursue her romance with my father."

" 'Tis good for her! For the first time in years she hasn't had to hover over me and worry about me and watch for plots against me and clear my way!"

He said nothing, and she blurted, "I'm not jealous of—" The words caught in her throat. Just yesterday she'd admitted she was jealous. She dropped her head and muttered, "I'm a petty little bitch."

"Nay, nay, not you." He put his arms around her. "You're finding your way. I just wish I could convince you to trust me. I trust you. Blubbering in your lap."

"You're over it now, aren't you?" she asked.

Startled, he searched his mind and found no remnant of panic. In wonder, he said, "Aye, it seems I am."

"That's good." She stood up and away. "Because I found a way to escape, but I need you to clear it out."

Her matter-of-fact pronouncement amazed him. "Wait a minute!" He reached out and knocked his wife into his lap, cradling her carefully. "You're a witch. A beautiful, raven-haired witch. I come to you in fear and trembling and by the time you're done with me I'm curing your ills."

"Are you angry?"

He laughed and hugged her close. "Nay."

"William, why did you come alone?" She didn't mean to, but her voice quavered pathetically.

"Why didn't I come with an army?"

"Aye." She dropped her head onto his chest, listening to his reply with her ear pressed to his breastbone.

"You must learn to trust me, dearling. If I'd come with an army, Nicholas would have dragged you up on the battlements and threatened to throw you over. 'Twas better to come alone, unarmed, with only my eating knife at my belt, and let them take me with no struggle."

"With no struggle at all?"

He shrugged. "Only a bit. Nicholas would be suspicious if he captured me too easily. He believes I'm so desperate for you, I have no plan."

"Foolish man," she murmured.

"Not so foolish," he corrected. "I am desperate for you. I always knew I must remove you from his grasp before I could start smashing skulls."

She started at his grim resolve, and he dropped a kiss on the top of her head.

"I'll teach you to trust me one day. One day, we will have to finish this conversation we've started."

Her voice was so tiny he bent to hear it. "I know. William, they killed Bula."

"What?"

He stiffened, and she wished she didn't have to tell him. "They captured me in the woods, where I'd foolishly gone."

"To cry, Nicholas said."

" 'Tis true. I couldn't bear to worry and wonder about you, about us, any longer. So I went where I knew I should not, and Bula paid with his life for me." Her voice shook with guilt.

"Bula gave his life for you because of your never-ending patience with him, because of your gentle devotion to him, because of your kindness. You mourn Bula, but think how much more he would mourn you."

Her pain was too deep for tears. "You comfort me, William, where no one else could."

"Sweet thing." He kissed her hair, came to his feet and set her on hers. "Now where is this escape route?"

Taking his hand, she led him through the darkness. "I explored this room, and found quite a few things. The builders of the castle took advantage of a natural cave, I'd guess, and used it for their dungeon. It isn't large, and while it isn't muddy, it feels humid."

" 'Tis close to the sea," he agreed. "I can taste the salt tang, even in here."

"Aye, can you not?" She grinned. "This place has been shut up for a long time. The walls should be mossy. The atmosphere should reek, but it's only stale. In fact, if you stand still and listen, you can hear the wind blowing off the ocean."

He tugged her to a stop and stood stock still. "By our Lady of the Fountain! You're right." Finishing her thought, he said, "A natural cave must have an outlet to the sea."

"Aye."

Chuckling, he swung her hand back and forth. "So how do we get out?"

"The ceiling gets low here," she warned. "Duck down. There's a tunnel."

He reached out and touched the wall. It was, as she said, clear of moss. It felt slightly moist and the rock left his fingers feeling itchy. Pulling them back, he rubbed them together and said, "Aye, that's the feel of chalk."

"It makes me shudder," she declared, her voice suddenly far below him.

He jerked back, but not quickly enough. His forehead hit the wall with a resounding smack, and he found her sympathy ended in a snap. "I told you to duck!" she said in exasperation, and he found himself remembering Madame Saura and her strictures.

"My skills have atrophied," he apologized, dropping to his

knees and easing into the tunnel. Almost at once he felt a fresh breeze; thin, but present. "God's teeth." He felt a surge of excitement. "We're going to get out of here."

"The cave's very tiny and there's a kink here." She sounded muffled, strained. "I can get through on my knees, but I don't know about you."

He grunted, already finding the space too confining, but the smell of the ocean lured him on. He ended on his stomach, crawling through the powdery dirt and hoping the rocks above him were stable. As if he were a babe at his own birthing, he pulled one shoulder through the bottleneck, and then the other shoulder, and wiggled up and out. Almost immediately he had room to sit up, and he could see. "Light!" he shouted. The sound bounced off the walls and bits of dust cascaded off the ceiling.

Saura shushed him, chuckling. "Aye, I knew there had to be light. I cleaned out all the cracks that I could, poking the pebbles out, and felt the wind on my face."

He stared at that wonderful illumination shining through in a smiling curve. They'd get out; he knew it now.

"William?" She touched his shoulder, her voice hushed and serious. "When we get out, what will we do?"

Twisting in the cramped quarters, he peered along the path of the tiny beam to his wife's face. Her features were barely discernible, but serious, thoughtful, and he squeezed around to hug her. "The first thing a warrior learns is to deal with one insurmountable problem at a time."

She chuckled.

"Charles went to fetch my father," he assured her. "Probably they're close to the coast right now."

Charles lay under the pile of brush and groaned. He was alive, but barely. Moss drooped into his mouth when he breathed and he wished he could move his hands to brush it away. They had wrenched his arms out of their sockets when they'd bound him, and he wished with all his heart he hadn't stopped at that wretched little alehouse for a drink. He thought of what William would say about his stupidity and groaned again.

Channing had objected with respect, and then with vigor, but Charles thought a wee drop couldn't hurt and he'd yelled the man into silence. William's sullen troops had milled around the inn, waiting impatiently, while his own less disciplined troops had joined their master. Thus it was when they left three hours later, they'd been easily overcome.

How could there be any doubt? It had been Nicholas's men who attacked them, a large force of heavily armed men. William's men had fought with valor; his own men had fled, and now he found himself face down in a ditch, wishing he'd been killed. 'Twould have been an easy death compared to what William would do to him.

He groaned again.

TWENTY-ONE

"What blocks us?" William asked, squeezing next to Saura and feeling around the wall.

"A boulder. A huge boulder. I couldn't budge it."

He grunted, finding the outlines of the rock.

"But God didn't place it. Whoever built the dungeon shoved it there, and I know it could be shoved away."

"By God, perhaps." His initial euphoria faded. "Is there aught in the cave? Perhaps a board I could use as a lever?"

"Nay," she said doubtfully. "There's nothing I found, nothing I can think of. Can't we both push?"

"Of course, my puny dearling, we can both push. Come and put your shoulder to it."

Eager to help, she wiggled up against him.

"Mmm, that's nice," he said. "But I think it would be more effective if you faced the same way I do."

Obediently, she eased away, twisted around and backed into him.

"This is nice, too," he teased.

"But 'tis no place to be trapped," she said severely. "So push."

The amorous husband dropped his banter and became Lord William. "On my word. One, two. . . ."

At last she slid down the boulder, panting. "We roll it a bit and it rolls right back into place. We need help."

" 'Tis on an incline. Go back out into the cave and see if you can find—"

"A lever," she finished. "Aye, sir."

As she crawled through the kink in the tunnel, she heard someone calling. She turned her head back, but it didn't come from William; she turned her head forward and wondered who could be in the cave. And why. And whether Nicholas had been unable to wait to kill them. She prayed. As the walls began to fall back and give way to the main room, she paused and listened.

"M'lady?"

She would always recognize that mournful, worried voice. "Bronnie?"

"M'lady? Where have ye been? I've been hollerin' and hollerin'."

"What do you need?"

"I brought food an' wine."

Suspecting the truth, she said, "Lord Nicholas is very kind."

"Ah, Lord Nicholas, he doesn't exactly know."

"You're a good man, and if I weren't so thirsty I'd make you take it all back. Toss it down." She ran to pick up the packages he slung down, and then asked, "Is there a bench we could have?"

"A bench, m'lady?"

"To sit on." Her voice trembled with melodramatic anguish. "The rats come right up and try to nibble on my fingers and I hoped for a bench."

"Migawd. At once, m'lady. There's a bench right here in th' wine casks where cook comes t' sit an' sip a bit of th' grape." He left and returned at once. "How can I get it down t' ye?"

"Drop it," she answered cheerfully.

" 'Twill break! Let me lower it."

"Nay, the dust is up to my ankles. It'll not break. Just drop it."

"Awright." He sounded doubtful, but obedient. Saura stepped out of the way and the bench came flying down to land with a splinter of wood. Bronnie heard it, complaining, "M'lady, ye said—"

"It must be farther to the ground than I'd realized," she explained blithely. Scurrying into the swirling cloud, she scavenged the pieces of bench and thanked God for opportunities. The long board that had been the seat seemed thick enough to move a boulder. It was still connected to one leg, but she knew that William could separate the pieces.

Above her, she heard a thump, like a branch falling on a hollow log, and suddenly the floor beside her exploded in a flurry of dust. Flabbergasted, she stood with the boards in her hands and wondered which way to run. "So I will deal with all who assist you, Lady Saura." Nicholas's voice chilled her with its intent, and then the door above closed gently and she dropped the lumber.

"Bronnie?" She scrambled and found his body, twisted in a distorted shape. "Bronnie?" Her fingers found a break almost right away. His collarbone had snapped, his arm twisted below him. Her hands skimmed over him. She found a swelling on his shoulder, put there by his angry lord. She found another lump, a bigger one, on his forehead.

From the tunnel she heard a cursing and grumbling, and then William demanded, "What in the name of Saint Wilfred was that? Are you hurt?"

"Nay, but I would have been if Bronnie had landed on me."

"Bronnie's down here? Oh, splendid, now we have to get him out, too."

"Not at the moment, we don't. He's senseless. Our friend upstairs caught him providing us with a meal and clobbered him, and knocked him in."

"God's teeth," William said blankly. "Will he live?"

"Aye, he landed in thick dust. But I'll need your help setting this collarbone and making him comfortable."

"In a prison we're going to make him comfortable? All we can do is bind his shoulder; there's nothing to splint with."

"We'll use the leg of the bench Bronnie dropped for me."

"A bench?" His voice rose in excitement. "How did you get him to give us a bench?"

"I lied," she admitted. "There's a good long piece to lever that boulder with, but first you have to help me with Bronnie." Sitting back on her heels, she sighed, "I never expected Bronnie to look like this."

"Like what?" William asked cautiously.

"Beautiful. At first, I thought he'd be a graybeard with eyebrows that met over his nose and hair that grew out of his ears. Then, when he hefted me around upstairs, I knew he must be a younger man, but still pictured him with long arms and knock-knees. My fingers don't lie, though. This boy is a god."

"Humph."

She sat forward to work on him, but William brushed her hands aside. "I'll do it."

"But I'm used to working without light," she objected.

"*I'll* do it."

Bronnie was bandaged with an efficiency that would have amazed him, had he been awake. As William finished, he assured her, "He'll be fine. Listen to him." Bronnie had slipped from unconsciousness to sleep with nary a pause between. His snores serenaded them as they squeezed into the tunnel, pushing the lumber ahead, pulling the food and drink behind.

William surveyed the boulder that blocked them with renewed hope. It was still too big, but with the lever Saura had obtained, they would do the job. First they had to move the stone enough to put the board beneath it, and so he commanded, "Put your shoulder against the rock, dearling, and we'll get this pebble moved."

"And then can we eat?" Saura braced herself between the boulder and the wall, he reached one arm beneath it, and together they heaved. It rolled just enough for him to shove the board under the boulder.

"We'll eat when we're out. 'Twill be incentive."

She scooted around to help him lean on the lever, but he pushed her gently aside. "I can do this. You're too delicate."

"But, William. . . ."

"This will take more muscle than you have. Trust me, Saura."

Silently, she crawled to the side and laid one hand against the boulder.

He leaned on the lever. The board made ominous cracking noises, but nothing moved. He stopped, got his breath, and tackled it again. He shoved, he struggled, he panted, all with no success. He groaned with the effort he used against their obstacle, but the stone hardly budged.

She let him try until she couldn't stand it any more before

she said, "I can't believe it wouldn't be easier if I pushed, too."

"Would you like to take over this operation?" he asked between his teeth.

"Nay. You're doing fine."

He leaned on the lever again.

"I just think—"

He roared, and it echoed around the tiny cavern. "Help me, then, Mistress Saucebox."

She flounced as she moved into place and couldn't resist asking, "Are you always this grumpy when someone comes up with a better idea?"

"Aye."

She decided to drop the subject with a murmured, "Oh."

She pushed and he heaved, and the boulder moved up a bit. Forgetting his pique, he shouted, "Hold it there!" and thrust the board deeper. In painfully small increments, the stone rolled out of its resting place until suddenly Saura lay flat on the ground and the boulder rolled away. Pebbles from the ceiling showered on her and William crawled forward after the rock as if he were afraid it would return. Surveying the scene outside the tunnel, he announced, " 'Tis out. The rest of the cave slopes down." Cramped from his kneeling, he raised himself to his feet and picked her up like a rag doll, hugging her in mighty pleasure. "We did it!"

She hugged him back, agreeing, "We did it."

William looked at her as she lifted her face to his and laughed and groaned. "Do you know what you look like?"

That was not at all what she expected, and she blurted, "Is it important?"

"Nicholas will never spot you in the scenery." He blew on her face, set her down and brushed at her clothes. "You're white," he pronounced. "And likely to stay that way until we find you a bath."

"Are you any cleaner?"

"Nay. Perhaps when I come for my vengeance, he'll think I'm a ghost haunting him."

"A very healthy ghost." She scoffed at his fancy and demanded her reward. "May we eat now?"

"My gluttonous wife," he sighed, reaching into the tunnel and dragging out the food and wine. "Come out toward the front of the cave. The sunshine will feel good."

"What about Bronnie?"

"One insurmountable problem at a time, wife," he reminded her.

She took his hand and let him lead her. She let him seat her and open the cloth bundle wrapped around their food. She let him tear off a chunk of bread and put it in her hand. She let him open the animal skin bag filled with wine and she let him dribble it into her mouth. Leaning her back against the wall, she sighed. "I'm tired."

"Such an indomitable warrior has the right to be tired," he soothed.

"Nay, 'twasn't being a warrior that wore me out. 'Twas *waiting* to be a warrior. I didn't sleep well last night. Not that I'm afraid of rats, you understand, but I don't like to think they're nestling with me. I was worried Nicholas would realize why I wanted you in the cave with me, and I worried he'd change his mind and take me to his bed." Her words drifted along, the spaces between them became longer and longer, and her head nodded and dropped.

William rescued the chunk of bread in her hand before it could dip in the dirt and carefully laid her down on her side. With a sigh, he stared at his wife. Blotted with chalk, unconscious with weariness, she was still an inspiration to him. If

not for her calm good sense, he'd never have escaped the
fear that held his mind prisoner. If not for her quick thinking, they'd never have escaped the prison where Nicholas
had them confined.

Now it was up to William. He would arrange for them to
escape this cave, this prison that was even more dangerous,
even more confining than the dungeon within. If Nicholas
found them here, he'd be furious they'd outwitted him so
well. If he found them here, their bodies would never even
wash up in the tide. Nicholas's men would toss them into the
surf and they'd be carried away, to become simply another
mysterious disappearance in this time of trouble.

They had to get up on the top of the cliff. But how? He
walked to the ocean side of the cave and looked down.
Waves battered the bottom of the cliff, foaming against the
toothy rocks. He looked up. Far above him a sheer cliff
loomed, an unbroken expanse of white. He looked to the
left, he looked to the right. No steps, no handholds.

No way out.

The sun shone directly overhead when William lifted
Saura into his arms. "Come, dearling, we have to go."

She moaned and snuggled into his chest, and he stroked
her hair. How he wished he didn't have to wake her. Exhaustion had claimed her, and her upper lip had quivered with
the heavy breath that sighed between her teeth. She'd never
turned over, never moved the whole time she'd lain there.

"Come, sweet, 'tis time to become heroes again," he
crooned.

"William," she complained, never waking.

He hugged her and thought, *Just a few minutes more.*

He glanced around the narrow cave. Defined by its high ceilings and walls hung close together, it was nothing more than a slot over the ocean. During the time she slept, he'd busied himself with preparations. He'd broken off jagged bits of board and tucked them in his belt. Sharp enough to scratch and pick, they'd be his only hand tools on their climb to the top of the cliff. The boulder he'd rolled back into its snug niche at the mouth of the prison. It was easier to move the second time, he'd discovered. It functioned as nothing more than a plug, but time counted, and the rock would slow Nicholas and his men. He'd hung far out over the ocean and studied their route up the cliff. It was just as far to the top—farther, perhaps, than he'd realized the first time he'd looked—but his second observation had yielded a few rays of hope. Scraggly bushes hung here and there, defying the salt spray to sink their hardy roots into the soil. Here and there, a tougher stone hung out to provide a toehold, here and there were indentions in the smooth expanse.

A difficult climb for him, but not impossible.

For Saura? He winced. The thought of directing her, step by painful step, up the smooth, upright surface made his hands shake. Clasping her closer, and closer still, he placed his mouth on the top of her head and prayed with all his might.

"William?" She still rested against him, and for a brief moment her arms encircled his waist to hug him. "William?" She tugged free and sat up. "Are you going to sleep all day? Hadn't we better go?"

With silent profundity, he reflected on how rapidly she could turn his sentiment to vexation. "You're a nag, do you know that?"

She stood and shook out her skirts. "I've been called worse things," she assured him, "but not by better men."

He grunted and dragged himself up. "Do you think to flatter me with compliments?"

"I think we'd better climb that cliff above us," she answered.

Startled, he studied her wide, innocent eyes and mobile mouth. "How did you know there was a cliff?"

"You would have never let me sleep if it had been an easy walk to the top."

"You're an annoying woman. I should leave you here." He studied the boulder blocking the way into the cave and sighed. "But I can't."

"I'll be fine, William." She reached out and stroked his cheek. "We'll be fine."

They were fine.

William lay on the coarse grass at the top of the cliff and held it clutched in his fists and panted. They were fine, except for the sweat that poured down his sides and the heart that beat out of his chest. Saura was fine. She'd been gallant, patient, awaiting his instructions before moving hand or foot, never faltering when he'd had to go on ahead and gouge a tiny toehold out of the bluff. She hadn't complained about the heat, although the afternoon sun beating on the unrelenting rock had baked them. She didn't seem to realize, although he warned her, that the slightest slip could end in a long fall. She'd just smiled and said, " 'Tis not falling that worries me. 'Tis landing."

He'd been in no mood for levity.

Now she sat just a little away from him, the sea wind blowing the chalk from her hair, waiting for him to recover from his fright. He didn't see the care with which she lifted the end of her sleeve to wipe the perspiration from her forehead before she asked, "William, are you well?"

"Aye." He turned his head and studied her. "Are you?"

She clasped her hands. They trembled slightly, and she tucked them into her lap. "My hands are sore from gripping the stones and I have a few bristles imbedded in my palm, but compared to—"

"Don't!" He reached out and shook her knee. "Don't even say it."

"Husband." Catching his hand when he would retrieve it, she stroked it in both of hers. "You must stop worrying. We're at the top now, 'tis time to move on."

"Most women would have been hysterical about such a climb. How can you be so calm?" He found himself perturbed by her unfailing good humor. Didn't she realize that nothing, absolutely nothing else he had to do, would compete with that crawl up the cliff?

"I never doubted you would bring me to the top." She paused to invest her words with significance. "You would never let anyone or anything endanger me. I trust you."

"Trust! What has trust to do. . . ." His words trailed off, and he sat up. Catching her chin in his hand, he questioned, "Trust?"

A slight smile danced about her lips, and she veiled her eyes shyly. "Trust," she confirmed.

He discovered he could knock down Cran Castle with his bare hands, stand flat-footed in the bailey and toss Charles over the curtain wall, and gallop to Burke with Saura on his back, sans horse.

"You trust me to take care of you?"

"Eternally."

"We have to go now," he murmured, entranced by his wife's confession.

"I know." She sounded vague. "If Nicholas should find us lying on the grass. . . ."

Like the jolt of a lightning flash, her words brought clarity back to him. "Correct." He stood, pulling her up after him. "We have to go. I must find a place close by where I can hide you."

"Hide me?" She jogged along behind him. "I thought I'd go with you."

He chuckled. "Foolish love. I couldn't care for you in a fight. There may be many men against me. It will take all my concentration to defend myself and destroy Nicholas."

Tugging at his hand, she said, "Nay. Nay, we'll just run and keep running."

"Nicholas has horses and men and a thorough knowledge of this land. He'd find us." He glanced around at the flat, clear land and grimaced. " 'Twould be too easy, I fear. There's that pile of rocks."

She set her heels and jerked him around. Knitting her brow fiercely, she yelled, "You can't fight a castle of men by yourself!"

"Now, dearling," he soothed. "I was with Charles when I realized you were right, did I tell you?"

"Did you tell me I was right? Nay, somehow that slipped from our conversation."

She resisted as he pulled her underneath his shoulder, but he dragged her along beside him. "Aye, Charles was quite indignant that I thought he'd try to kill me in such a cowardly manner. It humbled me to be so wrong."

"Oh, you are humble," she agreed sarcastically.

"And some of the incidents he told me about Nicholas cleared my mind. He's mad, you know."

"Nicholas?" She nodded. "Aye, he is. And quite without logic."

"Nasty little piece, aren't you?" Savoring her wit, he hugged her in a sweep that lifted her from her feet, and when he put her down she stopped struggling against his briskness and walked at his side. "You're cooperating," he said in surprise.

"I can take a hint." She ducked out from under his arm as his grip loosened and took his elbow. "You'll carry me if I don't."

She saw him more clearly than he saw himself, he realized. He hadn't meant to coerce her when he lifted her, but perhaps that was what he intended. "My men are probably close to the coast already."

"In only a day?" Skeptical, she slowed her step. "Your father never moved with such haste in his life."

"You've never seen my father go to war," he answered with unwavering faith. "I pity the men-at-arms who lost their sleep last night." Double-time, he towed her toward a stony knoll covered with scrub, and once more she gave up the struggle and hurried with him. "You'll know they're here before I do. Sit up on the top of this rock and listen, and when you hear the sound of battle you'll know we are victorious."

The three men rode toward Cran Castle, their troops trailing behind. Raymond and Lord Peter flanked the great lord, arguing across his saddlebow and never missing a stride.

"He bragged about it, I tell you." Raymond stripped off his helmet and ran his hands through his long, dark hair. "At the wedding, he hinted and I shrugged. So he suggested and I looked interested. Then he told me of his plans to murder William and I admired him with all my heart."

"He believed you?" Incredulous, Lord Peter glared at Raymond.

"Aye, he's so far gone he can only see his own greatness."

Lord Peter shook his head, interested in spite of himself, afraid it was the truth and feeling foolish for dragging his men halfway across England for a fairy tale. "Why didn't you come to me at once?"

Raymond turned his fine, dark eyes on Lord Peter. "Would you have believed me?"

Lord Peter's gaze dropped away.

"You don't really believe me even now. You don't want to believe that one of your nestlings has grown into a vulture."

"After Arthur kidnapped William and Saura—"

"What?" Raymond roared. "Was that ridiculous story the truth?"

"Assuredly it was the truth." Lord Peter stared at Raymond. "I thought William would have told you."

"When?"

"At the wedding."

Raymond threw his head back and laughed harshly. "At the wedding, William had only one thing on his mind. But I heard rumors."

"Arthur admitted that he and another lord worked together to kill William. I should have spoken to you."

"You were not consulting one another," the lord told them. "So too many battles go astray."

Fretting, Lord Peter said, "I should have stayed at Burke. What if a message comes about Saura while I'm gone? Maud's likely to lead the garrison into battle herself."

He glanced at the lord, who grinned and said, "My wife's like that. Too sure of herself and ready to let me know it."

"Women." Lord Peter sighed. "Maud almost took my ears off for being gone when Saura was kidnapped. Maud went looking for Saura, all by herself, when she suspected treachery."

"Was she hurt?" Raymond asked.

"Nay, only her voice ached from shrieking. She found the footprints of men and horses. She found a strange churl, mauled to death. Odder than that, she found our dog, Bula. You know the dog is nothing but a coward, yet the man lay dead beside that animal. Bula was tied with a stout rope and frantically chewing his way through it." Lord Peter shook his head. "How did that dog get tied?"

"He knew whoever tied him," the lord answered logically.

"Aye, so we surmised. When Maud released the dog, he took off into the woods and we haven't seen him since."

"I suspect you'll see Bula again," the lord comforted.

"Yes, on the day I see Saura again," Lord Peter agreed. "Someone has taken her, but why?"

"Nicholas did it," Raymond insisted. "This whole plot is one big sticky web Nicholas has woven. I told him to let me know when the time came to divide up the lands and I'd be there."

Lord Peter snorted. "I can imagine what he said to that."

"He said I'd have to help him to earn the lands. He had the idea I would do anything to have some income of my own and not be dependent on my sire." Raymond's mouth twisted into a bitter line.

Neither Lord Peter nor the great lord said a word. They looked straight ahead as they rode and offered neither sympathy nor understanding. What could they say? The way Raymond's parents treated him was shameful, yet it was Raymond's problem and he'd not welcome interference.

"I failed to pay attention as I should. Forgive me," Raymond apologized. "The events in London are so tremendous," he glanced at the lord, "that I let William slip from my mind. In sooth, I've always believed William could care for himself."

Lord Peter laughed. "Aye, he does strike you like that, does he not?"

"So it was until the last new moon, when the most extraordinary person arrived at my home in London. A big, beautiful man who insisted he'd run all the way from Cran Castle with a message from Nicholas. I was gone from London, trailing along after Prince Henry. The man never sleeps, Lord Peter, and he delights in unplanned trips."

"So I see," Lord Peter answered wryly.

The lord laughed, and Raymond shrugged at Lord Peter, indicating his own lack of responsibility for their bizarre situation. "My servitors didn't pay the runner a lot of notice. Just let him eat and sleep and brought him in front of me when I arrived. This fellow was none too bright, and when he repeated the message, it didn't make a lot of sense. Something about Nicholas wedding a woman to equal William's wife."

"What!" Lord Peter roared.

"It didn't make sense to me then," Raymond said, "but it scared me and made me decide 'twas time to let you know what I suspected, and what I knew. It makes sense to me now."

The lord turned to Lord Peter. "I couldn't resist coming along. I need to see the countryside, talk to the barons. I assure you, I've developed a second sense about treachery and deceit. You're doing the right thing."

Waving his hand, Lord Peter urged them to a gallop. The whole company rode hard, overtaking all other traffic on the road and passing through hamlets where the villagers cowered at their passing. Lord Peter paid little attention when they saw a small band of soldiers, battered and grim, riding toward them, but a shout from the group made him pull up. "Channing," he said, recognizing the man whose leg lay crooked across the saddle. "Damn, man, what happened?"

"Attacked, my lord, as we rode t' warn that ye must ride t' Cran Castle at once."

"How were you so distressed?" Lord Peter asked, displeased with the chief man-at-arms and showing it.

" 'Twas a large group of knights, m'lord, well-trained mercenaries. Charles was in no shape t' command us an' his men nothin' but cowards."

"Charles? You were with Charles?"

"I couldn't stop t' check him, m'lord. I saw him go down under a sword, but whether he lives I cannot tell."

"Are any of you uninjured?" Lord Peter swept his eyes over the group.

Channing nodded. "A few."

"Send them back to find Charles and discover if he lives. You, Channing, go on to Burke."

"I must return wi' you t' my Lord William," Channing said desperately. "He ordered us t' go without him. I argued, m'lord, but Lord William—"

"Never listens to reason. Where is William?"

"He went t' Cran Castle alone, m'lord, t' rescue Lady Saura."

Lord Peter's mouth formed a perfect O of horror.

"He thought he'd sent th' message soon enough that ye'd be there already t' help him, but th' warriors were from Cran Castle, there was no mistaking their shouts."

"Go home, Channing," Lord Peter ordered. "You've done all you could."

"Where did you get these bruises?" William asked as he dipped her handkerchief into the bucket of water and washed her face.

His understated fury made her wish they'd never discovered the well at the abandoned farm in the shadow of the knoll. The folk who lived there, he told her, had obviously left in a hurry, seeking the castle for protection. "Rumors of war must be flying," he had said.

Now chickens pecked around their feet as they sat on a bench in the yard, and she soothed his anger with a laugh. "My bruises are nothing. You didn't think I'd go along with Nicholas without a fight, did you?"

"He looked uninjured to me," he snapped.

"His bruises don't show," she snapped back.

He relaxed a bit. "Did you find a stone to use on his head?"

"If I had," she replied with assurance, "you wouldn't be seeking him now."

"That's my girl." He slapped her on the shoulder and she winced. He froze and then carefully peeled back her cotte. "Ah, Saura," he breathed, his gaze on the black marks against her pale skin. "What did the blackguard do to you?"

" 'Tis nothing, William." She smoothed his face with her palm.

"I'll make him pay for every bruise," William promised, dipping his rag once more and wringing it out.

"You're too sloppy, William." She caught at his hand before he could wash her further.

"And you're too dusty," he countered, evading her.

"You're slopping it down my cotte," she complained, but a note of shrill dismay alerted him.

"Is there something you don't wish me to see?"

She didn't answer, trying to appear relaxed. She hoped

fervently he wouldn't wash her neck, but she'd piqued his curiosity. The rag dripped water onto her clothes as he wiped her neck clean of its blanket of white chalk.

"Saura. Holy Blessed Virgin." He surveyed her clean neck as it emerged and swore. A necklace of fingerprints circled her delicate skin and the two dark marks close to her windpipe told him how close he'd come to losing her. "Is this his favorite method of extermination?"

"Nay, he also favors poison." She raised haunted eyes to his face. "Hawisa was a bitch, but I pity her her death."

"Is it sore?" he asked with murderous intensity.

"I feel a little raspy when I talk," she admitted.

"What stopped him?"

That made her smile. "Bronnie. If not for Bronnie, I'd be dead right now."

"You mean I owe a debt to that simpleton?"

His blatant dismay brought a chuckle to her lips. "Aye."

"Very well." William straightened like a man doing an unpleasant duty. "I'll care for him as if he were kin."

"He's really a very nice creature," she said. "Like Bula. Endlessly loyal."

"Unlike Bula, he's not intelligent." He added, "Nor is he endlessly brave."

"That's my Bronnie," she agreed, affection and mirth quirking her lips.

"I'll kill him."

She jumped at his sudden fierce vow. "Bronnie?"

"Nicholas. I'll kill him as I would a mad wolf."

"Wait for your father to arrive," she urged. "No one would fault you for that."

"I thought you trusted me?"

"So I do." A tear glistened on her lashes, and she leaned

her forehead against his chest to hide it. "I trust you to care for me. I doubt you have any such care for yourself."

"Dearling, listen to me." His finger under her chin, he lifted her face to his. "I'll have the element of surprise. With any luck, Nicholas hasn't realized we've escaped, and even if he has, he'll not expect to see me inside the battlements. Not now. I'm afraid to wait too long, don't you see? Once inside, I can open the gates to my father."

"Open the gates, when his mercenaries command the castle?" she scorned.

"I can do it. I'm not just a great mass of muscle, you know. I'm crafty and I never forget the first rule of combat. If I don't get that gate open, there'll be a prolonged siege and that madman will have the chance to worm his way out. Nay, I want him gone. I want the way cleared for us to have a life together without fear."

She closed her eyes in defeat. "You have a strange way of freeing me of fear, haring off to do single combat with a castle full of warriors."

"I can manage." He grinned.

Her eyes popped open. "Your modesty doesn't bear examination."

"I speak only the truth," he intoned solemnly.

Pushing against his solid shoulder, she chuckled with watery amusement.

"That's better," he coaxed. "Keep your confidence. We only have a little way to go and you'll be settled and I'll be on my way. I'm going to carry this bucket up for you and leave you the bread and cheese."

"You don't think you'll be back tonight," she said flatly.

"I don't know." He lifted her with one hand under her elbow. "We must be prepared for anything."

"I'll tell you, William." She tucked her skirts into her belt in anticipation of the climb to her perch. "My body is prepared for anything, but I don't know how much more bruising my heart can stand."

TWENTY·TWO

William trotted down the path on the knoll, looking back only once to check that his dearling was placed out of sight. She hadn't grumbled anymore about his plans to capture Cran Castle on his own; she'd been heart-wrenchingly brave. It made him wonder how tightly she'd have him wound around her finger when he'd finished disposing of this little problem. One tear from her eye and he almost tossed his plans into the dung heap.

Nevertheless, he had a battle to finish. He had to do it in these last hours of sunlight or he feared Nicholas would slip from his fingertips. He didn't ever, ever want to have to watch his own back again.

His long strides brought him close to the gatehouse in good time, and he halted and listened. He strained to hear the sound of many horses' hooves, but instead he heard only the whine of the wind off the ocean and the distant barking of a dog. In spite of his assurances to Saura, he'd hoped to have his troops at his back. Ah, well, he'd soon hold a sword again.

Coming to the edge of the motte, he hailed the castle and got a very surprised call back. "Who did ye say it was?" the man-at-arms hollered.

"William of Miraval," he shouted back. "I fell out of the dungeon, and I've returned myself to Lord Nicholas's kind care."

A confused discussion took place on the battlements, and then another man, the mercenary who commanded the garrison, and had tossed him into the prison, shoved the soldier aside. "We're checking the dungeon now," he called. "We'll let you back in, if you've really escaped."

William spread his hands wide. "Let me in now," he urged. "I have no weapon. I'm only one man. Surely you don't fear me."

For answer, the knight gazed beyond William at the plain that stretched empty clear to the forest's edge, and nodded. "What harm?"

The drawbridge creaked and William laughed inside at the care with which the rusty chains lowered it. Nervous, were they? Good. Nervous men made mistakes.

He strode across the drawbridge and stood waiting at the portcullis as the mercenary examined him through the iron slats. "I don't believe it," the knight muttered. "How did you escape that dungeon?" He nodded to the guards and the portcullis rose with awkward jerks. "And what in the name of good Saint Wilfred made you come back?"

William waited, smiling, until the last barrier had been pulled from between them, and then he leaped at the man's throat. Catching him by the neck, he snarled, "I came back to kill Nicholas with your sword."

Taken by surprise, the knight staggered back and then recovered, knocking William's hands aside. But he wore armor and William did not, and when William kicked his feet out from under him he went down with a crash. William had him!

He dove for the sword. The earth-bound knight fought to keep it in its scabbard. They rolled in the dirt, and William smirked. The mercenary was smaller, laden with armor, as easy to defeat as a turtle on its back.

Jerking the blade free, William leaped up and glanced around. The guards had recovered from their paralysis, and he thrust out with the point of his ill-gotten weapon. The shouting at the gate brought men and more men to the fight; they came at him in a tide. He slashed, using the sword to advantage and fighting for a shield. He saw one he liked: large, sturdy, wielded by an opponent who seemed intent on remaining a spectator. In a surge, he drove toward the un-willing warrior and cracked his skull with the flat of the sword. He wrenched the shield from the slack grip and turned.

"Burke!" he bellowed in his open-mouthed war cry, and the soldiers fell back for a moment. He managed to get his back to the wall beside the still-open gate. The outer bailey rang with shouts and the deep, angry barking of a dog, and William was deafened.

He didn't like the way these men fought. They fought as if they'd die if they let him escape. They fought as if Nicholas would kill them in slow, painful ways if he outwitted them.

Suddenly, like driftwood caught by a wave, the guards seemed to ebb away. They disappeared under the gigantic, hairy beast who attacked them with slavering jaws. "Wolf!" they screamed, fleeing or falling as their courage allowed.

"Just what I need," William muttered. Distracted, he braced himself for an onslaught, but the great beast raised its head from the leading knight's chest. "Bula!" William lowered his sword. "Bula, you magnificent animal, I thought you were dead." He had no time to say more, but he glanced out across the plain at the distant cloud of dust and smiled. "Can my father be far behind?"

Saura waited in dignified agony. As soon as she was sure William could no longer see her, she'd climbed out of the protected hole where he'd placed her and lifted herself to the top of the highest rock she could find. She didn't care who observed her in this deserted countryside; she wanted to hear the battle. And she could hear it very well. The flat plain, the lack of obstructions, made sounds carry far and clear.

So she listened. Straining her ears, she heard shouting. She heard the drawbridge lowered, she heard William's bellow, and she heard the sweetest sound in the world. 'Twas Bula's bark.

It couldn't be. She'd heard his fury and the blow that silenced it.

The barking boomed out again and she started with the pain it brought her. Could she mistake his bark for another's?

No, this was no mistake. That was Bula's bark.

For the first time, something stronger than hope stirred in her. Bula was alive? He was alive. Nicholas hadn't murdered him, and with Bula on his side, William had a fighting chance. The dog was large and loyal, and an almost human intelligence moved the animal to perform.

If Bula had found them, could Lord Peter and his army?

They could. At least, she thought they could. She heard

the distant drumbeat of horses, and she leaned forward. Was it the soldiers from Burke? As they rode across the plain, the clank and rattle of armor and the shouting of many men obscured any individual voices. It wasn't until they halted and called a challenge that one voice predominated, but it wasn't Lord Peter. Nor Charles, nor any person she'd ever heard before. Clenching her fist, she strained to to hear, wondering if William was in greater danger now. What could she think? What did she want to think? Any army coming to Cran Castle now must be hostile; ergo, they were an ally of hers.

But in these unsettled times, perhaps the army came to conquer, and innocent William, caught in the middle, would count for nothing. He'd better have a care for himself now.

One by one, the men attacking William dropped their swords and stared out their open drawbridge. "A great force," one man-at-arms muttered, his voice carrying in the sudden silence. The dust raised by the horses speeding across the plains awed them. "No foot soldiers," another said. "A greater force of knights than I have ever seen."

Neither William nor Bula took more than a moment to gloat before they returned to their work with sword and tooth. The dog had positioned himself beside William, snatching at the legs within his reach. Bodies had piled up around the dog who so deftly avoided the swords aimed at him. For William's part, he'd parried the most obvious blows to Bula and taken advantage of the attackers' preoccupation with defending their feet. The bodies piled deep around his side, too, and now he watched for a chance to leap out of the circle and find Nicholas.

Beside him, the drawbridge gave a crack and leaped, then fell back. Looking up, William saw the mercenary commander twisting the great wheel that operated the entrance. William roared with rage, the knight looked down, and smirked. Leaning all his weight on the mechanism, the lone knight slowly inched the heavy drawbridge up. Fresh blood coursed through William's veins, and he leapfrogged over the groaning men-at-arms with Bula at his heels. William ran up the tiny stairway to the landing while Bula stopped halfway and kept the pursuing men at bay.

The mercenary cranked and watched from the corner of his eye. William reached the top before the knight could close that gate, and he waved the weapon in his hand. "I have your sword," he called. "Come and get it."

The knight loosened his grip on the wheel and the drawbridge rattled back down. "I have no need for my sword." He snatched a lance off the arsenal on the wall and pointed it at William's chest. He charged, and William barely stepped aside, teetering on the edge of the narrow landing. He whacked the lance in half with the edge of his blade, but the knight had already retreated, securing a mace for himself and swinging it like a man who knew what he was doing.

Its spiked iron head could be deadly in such small quarters, bludgeoning with indifferent conviction, and William grinned. He liked this knight. He was inventive, loyal, willing to fight. "You're a mercenary, eh?" William asked.

"Aye." The mace swung in wide circles.

"There's a huge force outside who'll soon be inside, and Lord Nicholas, I promise, will be in no position to pay your wages."

The mace drooped a bit. "I don't betray the lord who pays me," the knight said tersely, but William's gaze was on that mace.

"He's a treacherous, shifty, lying man who has deserted friendship and personal honor. You're not bound to him, for he'd never do more than toss you to the dogs." The mace's swing diminished to a half circle. "And the dogs," William jerked his head toward the stair where Bula held sway, "are fearsome."

The sway of the mace creaked to a halt. William kept his eyes on the spiked head of the mace and eased toward the gate's closing mechanism. Jamming the wooden shield deep into the gears, he effectively disabled it. The mercenary watched, and William turned to him. "Find me when this is over. I have uses for fighters such as you." Turning, he called Bula and ordered him to stay. "Bula will protect you from my father's vengeance, if you protect Bula from the swords."

Running lightly down the stairs, William glanced around. The bailey roiled with armed men astride destriers. He spotted his father, Raymond, and another man. A leader; big, bold, shouting the commands that directed the battle.

Who was he?

William had no time to stop and question. Eager now, he raced toward the keep, knowing he'd find Nicholas there.

The castle relied on its position on the cliffs for defense. The outer curtain wall hung almost over the edge on the three sides; the gatehouse opened onto the plain. Within the walls, only one bailey surrounded the keep, and William smiled with grim satisfaction when he found the door to the keep open.

Perhaps that should worry him, but he knew Nicholas was such a poor strategist, such a dreadful excuse for a knight, that he'd never planned for the enemy inside the walls. All his men fought at the gate; all of them. William had seen the steady stream of mercenaries who emerged from the keep. Only Nicholas cowered within, surrounded by the weapons he'd never bothered to practice with; the weapons that would not save him.

William entered the keep and glanced around. The abrupt change from light to dark made it difficult to adjust, but no one lurked in the entry. Running on the balls of his feet, he mounted the stairs, his sword at readiness. Before he entered the great hall, he paused and listened.

Nothing. Only the sound of fighting outside disturbed the silence.

He strode into the room. The fire burned on the hearth, the table was set for dinner, but nary a soul stirred. All the servants, all the folk of the castle were gone.

But Nicholas wasn't. William's instincts tuned to the stones of the keep. The entrance to the undercroft drew him like a magnet; it was the entrance to the dungeon, too, and Nicholas's only remaining hope. William knew Nicholas would try to secure the prisoners he thought he held for ransom.

Had Nicholas already discovered his fettered birds had flown the cage?

Moving softly, William started down into the dusk of the undercroft. A lone torch sputtered in reluctant illumination. The trapdoor that hid the dungeon lay close to the foot of the spiral stairs, and William listened for the crash of its closing. It didn't come, and he wondered for the first time if Nicholas really lurked there.

Did Nicholas have a secret tunnel? Had he slipped out the postern gate? Had he lowered himself into the dungeon and found their escape route?

William remembered the climb up the cliff and smiled a most unpleasant smile. That, he thought, would be a fitting justice.

But rounding the last corner, he came face to face with his

nemesis. "At last," he said, his teeth bared through his beard.

"At last, indeed." Nicholas lifted the sword he held and pointed it at William's throat. "This time I will finish you. You see, I have the advantage."

Nicholas gleamed with chain mail. His sword was fully half again as long as William's. His belt sagged with the combined weight of mace and dagger, and he held a shield that covered him from his knees to his neck.

William laughed out loud. " 'Tis not arms that make the man," he jeered, "but ability."

"Then I shall win," Nicholas replied, too quickly.

William snorted. "I could beat you with my knees in a bucket and my feet in the well."

The tip of Nicholas's sword trembled just a bit. "Too true. If only you had a shield."

His false sympathy set William's teeth on edge. "I climbed the cliff that guards this castle. What makes you think I can't get a shield if I need one? The shield I earned before now holds the gears to the drawbridge open, and 'twas an investment well spent. Now if I were you, I'd worry about my own situation."

"Why should I?"

"These stairs wind around the wall to give the advantage to the right-handed swordsman who defends from the top. You see? I'm right-handed." William swished his blade with exultant freedom. "I'm at the top. So I have the advantage."

Nicholas grinned, his teeth brown and stubbled. "I am left-handed, and thus a hard man to fight." He also swished his blade, free from the need to watch the wall. "So I have the advantage."

"Left-handed because of a broken arm," William remembered. "Perhaps if you'd practiced more as a squire."

He shrugged, a bit of elegance, and Nicholas lunged at him.

William easily moved aside. "Practicing now?" he asked, bored.

Nicholas halted, breathing hard, thinking hard. Sliding down a few steps, he mocked, "I'd be respectful if I were you. The last time I practiced on you, you were blind for months."

"*You* struck the blow?" Astonished, William thought about it and then shook his head. "Nay. You weren't even in that battle."

"You fought that battle because of me. I did it. I did it all."

The ring of pride in his voice forced William to evaluate his scorn. "How so?"

"I urged your neighbor, what was his name?"

"Sir Donnell."

"I told that old fool Sir Donnell that you were involved elsewhere, that he could take that land of yours, and by the time you discovered it, it would be accomplished. I knew you'd come running, I knew you'd attack, and I knew I could wear a helmet that guarded my whole face."

" 'Tis difficult to fight in a helmet that so diminishes your vision," William commented, not yet convinced.

"I didn't fight. I just rode up behind you and—"

"You *don't* fight. You play dirty, underhanded, treacherous games."

"Games where the forfeit is death."

Moving with well-oiled speed, William reached in and slashed Nicholas on the wrist that held the sword. He stepped back with insulting ease and watched as Nicholas stood and shook the drops of blood from his hand. "You're playing my game now," William pointed out softly.

Nicholas recovered his wits and made an attack of his own.

"Who commands the troops that unfairly besiege me? Not your father. I never heard his braying voice nor saw him from the arrow slits."

"If you'd ceased your cowering and come into the light, you'd have seen my father. And Raymond, too."

"Raymond!" Nicholas shouted, his face mottling. "Raymond! That traitor. He was willing to kill you for a cut of your lands, but when the tide turns he bellies up like a dead fish."

"Raymond would never kill me." William spoke with the same assurance he always used. "Raymond is my friend."

"And Charles?" The note of evil amusement crept into Nicholas's voice. "Did you see Charles in my bailey? Is Charles your friend?"

"He wasn't there." William thought about that. "I wonder what happened to Charles."

"He lies under a gorse bush and bleeds and dies," Nicholas said harshly. "I know all. I know everything. I know you sent him to tell your father to rescue you. I arranged a little accident for Charles."

With a shout, William leaped at him. He slipped under his guard, cutting a slice into his cheek and then jumped over Nicholas's swing like a boy with a jump rope. He backed up the stairs out of reach, and counseled, "Hold that sword a little higher. Didn't my father teach you any better than that?"

Tight-lipped with pain, Nicholas snarled, "He taught me never to fall for the same trick twice."

"I don't know how you can help it. That's a man's sword you carry, and you haven't the muscles to fight with it." Studying the agony that marred his enemy's face, he asked, "Is that the first time you've been blooded, dear boy?"

The trickle of red dripped off Nicholas's chin and matched the fiery glare of his eyes. "On my face, you bastard."

Nicholas came up the stairs after him, sword clenched firm by fury, and William backed up with slow deliberation. "Don't worry about your face," William said softly. "You won't be needing it any more." That checked the forward advance, and William chuckled. "Didn't you find what you sought in the dungeon?"

"How did you know I'd been down in the dungeon?" Nicholas asked.

"Where else would a spineless worm find his pass to freedom?"

"I should have known better than to trust that bitch you call your wife." He stepped back. Awkward with the weight of chain mail, he tipped back, waving his arms for balance, and righted himself.

William waited, watching with a seasoned gaze. "Trust her?"

"Asking me not to put you in with her when she knew you'd find a way out." He spat off the edge of the stair into the air.

"I'd find a way out?" William said incredulously. "You have it wrong, dear boy. Saura found the way out of your impregnable prison, not I. All I did was push the damned stone aside, and that only with her help."

"I see you managed to leave Bronnie behind, like a used rag."

"He's injured," William snapped. "You injured him."

"But I thought any man of exalted honor would find a way to save the boy from certain death. You certainly bandaged him well. It seemed almost a shame to pull my knife and slit his—"

This time Nicholas was prepared for the swing. He parried

and drove his blade at William's heart, but William faded beneath the attack. Nicholas had the satisfaction of knowing he'd met flesh, for the tip had caught, but the vexation of realizing William fought like a wraith.

William wiped the drop of blood from his chest. "Saura's going to be very upset at you, Nicholas. She liked that boy."

"She'll be more upset when I've killed you."

"I wait here with no shield, no armor, no helmet." William spread his arms wide, expanding into the space around him. "You have the advantage, you say, but you don't attack."

"I've beaten you in every battle we've fought."

"Talk, talk."

"I have!"

"Only because I didn't know we were fighting." William gripped the short blade, tip up, its point a dim spark of menace.

"I'll always win these kinds of fights." Nicholas smiled in a sneering triumph.

"Nay. You've forgotten the first rule of combat."

"What's that?"

With creeping caution, Nicholas moved closer, and William's eyes glinted in pleasure. He smiled in invitation like an overconfident youth, but his heel seemed to slip off the step. His arms flailed madly, he danced to recover, and with a cry of triumph Nicholas lunged at him. With lightning reflexes, William's sword streaked up and speared Nicholas between the chin and neck. Blood gushed as he jerked his sword back. Nicholas teetered there for one ghastly moment before he crumpled and rolled with increasing speed down the stairs to the cold stone floor.

Serious now, William followed him down and checked the eyes that stared with the true blindness of death. "The first rule of combat, Nicholas. Do you remember it now? *Battles are fought to win."* Still staring at the lifeless body, he wiped his sword and thrust it into his belt.

Turning away, he strode to the open door of the dungeon and peered down. He could see nothing, hear no sound of life, and he sighed. Lifting a torch from the sconce on the wall, he waved it down the hole. Deep in the earth, he could see the outline of Bronnie, dark against the white chalk. The man lay still as death; William knew he was dead, but he could never go back to Saura and tell her he hadn't tried to rouse him. He yelled, "Bronnie! Lady Saura needs you!"

Nothing. It was as silent as a tomb.

"Bronnie! Fire's destroying the castle. We need help."

Nothing.

"Bronnie! Lady Saura wants you to come and live with us and be her serving man."

Reviving like a knight offered the Holy Grail, Bronnie sat straight up. "M'lady wants me . . . t' wait on her?"

Startled, William dropped the torch down and it illuminated the man where he sat. Bronnie rubbed his shoulder and looked vacant with delight, but clearly it took more than a fall to rout him. "Aye, Bronnie, the lady wants you to wait on her."

William sighed, stood, and dusted his hands, muttering "Somehow I knew it would be too easy if Nicholas had slit your throat."

He started toward the stairs only to hear the click of claws coming down. "Bula," he said, more glad to see the great dog than he believed possible. "Well met, my friend."

The animal stopped at Nicholas's side and sniffed, and then with seeming contempt leaped over him and trotted to William. William smoothed Bula's head and found a dozen tiny cuts. Dropping to his knees, William examined the dog from ear to toe. A huge swelling over one eye almost closed it. "Did Nicholas believe this would kill you?" he marveled. Bula winced beneath William's probing fingers, but the lump rested on the hardest part of the dog's stout skull. "If your performance above stairs was anything to judge by, it's clear you weren't even seriously injured." Dried blood matted Bula's hair here and there where he had been nicked with a sword, but nowhere was there any great wound. "To think we believed you were a coward." William patted him firmly. "You just waited until you could fight for someone you loved. Bula, my boy, your beauty will return and until then, you'll be the most pampered creature at Burke."

Bula whined and nosed his master's cheek, and as William rose he heard, "Are you there? William?" The shout echoed down from the great hall, and Bula responded as if he had been hailed. He bounded up the spiral stairway and the still-unseen caller scolded, "Damned dog," as he whirled past.

William roared, "Raymond?" He stared up through the gloom and spied his comrade, halfway up the stair and peering around the corner. With lightened heart, he stepped over Nicholas and sprang up to his friend. "You're the best sight my eyes have feasted on for the last three hours."

Raymond laughed and grasped his outstretched hand. "You must have Saura hidden somewhere—she's the feast you prefer."

"You've divined my secret," William admitted.

Peering over William's shoulder, Raymond shook his head sadly. "Nicholas?" he asked, nodding at the body lying in sprawled repose at the bottom of the steps.

"Aye." William turned to look back down to the stones where his secret enemy lay, exposed in his falsehoods and vanquished. "He died with a sword in his hand."

He looked at Raymond and smiled grimly, and Raymond nodded in condolence and congratulation. "If anyone could ever persuade him to take up a sword, 'tis you." Edging around to stand below William, Raymond put a hand on his friend's back and pushed him toward the great hall, but William seemed to have grown roots where he stood.

" 'Tis such a waste," William mourned. "He could have been the greatest man in England, chancellor to the king. He was richer than you, craftier than I, and he lies dead with not a soul to mourn him."

"He forced you to kill him. As the twig is bent, so grows the tree, and Nicholas had been bent the first time I met him. You're not to blame yourself for his death," Raymond admonished.

William faced him and glared. "I'm not such a fool as to lose sleep over it." He marched ahead and they climbed the steps single file. On the landing, he paused. Without turning, he instructed, "Make sure a priest is sent down, won't you?"

"Of course." Raymond slapped his shoulder, holding it with an understanding grip. "Of course, I'll see to it."

"And for the sake of my soul, see that someone gets that idiot Bronnie out of the dungeon." He swung on Raymond. "I've sworn to care for the boy as if he were my kin." Before Raymond could question his droll resignation, he added, "That reminds me, is my father well?"

"He's fine," Raymond assured him.

"Are you well?"

"I can't complain."

They reached the great hall, and William turned to see a broad smile on Raymond's face. "Then why didn't you command the attack? Why didn't my father?"

"Come. Let me show you."

TWENTY-THREE

Raymond took his arm and led him to the strange knight who stood talking to Lord Peter. Lord Peter saw them approaching and he smiled the same satisfied smile that Raymond wore. Touching the stranger's shoulder, he directed his attention to William. The stranger immediately stepped forward to meet them, his stride broad, his manner vigorous.

Watching him, William was struck by the majesty that tempered the air of friendliness. He glanced at Raymond and saw awe, glanced at his father and saw approval. "Duke Henry," he guessed, but it wasn't really a guess. "Nay, it's Prince Henry, now."

"Quite right, Lord William." Prince Henry grinned as he reached them, stopping William's bow with a sweep of his arm. "Please, let's save the formality for the court. I'm delighted to meet you. All I've heard since we left Burke is William this, William that. I'm pleased to see your stature is not a giant's, as I've been led to believe."

"My father exaggerates, my lord."

Prince Henry bent a look of amused inquiry at his new subject. "Raymond sings your praises, too. Does he exaggerate, as well?"

William grinned back with full-bodied enjoyment. "I hope not, Lord, for he sings your praises, also."

Slapping his hands on his ribs, Prince Henry leaned his head back and bellowed with laughter. William followed him, his own amusement combining with his prince's to shake the rafters. Unable to restrain themselves, Lord Peter and Raymond laughed, also, as did the men who trickled in from the battle. Bula barked and circled them, herding them closer.

At last, Prince Henry wiped his eyes. "We'll deal well together, William. You'll have to come to London when I'm in residence. Bring your wife."

"Saura!" William straightened at once. "God's teeth, I must—"

"There's going to be a new order in England," Prince Henry boomed, "and a place for honest men like you."

"Thank you, my lord. I look forward to that." William bowed slightly. "Now, I must—"

"A new order! Of course, I'm not the king of England yet, but with the succession secure at last, I'm making plans." Prince Henry stepped up on the dais and clasped his hands behind his back.

"I'd love to hear them, my lord—"

"When, by God's favor, the crown is firmly on my head and I hold the scepter in my hands, the first thing I'm going to do is expel those foreign mercenaries of Stephen's." Prince Henry paced across the dais. "He's been paying them to quell rebellion, and all they've done is teach rebellion."

"That's God's truth," Lord Peter agreed.

"Law will return to the land. The courts set up by our forefathers have been made puppets of the robber barons. The barons, too, have forgotten that they owe their lands and castles to the king. The king grants the land in return for obedience and fealty. These barons who used this unsettled time to seize land and build castles have a surprise in store."

"Good tidings, my lord." William nodded with hearty encouragement. "Now if I could—"

Swept along on a tide of his own enthusiasm, Prince Henry said, "I'll have those castles confiscated. Those barons seek only to prey on the unprotected populace. I ask you, how can the people of England produce flax and wool, raise corn and barley, without peace? How can my loyal nobles collect their portion of the proceeds without peace? How can my government run without the king's portion of their revenues? This country is in such disorder, the local sheriffs no longer come to present their accounts at the Royal Exchequer." Prince Henry poked his finger toward each one of them individually. "There are too few barons who retained only the lands due them through my grandfather's grants. Noblemen like you, Lord Raymond, will be the king's right hand. Barons like you, Lord Peter, and you, Lord William, will be the backbone of my kingdom." Prince Henry puffed his chest with the pride, and announced, "A kingdom we have secured in every way possible. Have you heard that I'm the father of a son?"

Delighted, William let this great news distract him. "A son? Prince Henry, congratulations. A son will secure your dynasty. Never again will such a dark time return to England. Long life to him!"

"Long life, indeed." Prince Henry grinned and hooked his thumbs in his belt. "His name is Guillaume, and Eleanor writes he's a strong and healthy boy. She's already designated him to be her heir, the future Count of Poitou."

"You do bring wonderful news, my lord," William said. "But if you would excuse—"

"Eleanor and I will have many sons. Many sons! Call for the wine, Raymond, and let's drink to the health of my son."

The signs pointed to a long and cordial night, and William interrupted in desperation. "Prince Henry!"

Prince Henry turned to William in surprise. "Aye?"

"I'm honored by your trust, and I hope to discuss these blessed changes tonight at the evening meal. But my lord, I must go fetch my wife."

Prince Henry reared back, offended by the interjection of such a trival matter. "Where is she?"

"I left her on the knoll overlooking the castle. Excuse me, Lord, I must go to her." He bowed with no grace and began to retreat.

"Your wife will forgive you for forgetting her. She observed the battle from her outpost, I'm sure," Prince Henry said coldly.

William stopped. "Nay, my lord. My wife is blind."

Prince Henry's brows raised, and his attitude changed immediately. He dropped the facade of provoked king and became a curious man. "She must be an extraordinary woman to have earned your devotion so thoroughly."

"So she is," William said.

Prince Henry looked around. Lord Peter grinned proudly, as if they discussed his own daughter. Raymond smiled with infatuated delight, and William smirked like a man who'd found the key to paradise. With pleasure, Prince Henry said, "Then I must meet this wife of yours, William."

"Right away, my lord. I'll have her spin you the tale of how she escaped the dungeon and routed the dragon." He bowed again, whipped around and bounded away.

"I'd take that wife of his away from him," Prince Henry confided to the two men beside him, "but Eleanor would have my ears."

Saura no longer perched up on her rock. As the sounds of battle had died, she'd crept back into the hollow where William had placed her and huddled out of the wind.

Someone had won; someone had been vanquished. The whole fight had taken only a few hours. Only now the fall sun had begun to cool and the breeze from the sea to freshen.

She knew it would take William time to come for her.

First he'd have to consult with the leader of his winning forces, then he'd have to decide what to do with the prisoners, then he'd have to liberate Bronnie. He'd have to stride from the keep in his fine, long steps and go to the stables. He'd commandeer a steed, ride to the knoll, walk up the path. She cocked her head, but he wasn't here yet.

Fine. She wouldn't panic. She began again, imagining William discussing the battle with his men. She imagined him waiting for his father to ride up, and roaring at him for being late. She imagined him ordering dinner for her.

She put her head down on her knees.

He'd never ordered dinner in his whole life; he wouldn't know what to say. He was a useless male creature with no idea of the labor involved in making a household work, and she wanted him with ridiculous passion. She wanted him with her *now*.

A footstep and then a rock rattled down the path behind her.

"William!" She almost shouted it, almost leaped around, but belated caution froze her where she sat.

How would she know this was William? Recognizing his footstep on the floor of the keep was not the same as hearing it on the pebbley surface of a path. William had instructed her to stay out of sight for her own safety, and she had ignored him. What if someone had seen her and decided to rape her? What if Nicholas had escaped and sought her as a hostage?

Another shower of stones sounded closer, and her heart beat with mighty rhythm and her hands clenched her skirt. What should she do?

Then right on the other side of her rock, William's voice blasted, "Saura! Where are you?"

Scrambling up, she called, "Here! Oh, William, I'm here."

"God's teeth." He vaulted onto the boulder and slid down into her arms. She trembled with worry and restrained hysteria, and he said hastily, "He's dead."

"I know."

"And Cran Castle's been captured."

"Are you hurt?"

"A scratch." He put her hand on his chest and she felt the drop of blood dried there.

"I was so worried. What took you so long?"

She was panicked, he judged. He took a breath, calming himself. She'd been through a terrible time, she'd been unable to see the events unfolding at her feet. Later he could express his concern for her; right now she deserved a patient understanding. Taking another breath, he snarled, "Why didn't you wait where I put you?"

"This is where you put me," she insisted.

"Nay," he said, sure and terrible. " 'Tis not. What have you been doing?"

"Nothing."

"Saura." His very tone was a warning.

"I sat where I could hear," she snapped defiantly, gripping his shirt in her fists. "Is that a sin?"

His arms squeezed her, taking her breath away, and he was torn between hugging her and smacking her. "Aye. I put you down below the level of visibility for your own safety. Woman, can't you follow directions just once in your life?" He started with a steady self-possession, but his voice rose until he was shouting.

Take a breath, she counseled herself. He had a right to irritation, he'd been through a rough few days. He'd besieged one friend, fought and killed another, been faced with his own fears. Last but not least, he'd had to admit he was wrong. He deserved a gracious apology and assurance she'd done it only because she worried about him. Taking another breath, she blasted him with all her lung power. "Not when I'm troubled for a stubborn, beetle-headed malfeasor who frightens me every time he fights and yells at me when I'm independent and who," her voice suddenly dropped to a whisper, "who makes me happy and whole."

He had to lean down to hear her, but her words deflated his indignation. "Do you love me, then?"

"Too much."

"Too much?" he questioned tenderly, his worry and distress melting under her whispered confession. "Like a good wife should love her husband?"

"Not like that, better than that." She never knew she could be so embarrassed, so afraid to speak the truth. Still, she owed it to him; she owed him everything. She raised her head so he could see her face, could know with all his senses that she spoke the truth. "I've loved you for so long." She held up her hand for silence. "You were right, though, I didn't trust you. How could I? It seemed as if all the needs were on my side and all the providing was on yours. If you didn't need me in any way, what would happen if you tired of me someday?"

Clasping her in his arms, he slid down the rock and settled her onto his lap. "Well, first of all, I could never leave you. Your mind is quick and clever, your conversation delightful. You have the kind of beauty that grows with maturity, blossoms with age. You're a noble lady, a chatelaine. Intelligence, beauty, domestic skills. A man would be a fool to tire of such a woman." She opened her mouth to contradict him, and he put his big hand over her lips and said swiftly, "I agree, men are fools. That's why I insisted on marriage, Saura, even when you fought against it. I wanted you to feel secure."

"What security is there in marriage? Men beat their wives for intelligence, for beauty." She considered. "Not for being a good chatelaine, though. I'm trying to tell you a good marriage depends on mutual needs."

"I need you!" He reared back in astonishment.

"Why?"

"Why? You silly woman."

He sounded resigned, and she agreed. "I know, but I couldn't see that the old needs had been replaced, not reduced. It used to be easy. You used to need me. When you were blind, you needed me so much. That's when I first loved you." Her smile wrapped itself in mystery as she remembered. "That golden voice, that blaring rage."

"Don't forget my kisses," he teased.

"Nay, I could never forget them." She patted the side of his face. "Did you realize my first reaction when you recovered your sight?"

"Tell me," he coaxed.

She sighed and blushed. "This will tarnish your image of me."

"Nay." He recalled her as she sat on Arthur's palliasse on the bright spring morning he'd first seen her with his restored eyes. He remembered how the pain on her face had broken her serene brow, and now he assured her, "I don't think you'll be tarnished by a very human reaction."

"You already know," she accused.

"If I could read your mind, love," he put his lips close to her ear and murmured, "we wouldn't spend so much time shouting at each other."

She laughed with reluctant amusement and realized the lump in her throat had diminished. "That morning, that awful morning after that glorious night, when I realized you could see, I wanted to scream with rage. I felt I'd been cheated, dreadful bitch I am."

"Tsk."

He clicked his tongue in mock amazement, and she turned on him. "But 'tis true. I wasn't needed anymore. I was useless."

"I've made a mistake with you, dearling." His lips brushed her forehead.

Bewildered by his lack of reaction and his comment, she queried, "Why?"

"When I recovered my vision and realized how terrible a life you'd had with your stepfather, I wanted to take care of you, never let you struggle again. Instead," his amusement deepened, "I should have tossed obstacles in your path."

"Not my path. Our path. There seemed to be nothing you needed my help with."

"You run my household and care for the children. What else do you want to do? Go into battle beside me?"

She pretended to consider that, and he cuffed her playfully. "Forget I asked."

"A single instance, William." Serious deliberation wiped her face clear of amusement. "I wanted you to believe me when I said 'twasn't Charles."

"I suspected I'd hear about this." He groaned.

"I'm not nagging about past mistakes," she insisted. "I'm trying to tell you where you hurt me, why it seemed I was of less importance to you than . . . than Bula. I have a talent. 'Tis not a great thing, but 'tis useful and never fails me. I can hear the truth in voices. You knew the value of it when you were blind, but when you regained your sight you lost some of your sense. You didn't believe me when I tried to tell you you were wrong, because I'm blind and because I'm a woman. And because you believe women aren't logical."

"Ah, Saura, you wound me with my own stupidity." He took her hands and laid them on his chest, and she laid her head there too.

His heart throbbed; she could almost feel his pain. "That was the biggest thing, I suppose. It hurt to be so wholly ignored. I'm no fool. You married an heiress, but you're so rich you don't need my money. You could do without it."

"Money can never be dismissed lightly."

"You told me yourself money wasn't the reason you married me," she explained with meticulous patience.

"God's teeth. You're throwing my own words back at me," he protested, his legs moving restlessly beneath her.

"Aye, and you could always find another woman. You're so big and strong and beautiful."

"Only you think that," he assured her.

"Oh, at our wedding I heard the way the women simpered when you came near. I don't need a block to fall on me." She made a moue of disgust. "Those women made it clear you don't need me in bed, any one of them would have gladly been a substitute." She knew she shouldn't care what anyone else thought, but she did.

William cared what someone else thought; he cared what *she* thought, and his chest swelled with indignation. "Do you think I'd use one of them as a substitute?"

"Nay!" Her throat hurt from the talking. Her chest hurt from the tears that wanted to escape. "Nay, that's not it at all. 'Tis just that, if I died tomorrow, you'd live through it."

"Well." He shifted and she felt him reach up and comb his beard. "Aye, I would. I wouldn't be happy for a long time, and I'd never find a woman who fits me as you do. Still, I'd live and prosper, teach my son, help my father. But tell me something. If I had been killed down there, did you plan to throw yourself off these rocks?"

She froze. "Ah . . . nay."

"Did you plan to immure yourself in a nunnery and never seek the world again?"

"I hadn't considered."

"Would *you* live if I died today?"

She didn't want to think about life without William, but she forced herself. If he died, would she go back to being that sheltered, mild woman she'd been before? Or would she still shout when she was angry and dance to a bramble and laugh out loud at a joke? Would she still insist on the freedom to walk where the sun could warm her face? She trembled from the pain of the truths she told, but she kept on with valiant insistence. "I would. I could stand on my feet without you."

"And the tide would still go out without my pushing it. The spring will still melt the snow without my warm breath nagging it. You're a person, all on your own, with hopes and thoughts and dreams completely separate from mine. Do you think I want a woman who needs to lean on me to be complete? I don't, dearling, I want only you, as whole and self-sufficient and tender as you are. I want to know that if I die tomorrow, you can support my father's grief and raise my son to manhood."

She didn't admit he was right, but the body beneath his arm relaxed from its rigid restraint, and he smiled a little and rubbed her hair with his cheek.

"That's another thing," she complained. "You don't need heirs of my body, for you have a son."

"True, I don't need a child of yours to inherit my lands. My feelings have nothing to do with need, however. I want to hold your babe in my arms. I want those childish arms around my neck."

She made a yearning sound, and William rocked her back and forth. "Kimball adores you."

"And I adore Kimball. But he's of an age to be fostered. You must admit he doesn't need me."

"Kimball is so confident, he doesn't even need me," he pointed out. "When our children come, he'll be so happy for us. He'll be a good brother and never begrudge them your lands at all."

"I know. He's a good boy. I like Kimball."

"So tell me what great revelation made you confess your love, really confess it, not toss it out like something you thought I wanted to hear." She didn't answer, and he pressed her like a priest urging a confession. "Tell me what made you trust me at last."

"You'll like it not," she warned.

"I haven't liked the whole conversation," he declared. "Nevertheless, it needed to be said. We've established that I will not strike you, nor will I crumple into dust, so tell me, please."

Her smile dripped with honey, pleasured with a sweet and toothsome memory. "Until today, I didn't think you needed me, but you do."

"What brought this great revelation, my lady?"

"In the dungeon you needed me."

She felt his flush heat the chest beneath her hand. "In the dungeon? In the dungeon, I cried like a babe deprived of its tit. I shook, I trembled, I clung to you."

"Aye."

"I hoped you'd forget the dungeon."

"Never. I'll never tell anyone, but William," she took his face between her hands, "for those tears and those fears I love you all the more."

"Woman!" He wanted to shout at her, but his exasperation evaporated beneath the sun of her smile. "Woman, I want you to forget."

"I'll never forget." Her smile vanished, and the lump in her throat reformed suddenly. The highs and lows, the death and the joy seemed too much to bear, and her tears suddenly soaked his chest. She held onto him with clenched fists as if he'd float away, and he hugged her and made soothing sounds. The comfort was more than she could bear; her weeping accelerated until she shook with anguish.

Petting her with the tenderness of a desperate man, he begged, "Please stop crying."

She nodded and sobbed.

"Please stop." He scrubbed her face with his big palms, erasing the tears before they could drop. "I can't stand this, Saura."

She nodded and held her breath, trying with all her heart to halt the flow. Shudders racked her, she fought for air, she rubbed her eyes with her fists.

"If it's going to hurt to stop," he said in exasperation, "go ahead and cry."

She laughed in small, gasping chuckles.

"I'll never understand women," he grumbled, clearly relieved by the break in her clouds. "I beg you to stop and you cry harder. I tell you to cry and you laugh."

Snuggled in his arms, she recovered in the heat of his embrace. When she could speak, she said, "This is the way it always is. It's always seemed when I'm afraid and you're with me, my fright disappears in your confidence. And now I know I can absorb your troubles, too, turn them around and transform them into strength. You clung to me, you cuddled in my arms, you needed me. At that moment, I knew the truth of your pronouncement. We are two halves of a whole. We do fit. No one is ever going to tear us apart."

"You foolish, idiotic woman." From his lips, it sounded like a choked commendation. "Did it take you this long to discover the truth?"

Saura's throat tightened, her heart beat with his, and she lifted her mouth to meet his as it descended. They kissed as if they were the first two people to discover the joy of kissing; they kissed as if they had done it for a millenium. They kissed and parted and kissed again, straining against each other in demanding need. She turned in his lap and wrapped her legs around him, fierce with her love and her pride and her joy. He pulled her close, wanting her with a mighty deluge of pleasure. He'd won his victories; victory over the evil that threatened them, victory over Saura's fears. He wished he could tell her everything in his heart, but the surge of her body against his distracted him, and his thoughts scattered in the insistent breeze.

Together, they clutched and parted and clutched, frustrated by clothing and frantic with love, and only a sudden cold gust of sea wind woke William to good sense. "Saura." He held her hips still. "Saura. It's getting dark, it's going to rain, and my father will send Bula if we don't come back soon."

"Bula?" She grabbed the front of his shirt. "My dog? I heard the barking, and hoped. Was it really Bula?"

"It was," he confirmed. "But it was a new Bula. He fought like a warrior. It seems Nicholas had an exaggerated faith in what a blow to the head would do to that dog's hard skull."

"To his master's hard skull, also." She grinned at him with saucy delight. "I should have known it was him. That deep, threatening roar that reminds me of your rage in canine form."

"Have I been insulted, I wonder?" He leaned into her neck and nipped her ear.

She gasped, and laughed shakily. "If we don't find a bed soon, Kimball won't have any siblings to worry about."

"Aye." William drew a ragged breath. "I'll wrestle my father for the master bed. Oh, nay!"

She stopped rubbing his chest. "What's wrong?"

"I can't take you to a bed." He stood and set her on her feet, brushing her skirt and finger-combing her hair. "But I can introduce you to a prince. He longs to meet you and hear the tales of your courage."

"A prince?"

"Prince Henry is here." She gaped at William, and he laughed. "Yes, the heir to all England awaits us in Cran Castle. He has great plans for England. He has great plans for peace, and I believe he's the man to bring it about. Our sons and our daughters will have a place in the court of the king, and you'll be one of the jewels of the kingdom."

"Prince Henry?" she faltered. "I'm not a jewel of the kingdom, I'm a beggar. I can't meet Prince Henry. I'm dirty, my hair is in snarls, and my clothes—"

"Your clothes look fine for a woman who's just routed an army," he assured her. She looked unconvinced, and he offered, "I'll gladly sneak you into the keep and play lady's maid until you are your usual comely self."

"I would be satisfied with my usual tidy self," she answered tartly.

"I offer you a chance most women would jump at," he grumbled, "a chance to meet a prince, and you are unimpressed. Well, if I can't tempt you with a chance to meet our future king, perhaps you'll go down to the castle for the chance to salute your heroic dog."

She touched his cheek with her hand. "Am I such a trial to you?"

"Aye, but God never gives me more than I can handle."

He sounded so naughty, she laughed and raised her arms to him. "As long as you're with me, I can face anyone. Let's go, then, and while we go, tell me how to behave for a prince."

He swept her into his arms and began to descend the path toward the lights of the castle. "Be yourself. He'll be overwhelmed, and jealous of my good luck." He stopped and looked down into her dear face. The chalk that covered her couldn't hide the beauty of her features nor dim the beacon that shone from her soul. He held her close against his body and brought his lips against her cheek. "Stand tall, show your pride, and never forget. If it weren't for you, I'd still be cowering in my own castle, afraid to move for fear of the dark. In this world you are my light, my candle in the window."

New York Times bestselling author

Christina Dodd

The Barefoot Princess
0-06-056117-3/$7.99 US/$10.99 Can

Since the powerful and wickedly handsome marquess of Northcliff has stolen the people's livelihood, Princess Amy decides to kidnap him for ransom.

My Fair Temptress
0-06-056112-2/$7.99 US/$10.99 Can

Miss Caroline Ritter, accomplished flirt and ruined gentlewoman, offers lessons to any rich, noble lord too inept to attract a wife.

Some Enchanted Evening
0-06-056098-3/$6.99 US/$9.99 Can

Though Robert is wary of the exquisite stranger who rides into the town he is sworn to defend, Clarice stirs emotions within him that he buried deeply years before.

One Kiss From You
0-06-009266-1/$7.99 US/$10.99 Can

Eleanor de Lacy must have been mad to agree to exchange identities with her stronger-willed cousin. Worse still, she finds the man she's to deceive dazzlingly attractive.

Scandalous Again
0-06-009265-3/$6.99 US/$9.99 Can

Madeline de Lacy can't believe that her noble father has lost his entire estate—*and her!*—in a card game.